BREACH OF TRUST

BREACH
OF
TRUST

DAVID
ELLIS

Quercus

First published in Great Britain in 2011 by

Quercus
21 Bloomsbury Square
London
WC1A 2NS

A CIP catalogue record for this book is available
from the British Library

ISBN (HB) 978 1 84916 199 2
ISBN (TPB) 978 1 84916 200 5

10 9 8 7 6 5 4 3 2 1

Printed and bound in Great Britain by Clays Ltd, St Ives Plc

To Julia Grace Ellis, my little treasure

Keep your friends close and your enemies closer.

—SUN-TZU, CHINESE GENERAL AND MILITARY
STRATEGIST (ATTRIBUTED), FIFTH CENTURY B.C.

Unless your enemy's wearing a wire.

—CIRIACO "CHARLIE" CIMINO,
POLITICAL FUNDRAISER, 2007

OPENING STATEMENT

I AM RECOUNTING THIS STORY IN CASE I AM NOT AROUND WHEN THE dust settles. If some unfortunate accident should befall me, as they say, and I am unable to testify, I want to have some account of what I did and why. I will not try to justify my actions. I could tell you that they made me do it, but that's hardly the point, and it may not be entirely accurate.

I won't lie to you, which is to say I will not deliberately mislead you. I will give you the most accurate account of events I can muster, but I can't promise it will be the truth. Truth is a matter of perspective, and if you don't believe me, then just watch how this whole thing plays out. Everyone who is a part of this story will tell a different version, when their time comes. In most of those versions, the hero will be whoever is telling the story.

In many of those versions, no doubt, the villain will be me.

TRIALS

March–June 2007

1 IF ERNESTO RAMIREZ HAD BEEN A BETTER LIAR, HE'D still be alive.

If he had told me right off the bat, or never given me the slightest indication that he had anything to tell me, I would have been on my merry way.

Joel Lightner was the private investigator. I was the lawyer. We were in Liberty Park, by which I mean not the southwest-side neighborhood bearing its name but the actual park itself, a city block of unhealthy grass and broken-down playground equipment, with a war-torn aluminum fence on the perimeter and a large wooden park district building with more graffiti on it than actual paint. The spray-painted gang insignia was an even split between the Columbus Street Cannibals and the Latin Lords. This was *La Zona,* disputed territory claimed by each of the gangs.

Almost two years ago to the day, exactly a half-mile straight west from this park, a small business owner named Adalbert Wozniak took five bullets to the chest, neck, and face. My client, State Senator Hector Almundo, was charged with his murder.

Nobody thought that Hector had pulled the trigger, of course. The Wozniak murder was part of a larger federal prosecution that went like this: Senator Almundo, harboring ambitions to be the state's next attorney general, had cut a deal with the Cannibals street gang to shake down local businesses for monthly payments—an old-fashioned street protection tax—which the Cannibals then shared with Hector's campaign fund. The government figured that the take was roughly a fifty-fifty split between Hector and the Cannibals. That meant that, over an eighteen-month period, Citizens for Almundo took in about a hundred thousand dollars courtesy of the Cannibals' extortion of local businesses.

Anyway, Wozniak was one of those business owners but refused to pay. The feds figured that the Cannibals decided to teach Wozniak a lesson and send a message to other like-minded dissenters that the street tax wasn't optional. The message was sent well enough that Wozniak's family couldn't have an open casket at his funeral.

But the feds charged the whole thing, from the shakedown to the murder, as a conspiracy—their favorite word, that one—which meant that all of the crimes that were a part of the overall scheme could be attributed to all of the co-conspirators. Thus, State Senator Hector Almundo, as the supposed architect of the whole extortion scheme, was on the hook for the murder of Adalbert Wozniak, regardless of who pulled the trigger or who made the ultimate decision to pull it.

Joel Lightner and I passed a group of kids playing soccer, using anything they could find—a stone, a brick, a backpack—to frame their goals. I narrowly missed an appointment with a flying soccer ball, which made the kids howl in laughter almost in unison. I felt more than a decade and a half removed from that carefree bliss, having no other responsibility than to run around in a field chasing after a ball, though my sport was the American version of football.

Ernesto Ramirez was standing near the basketball court, in part observing and in part refereeing a four-on-four game of half-court hoops. The backboard was tattered and the rim had no net, but it didn't seem to dampen the enthusiasm of the kids, who looked to be ages six through mid-teens. Ernesto was shouting something to them in Spanish I couldn't place. I spoke the language pretty well but had trouble keeping up with native speakers.

"We can talk right here," he said to us, which wasn't our preference but we didn't have any leverage over him. I wasn't used to that. Until recently, I'd been a county prosecutor, where the failure to cooperate meant an arrest for obstruction.

It didn't take long to learn that Ramirez knew of Senator Almundo, the criminal case, and Adalbert Wozniak. "I didn't know Wozniak," he said. He spoke well but it was clear that English was his second language.

"Did you know Eddie Vargas?" asked Lightner.

After Wozniak's murder, eyewitness accounts of the make and model of a Chevy sedan, together with partial license plate identification, led police to discover what they believed to be the killer's vehicle in a dump several miles away. The feds used some of their fancy forensic technology to conclude, from sediment found within the tire tracks, that the vehicle had spent some time parked behind a housing project controlled by the Columbus Street Cannibals. They also found a print on the rearview mirror that belonged to a sixteen-year-old Cannibal recruit named Eddie Vargas. When the FBI raided Vargas's home, they found a small pistol, a Kahr MK40, which could be mistaken for a metal spray nozzle on a garden hose, and which they confirmed was the murder weapon. Young Mr. Vargas has never been located and is strongly believed to have suffered an unfortunate accident of one kind or another, probably involving a machete, the Cannibals' weapon of choice when silencing potential talkers. Bottom line, the feds had their shooter, and he was a Cannibal, but that shooter wouldn't be talking.

Ernesto Ramirez stared forward in the direction of the hoops game, but his eyes weren't tracking the players or the movement of the ball. He'd drifted away momentarily at the mention of the name.

"Eddie was a sixteen-year-old kid," he said. "A sweet kid."

Though Ramirez was only thirty-two, his skin was weathered and his wavy dark hair was flecked with gray. He was a former Latin Lord member and drug addict who had managed to break free of both problems, but not without some residual wear. He spent his time these days running youth programs to provide alternatives to gangs. Eddie Vargas had been one of those youths.

"He didn't shoot nobody," Ramirez added.

Lightner shrugged. "The federal government is saying he did. Can you help us out?"

Ramirez's jaw clenched and his left eye twitched. He was still making a show of watching that stupid basketball game. But I thought he was thinking. His mouth parted and his tongue moistened his lips, like he was on the verge of speaking.

"Senator Almundo shouldn't have to go down for something he didn't do," Joel said.

Ramirez snapped out of his trance, turning on Joel. A vein throbbed near his left eye. "Hector Almundo can go to hell. I don't know nothin' about this, anyway. I can't 'help you out.' Okay, guy?"

Another satisfied customer, Joel would say; I'd done a few of these interviews with him. Joel tried a couple more times, but Ernesto Ramirez wasn't going to budge.

"Almundo shouldn't go down for something he didn't do?" I said to Joel, when we got back in his car.

Joel laughed. "It sounded good at the time." Neither of us thought we were representing an innocent man. We didn't think Hector had ordered a hit on Adalbert Wozniak, but the part about working out a deal with the Cannibals to shake down the local businesses? We figured the government had that part right.

" 'He didn't shoot nobody,' " I said, quoting Ramirez.

"He was speaking well of his friend. Doesn't mean he has any information. A dead end, kid," Joel pronounced. "Mr. Ernesto Ramirez doesn't know anything."

Maybe. But I thought differently. Joel was pretty good with these things, but I thought he'd made a misstep. I thought Ernesto was about to tell us something back there, before Joel had invoked a name that clearly upset Ramirez and knocked him off the rails.

Joel kicked his Audi into gear and drove off. I looked back at Liberty Park.

Ernesto Ramirez was watching us drive away.

2 I REACHED OVER WITH BLEARY EYES AND TOOK A GOOD whack at my alarm clock. My head sank back into the pillow until I got a nudge in my rib cage.

"It's five, babe."

I rolled over and peeked up at my wife, Talia, who was sitting up in bed, wide awake.

"Can't sleep?" I moaned. "Your back still?" I nestled up against her warm body and moved my hand onto the hump of her belly. Technically, the due date was ten days away, but Doctor Waite said it could be anytime. "Hurry up, Emily Jane. Daddy's big trial is starting soon. I want to see you as much as possible before— She kicked." I popped up in bed. "I felt her."

Emily Jane—we'd already named her—had made an art of kicking for her mommy but never for me.

"She's been doing that for over an hour." Talia ran her hand through my hair. "Did you sleep at all?" she asked.

"A few hours." I was trying to get as much done for the Almundo trial as I could before I had to take some time off for the arrival of Emily Jane. Her due date was five days before jury selection.

There were all sorts of reasons for me not to work as second chair on the Almundo trial, given Emily's impending arrival. But there were even more reasons for me to take the assignment. Starting with this: Every single associate at Shaker, Riley and Flemming would give a major organ to be in my position. This case could make my career if it went well. And it was the chance to work alongside Paul Riley, our senior partner and, by most people's accounts, the best trial lawyer in the city. I was new to Shaker, Riley and to private practice in general when Hector Almundo walked through the door and hired Paul to defend him in one of the biggest public corruption cases the city had ever seen. I don't know what I did to catch Paul's attention. I'd handled a few projects for him but nothing huge. Maybe he'd asked about me at the county attorney's office, where I'd cut my teeth before landing at the firm. I didn't know and didn't care. I said "yes" to this assignment before it was out of Paul's mouth. I couldn't have known at the time that my wife and I would be expecting our first child just as the trial opened.

I warmed up a couple of breakfast sandwiches in the microwave and brought them up to Talia before I left for work. Last week, these sausage-and-egg biscuits would have made her gag; this week she couldn't live without them. "I miss coffee," she told me. She'd forsworn it, even though her doctor told her she could have a little caffeine now and then. This was our first, and Talia was taking no chances.

Even sleep-deprived and uncomfortable, my wife was a classic Italian beauty. I wiped her flattened bangs off her forehead and kissed her there, then her nose and cheeks and soft, warm mouth. "I miss sex," I told her. "Unless—"

"Sorry, mate. If you touch my boobs, I'll scream." She pulled on my tie. "Get home early, okay?" By *early,* she meant some time before she went to bed.

"And keep that cell phone handy," she added.

3   "THE TAPES, THE TAPES, AND THE TAPES," SAID PAUL Riley, his feet up on his desk and his tie pulled down. "That's what it comes down to. Hector's own words caught on tape."

"And Joey Espinoza," said our investigator, Joel Lightner. Joey Espinoza was Senator Hector Almundo's chief of staff. The feds, who had caught wind of the Cannibals' shakedown scheme as early as February of 2005, liked Espinoza for one of the ringleaders. Thus, one early morning in April of 2005, as Joey Espinoza carried a mug of coffee and briefcase to his car, FBI agents stormed his garage and did what FBI agents do best—they scared the shit out of him. They told him his life, as he knew it, was over. They had him cold. His only chance of survival? Wear a wire and help them nail his boss, Senator Hector Almundo.

Joey eagerly complied and covertly recorded four conversations with Hector before Adalbert Wozniak's murder in May. At that point, the feds made the call that they couldn't continue to lie low and risk more bloodshed, so they closed in, arresting eleven gang members, fourteen co-conspirators, and the illustrious Senator Almundo.

"Joey's not the problem," Paul argued. "He's a scumbag, but that doesn't change what's on the tapes. Hector still said what he said."

Hector's words on the tapes were pretty damning, instructing his chief of staff, Espinoza, to continue working with the Columbus Street Cannibals and their extortion scheme. We didn't have much to refute it, other than to argue that Joey was really calling the shots, and Hector was an absent-minded leader who didn't sweat the details. That wasn't the easiest sell, however, when he was on tape telling Joey to keep doing what he was doing with the street gang.

"So find a way to refute it," Lightner said.

"Oh. Thanks, Joel." Paul turned to me. "You get that, Jason? Lightner says we should find a way to refute it. You can't put a price on those pearls of wisdom."

Paul and Lightner went back to the eighties, during a mass murder in the south suburbs, when Paul was the prosecutor and Joel the cop. Lightner left the job fifteen years ago and opened a private investigation agency that has benefited mightily from its association with this law firm.

"Jason," Lightner said to me, "you're new, so you may not know—when Paul gets frustrated, he takes it out on poor underlings like me. What he really means is he appreciates my contribution to this case. Also, I don't know if he told you yet, but as a condition of working on this case, you have to name your child after Paul."

"Jason's child is going to be a girl, Lightner, which you would know if you didn't start drinking before noon every day," Paul replied.

"Okay, Paulina, then. Paulina Kolarich."

This usually happened at the end of the workday, these two getting on each other before they went out for steaks and martinis that night. They were both bachelors, Paul once-divorced and Lightner twice. They could be pretty amusing when they got going. Their deliveries were so dry that it still took me an extra moment to separate sarcasm from sincerity.

"And I don't start drinking until three o'clock, at the earliest," Lightner protested.

I felt something pull at me, a clearing of some clouds in my head. *Maybe . . .*

"What kind of a name is Kolarich, anyway?"

Could that work? Was it that simple . . . ?

"He's in a state of shock," Lightner went on. "He's so mesmerized by your intelligence, Riley, that he can't speak. You're gonna have a long career at this place, Jason. Just repeat after me: *Paul, you're so brilliant. Paul, you're so brilliant.*"

I looked at Lightner, then at Paul. Riley nodded at me out of curiosity.

I cleared my throat and gave it one more thought.

"Hang on," Lightner said. "I think he's about to say something."

"Yeah, I am," I said. "I think I know how to defend this case."

4 As the second chair on the Almundo defense team, I had to serve dual roles. I had to be prepared for my portion of the trial work, less than Paul's but still significant. Then I had to oversee the other lawyers on Team Almundo—six lawyers, six paralegals, and four private investigators—ensuring that all operations were humming along in synch. We had meetings twice daily, first in the morning and then at five o'clock, confirming that the documents had been cross-referenced accurately in the database; that all motions *in limine* had been drafted; that drafts of direct and cross-examinations had been prepared. We were two weeks out from trial now, and all those assignments that looked like we had plenty of time to finish suddenly seemed desperately incapable of timely completion.

My own personal to-do list was moving quite nicely. I had tasks scribbled on pieces of paper plastered haphazardly on my wall and most of them had been completed. But one prominent item remained: Ernesto Ramirez. Joel Lightner had once again labeled it a lost cause—"Either he doesn't know anything or he does, but he won't tell you; a dead end either way"—but that only motivated me more. I was sure I saw something in his face, and I let my imagination take me to places where his revelation was a game-changer at trial, a Perry Mason moment. If everyone else on Team Almundo doubted me, so much the better; the glory would belong only to me.

"How we doing?" I spoke into my cell phone.

"It's going to be soon," Talia said.

"Wishful thinking."

"When are you coming home?"

"One thing I gotta do first."

My one thing was Ernesto Ramirez. I'd made Lightner assign someone to give me a full workup on the guy in case I wanted to pursue him further. Ernesto Javier Ramirez, former member of the Latin Lords street gang; working for a nonprofit off-the-streets program called *La Otra Familia* that tried to pull kids out of gangs; wife Esmeralda and two kids, ages six and nine. He pumped iron at the YMCA three times a week. He had dinner with his mother once a week. He took a shop class every Tuesday. Otherwise, he went to work and spent time with his family.

Most important, he still had ties to the Latin Lords, which was promising because that gave him access to on-the-ground information about all sorts of criminal activity should he desire it. I was working on the assumption that if he knew something about Wozniak's murder, the information might well have come from the Lords—and play that out another step and maybe it was the Lords, not the Columbus Street Cannibals, who killed Wozniak. A wild thought, maybe, but imagine the bombshell at Hector's trial: *The government got the wrong street gang.* It would blow a hole in a big part of their case, the Wozniak murder. It wouldn't exonerate Hector from the part about the street shakedown, but once we knocked out one leg, that other limb would look mighty shaky.

His branch of the YMCA was over in the Liberty Park neighborhood, close to his office and his home. I drove there. The sun had fallen behind the buildings on the city's southwest side but it was not yet dusk, casting a dull glow over the broken streets and run-down shops—check-cashing facilities, liquor stores with chains over their windows, a bakery, and a couple of *carnicerías*. I didn't know this neighborhood well. I grew up only a few miles to the south and east, in Leland Park, but it might as well have been a thousand miles away. Back then, the white Catholics didn't cross the unofficial borders, and nobody else crossed theirs unless they wanted a beating.

I turned onto Knapp Avenue, which for wealthy whites served as nothing more than a major westbound artery to the interstate highway. The area was teeming with pedestrians, mostly brown faces, some kids darting suicidally between cars across the avenue like a real-time urban video game.

I didn't have a membership to the Y and I didn't know what I'd be able to manage at the front desk. But it couldn't hurt to try. A pleasant young woman told me I could have a one-time pass as a try-out. I gave her my driver's license so she could be sure I wasn't living off of free passes, and once she typed in my name and confirmed I was a first-timer, she handed me a green ticket and a couple of towels. If she'd noticed that I had no gym bag or any other evidence of workout gear, she didn't say so.

I went downstairs to the workout facility and found Ernesto Ramirez pretty easily. There were only five people pumping iron. He was wearing baggy shorts and a gray tank top stained with his sweat. He was bench-pressing two plates on each side of the bar—two hundred twenty-five pounds. The bar is forty-five and each plate is forty-five. A standard test in the NFL draft is bench presses of this weight, with your hands no wider than your shoulders, emulating a lineman's shiver block. Or at least it was a standard test when I was playing college ball. I managed eleven presses my freshman year. I didn't make it to the end of my sophomore year, having settled a disagreement with one of our team captains by breaking his jaw and ending my football career.

Ernesto managed one shaky press, with his arms spread wide and his back arched for additional leverage. Not bad for a little guy in his early thirties. Not bad for anybody.

His eyes swept past mine but quickly returned. I was a white guy in a suit, not exactly fitting in, and then his eyes registered that I was a white guy in a suit whom he knew. It probably spooked him a little that I knew where to find him. I'd obviously done my homework. But I didn't want to catch him at home, where he could close a door in my face, and the time for diplomacy had come and gone.

He picked the towel up off the weight bench and wiped his face. He said something in Spanish to the guy spotting him, who was just as short as him but much stockier.

"I told you," he said before he'd even reached me, "that I got nothing to say to you."

"You have something to say to me. You just don't want to say it."

Fresh sweat broke on his forehead. He wiped at it with his hand towel. "Either way," he said, "I'm not talking to you anymore. Don't contact me. Leave me alone."

"Whoever killed Bert Wozniak is going to walk from it," I said. "You okay with that?"

"Not my problem."

"Your whole life is worrying about other people's problems."

"Well, not this one."

"You stay quiet, everyone blames your friend, Eddie Vargas. That okay with you?"

"Now you got me worrying about a dead man's problems."

I nodded slowly, watching him. He looked over his shoulder. All four of the other weightlifters, especially his spotter, were watching me. Ernesto was scared. I could read it all over him. And that was meaningful. Ernesto was clearly a proud man. Nobody who puts up vanity reps at a weight bench is anything but proud. You work out, at his age, to stay in shape. You choose weights that you can press eight, ten times. You don't go for your max weight unless you take some pride in how much you can press. Nothing wrong with that, but it meant he wouldn't want to show anyone his fear, and he wasn't doing a very good job of hiding it right now.

"I can protect you," I said.

"Oh?" He laughed at me without humor. "Who you gonna protect me from?"

"Whoever."

His eyes narrowed. "You know anything at all about my world?"

"Then tell me confidentially. I won't disclose you as a source. Give me a name—give me something—and I'll take it from there. Nobody will ever know."

He was quiet for a long moment. I couldn't tell if he was considering my proposal or considering the best way to blow me off. Finally, he squared up and spoke to me in what he intended to be a conclusive statement on the matter.

"They'll know," he said. "Now good-bye."

I called after him, my heartbeat escalating. "Who's *they*?"

"Excuse me," said some muscle-bound guy wearing a Y t-shirt that was two sizes too small. "If you're not here to check out the facility, we need to ask you to leave."

"Who's *they*, Ernesto?" I tried again, speaking to his back as he returned to the bench press.

"Sir, c'mon, now."

I worked my arm out of his grip. But there was no sense making a scene.

They'll know, he'd said.

There was something there. I knew it.

My cell phone rang. I fumbled with it, revealing some nerves. I might actually be onto something big here.

The caller ID said the call was coming from home.

"My water broke," said Talia.

Assistant U.S. Attorney Christopher Moody, lead prosecutor in *United States v. Almundo,* stood at the prosecution table, leafing through some papers. He had about five years on me—roughly forty—and his tightly cropped reddish blond hair and boyish features struggled against the sober demeanor required of any federal prosecutor. He had the look of someone who had just finished a stressful assignment.

In fact, the government was all but done with their case now. They'd put on more than thirty witnesses. Eleven members of the Columbus Street Cannibals, each of whom had pleaded guilty, had testified to shaking down local businessmen. Nine intermediaries, "straw" contributors who pocketed the extorted cash and then wrote a check in the same amount (minus a small fee for their troubles) to Citizens for Almundo, all had taken pleas and testified as well. There was no doubt about the extortion; the defense, in fact, had agreed to stipulate to it, but the federal government, in its typical flair for overkill, had scorched every last plot of earth, calling many of the shopkeepers as well and providing all kinds of colorful, fancy charts and PowerPoint presentations matching up the extortion payments to contributions to Hector's campaign fund.

As for the Wozniak murder, the government showed that Wozniak refused to pay the street tax and introduced plenty of forensic evidence linking the fine young Cannibal, Eddie Vargas, to his murder.

But the government had a problem. For all this evidence, none of the witnesses could point the finger at Senator Almundo himself. None of those witnesses would testify that they ever spoke to Hector. And it wasn't a crime to accept a contribution that was the product of extortion unless you *knew* the source of the money was illegal. If we could detach Hector from this criminal enterprise, he would walk free.

Enter Hector's chief of staff, Joey Espinoza, the sole witness who could tie Hector to all of this, and who wore a wire to help the government do so. A polished, well-groomed man in his early forties, Joey Espinoza had just spent the last three days testifying that the entire neighborhood shakedown was orchestrated by his boss, the senator, from the comfort of his district office.

Finally, after conferring with his fellow assistants—other white Irishmen—Christopher Moody unbuttoned his blue suit jacket, signaling he was about to take his seat. I felt the familiar adrenaline spike.

"Thank you, Mr. Espinoza," Moody said. "The United States has no further questions, Your Honor."

"Cross-examination?" asked the judge, looking at Paul Riley, not me.

I felt the courtroom brim with fresh energy as the prosecution passed the witness to the defense. Espinoza had been on the stand for the government for three full days, so the buzz had subsided. But now the defense was going to get its shot, and expectations were high. We had to be aware of that from the outset. After Espinoza's testimony, the jury would be expecting us to put a big hole in his testimony, or Hector Almundo would be convicted.

Paul Riley gave a very curt nod in my direction, a vote of confidence. I rose from my seat and felt a hushed surprise behind me. I assumed almost every spectator had anticipated that Paul, a celebrated lawyer, would handle the cross-examination of this witness. I'd been surprised myself when Paul tapped me. It certainly wasn't charity on his part. There was no way that Paul would let me cut my teeth in a situation where the stakes were so high. Something had told him that I was the better choice. I think he wanted to stay "clean," so to speak, for the closing argument. He wanted to remain the good guy, the earnest advocate, and not the one who tore a hole in the prosecution's chief witness.

In any event, all that mattered now was that I took this witness down.

"Good afternoon, Mr. Espinoza. My name is Jason Kolarich."

"Good afternoon," said Espinoza.

The witness was inherently unlikeable: dressed too immaculately, bountiful dark hair styled just so, overly impressed with his careful enunciation—*slick* was my preferred term.

"If Senator Almundo had been elected attorney general, he would've had to resign his state senate seat mid-term, isn't that true? He'd have two years left on his four-year term."

"Yes, of course," said the witness.

"And you wanted to be appointed to fill that vacancy."

The witness angled his head ever so slightly.

My eyes moved to Chris Moody, who was scribbling a note. This would be a surprise to Moody, I assumed. Espinoza had said nothing of this in the direct examination, and he probably hadn't volunteered this information to the feds. Espinoza had cast himself as the faithful aide, the loyal servant acting at the behest of his master. The obvious point I wanted to make was that Espinoza had an independent motivation to engage in the extortion plot; Hector's move up the ladder would leave a rung open for Joey. And given that Espinoza probably hadn't shared this information with the prosecutors, they hadn't had the chance to prepare him for this line of inquiry.

"I don't know about that," said the witness.

"Well—" I looked at my client, Senator Hector Almundo, then back at Espinoza. "Didn't you tell Senator Almundo that you'd want to be appointed to his seat? That you wanted to be the next senator from the thirteenth district?"

Espinoza restrained himself from looking in the senator's direction. He took the whole thing like it was amusing. "I might have expected to serve as his chief of staff at the attorney general's office, but senator? I don't know about that."

"That's not what I asked you, sir." Always a favorite line of a defense attorney—pointing out a witness's evasion. It puts a small dent in his credibility and also highlights the importance of the question. "Did you not *tell* Senator Almundo that this is exactly what you wanted? To take his place in the senate?"

The witness, I thought, was calculating. Would Senator Almundo take the stand and testify to such a conversation? Had anyone else heard him utter this desire?

"Mr. Kolarich, the senator and I spent a great deal of time together. Often sixteen-hour days. Many things came up from time to time. If you are asking, did we ever discuss my future, the answer is probably yes."

This was going well. The witness was giving a political answer, but this wasn't a press conference. A chance for another indentation in his façade of credibility. If a witness is a brand-new car on direct examination, you want him to look he was in a head-on collision by the time you're done crossing him.

"No, that's *not* what I'm asking. Let me ask it a third time, Mr. Espinoza. Did you not *tell* Senator Almundo that you wanted to take his seat in the senate if he were elected attorney general?"

The witness smiled at me, and at the jury. "Mr. Kolarich," he said, as if exhausted, "I cannot sit here with certainty and say yes or no to that question. It is possible that I said that, and it is possible I did not. I don't recall with any certainty."

"A conversation concerning whether you would be the next senator from the thirteenth district—you *aren't sure* whether you had that conversation or not? You're telling this jury you wouldn't remember that?"

It sounded ridiculous. Espinoza had ambition written all over him. There was no way that he would have discussed this topic with the senator and not recalled it. Best of all, it was clear that the jury was not buying it.

Appearing to recognize as much, Espinoza tried to recover. "Let me say it this way, Mr. Kolarich. It is possible that I said such a thing but only in jest. I've been accused of having a dry sense of humor. I may have made the comment but not been serious."

I gave him my best poker face. Espinoza never really had a good answer to this line of questioning. You're at your best as a defense attorney when the witness is damned either way he answers, but Espinoza had made matters worse with his rationalization. I did my best now to look confused, maybe flustered, even disappointed, all to embolden Espinoza, to make him think he had won this small battle. I wanted him to think that he'd just stuck a knife in me, so he'd be encouraged to plunge it deeper still.

Espinoza, after all, was a smooth talker who'd had great success in that regard. He'd probably been nervous about facing the famed Paul Riley in cross-examination, and no doubt let his guard down ever so slightly when a young guy like me stepped up instead. I discovered, at just that moment, that probably this had been Paul's intention in tapping me all along—to sneak up on this guy.

"So you're saying that you and the senator would have discussed such a thing in jest? An exchange of dry senses of humor?" My tone was far less confrontational than my previous inquiries. To Espinoza, in fact, it probably sounded like I was flailing, losing the argument.

"Certainly. We share that trait."

"A dry sense of humor?"

"Yes, sir."

I nodded meekly and sighed. "Well, would it surprise you to learn that the senator didn't take the comment as humor? That he might have interpreted your comment as serious?"

Out of the corner of my eye, I saw the prosecutor, Chris Moody, stir. There would be a temptation to object to this question, but Moody decided against it. The reason was that the only way I could prove that the senator took this comment seriously was for the senator to take the witness stand and say so—something Moody was correctly assuming would never happen. So it would be left hanging, unproven, which Moody would be happy to point out in closing argument.

Neither Moody nor the witness seemed to recognize my ulterior motive.

"It would not surprise me at all that he might have misinterpreted it," said Espinoza.

"Even someone who has known you for a long time, like the senator?"

"Yes, sir," he said, gaining momentum now, going for the kill. "Most certainly. If Hector took a comment like that as serious, then he was simply mistaken. It happens." Espinoza bowed his head. "That is the hazard of a dry sense of humor, sir. Sometimes you are taken as serious when you are not."

I paused, to give the appearance that I was defeated, drowning, unable to counter his answer. This played directly into his ego. He was smarter than the high-priced lawyer. "But—if you were joking, being sarcastic as opposed to being serious, wouldn't your voice change inflection or something?"

"That," said the witness, entirely pleased with himself, "is the very definition of a dry sense of humor, Mr. Kolarich. You deliver the sarcasm with a straight face. With an even tone."

"So it's a joke, but it sounds serious."

"Yes."

"Or serious, but mistaken for a joke."

The witness opened his hand to me. "Precisely. Sarcasm is sometimes harder to detect than we realize."

Oh, Joey, I thought to myself. *Thank you for that.*

Joey had beaten me up pretty well on that point, and I wanted it to soak into the jurors' minds for a bit. An awkward silence hung for a moment. I thought that some of the jurors were actually feeling sorry for me. Then I shrugged and said, "Government's 108, Your Honor." I walked past the prosecution table to the small table where the recorder sat. I'd cued it up during the last court recess, so it was ready to play right where I wanted it. For the fourth time in this trial, the jury heard a secret government recording between the senator and Espinoza, poring over a campaign finance report:

ESPINOZA: At least fifteen thousand of the take from last month is from the Cannibals, Hector.

ALMUNDO: Great. Terrific. You know, ah, Flores, look at this guy. A lousy five grand after everything I did for him last time around. Five fuckin' grand. And the carpenters didn't exactly come through, either. Where the hell is all this union money I've heard so much about?

ESPINOZA: Hector, we have a problem.

ALMUNDO: Problem? Where the hell are my glasses? And where the hell is Lisa? What problem?

ESPINOZA: The Cannibals, Hector.

ALMUNDO: The Cannibals—

ESPINOZA: Some of the store owners are complaining, Hector. Should we tell the Cannibals to lay off them? Stop squeezing them for campaign money?

ALMUNDO: Hell, no. They're performing a public service, right? Tell 'em I want double next month.

I turned off the tape. "I've lost my place, Your Honor," I said. "Could the court reporter read back the witness's last answer?"

Several of the jurors, who had been hit over the head with the government's theory of the case throughout the trial, now stared at the recording equipment with furrowed brows. I would gain nothing from further debate with Espinoza on this issue. I had made my point: Senator Almundo hadn't taken Espinoza's comments about the street gang seriously; he'd thought it was a joke and his response was as sarcastic as he thought Espinoza's comment was. Two of the jurors nodded as they listened to the court reporter read back Espinoza's last bit of testimony:

"Sarcasm is sometimes harder to detect than we realize."

It had come to me while listening to Paul and Joel Lightner give each other the what-for in Paul's office. I could imagine the two of them having this very exchange, in jest. I just needed Joey Espinoza to confirm for me that he and Hector engaged in similar sarcastic jabs, and he'd been kind enough to oblige me.

I had nothing else to gain from further exploration of this topic. Paul Riley, in his closing argument, would dissect each of the four recorded conversations, making two simple observations: first, in each case, Joey Espinoza had forced the topic of the Cannibals into the conversation; and second, each of Hector's responses could plausibly be interpreted as sarcasm. That, plus Joey Espinoza's political ambitions, painted a nice picture: This had been the Joey Espinoza Show, from start to finish, and the only reason Hector Almundo was standing trial was that Joey had to finger someone to try to save his ass from twenty years in prison.

I smiled as the jury heard the read-back of Joey's testimony. I looked over at Chris Moody, who apparently had failed to find the humor in it.

6 I SPENT THE REST OF THE AFTERNOON GOING AFTER Joey Espinoza a bit more aggressively, having sucker-punched him on the main point we wanted to make. It wasn't hard, after that, to establish that Joey had actually spoken with several elected officials about assuming Hector's senate seat if he became attorney general—Joey probably figured I would call those other officials to testify, so he couldn't very well deny it. And then, of course, the obvious motivation that a man looking at twenty years had in cutting a deal that landed him only eighteen months in Club Fed. The only thing he could give the feds, that they didn't already have, was Hector, so he embellished and tried to manufacture carefully crafted conversations to make it look like his boss was part of the criminal enterprise.

Back at Shaker, Riley afterward, the atmosphere was subdued celebration. "I'd offer you lunch," said Paul, "but I think you just ate Joey Espinoza's."

"Outstanding, Jason." My client, Hector Almundo, nattily attired in an olive suit, was jubilant.

"The Joey Espinoza Show," Paul continued. "They saw it today, Hector. They watched him and they saw him as manipulative. And the 'dry sense of humor' stuff? Priceless."

"The cocksucker." Senator Almundo, favoring a more concise summary in his own lyrical way, collapsed into a chair in the conference room. What angered him about Espinoza was not the criminal actions of Espinoza or the Columbus Street Cannibals; neither Paul nor I had much doubt that Hector had known exactly what was taking place on the west side. No, his anger toward his former aide was based on one thing, and one thing only—the betrayal.

"We still have a lot of work ahead." I said, opting for the humble voice of reason.

"Maybe," said Paul. "After today, I'm not sure we put on a case at all."

Inside, I was doing leaps. I felt my new position in the private sector greatly enhanced with today's events. My secretary had pulled up early Internet accounts of the trial on his BlackBerry and the verdict, pardon the pun, had been a knockout for the defense. When we walked back into the firm tonight, we'd been greeted by other lawyers at the firm, who had been reading about it blow-by-blow online, with the customary mix of congratulation: sincerity blended with envy.

But all I wanted to do was go home and see my wife and daughter, Emily Jane. I threw my notepad on the conference table and reviewed my checklist, to make sure I wasn't missing anything. My big cross-examination was over, the jury instructions were done, the post-trial motions as ready as they could be for now. But there was one thing left.

Ernesto Ramirez.

One of those things, not slipping through the cracks exactly but never making the cut as the top priority. He'd told me to go scratch my ass when I'd visited him at the YMCA—what was that, three months ago now? I told him I'd keep his information anonymous, and he'd had a ready answer: *They'll know.*

Right. It was the night Emily was born. I'd driven straight home from the Y and taken Talia to Mercy General, where she spent eleven hours in labor before our little gift showed up, red-faced and fussy.

I was feeling a surge of momentum. Things had gone perfectly today. If I could just pull this one last rabbit out of the hat—

I meandered to the corner of the conference room and dialed him on my cell phone. The phone rang twice before he answered.

"Hello?"

"Ernesto? Jason Kolarich. The lawyer who—"

"Yes, Jason." Curt and hostile.

"I'm out of time here, so I'll be blunt—"

"I don't have anything to say to you. You understand? Nothing."

"Wait. Just—hang on. I can protect you. I can have the government protect you as a material wit—"

"The *government*. Yeah, the government. Man, you don't get it."

"Then *help* me get—"

"Listen to me. Listen. Don't ever call me again. I got nothing to say."

A loud click followed. I sighed and closed up the phone. I turned to find Riley, Lightner, and Hector Almundo staring at me.

"Ernesto Ramirez," I explained.

"Ernesto—oh, Jesus, kid." Lightner chuckled. "Dead . . . end."

Hector looked up from his plate of chicken and rice that we'd catered in. He was looking better today than he had for a while. We'd taken blow after blow in the prosecution's case-in-chief, but things had gone well today, and his expression seemed to reflect the turn of events. Hector generally liked to keep up a brave front. He was a stubbornly proud man who did not like to show weakness; it made our relationship with him difficult at times. He was quick to anger and seemed to hold grudges, which probably made him an effective politician. It also explained, in my mind, the reason for his divorce almost eight years ago, though Joel Lightner had favored another theory—that Hector's true tastes didn't run toward the female gender.

He had a good politician's story. He'd grown up on mean streets and dropped out of high school but eventually returned and got a college and legal education to boot. He started at the bottom of city government but worked his way up quickly, having thrown in a few extracurricular hours on the mayor's political campaign to win a few chits. He got fairly close to the mayor—as close as he could, probably more an alliance than friendship—and ultimately took a shot at the senate seat and won. He was a street fighter. He went after his opponents ferociously. He'd put Joey Espinoza's head on a stick if he could. And yes, we figured he probably did engineer this extortion scheme with the Columbus Street Cannibals, though we thought the murder of Adalbert Wozniak was beyond even Hector's capacity.

"Who's Ernesto Ramirez?" Hector asked.

"Guy we met during the canvas," said Lightner. "He runs a non-profit called *La Otra Familia* or something. He was a mentor to Eddie Vargas. We asked him for information and he said he didn't know nuthin-bout-nuthin. Like a hundred other people said. But this guy Ramirez, he must have scratched his cheek or averted his eyes or something when he answered, so young Jason here is convinced he holds information that could break the entire case wide open."

Paul smirked. Lightner and Riley liked to point out my youthful vigor—read näiveté—from time to time.

But I had built up some additional credibility after today. Hector looked at me quizzically.

"The guy's a former Latin Lord and he's still close to them," I explained. "Whatever it is he knows—"

"If he knows anything," Lightner interjected.

"Whatever he knows, he probably knows from the Lords," I said. "I think maybe the Lords shot Wozniak, not the Cannibals. Now wouldn't *that* be a nice thing to share with the jury."

"The Lords? Why would they do that?" Hector asked. "It's not their turf. It's not even *La Zona*."

"I don't know why," I said. "But Ernesto Ramirez does. I just know it."

"And how many times has Ernesto Ramirez told you to go fuck yourself?" Lightner asked.

"Only twice," I conceded, to the amusement of the other lawyers. "But I haven't turned on the charm yet."

7 I DROVE HOME, MY EYELIDS HEAVY, EXHAUSTED FROM the comedown after an intense day but propped up on electricity. This had been probably the best day of my professional life. After today, I thought we had a great shot at an acquittal, which three months ago would have been unthinkable. It wasn't lost on me what this could mean for my career, for my family. I'd never had money, and until a year ago served as a county prosecutor making shit for a salary. This case could make me. Driving home, I let it swim over me, ambition mixed with fantasy, fancy cars and a second home and an Ivy League education for Emily Jane, foreign things to me, all of them.

I found them both in the nursery when I came upstairs. We had done up one of our spare bedrooms into a nursery for a little girl, pinks and greens with bunny wallpaper. Talia was seated in the rocking chair that her mother had used for her. She had been breastfeeding Emily, and the little one seemed to have settled down for the moment. Talia managed a weak smile but didn't speak, not wanting to wake the dozing munchkin.

"How's she doing?" I asked.

Talia simply nodded. She looked beautiful and awful at the same time. The shape of her coal-black hair, which she had cropped in anticipation of Emily's birth, still looked new to me, though tonight it was unwashed and flat against her head. Her eyes were puffy and lifeless. Maybe four hours, tops, of sleep over the last two days will do that.

"How are *you* doing?" I whispered.

"I'm fat, tired, and my nipples are killing me."

"Other than that, I meant."

"We're still on for my parents tomorrow?"

"Sure, yeah." Tomorrow—Friday night, we were heading out of

town to see Talia's parents, who lived ninety miles south. Talia's mother had MS, and it was hard for them to make the trip up to the city.

Talia managed herself out of the chair with Emily cradled in her arms and began the transition. Emily let out a soft moan, and those large, expressive eyes opened. When she saw me, she grimaced in that unsubtle way that babies possess. Pure horror might have described it better. She wasn't in favor of the transfer from Mommy to me.

"She had a dirty diaper an hour ago and I just fed her," she said.

"Okay. Hey, beautiful."

Now safely in my arms, my bellicose beauty broke into a full-out cry, the tiny red face collapsing into utter revulsion. I bounced around the nursery, humming to her and bringing my face close to hers, but she wanted Mommy. I wasn't good at this yet. I hadn't developed a rapport with her, a rhythm. With the amount of time I'd spent at work these last ten days, I was hardly different from a guy off the street. I pulled out my bag of tricks I had developed to date. I changed my tone of voice. I closed my own eyes to see if she would mimic. I cited the preamble to the Constitution. I recited her a poem I'd memorized in junior high ("It was six men of Indostan to learning much inclined, who went to see the elephant though all of them were blind"). I held her up at my shoulder, in the crook of my arm, on my legs while seated. I tried a few songs I knew. "Catch" by the Cure. "The Riddle" by Five for Fighting. "Verdi Cries" by 10,000 Maniacs. All over the board, but all slow and soothing, at least when sung properly. If I was any kind of a vocalist, it might have worked, but I wasn't, nor was my voice a source of calm to her. That, in the end, was the real problem. It wasn't what I was saying or doing, but the fact that it was me, not Talia, saying and doing it.

And then it just happened; she ran out of steam. Her eyelids fluttered and she was asleep, her head resting in the crook of my arm. She looked like her mother, the almond shape of her eyes, the tiny nose and full lips. Asleep, at peace, she had Talia's placid expression, too.

Time passed. Her tiny, warm body rose and fell, short breaths escaping from her mouth. I couldn't take my eyes off her. Until I couldn't keep my eyes open.

We got two hours like that, sleeping together on the couch. I was startled awake by her stirring, a moment of panic as I realized I'd been responsible for holding her while I slept, never a good idea. My head had fallen forward during sleep, and now I had a crick in my neck as a reward.

Once Emily realized who was holding her, it was back to the horror movie. I couldn't keep my eyes open, but I tried to sweet-talk her, which never worked on any other female in my life, so I don't know why I thought it would now.

"I'll take her." Talia was at the landing, looking in on us in the family room. "You need sleep." Her hair was all over the place and her right cheek showed a crease line from her pillow.

"You need it more," I noted. I had no idea how she could have awakened on her own, at her level of sleep deprivation.

Emily wailed at the sound of her mother's voice, but as soon as Talia had expertly scooped her from my lap, the cry shut off in an instant, like an alarm clock after hitting the snooze button.

"I don't know how to do that," I said.

Talia kissed Emily's forehead and tucked her into the nape of her neck. "She just doesn't know you yet, that's all. She will." She put her hand on my cheek. "She will, Jase."

I LEFT HOME THAT MORNING ESTIMATING THAT COURT would adjourn early on Friday, and that I'd be able to hit the road with Talia and Emily by no later than five to go to her parents. Evening rain was predicted, she'd told me, so the earlier the better.

Court actually adjourned even earlier than that. Chris Moody, re-directing Joey Espinoza, had wanted to run through the recorded conversations of Hector several times, stopping at various intervals to ask Joey, "Did it sound to you like the defendant was joking *there*? Did *that* sound like sarcasm?" That kind of thing. But I made the point that Joey had testified on cross-examination yesterday that they sometimes misunderstood each other's sarcastic exchanges, so how could Joey really say if Hector was kidding or not? It became enough of a distraction that Chris Moody dropped it altogether, opting to make his pitch in closing argument.

When Chris Moody sat down, he looked awful. He'd had a rough night, I imagined. His star witness hadn't done well, and there wasn't a whole lot he could do to rehabilitate him. This case was far more important to him than it was to anyone else in the courtroom, save Hector. This, I assume, was going to be his crowning achievement before he went for the big bucks in a major law firm, not starting as a junior partner like me, but at the equity level, the really big bucks. But if this went the other way on him, it would be a pretty black mark. And at this point, I figured it was even money, at best, that Chris Moody would convict Hector Almundo.

After court recessed at two o'clock, we retreated to the law firm. Hector's spirits were relatively high. Paul tried to dampen enthusiasm, but I could see it in his eyes, as well. The prosecution hadn't proven Hector's knowledge of, much less involvement in, this conspiracy. There was no concrete evidence that he had any idea what was taking place. Joey Espinoza simply was not credible, and the tapes reeked of staging—Espinoza forcing the conversation, discussing the topic when Hector was distracted or making it sound like a joke so Hector would agree, sarcastically. Though Paul didn't want to raise expectations, he had to acknowledge the current state of affairs, because we were debating whether we should call any witnesses at all or just rest.

"I'll be back Sunday," I told him. "If you're sure it's okay I go."

"It's more than okay. It's an order," said Paul. "You did a great job, kid. Go have fun and we'll talk Sunday afternoon."

I looked at my watch. It was half past two. I still had time for one more errand before I hooked up with Talia and we drove downstate.

I drove to Liberty Park, where I knew I would find Ernesto Ramirez. I got out of my car and passed through a tall chain-link fence at a spot where someone had torn open a human-sized portion. Why rip into this fence when there was a gate just down the way? Because kids are stupid. It's the kind of thing I did, too, when I was a kid.

I walked across the wide expanse, grass and concrete. A grown man, without a child in tow, feels funny these days walking among children in a park under any circumstances, and throw in that I was wearing a suit, and I had white skin, and I pretty much stuck out like oil on snow. I was headed for the basketball court, where I'd previously talked with Ernesto.

They'll know, he'd said.

Ernesto was with two other Latino men who looked to be in their mid-twenties. One of them was wearing a ripped tank top, long shorts, and court shoes. The other was scrawnier and wore an oversized shirt and blue jeans. I'd seen enough of them in my time as a prosecutor, the posture and cocky chin. Gangbangers, or I wasn't a south-side Irishman.

The scrawnier one saw me first and said something to Ernesto, who looked my way. When he saw me, he started to come toward me, presumably to separate the two of us from his friends. But I was so close I could almost touch him, and for this function I was performing, I literally had to make contact with him.

He managed to say, "The hell are you doing," before I slapped the envelope against his chest.

"A subpoena," I told him. "You've been served. You must appear in federal court next week to testify in the case of *United States versus Hector Almundo.*" It was all very formal and unnecessary. The subpoena inside would tell him all of that. But I wanted the drama. I didn't have anything left.

Instinctively, Ernesto had accepted the envelope before I'd explained its contents. He stared at it and then looked up at me, shaking his head. "No," he said. "I don't—I won't—"

"It's your decision," I said. "You can appear at that date and time, or federal marshals will come and escort you. And then you can explain to a federal judge why you're different from everyone else who is subpoenaed."

"No," he repeated. He seemed to be in shock, only now catching up with what was happening.

"And if you lie about what you know," I went on, "you could be charged with perjury."

"You threatening my friend?" It was the bigger guy, the one with the torn tank. Up close, I could see the tiny tattoo of a dagger on the inside of his upper arm. He was a member of the Latin Lords. He had only a slight trace of an accent. He'd learned English and Spanish simultaneously as a child, I assumed.

Standing face-to-face, as we were now, I towered over him. I was six-three and he was five-ten at best. He had wide shoulders and some muscle tone, a scar across his forehead, a crappy goatee. He was meaner and tougher than me, but only one of us knew that for sure. I looked down at him, making eye contact for a long moment before I uttered two words with sufficient conviction that I was making it clear, I'd only say them once. "Back. Off."

It threw. him momentarily. He'd expected retreat. Now he was reassessing. In my experience with the gangs, they respect the well-dressed white man who marches onto their turf, because they assume he's law enforcement. For all this guy knew, I was an FBI agent.

"*Oye*," said Ernesto, placing a hand on his friend's arm. "*Permítame.*"

"*Buen consejo*," I said. Listen to Ernesto and back off.

"You can't make me say something I don't want to say," Ernesto said to me.

I slowly took my eyes off Ernesto's friend and looked at Ernesto squarely. "I can put you on the stand and ask you questions all day. I have a pretty good idea of where to start. I'll get there sooner or later. If you lie, I'll know. And if you refuse to answer, you'll go to prison for contempt."

"No," he said. "No, you can't—"

"I can and I am. My card's inside that envelope," I told him. "Including my cell. You talk to me now or I'll see you in court."

It was my best pitch. I drove back to my office. I wasn't feeling great about what I'd done, but I was out of options. I was betting that compelling his testimony would ease whatever conflict was plaguing him. I'd be making the decision for him. You can't ignore a federal subpoena. So with his back against the wall, he'd come clean. Maybe.

My cell phone buzzed as I was exiting the highway into the commercial district. Traffic had been murder at four o'clock on a Friday night. It reminded me of our trip to see Talia's folks tonight. But the phone call wasn't from Talia. The call was from Ernesto Ramirez.

"Hello," I said with as little feeling as I could muster.

"You said before—you made me an offer before. I tell you what I know and you keep me out of it."

"Right, I said that. The longer you take to tell me, the harder it will be for me to use the information, the more I'll need your live testimony."

"What does that—"

"It means tell me right now, Ernesto. Right. Now."

There was a pause. Electricity shot through me. I thought it was actually coming.

"Not over the phone," he said.

"Okay," I said, trying to conceal my reaction. I'd broken through. Easy and calm was now the right approach. "Where and when?"

"Later today," he said. "I'll have to figure out how. No phones, though. Face-to-face."

"Then make it very soon. I'll meet you anywhere. Don't keep me waiting, Ernesto," I told him. "Do not keep me waiting."

9 I HUNG UP WITH ERNESTO AND TRIED TO KEEP MY expectations low. He seemed ready to play ball, but a promise wasn't anything more than a promise. Still, the more he'd held out, the more valuable his information appeared to be, the more my hopes rose in the air like they were filled with helium.

Talia called my cell as I was walking back into my office building. "Hi, babe," I said. "I'm trying to wrap everything up. I'm at the finish line."

"Great. Okay," she said, somewhat distractedly. I could hear Emily making a yelping sound near the phone. "Remember it's supposed to rain tonight. It would be good to get on the road as early as possible."

"Right. I just have to wait to hear from that guy I told you about, Ramirez. I'm on his schedule, not the other way around." Talia and I had been over this briefly this morning, but like most disjointed conversations while caring for a newborn, there had been no real resolution.

"And this matters, even if you're at the finish line?"

"It depends on what it is he gives me," I said. "We haven't formally decided to rest our case, and even if we do, if I uncover something huge, the judge would let us reopen."

Talia tended to Emily a moment. I was used to such interruptions. I waited her out.

"Does that mean you're planning on working this weekend, too? I mean, if this is 'something huge,' does that mean you aren't coming?"

I didn't have a good answer to that. "I don't know. He said he'd call me soon. I don't know 'til I know."

"That's not very helpful, Jason."

"I don't know what else to say. These are unusual circumstances."

"Are they?" Talia's tone sharpened.

"Yes," I said. "They are. This guy's life is hanging in the balance,

Tal. He's being accused of murder and I might be coming upon evidence that proves it didn't happen the way they say. I'd put that down as unusual circumstances. Wouldn't you?"

"I'm just wondering if we're going to have an evolving standard of 'unusual.' That's all. Is there always going to be something? Am I going to be raising our children alone?"

"That's not fair—"

"You know what? I'm tired and nauseated and cranky, and right now I'm not in the mood for *you* to tell *me* what's 'fair.' I believe you told me last night that Paul told you to go with us this weekend, not to worry about anything else."

"But that was before Ramirez agreed to—"

"Okay. Jason? Just—stay here, okay? Stay here and go the extra mile for a man who you think is guilty of just about everything they're accusing him of doing."

"Talia, just—just give me an hour or two, okay? Two hours," I decided. "Two hours."

*   *   *

NINETY MINUTES CAME AND WENT. No call from Ernesto Ramirez. Paul Riley called my cell with a quick question about a document. Then, sensing something, he asked, "Where are you?"

"Office," I said.

"I thought you were going with your wife this weekend."

"I am. I'm just waiting for somebody."

"Tell me what you're doing."

I sighed. "Ernesto Ramirez. You remember that guy I told you about?"

"Jason, Jason. He's waiting to talk to Ernesto Ramirez," Paul said to someone. I heard Joel Lightner laugh and call out, "Dead end, kid!" I heard our client, Hector Almundo, say, "Tell him to go with his family."

"Well," Paul summarized, "the universal conclusion of your senior partner, your client, and your private investigator is that you should forget about this guy and go be with your family."

"I'll take that under advisement," I said.

"Hey kid—seriously. I know what you're trying to do. You're trying to pull a rabbit out of a hat. I've been you. But it's late in the game, and I think your part is done. You've done a phenomenal job and your family has earned a day or two of your time."

"Understood," I said. "But if—"

"That's an order, kid." The last thing I heard, before Paul hung up, was the sound of Joel Lightner and Hector Almundo laughing.

Well, laugh, I thought. *It will just make that rabbit all the more magical.*

*   *   *

HALF PAST SIX. Still no call from Ramirez. I was back on the phone with Talia.

"What's the delay?" she asked me.

"I don't know. He— I don't know. I tried his cell and he didn't answer. But I think it will be soon."

"You think it will be soon."

"Maybe 'hope' is a better word. What if—"

"Jason."

"—we waited until tomorrow morning—"

"Jason."

I stopped. There was an icy calm to my wife's voice.

"Emily and I are going now. You feel like you have to wait there, and I feel like I can't wait any longer. I'll call you when I get to my mother's."

I let out a long, sorrowful sigh. "Talia, baby, I swear that this won't always be like this. I promise."

There was a long pause. It sounded like my wife was crying. I wanted to fill the space with more promises, but I wasn't sure they helped. A promise never made is better than a promise broken, and I'd fractured plenty of them since this trial started.

"Say good-bye to Em." Talia's voice had choked off; she barely got the words out with emotion filling her throat. I heard her away from the phone. "Daddy's saying bye-bye, honey."

"Bye, sweetheart," I called into the phone. "Have fun with Grandma and Grandpa, Em. I love you, sweetie."

"Okay." Talia took the phone back. "Bye."

"I love you," I said, but the line had already gone dead.

And that was the last I heard from my wife. I spent the next four hours bouncing off the walls at my law office, cursing Ernesto Ramirez for the delay, making silent vows to Talia and Emily Jane, going online to investigate possible vacation spots for after the trial. Things would be better after this case. I would make it up to both of them. It wouldn't always be like this. This trial was the exception, not the rule.

When the phone rang four hours after we spoke, I thought it might be Talia, safely at her parents' house. Or I thought it might be Ramirez, finally agreeing to meet with me. In that brief flash of time as the phone rang, it didn't occur to me that she always dialed my direct line or the cell, not the general line that was ringing, nor did it occur to me that Ramirez would have probably used the cell phone number I'd given him.

Mr. Kolarich, I'm Lieutenant Ryan with the State Troopers.

I'm afraid I have some bad news, sir.

I don't remember with any specificity the next two hours. I remember my dumbfounded, illogical comments to the state trooper—she couldn't be dead, I just spoke to her a few hours ago; are you sure it was *my* wife and child in the SUV bearing our license plate, on the route we always took to her parents' house? I don't remember driving until I got to the backup on that county road, at which time I pulled the car over and jogged over a mile to the scene, blocked off with cones and tape and squad cars. The story was easy enough to discern without explanation; no doubt the other drivers, sitting idle in the traffic jam behind us, could have figured out what happened, too. That tricky curve in the road, the incessant rain bringing a one-two combo of poor visibility and a slick driving surface: Some car had gone over the embankment.

Looks like they died on impact, another state trooper told me, as we stood at the curve in the road that Talia had missed, by the side railing that had a large piece torn out of it, down at the ravine out of which they had fished Talia's SUV. I remember saying those words over and over for comfort, *they died on impact,* not believing them, trying to push out the image of Emily restrained in a car seat, under-water, struggling to breathe. *No, they died on impact. Painless. No pain.*

I remember rain, slapping unapologetically on my shoulders and hair. I don't remember calling my brother, Pete, but I do remember him being there, gently pulling me away, smelling his damp, musty windbreaker as his arm went over my shoulder.

I remember my cell phone ringing, and I remember taking it out of my pocket and throwing it into the ravine.

Various snippets follow: Arguing with the mortician about the amount of makeup on Talia's face as she lay in rest. The wake for my wife and daughter, surrounded by hordes of conservatively attired people, members of my law firm whom I didn't even know, still being a relative newcomer, and deciding that I had no interest in ever knowing them. Paul Riley, in that laid-back style of his, men-tioning offhand the acquittal of Senator Hector Almundo on all counts, all thanks to me, and telling me to take all the time I needed before returning to work. Paul cautioning me not to rush to judg-ment, after I told him that I'd never be returning to Shaker, Riley and Flemming at all. Talia's father, indirectly reminding me, more than once, that I was supposed to be driving Talia and Emily Jane the night they died. Thinking that I should be crying when I wasn't, and shouldn't when I was. Being tired, exceptionally tired.

In hindsight, I was probably a ripe target for them, for everything that happened. After that phone call from the state trooper, after burying my wife and daughter, I had nothing left that I cared about in this world. I had nothing left to lose.

That, more than anything, is why I did what I did. And that, more than anything, is why they wanted me.

ADVICE OF COUNSEL

Six Months Later:
December 2007

10 I STOMPED MY SHOES OUTSIDE THE DOOR OF MY OFFICE to shake off some accumulated snow. The frosted glass on the door read, in the appropriate order, SHAUNA L. TASKER, ESQ. and JASON KOLARICH, ESQ. "Hey," I said as I passed the administrative assistant whom we share, Marie, who has put her archaeology degree to fine use.

"What's the occasion?" she asked. I didn't feel the need to respond to her commentary on my attendance record. If this law office were a school, I'd have been expelled long ago for truancy. It's not that I don't like practicing law; I just don't like clients very much. They are needy and ungrateful.

"Why don't you go dig under your desk for some Incan deposition transcript or something," I suggested.

After I had spent a few months in a funk, Shauna basically dragged me to this firm and demanded that I rekindle my romance with the legal profession. I have no idea how to be a solo practitioner. Since law school, I'd been a prosecutor—where the cases come to you, thanks to a reliable slew of criminal activity in our fair city—and then a junior partner at Shaker, Riley, where partners like Paul Riley reeled in the clientele and I just did the work. The pattern here is I got to focus on the work without having to stroke some idiot for business and tell him how honored I was to represent him.

Shauna, bless her heart, has thrown a few cases my way, and I have benefited from a few cases courtesy of our upset victory in *United States v. Hector Almundo*. Most of them are criminal cases, which is fine as long as you get the retainer up front, but few of them are particularly interesting. The heaters—murders or white-collar cases—typically go to larger firms where the lawyer has gray hair.

"Hey," I said, popping my head into Shauna's office. She had her feet up on her desk, reviewing some transactional document. She does courtroom work like me, but she has wisely broadened her practice to handle basically anything else—real estate transactions, start-ups, trusts and wills, any number of commercial transactions. I refuse to do any of that. Put me in a courtroom, in the battle, or leave me alone. She is also active in three different bar associations, which allows her to "network," meaning she has to socialize with other attorneys, which is something else I detest with an intensity I normally reserve for brutal world dictators, or the Dixie Chicks.

So, to summarize: I don't like clients. I don't like transactional work. I don't like small-caliber criminal cases. And I don't like talking to other lawyers. I'm hoping to create a niche in the market for people under indictment for serious felonies who don't require that I converse with them.

"Twice in one week," Shauna observed upon my arrival. "Wow."

"I'm looking to set a personal best," I explained.

"That's the spirit. Just don't overextend yourself."

The attitudes on these women. I started back to my office but then popped back in, wondering what was different about Shauna today. It was the glasses, black horn-rims instead of her usual contacts, and her blond hair was pulled back. "The naughty-librarian look," I noted.

Shauna paused, to show her disapproval, then glared at me over her glasses. "Charming. Very mature." Shauna was easy on the eyes, as they say, more for the sum of her parts than any particular detail—smartly dressed, fit, intelligent—but like most professional women, she didn't like to be thought of as a slab of meat by the knuckle-dragging males in the profession. The reason she'd left her former law firm, in fact, was because the senior partner had certain ideas about the employer-employee relationship that were, let's say, inconsistent with Title VII.

Shauna and I had a few go-rounds in college ourselves, but we quickly recognized that animal sex and compatibility were two different things, and we managed to stay buds afterward. We really didn't have much of a choice back then, because there was a whole gaggle of us packed into a house off-campus, forcing people to double up on rooms, and somehow Shauna had drawn the short straw and gotten me as a roommate. That was after I got kicked off the football team for punching out the team captain, and I was lucky not to have been expelled from the university altogether. Had the team captain pressed charges, I would have been toast, but I think he found the whole thing embarrassing, considering he was an all-conference offensive lineman who was flattened by someone a hundred pounds and four inches his lesser.

My office would appear, to the untrained eye, to be abandoned. I had a couch that my brother had spotted me in one corner, shelving with law books, and a desk with nothing on it but a computer. I didn't like coming here, because it reminded me that someday soon, I was going to run out of money from my days at the silk-stocking law firm, and I'd have to get off my ass and restart my career. It was hard to imagine doing it here, but I didn't have a better idea. For several months after the bottom fell out, I'd received weekly calls from Paul Riley or someone else from the firm, asking me back when I was ready. But I couldn't go back there. And I couldn't stomach the idea, at this point, of answering to anyone else. As surprising as it may seem, given my overall sunny outlook on life, I don't like being told what to do, and I don't like having to be nice to people.

To summarize: I don't want to work for anyone else, or for myself.

My intercom buzzed at about ten o'clock. "Someone to see you," said Marie.

I hadn't expected anyone. "Do you want to give me a hint?" I asked. "We could play twenty questions."

"No, I'm happy to tell you, if you'd like."

Always the attitude.

Marie said, "Her name is Esmeralda Ramirez."

 I HADN'T THOUGHT OF ERNESTO RAMIREZ FOR SIX months. After Talia's and Emily's deaths, I had dropped out of society. The trial finished without me. I hadn't followed up with Ernesto and, presumably, neither had anyone else.

That was kind of funny, as I thought about it, because I had spent the last six months blaming myself for not being the driver of that SUV that night, allowing my sleep-deprived wife to navigate a winding road in the rain, but I had never included the reason for my absence—Ernesto—in the equation.

It came flooding back now, images from that time, mostly the haunting ones by the roadside, the identification of the bodies, the phone call to Talia's parents, but also Ernesto—his ambiguous expression when we first interviewed him about the Wozniak murder; the fear in his voice later on, as I homed in on him.

And most of all, the panic in his eyes when I'd slapped him with a subpoena, forcing him to testify to whatever knowledge he possessed. I wondered, for no particular reason, if Ernesto had shown up in court that following week. I was bluffing more than anything. The subpoena was real, no question, but I had threatened to put him on the stand and question him all day long, when in fact I wouldn't have done so. I wouldn't have flown blind in front of the jury. I hadn't even given notice of the subpoena to the federal prosecutors yet. I was just trying to force Ernesto into a corner.

Esmeralda Ramirez walked in behind Marie. She was a tiny

woman with long black hair pulled back, a youthful face save for prominent worry lines dancing along her forehead, and what appeared to me to be a very modest demeanor, gripping her purse with both hands in front and only briefly making eye contact as she walked in. I took her hand and she squeezed mine softly.

"Thank you for seeing me," she said. "Do you know who I am?" She was from Mexico, I recalled, and the accent confirmed it, but she spoke English comfortably.

"I know your husband."

She watched me a second. Her expression changed a bit. "You *know* him?"

"A bit, yes." I didn't understand her inquiry.

"My husband is dead," she said.

"Oh, well, I'm very sor—"

I didn't, I couldn't finish that sentence. Dread filled my chest. Ernesto Ramirez was dead, and here was his widow in my office. And she wasn't here, I gathered, to have me administer his estate.

"You didn't know," she said.

I shook my head, no.

"But you were the lawyer, weren't you?"

The lawyer. I put my hands flat on my desk. "Six months ago, I was trying to get some information about a case from him, yes. Is that what you're referring to?"

"I don't know what I'm referring to." A trace of frustration had crept into her voice. "My husband, his way—he wouldn't talk about something like that with me. It would be *his* job to worry about things like that, not mine. I knew only a little bit."

"Tell me how he died, Mrs. Ramirez."

"He was shot to death." Her dark eyes trailed off.

I steeled myself, not wanting to ask the next question. I felt like I knew what the answer was going to be before I asked. "When was he shot?"

"June twenty-second. A Friday."

I closed my eyes. June twenty-second was the day I served him with the subpoena. June twenty-second was the day I waited in my office for him to call, rather than traveling with Talia and Emily to my in-laws. June twenty-second was when life, as I knew it, ended.

"Does that mean anything to you?" she asked me.

"Maybe," I said, but it seemed like a whole lot more than *maybe.* "Did they catch the shooter?"

"No. He was killed in Liberty Park. That's in *La Zona.* Do you know what that is?"

I nodded. And I could see where the police would have a hard time making a case. "They figure it was a gang shooting," I said. "But in the 'zone,' that gang could be the Cannibals, could be the Lords. Could be random gang violence, could be intentional because your husband was trying to steal away their recruits from gang life. No way of knowing, and next to impossible to get anyone to admit they saw anything. Is that about how they explained it?"

Her eyebrows rose, almost imperceptibly. "Pretty much exactly."

"But you think they're wrong."

She was quiet for a while. No, of course she hadn't accepted the cops' conclusion. That's in part because no one ever really accepts an unsolved murder of a loved one. The crime becomes all they have left of their spouse or child, whatever, and knowing that your loved one was murdered, but that nobody will pay for it, is like walking around with a missing limb.

But the other reason Esmeralda Ramirez wasn't buying the cops' theory was, in a word, me.

"I knew there was something wrong," she told me. "I didn't know what. He mentioned a lawyer. I didn't understand. I asked him if he was in trouble with the law or something. He told me, 'Not in the way you think.' He talked about a lawyer but said it wasn't a lawyer for him. It was just a lawyer who wanted to know something. A lawyer who was persistent."

I didn't want to interrupt her, but when it was clear she was done, I said, "And he was reluctant to talk to that lawyer. To me."

She nodded. Her eyes trailed up and she started to speak, then stopped.

"Go ahead, Mrs. Ramirez. Ask away."

"Call me Essie." She thought for a moment. "You talked to him and then left him alone for a while. And then, after a time, you came back. Is that right?"

It took me a moment, but I realized that she was correct. I'd worked on Ernesto pretty hard about a month out from trial. Then I gave him some space, a few weeks, and called him, at which time he told me to go jump in a lake. I let it lie for months before returning near the end of the trial to make a final, full-court press.

She said, "Whatever it was you did worked, I think. At first, I mean."

"When I first approached him."

"Yes. He wouldn't say much to me. He was so protective, Ernesto. So protective." Her eyes welled up but she kept her chin high and her voice strong. She cleared her throat. "I think you convinced him to talk about what he knew."

"But he didn't."

"Apparently not. I remember he came home one day—he was very upset."

"Scared?"

She angled her head. "Upset more than scared. Kind of— *decepcionó*. I don't—"

"Disappointed," I translated.

She nodded. "Thank you. He said to me, *'La verdad no importa.'* The truth doesn't matter. He said it wasn't worth prison. And then he said he didn't want to discuss it with me or with the lawyer or with anyone. That was it. He never brought it up until a few days before—before the—"

Before I returned, accosting him and hounding him.

"And what did he say then?"

She shook her head. "Little. Just that the lawyer was back, and he didn't want to tell him anything. He couldn't," she corrected herself. "He said he couldn't tell you."

I put a hand over my face. I couldn't believe this was happening.

"I tried to talk about this to the police after he was killed, but there was nothing to tell them. They kept asking for details and what did I have? I didn't even have your name."

It raised a question that hadn't yet occurred to me. "How *did* you get my name?"

She nodded and reached into her purse. "It's funny, how long it took me even to clean out his drawers. You don't want to do those things because it's so—final, I guess."

I understood her completely. Talia's clothes still hung in our closet. Emily's room was exactly as it was the day she left with her mother for the trip to see Grandma and Grandpa.

"I found this, of all places, as a bookmark in a book he was reading." She produced a business card, and even across the desk I recognized its style. It was a business card bearing the name of Shaker, Riley and Flemming. She handed it to me. "Your card. Turn it over."

I did. On the back of my card, in black ink, a small diagram had been written:

$$ABW \rightarrow PCB \rightarrow IG \rightarrow CC?$$

"Do you know what that means?" she asked.

I put the card down and blew out a sigh. I didn't want this. I didn't want a mystery. I didn't want to go back. A door that I'd been trying to close was now opening, a crack at a time, only it wasn't sunlight pouring through but an ugly, lethal darkness. I didn't want to think about Ernesto Ramirez because it made me think of my wife and daughter.

"ABW is the name of Adalbert Wozniak's company," I managed. "I have no idea what the rest of this means."

"Adal—? Who's that? Was he a friend of my husband's?"

"Not particularly, according to your husband." I gave her the

Reader's Digest on Bert Wozniak, including that I had been investigating his murder and thought that her husband, Ernesto, had information on that subject. "But I never knew what he knew," I said.

"So we know nothing," she said, bitter and disappointed. Another dead end.

Her composure was on the verge of crumbling. She was a proud woman, I could see. Proud like Ernesto as I remembered him. They made a good couple. Ernesto had beaten some odds and made a decent life for himself and Essie and their two kids. He'd come upon some incriminating information, undoubtedly, something dangerous, and he wouldn't have been the first person who would choose, in that instance, to keep his mouth shut about it. He would have been thinking about his family.

But Essie Ramirez was wrong. I knew two things.

I knew that I got her husband murdered.

And I knew that I would find the person who killed him.

I DON'T BELIEVE IN FATE, PER SE, BECAUSE THAT WOULD be giving more credit for a higher being than I have been willing to concede of late. I grew up a God-fearing Catholic but with a healthy dose of skepticism that was allayed only briefly, when I met Talia and we had little Emily Jane. But if I don't believe in a predetermined order of events, I do believe there is some higher order in play, that we are one gigantic chemistry experiment, with various actions causing reactions that we often chalk up to coincidence.

Was it divine intervention that former state senator Hector Almundo called me later that same day, after I spoke with Essie Ramirez? Probably more like happenstance. It's not like he hadn't reached out to me before. He'd stopped by the funeral back in June. He'd called after the acquittal, though my cell phone was swimming with the fishes, so to speak, at the bottom of a ravine off of County Road 11. He'd even sent me a note after I rejoined the legal community at my own shop.

He'd been facing the possibility of a life sentence, after all, had he been convicted on all counts. Instead, he walked out a free man, however bruised his political career had become. He'd been forced to abandon his run for attorney general and he didn't bother running for reelection to the senate, having faced a formidable challenge in the Democratic primary while he awaited trial.

But that was then. Having stood up to the G and actually won, Hector Almundo had become a hero of sorts to the city's Latino community, which often felt as if it drew the short stick on law enforcement's pursuit of justice. Statewide ambitions were probably permanently erased. No matter the result of a multiple-count felony prosecution, you're smeared. But more locally, where Hector was within his base constituency, he undoubtedly harbored new ambitions. Certainly another run for the senate seemed in the cards. The county board, perhaps. Maybe the first Latino mayor?

"You never write, you never call." He gave me a warm smile as the waiter filled our water glasses. The joke fell a little flat, but the gesture was nice enough. I never decided how I felt about Hector. Though he'd never outright admitted as much, I was relatively sure that Hector had enlisted the Columbus Street Cannibals to, shall we say, conduct voter outreach. I figured, at least before Ernesto Ramirez came into my life, that the Cannibals gunned down Adalbert Wozniak, but I didn't put Hector next to that. Didn't seem to be his style; Paul and I assumed that the Cannibals had simply taken matters into their own hands. In the end, Hector Almundo had a politician's lust for cash and power, but I wasn't sure that put him permanently on the side of evil. I didn't see the world in black and white. And there is something about being someone's defense attorney, his protector, that puts a paternalistic gloss on the entire relationship. My role was to be on his side, so the emotions tend to fall in lockstep.

"I'm doing great," I told him, in response to his question, hoping the crisp answer indicated I wasn't interested in elaborating. "What are you doing these days?" Hoping my return volley would underscore that point.

Whatever he was doing, he was doing relatively well. He was always a flashy dresser, today in a gray suit and light purple shirt, a pin propping up a tie only a shade darker than the shirt. I never understood the monochromatic thing.

"I'm the deputy director for the Department of Commerce and Community Services," he said. "Say that three times fast."

I couldn't even say it once. I had no idea what it meant, but I wasn't surprised that Hector had landed a bureaucratic post. I couldn't imagine him doing an honest day's work.

"State government," he said. "Governor Snow tapped me for the post."

Carlton Snow had been our governor for all of a year. The previous governor, Langdon Trotter, had resigned from office when he was appointed the U.S. attorney general. Unlike Trotter, Snow was a Democrat; in our state, the lieutenant governor runs separately from the governor, and in our typical political schizophrenia, we elected a governor and lieutenant governor from different parties. When Trotter took the federal job, Snow became the governor for the remainder of the term.

"You know," he said, "I wouldn't have made this offer while you were at Shaker, Riley. But since you're out on your own and all—there are opportunities for lawyers in state government. I could work out a contract for you, if you like."

Right. I imagined a guy in a short-sleeved shirt and polyester tie, denying a claim because someone forgot to check a box, and the-rules-clearly-state-that-if-you-don't-check-the-box-we-can't-process-the-application.

Hector seemed amused. "You can stay in private practice," he said. "The state would just be another client you have. You have any idea how many outside law firms have contracts with the administration?" he asked me. "Litigation. Transactional work.

There's a lot of money to be made there. And some of the work is interesting."

"I suppose. How does that work, exactly? Is there a list?"

A waiter took our orders. Hector had a chef salad. I had a turkey sandwich and soup. When the waiter left, Hector sliced open a roll and buttered it. "No list," he said, as if that were an understatement. I didn't catch the point and didn't ask.

"Now, a referral from someone the governor trusts," Hector said. "Someone who thinks you're an excellent attorney and who would be happy to sponsor you. That would help."

"Now I just have to find someone like that," I quipped. It was nice of Hector to make the offer. He probably felt like he owed me. In fact, he did not. He'd paid his considerable legal fees to the firm, and that was all that was required. But I could see it from his perspective. We did more than perform good legal work. For all practical purposes, we saved his life. He surely felt the same toward Paul Riley, but Paul was wealthy beyond need and had a nomination to the federal bench pending. I, on the other hand, had just suffered a personal tragedy and, from an outside viewpoint, my life probably seemed to be off-track. Actually, that sounded pretty accurate from an inside viewpoint, too.

"Snow is the new game in town," he said. "He's going to run for a full term and he thinks he's going to be president someday."

"Is he right about that?"

Hector deferred on that. "He's raising a helluva lot of money," he answered, which seemed to be his way of saying, *maybe*. "It might not be a bad train to get on, Jason. Just as it's leaving the station." He nodded to me. "Are you a Democrat?"

I drew back. "Does that matter?"

"Yes, of course it does. Are you?"

"I'm a south-side Irish Catholic, Hector. It's a prerequisite to baptism." The real answer was, I generally dislike both political parties and don't feel loyal to either one.

"In the primaries," he said. "Do you pull a Republican or a Democratic ballot?"

"I'm not sure I've ever voted in a primary."

"Oh, for God's sake." Hector shook his head, as if I were hopeless. "Okay, well, I'll see what I can do. This is something you'd want?"

I told him the truth: I wasn't sure. But the clients weren't exactly streaming through the door, and maybe Hector could find me something interesting.

I had no idea just how "interesting" it would be.

THAT AFTERNOON, I PUT IN A CALL TO JOEL LIGHTNER, private eye extraordinaire—just ask him—and put in for a favor. Then I stared at the ceiling and thought about Adalbert Wozniak and Ernesto Ramirez. I had to start with the safe assumption that their murders were related. And the federal government had more or less conclusively fingered Wozniak's actual killer. It was that teenage Cannibal—Eddie Vargas was the name, if memory served. But a sixteen-year-old gangbanger didn't commit that murder without say-so, without some direction. And that same person saw Ernesto as a threat and ordered his death.

Good. I had mastered the obvious. Also, one plus one equals two.

What had Essie said? She thought my initial visits with Ernesto had been successful. I'd appealed to him. But then one day he returned home upset. *Decepcionó*. Disappointed. Upset. *La verdad no importa*, he'd told his wife. It wasn't worth prison, he'd told her. Prison—for Ernesto? Had he been part of something illegal? I didn't know. But clearly, my powers of persuasion had moved him to talk to somebody. And more to the point, somebody had talked to him. Threatened him. He'd gone from wanting to come forth with his information to sealing the vault. He'd cut me off at the knees when I'd called him.

The truth doesn't matter. It's not worth prison.

Whatever it was, clearly someone, at that point, knew that Ernesto had information and had discouraged him, to put it mildly, from sharing it with me.

And then I'd returned. I caught him at the YMCA working out with some friends. I walked into Liberty Park and slapped a subpoena against his chest. Highly visible, each of those encounters. A mistake on my part. A fatal mistake. Born of necessity at the time, I thought.

I had three avenues of pursuit. One was to figure out who ordered the hit on Bert Wozniak. Find him and I'd find Ernesto's killer. No problem, right? Piece of cake. Except that the federal government had marshaled all of its considerable resources and couldn't pin it on anyone. Christ, they even knew who the shooter was, and still they couldn't crack that nut. And that's to say nothing of our investigators, led by one Joel Lightner. We would have loved to come up with an alternate theory for Wozniak's murder, obviously, and we'd come up dry.

The second line of pursuit was to figure out what information Ernesto possessed. Same result, if successful. But difficult. He didn't tell his wife, presumably for her own protection. Maybe he told a friend. But if that person were any kind of friend, he would have told the *policía* investigating Ernesto's murder. Even anonymously. One way or the other, he would've gotten the word to the cops. So it felt unlikely that Ernesto had told anyone at all.

The third avenue was to forget about Wozniak and answer this question: Who knew that I was hounding Ernesto at the end of the trial? That was a critical two-day period of time. After all, nobody killed Ernesto after I first spoke with him. It seemed, in fact, that someone gave him a stern warning. But they didn't kill him. Then, suddenly, come Friday, June 22, they take him out in a drive-by at Liberty Park. The intervening cause was me. So they got word, somehow, that I reinitiated contact.

I remembered two gangbangers, Latin Lords, standing with Ernesto at the basketball court at Liberty Park. One stockier guy in a tank top with a scar across his forehead; one younger, scrawny kid in blue jeans. Could I remember their faces if I saw them again? Maybe. Then there was the YMCA. A handful of guys there, at least one of whom knew Ernesto well enough to be spotting him during bench presses. I didn't know their faces well at all. But I could find them again easily enough and get their names, unless they dropped out of the Y.

And what about that diagram Ernesto had written on the back of my business card:

$$ABW \rightarrow PCB \rightarrow IG \rightarrow CC?$$

"ABW" was Wozniak's company. "CC" probably meant the Columbus Street Cannibals. Other than that, I was at square one. I don't like being at square one.

"Hello, Sunshine." Joel Lightner strode into my office, pulling a wheeled cart that held three bankers' boxes of papers bound together with a thick elastic strap. "If there's anything, it's in here," he said. In the workup to Hector's trial, we had pulled records of every phone call made by Wozniak in the six months preceding his death; every document from his corporate and personal computer; every website he'd ever visited; every contract his company, ABW Hospitality Supplies, had ever entered into. Any of that information, theoretically, could have been a lead, but only if you had some hint of what you were ultimately seeking. We didn't. We'd taken several shots. Employee grievances at ABW. Disputes with other contractors, even a couple lawsuits over time. Nothing that panned out. Nothing worth killing over.

But now, at least, I had something. Cryptic initials on the back of a business card, but at least something.

"Say thank you to Riley for this," said Joel, pulling a laptop computer out of his shoulder bag. "This is the database." High-tech firm that Shaker, Riley was, we'd had a paralegal scan in every document obtained from ABW and put them on a searchable database. "The hard copies are there if you need them, but the computer should be all you need. Return it in good condition. He says hello, by the way."

The database made my job infinitely easier. I could do word searches for the initials Ernesto had written down and see what hit.

"So, you were right about that guy Ramirez? He had some information?"

"Never felt so wrong to be right."

Lightner nodded and appraised me. I don't like being appraised. "You didn't put the information in the guy's head," he informed me. "You just asked for it. That was your job."

"Roger that."

"Not your fault, I'm saying."

"Heard you the first time. Understood you the first time."

"Yeah, well, aren't you full of piss and vinegar today." He looked around the office. He didn't look impressed. I wasn't, either. He looked at his watch. "Let's go have a pint across the street. My treat."

"Joel, in contemporary American society, the phrase 'my treat' indicates that you are willing to pick up the tab for the other person. I realize there's a first time for everything, but I wanted to make sure you intended to convey that message. Would you like to rephrase?"

He hitched his thumb toward the door. "Before I change my mind."

I patted the computer lightly.

"C'mon, Kolarich. It can wait. It's got nothing to—well, anyway."

I could have finished the sentence for him. *It's got nothing to do with what happened to your wife and daughter.* He wasn't completely off base here. I was motivated to investigate this by Ernesto's death, because it sure seemed like he had correctly feared retribution if he gave up his information, and I forced him past the point of no return with the subpoena. But it wasn't lost on me that the reason Ernesto never got back to me on that fateful Friday was that someone put a few bullets into him, and that delay led to my waiting pointlessly in my office instead of traveling with my wife and daughter.

Yes, that was part of it. But not all of it. This morning, I looked into the eyes of a woman who lost the love of her life, and who would now raise her two children alone. Ernesto Ramirez had the right to keep whatever information he had to himself. But I publicly confronted him and got him killed.

"Have it your way." Lightner stopped on his way out. "Okay, so you've never taken my advice before, but I'll give it, anyway. Have that hot little partner of yours handle this matter. Let this one go."

"That's probably good advice," I conceded. "And I'm sure Shauna will be flattered beyond words."

As soon as he walked out the door, I booted up the computer.

14

BLESS THESE COMPUTERS, BUT THEY'RE ONLY AS GOOD AS the moron directing them, and I didn't have much to go on other than conducting searches for the "PCB," "IG," and "CC" initials that Ernesto Ramirez had written on the paper. My money had been on "PCB," because it sounded more like an acronym. What it stood for, I had no idea, and the search came up empty. I'd had a fleeting thought that it referred to that chemical that had leaked into public drinking water supplies years ago, causing death, mayhem, and barrels full of money for lawyers. I briefly warmed to the notion of a grand conspiratorial cover-up about poisoned water in our city's sanitation system.

I tried a Google search on my office computer with the initials "PCB" and found all sorts of hits, but I didn't think Adalbert Wozniak had been killed by the Pakistan Cricket Board or because of a printed circuit board in a video game.

My curiosity and, more to the point, stubbornness kept me in my office well past normal hours, poring through the database until I finally got lucky. I decided to look at lawsuits involving ABW Hospitality, because, by definition, those cases involve two things that can lead to murder if pushed to the extreme—hostile feelings and money. Turned out that ABW Hospitality Supplies had filed suit in April 2003 over the denial of a contract to supply beverage and vending services to the state's Department of Motor Vehicles' affiliate offices. As a governmental contract, it was let out for public bidding, and the entity handling the bidding—also one of the defendants in the lawsuit—was the Procurement and Construction Board—the "PCB."

These days, as someone recently reaffirmed to me, litigation is part of all public contracting. You get passed over on the government contract, you sue. Why not? Take a shot at getting the contract. You're no worse for trying. So I didn't see a lot of significance here.

But then I said out loud, "The government," and it appeared to me from the recesses of my memory, my conversation with Ernesto Ramirez over the phone. I'd told him that if he talked, I'd cover him, that I'd have the government protect him as a material witness.

The government, he'd repeated, emphasis on that last word. *Man, you don't get it.*

I'd meant the federal government—the U.S. attorney—not state. But maybe Ernesto wasn't splitting that hair. Regardless, his emphasis on that word, which I hadn't appreciated, had to be significant. He was saying the government was part of the problem here. Surely, it deserved further inquiry.

I switched back to my office computer and did some due diligence on the state's Procurement and Construction Board. It listed all kinds of contracts for work performed throughout the state, ranging from consulting and professional services contracts to road repair work to building construction and everything in between. It was rather staggering, the number of contracts our state entered into with outside vendors ("Child Care Technology Project Manager;" "Nastrum Center Elevator Repair and Maintenance;" "PSD Foam, Mattress Core for Marymount Penitentiary"). The list reached the thousands.

Lots of money. Hundreds of millions, possibly billions. All running through the Procurement and Construction Board.

I looked up the members of this board, hoping that it would net me the initials "IG" or "CC." No luck. Gregory Connolly was listed as board chairman. The other four members were Alex Morris, James Clark, James Hathaway, and Antonia Harris.

I read through the allegations contained in ABW's suit against the PCB, which had been dismissed after Wozniak's death and the close of his company. According to the complaint, ABW had been the lowest bidder on a beverage contract, but the PCB had rejected its bid and given it to the next lowest bidder, Starlight Catering.

I sent an email to Joel Lightner, asking him to take a look under the hood of Starlight Catering. Then I looked through my Rolodex— and by Rolodex, I mean a mess of business cards shoved into the drawer of my desk—and found Hector Almundo's cell phone number. I dialed it up, not expecting him to answer, and I wasn't disappointed. I left him a quick message.

"Hector, it's Jason Kolarich. About that thing we discussed," I said.

15 I SPENT THE NIGHT IN, READING WITH THE TELEVISION on, but I spent more time simply looking out the window. A light snow had dusted everything, casting a serene blanket over my neighborhood. I don't ordinarily welcome winter, but the change of seasons felt oddly cathartic. And I'd grown tired of summer and fall. I used to think that if grief were a color, it would be gray. Not black—too extreme, too intense. Gray is that fuzzy compromise, lacking its own identity. But after I lost my wife and child, I colored it green—vibrant, flourishing life mocking us, highlighting our irrelevance, cruel and indifferent to our pain. I wanted to cut down every tree, uproot every plant and flower. I wanted to pull the sun down out of the sky, bathing the earth in darkness. Even the orange and browns of our brief autumn disgusted me, its simple beauty a grotesque and sniggering insult.

But it was becoming different now. Maybe not better, but different. The cymbals did not crash as often between my ears. The nightmares had subsided. The throat-gagging, pulse-pounding, breathtaking pain was replaced with a quiet ache, a soft echo in a large, empty house.

*   *   *

HECTOR SAID HE COULD spare fifteen minutes for me in the late morning. I went to the monolithic state building in the city's downtown and found the Department of Commerce and Community Services on the thirteenth floor. An elderly uniformed man sat at a desk, under a large photo of a beaming Governor Carlton Snow—his thick mane of brown hair and that goofy smile. I showed my identification and he made me fill in my name and purpose-of-visit in a schedule book.

These offices could not be mistaken for anything other than government—thin carpeting, unimaginative beige walls, cubicles made of a cheap cloth. But I'd spent most of my career in the county attorney's office, so this was more what I was accustomed to than the princely surroundings of Shaker, Riley and Flemming. After winding my way through the maze, I was inside Hector Almundo's office, nothing fancy but a decent picture-window view of the commercial district's north side. Hector was done up like always: bright yellow shirt, chocolate-brown braces over his narrow shoulders, a tie the color of a falling sun, propped up by a collar pin.

"The PCB," he laughed, after I made my request. "You've been doing your homework. Definitely where the action is."

"If it's a string you can't pull," I started, appealing to his ego.

"No, no. No, no." Hector, I had gathered for some time now, wanted to impress me. I had seen him at his worst, at his most terrified. I had listened to his darkest secrets. If there was anyone in the world who might think ill of Hector—aside from the federal prosecutors—it should be me. He wanted to please me. He also wanted to show me how much power he still had. Hector was in

rebuilding mode, having overcome the wrath of the federal government but losing his senate seat in the process. Some people in his
situation would just be happy to have avoided prison and would opt
for the quiet life. But Hector wanted everyone to know that he was
back—or at least on his way.

"How would this work?" I ask. "I put my name on a list? Fill
out some application? Do an interview? Do we even know there's an
opening?"

Hector was giving me a paternalistic smile before I'd even finished. "There's an opening if we say there's an opening. A list," he
chuckled. "I'm sure Charlie will want to meet you."

Charlie. None of the PCB board members were named Charlie.
"Charlie Cimino," Hector said, in response to my inquisitive look.
"Everything goes through Charlie."

Charlie Cimino. So maybe the "CC" Ernesto had scribbled on
the back of my business card hadn't been the Columbus Street Cannibals, after all. "He's some director of something?"

"Charlie? No, Charlie's the—well, call him an unofficial adviser.
Be nice to Charlie, Jason. He can . . . make life difficult."

That last piece of advice was intended to be lighthearted, but
I sensed a tension behind the words, that Hector wasn't really kidding. I didn't know this guy Cimino, but he already had an ominous
aura given his presumed inclusion on Ernesto's diagram.

I left with the promise that I'd be hearing from someone soon.
I got a call later that afternoon, setting something up for tomorrow.
So much for inefficient government—it had taken two hours to work
my application, such as it was, through the channels. Tomorrow,
I would meet Charlie Cimino.

16

I TOOK A CAB OVER THE RIVER THE NEXT MORNING TO the near-north side, where the streets were mobbed with shoppers at the high-end boutiques just two weeks before Christmas. I had a headache from lack of sleep and my back was sore from the three-hour interval in the dead of night when I actually did nod off, albeit in the love seat in my family room. I do that a lot these days. Sleep is easier when I'm not in our bedroom. Because now it's just *my* bedroom. I knew I'd have to sell that townhouse one of these days—meaning my brain was telling me that, but so far I had resisted.

Suffice it to say, I wasn't looking forward to Christmas, my first without what we affectionately dubbed Team Kolarich. I didn't connect any memory of the holiday with Emily Jane, as this would have been her first, but Talia and I always enjoyed that time of year, jealously reserving some time just for us and away from our families. My brother, Pete, was down in the Caribbean right now nursing some wounds from a rough few months—long story—and he'd asked me to join him for that week through the New Year. Maybe. Otherwise, I had no family with which to spend the holiday, unless I drove up north to visit my father in prison, the probability of which I put just below the likelihood I would shave my head and become a Tibetan monk. Although I hear Tibet is lovely this time of year.

I missed the warmth of the cab, though not the smell of body odor, once I stepped into the frigid air outside. What little snow had fallen over the last day had been ground into dirty slush, which I tried to avoid because I hate wearing rubbers over my shoes but I also hate wet shoes. Life's full of conflict.

Ciriaco Properties was out west, a ways from the lake, away from the boutiques and closer to the trendy lofts and restaurants as the city gentrified west. I signed my name with a doorman and took a gold-plated elevator to the twenty-third floor. I checked the walls for a sign, which direction to turn, when I realized that the entire floor was this one company. I pushed through a glass door and found a woman at a tiny reception area who could have been plucked out of a swimsuit competition.

The place could best be described as hip modern, with abstract art filled with primary colors along the walls, designer rugs, sharp geometric angles. I followed the receptionist—about six feet tall, maybe a hundred twenty pounds after a full meal, which to her was probably a couple of celery stalks; shiny blond hair; a simple, form-fitting black dress—down the hallway to an office with a gold plate stating MR. CIMINO.

The guy had the entire south wall for an office, floor-to-ceiling windows showcasing the city's south and east, a view to the suburbs on the west. The north side was a paneled wall featuring a gigantic flat-screen television carrying a cable news channel, as well as a door that, I assumed, led to a bathroom. I thought I should look both ways for an airplane to land before I approached the desk.

Ciriaco "Charlie" Cimino's primary business was real estate development. From what I could gather online, he held property all over the city, as well as other places in the country and overseas. He had something like twenty or thirty million dollars' worth of real estate, but that didn't mean he was worth twenty or thirty million. It might, but it could also mean he was leveraged to the hilt. The real estate market wasn't so great these days, and wealth on paper did not translate to wealth in your pocket. It meant you were always making deals, always juggling a lot of balls, living and dying with the roller-coaster market.

Cimino was talking on a headset, his hands moving expressively, as he stood looking out the south window. It was the portrait of the man looking over his city, which I suspected was exactly the profile he'd hoped to convey.

"Let me know," he concluded, then turned to face me. He didn't smile. He was a barrel-chested Italian, olive complected, dark through the eyes, with a thick mustache that lent an overall scowl to his face. He was dressed in a suit that looked like it had been tailored for him overseas, a glossy smoke-colored piece of silk.

"Jason," he said, without a hint of warmth. He tried to shake my hand more strongly than I did his, and I let him. "Have a seat."

His desk was modern, a long slice of steel with thin legs. He sunk into a high-backed leather chair and crossed a leg. He trained those hawkish eyes on me. I saw no reason to speak until he did.

"Tell me about me," he said.

"I've been practicing—" It took me a moment before I realized what he'd said, another moment to be sure I'd heard him correctly. "You have more than a dozen corporations under Ciriaco Properties. You own several million dollars' worth of property. And Governor Snow trusts you."

He nodded, just once. "What else?"

"You have excellent taste in receptionists."

One side of his mouth budged, maybe a centimeter. "About forty million. Depends on the day." He glanced at his bare desk and tapped his fingers. He wanted to show me that he was unimpressed by that gargantuan figure. "So you saved Hector's ass."

"The jury did."

"To listen to Hector, you turned water into wine. Did you?"

"The feds overcharged."

That comment seemed to find a soft landing. "The feds always overcharge. It's a negotiation. An opening bid."

I couldn't disagree with that. But I didn't take it personally, and it sounded like Cimino did.

"And now you want to work for the PCB."

I lifted a shoulder. "Hector and I discussed some options. It sounded interesting."

"Why?"

"It's one thing to help someone once they're in a jam. I like the idea of helping people avoid it in the first place."

That, I thought, was my best sales pitch. If I was in simply because I was Hector's friend, then I had this job as long as I didn't pull my dick out during the interview. But if he was actually evaluating me, then here I was, a former prosecutor and current defense attorney, with no experience in government bureaucracy, no time spent dispensing legal advice on how to do this or that, really very little to offer other than my charm and good looks—except that, if I knew how to charge people with crimes and how to get them off those charges, then I could probably also help steer people from crimes at the outset. As far as I knew, that's what non-litigator lawyers did—steer clients through the legal land mines. Who better than someone who'd been there when the mines exploded?

Cimino nodded slowly. He didn't speak for a long time. Sometimes people do that as a test to see if the other guy will fill in the dead air by babbling. I used to do that in interrogations all the time. I once got a confession on a B-and-E just by shooting looks at the suspect. "The contract would pay you three hundred an hour," he said. "No limit. Bill every hour you work. You'll make a lot of money."

Wow. Three hundred an hour, no cap, for government work sounded awfully generous. It was the first time that morning that I had been surprised.

"You'll need to raise twenty-five thousand for the governor by the end of next year," he said.

And that was the second time. I met his eyes. He was wondering how I would respond. So was I. I couldn't find the words to best express how I felt about having my wallet picked. A couple of expletives might have found their way into my response, along with general suggestions of where the demand for money could be inserted—certain bodily orifices leapt to mind.

Cimino seemed amused by my reaction. "You've never raised money before. You'll learn. It will be worth it to you, believe me. You do your part, you'll get a lot more back. A lot more. Understand?"

I nodded.

"You prove yourself to us, you'll be rewarded."

"Fair enough."

"You fuck me, I'll fuck you harder. Understand *that*?"

Jesus, this guy. I've never had much time for people telling me what bucket to piss in, but I wanted this contract. I wanted in. The more time I spent in this office, the more I knew that this had something to do with Ernesto Ramirez's death.

It seemed to me that the entire reason for meeting with Cimino was these last exchanges: the money, the promise, and the threat. Hector had already greased the wheels for me. This guy just wanted to see whether I was willing to kiss the ring.

"Then I better not fuck you," I said.

And that was it. One request to an acquaintance, ten minutes with this stroke-job of an egomaniac who made me feel like taking a shower after I departed, and I had a contract for legal services with the state's Procurement and Construction Board. My radar was buzzing, but that was the point. I was, in a very real sense, looking for trouble. Something told me that it wouldn't take me very long to find it.

17

"How uncharacteristically enterprising of you, young man." Shauna, my law partner and probably best friend, if I thought about it, seemed genuinely surprised. She took a healthy drink of wine from the bottle and passed it to me. "It's almost like you want to have a legal career, after all."

Shauna had been on me to pick things up at the firm, starting with showing up on a daily basis and using my celebrity as Hector Almundo's lawyer to drum up business. Technically, I was just renting space from Shauna and she had no financial connection to my success. But she was hoping that jumping back into the pool would help me recover from whatever it was she had diagnosed as ailing me.

Maybe I was, too. I was taking this gig because I wanted to look into what happened to Adalbert Wozniak and, by extension, Ernesto Ramirez. But I couldn't deny that I was intrigued. It always seemed like a dark and murky world, this backroom political thing, and if it had escalated to a murder or two, so much the more enticing. It was reckless of me, sure. Nothing that I would have done, had I still been married to Talia and a father to Emily Jane.

Then again, it could have been the wine emboldening me. Shauna and I were camped out on her living room floor, listening to old R.E.M. music on the iPod hooked up to her stereo and splitting a bottle of red wine with our spinach and garlic pizza. This was basically how we spent our junior and senior years at State, only back then we had about a dozen other roommates, and if you wanted to lie on the floor, you needed a tetanus shot. Shauna now had a condo in a high-rise on the near west side, which was pretty small (about a thousand feet) but with a terrific view west that made the place seem twice as large.

We'd fallen back into this routine of late, hanging together the majority of evenings and listening to music or watching the rare show worth viewing on television—a list that grew smaller each year—or sometimes clicking on one of the inane shows that passed for entertainment just so we could ridicule it. Some nights, I'd just slept on her couch rather than make it home. It was always her place, never mine; there was something haunted and unspoken about my townhouse.

Shauna, with her short blond hair, blue eyes, and small frame, had a bit of an angelic look about her, but she could dissect me like a frog in biology class. "So what's the catch?" she asked, leaning back in the chair behind her desk. "Why this government thing?"

"Steady work between high-profile murder cases."

"I see." She wasn't buying it, and the tone of her voice was her way of saying so. "But this is just a contract, right? Just a client? You're not becoming a state employee."

"And leave behind this dynamic private practice I've built up?"

"Hey, listen." She pulled her oversized sweatshirt over her knees.

"Christmas. What do you have going on?" She always did this, since Talia's death, asking after me but in a casual way that tried to deflect her concern.

"I might go down to see Pete. Otherwise, I don't know. You?" I passed her the bottle.

"My family's coming. My parents and my brother's family. I think it's more an intervention than Christmas dinner."

"Ah," I said. "You're over thirty, and not even a boyfriend, Ms. Tasker." Shauna grew up on the city's south side, like me, though we didn't meet until college. I couldn't even call myself Catholic compared to her. Her parents were outfitting her for a nun's habit when she informed them she was heading to law school. She never told them that I was her roommate in college. They wouldn't have survived it—dual coronaries within minutes of each other.

"Anyway, I could use a lawyer for the interrogation," she offered.

"I'll pretend to be your boyfriend. We'll say we're living together."

She laughed, but the offer still stood and I hadn't answered. "Maybe," I said. "Thanks."

She let it go, nodding toward the iPod resting on her stereo system. "You can't group them by twos the way you're saying."

"Sure you can. *Murmur* and *Reckoning,* obviously. *Fables* and *Pageant,* when Michael started feeling confident in his voice."

"He wasn't confident in his voice during *Reckoning?* Ever heard 'South Central Rain'?"

"An anomaly." I took the wine from her. We'd had this debate over R.E.M.'s music since State. She had trouble admitting she was wrong. I was fortunate not to have that problem, because I was always right.

"You know, Lynette asked about you the other day," she said.

"Lynette from law school? Jewish girl with the nice rack?"

Her head fell back, resting on her shoulders. "Why are men such single-cell organisms?"

"You like us that way, Tasker. You can manipulate us and turn us into groveling dogs."

She smiled, still looking up at the ceiling. "That's true. We can."

She didn't move, but I felt her eyes fall on me. She was constantly poking around with this kind of stuff, gauging my progress. She wasn't lying, I suspect; Lynette from law school probably had made a comment, but Shauna chose her words carefully and wouldn't have mentioned it unless she'd had a reason.

I loved Shauna. The way she watched over me, while challenging or insulting me in the same breath, was downright touching. But sometimes her protectiveness landed the wrong way, like an off-color comment made in mixed company. The slow unraveling of my senses, as the second bottle of Cabernet lay empty on the carpet, on this particular evening put me into the early stages of edgy belligerence.

"Next topic," I suggested.

"I'm drunk is the next topic." Shauna eased herself down to the carpet. "On a weeknight."

"There, there, pet." I stroked her hair. I played some of my early favorites—"Harborcoat" twice, then "Wolves, Lower"—and Shauna grew quiet, her body rising and falling with ease.

"Next year'll be better, Jase," she mumbled. I'd thought she was down for the count. I tried to coax her up and, failing that, lifted her up and carried her to her bedroom. She smiled and moaned with pleasure when her face touched the cool pillow. Moments later she was in a deep slumber. I kissed my hand and planted it on her forehead, then went back to the living room and played the same songs all over again.

18 THE FOLLOWING WEEK, I REPORTED FOR DUTY AT THE state building. An efficient older woman showed me into a small office that I'd be able to use. She showered me with forms to fill out and various bureaucratic idiosyncrasies (I had to take an ethics test; I had to promise to disclose any securities I might sell) and left me for a couple of hours. I had about twenty questions about what I was filling out, but I just did the best I could, or left something blank, figuring they knew where to find me if there was a problem.

The last document I came upon was a confidentiality agreement. I had to swear that I would keep all official business confidential, and that I would not remove any items from the state office. It put a little acid into my stomach to sign it, but it made sense that an office that oversaw hundreds of millions of dollars in state contracts might want to keep the wall up at all times.

The day before, I'd put in a call to Jon Soliday, a lawyer I knew in state government. He was the lawyer for Senate Majority Leader Grant Tully, his lifelong friend. Jon was one of these friends of a friend, but he'd always seemed like a pretty straight-up guy. More recently, I'd come into contact with Jon by virtue of Hector Almundo's prosecution. Nothing hot and heavy, just some general background information from Jon about things the senate did, and some questions he'd had for me, always deliberately vague. I'd sensed that Jon hadn't wanted to get too close to the hot iron. I'd also sensed that, as professional as Jon tried to keep it, Hector Almundo hadn't been his favorite senator.

We met for lunch at the Maritime Club, an old boys' club just a few blocks south of the state building. His hey-how-*are*-you was overly punctuated, given the circumstances, and I thanked him for the note he'd sent after Talia's car accident.

I liked Jon, because he kept most of his thoughts to himself, and when he spoke, he had a good reason. I'd first met him several years ago, and compared to then, he'd showed some signs of age—more wrinkles carved in his forehead, more snow at the temples—but otherwise hadn't changed a bit.

"So what's this opportunity?" he asked me, as he worked some Caesar dressing through his salad with his fork. I can't do that, the salad thing. It's not just a philosophical opposition, although that's part of it; roughage just doesn't fill me up.

"The Procurement and Construction Board," I said. "I have a contract for legal services."

He paused for only a moment, long enough for me to see that I'd struck a chord. With a poker face, eyes diverted, he asked, "Is that something you've already accepted?"

I almost laughed. He'd already given me the answer I'd sought. He didn't want to shit all over my "opportunity" if I had already signed up. If I hadn't, he was going to warn me off. "Give it to me straight," I said.

"I'm not sure I'm the right person to do that." He smiled. "Our current governor and the legislature aren't exactly the closest of friends."

Thinking back, I guess I'd read something along those lines. I didn't follow local politics all that closely, though representing a state senator had attuned me slightly more. The media, always more interested in the conflict than the policy, had covered the fight this past year between the governor and both the house and senate—but especially the senate, and especially Jon's boss, the senate majority leader, Grant Tully.

"The straight scoop, Jon. Please. I'm no partisan. I'm just a lawyer."

"Carlton Snow is an idiot." Jon opened his hands. "That straight enough?"

"Go on."

"He was the city clerk here—meaning you got your marriage license from him—who somehow managed to finagle his way into the nomination for lieutenant governor and then, by some God-forsaken twist of fate, actually won. And then he fell ass-backward into the governor's mansion when Lang Trotter went federal on us. I mean, Snow has absolutely no idea what he's doing, but he thinks he's going to be president some day."

Hector had said the same thing, the presidential ambition. "So—"

"He waltzed in on day one like he's Winston Churchill, having absolutely no idea about the legislative process or how to do anything other than issue a press release. He punched everyone in the capital in the face, refused to compromise on anything, and then wonders why nobody likes or respects him. He surrounds himself with yes-men who tell him he walks on water. See, you got me started." He took a drink of water.

"Don't sugarcoat it, Jon."

Jon's smile quickly evaporated. "The Procurement and Construction Board," he said. "That was initially something Snow created in the governor lite's office."

"The governor—?"

"Sorry, the lieutenant governor's office. Basically, your job as lieutenant governor is to sit around and be ready if the old man croaks, but the one thing that falls under the lieutenant governor is driver's licenses. He oversees DMV."

I'd seen that. Adalbert Wozniak's company had sought to provide hospitality supplies to the affiliate Department of Motor Vehicles offices.

"So, Snow falls into the governorship, and he decides to use that same model. Only the governor doesn't just preside over one agency—he oversees dozens of administrative agencies with millions upon millions of dollars' worth of contracts. Each agency doles out contracts, right? For anything you can imagine. Well, now Snow says, all of those agency contracts—all of them—are going to fall under a single board, the PCB. That's over a billion dollars in contracts, with five people appointed by Snow deciding who gets what." He looked up from his salad. "You get this contract through Hector?"

I nodded.

"Right. And who interviewed you? Derek Bruen?"

"Who's that?"

Jon shook his head. "The guy who'd normally be interviewing you," he said. "Anyone other than Charlie Cimino?"

I drew back. He seemed to have a pretty good handle on things. "Just Cimino," I answered.

"Sure." Jon shook his head and smiled. He seemed to be sensing that he was coming on too strong. "Well, hey, I'll say this much—there's lots of work with the PCB. Lots of money for a private practitioner. I'm sure it'll work out fine."

"Are you?"

He wiped his hands with his napkin and took a long drink of water. "Jason, you're a big boy, and a smart guy. Smarter than they'll be used to over there. Just call it like you see it, and document everything. Paper the files."

"Cover myself."

"Cover yourself, exactly."

"Jeez, Jon, is it that bad?"

He took a long time thinking about that. "The truth is, I don't know. I hear things. But the capital, I mean, it's like a sewing circle. Who knows? But when I say names like Governor Snow and Charlie Cimino, I don't usually use words like 'ethical' in the same breath. Know what I mean?"

I wasn't particularly surprised by what Jon was telling me, but hearing him say these things, I admit, gave me some pause.

"Look, I'll just say this once, Jason. Because you're asking. And then I'll shut the hell up."

"Okay." I opened my hands. "Hit me."

"The second best thing you can do is be careful, like I said. Cover yourself."

"And the best thing I could do?"

"Walk away," he said. "Walk away, Jason." He wagged a finger at me and did not smile.

19 "THIS IS WHERE EVERYBODY WHO WANTS SOMETHING comes. And we're the ones who decide whether they get it."

Patrick Lemke was the executive director of the Procurement and Construction Board, which meant he oversaw the daily operations and prepared the board for its meetings every other week. Lemke was tall and out of shape, with half a head of unpredictable hair and thick glasses and no shortage of nervous energy. He generally avoided eye contact but, every now and then, those beady pupils shot glances in my direction. His forehead was glossy with sweat, even though I found it rather frigid in this office. I hoped it couldn't be chalked up to nerves, but after listening to him ramble for a few minutes, I concluded that his natural equilibrium was hot-nervous.

A few minutes turned into ninety, as Lemke gave me an overview that was essentially a repeat of what I'd already read in a thick manual. The state gives out hundreds of millions of dollars in contracts annually, and they can give them out all sorts of ways. They can do the traditional "blind" bid—everyone makes their best offer, under seal, and the lowest bidder gets the bid, regardless of who they are or whom they know. That was the easy part; the rub was all the different exceptions to that rule, where it was impractical, impossible, or unnecessary to go through the sealed bidding process.

Only one of us grew tired during this lecture. This guy was like the Energizer bunny, and I was getting a headache. Finally, after offering to answer any questions several times, and appearing disappointed that I had none, he told me that he was "very busy" and "really had to go," as if I were clinging to him to stay, and rushed out of my office.

It was my office but I was sharing it, or at least it was big enough to share. There were two desks and five file cabinets and a small window that looked into another building and a radiator with peeling yellow paint that appeared to cough and hiss more often than it provided heat.

"Oh, and one more thing," Lemke said, bouncing back into the room and startling the bejeezus out of me with that high-pitched voice. "Nothing leaves this office. You can't take any of the documents out of here. And no emails."

"No emails? Isn't this the twenty-*first* century?"

Patrick didn't seem to be one for humor. He stared the wall and said, "Don't email documents or say anything sensitive over email. It can get hacked. Okay, I really gotta go now. Oh, and you have your ID? You have to have an ID to get in and out—"

"I have my ID"

"You have your ID, okay, good. I'm going to be late now—"

Out he went. I'd been given five contracts to review for next week's meeting. I calculated the amount of time it would take to pore over these specifications, multiplied by how boring it would be, and came up with multiple headaches and many cups of coffee. I had a purpose for this gig, and it wasn't driven by money, but as I thought about it, I was taking a real flier that any of this would even result in anything that would give me a hint as to who killed Ernesto Ramirez. Well, at a minimum I would do some legal work and make a few bucks—

"Oh, and do you play music loud?"

"God, Patrick." I turned away from the box I was emptying and looked toward the door. This guy moved around so quickly, his footsteps didn't even make noise. "Do I—"

"They don't like it when you play music too loud. If you have a stereo or whatever." He was staring at the carpet.

"I won't play music at all."

"No, you can play it, just don't play it loud."

"I'll just hum to myself."

"Okay, so, I should go."

I waited patiently, hands folded, humming to myself quietly, for Patrick to return. It took three minutes.

"Oh, so this is the last thing, unless you have any questions."

"I do have a question," I said, startling him. His face lit up. He even looked at me for a brief second. A question!

"How far back do the files go for the PCB?" I asked.

"Okay. The governor just started this board when he took office a year ago. I mean, he had it in the lieutenant governor's office, but he transferred the PCB—"

"Patrick. I was just wondering, if I needed to refer to past practices, if I would be able to access prior documents. Maybe even back to when the PCB was under the lieutenant governor's office."

"Oh, sure you can. I can show you where to look. It's in one of these cabinets, the hard copies I mean, but it's also online, and I really have to go."

"Sure. We can talk about it later."

"Okay, good."

I couldn't be sure if Patrick was gone for good, but I had the sense that I would never know that in this job. I considered closing the door for some privacy, but it was my first day, and the other offices had their doors open, so it didn't seem like a good idea.

After giving Patrick ten minutes to pop back in, I started looking through the files for the contract Adalbert Wozniak's company, ABW Hospitality, bid on in 2005. I looked through all of the file cabinets and even made a passing attempt at finding things on the computer, but I was out of luck. I'd have to wait for Patrick to scare the shit out of me again and show me where to look.

I had to prepare memoranda on the five contracts by the day's end. If you had looked up "bureaucratic hell" in the dictionary, you would have found my assignment, which included these thrilling topics: "Asbestos Abatement Materials" for the Department of Corrections; "Collection Cups for Random Drug Testing" for the Department of Corrections; "HIV-1 Oral Fluid Transmucosal Exudate Collection Devices" for the Department of Public Health;

"Asphalt Crack and Joint Filler" for the Department of Transportation; and "Passenger School Buses and Wheelchair Lift Buses" for the State Board of Education. I would've had more fun watching water freeze. The Internal Revenue Code was a coloring book by comparison.

Just as I'd finished the final memorandum for Patrick, he popped back into my office. "One more thing, Jason, okay? Mr. Cimino might call for you sometimes. He likes you to go to his office."

"He has some official position here?"

That one stumped Patrick. He stared at the carpet for a long time before saying, "He'll give you instructions sometime."

"At his office."

"Yeah, you have to see him in person. He doesn't like phones."

"A man of mystery," I said.

His eyes shot up, briefly, to meet mine. "Okay, I have to go."

He vanished. I'd have to wait to access the ABW file I was seeking. I gathered my stuff together, including the memoranda I had drafted, calculating a full day's work at three hundred an hour—a nice pocket of twenty-four hundred dollars, which rivaled what I was making in a month thus far in my erstwhile law practice.

As I was gearing up to leave, my phone rang. I hadn't even noticed the archaic black contraption in the corner of my desk.

"Mr. Kolarich?" A woman's voice. "Mr. Cimino would like to see you tomorrow at ten A.M."

 I MADE IT INTO THE LOBBY OF CHARLIE CIMINO'S building at the appointed hour, 10:00 A.M. I picked up a pack of gum and looked over a newspaper for fifteen, maybe twenty minutes. Then I took the elevator up to his office.

Don't ask me why I do some of the things I do. After all, my whole reason for doing this job with the PCB was to get inside and see what I could discover about Adalbert Wozniak's and Ernesto Ramirez's murders. You'd think, with that mission, I'd be looking to get along with people like Cimino. But I didn't like the guy, and I didn't like being summoned to his office, so I decided that a little tardiness was in order.

At least I got to follow the swimsuit model down the hallway again to his office, which made the whole trip worthwhile.

"You're late." Cimino was wearing that headset again and standing at the opposite end of his airplane hangar of an office. He started talking again into his headset, something about a general contractor running behind schedule. I helped myself to a chair and waited for this asshole to finish trying to impress me, himself, and the guy on the other end of the phone call.

"The bus contract," Cimino said. "Hey, the bus contract." It took me a moment before I realized he was talking to me. "The bus contract? The Board of Ed? Hang on, Henry." He snapped his fingers at me. "Kolarich—"

"The bus contract, right." One of the contracts I'd reviewed was the State Board of Education's contract for passenger school buses and wheelchair lift buses.

"That's a sole-source," he said, before spinning back toward the window. "I don't give a fuck about a letter of intent, Henry. If I have Citibank as a tenant, the price goes up. So get me out of it." Then he looked back at me. "Okay, kid? A sole-source."

"Sole-source" bidding meant that the contract was asking for something so unique that only one company was capable of performing it, so going through the rigmarole of sealed bidding was a waste of time. But we were talking about providing school buses. There were probably hundreds of companies in this state that could do that.

I shook my head. "The bus contract has to go through sealed bidding."

"Hold on, Henry." Cimino yanked off his earpiece and stared me down. "What the fuck did I just say?"

"You said it's a sole-source."

"Right."

"And I said it's a competitive bid."

"Yeah, and you're a lawyer, right? You argue. Okay, so I see you know how to do *that*. Now argue my side, kid. Give Patrick a memo by the end of the day. Sole-source." He fit the earpiece back on. "Henry, I don't give a shit if they're gonna sue. It's a negotiation. What the fuck is a letter of intent, anyway? I mean, what does that even *mean*? Tell them my *intent* is to fuck them in the ass if they fight me on this."

He went on for a while, and it seemed to me that I had been excused. I wanted to have a few more carefully selected, four-letter words with Mr. Cimino, but I forced myself to stay true to what I was doing. If I'd acted in character, I'd be off this job after less than a week, and none of my questions would be answered.

"Wait, kid, there's something else." Cimino rifled through some papers on his desk. "Right. Here. This was a contract that Corrections put out for sanitation. I don't have the details but Patrick will. The two lowest bidders on the job—I think there are questions about their qualifications. Okay?"

I wasn't sure how to answer that.

"I need a memo discussing whether they're responsible bidders, okay?" he said, as if I were trying his patience. "Make one of those arguments Hector says you're so good at. That's all." He waved at me like I was a peasant and turned back to the window.

On my way back out, I passed an office where a woman was talking on the phone while she typed on a computer keyboard. Something struck a chord, but I couldn't place her, on the cloudy periphery of my memory. She didn't notice me, providing me a moment to stare at her. Nothing particularly remarkable about her—late twenties, light-brown skin, pretty features, typical work attire. Something told me not to linger, to avoid a face-to-face with this woman, which made me even more curious—my subconscious was signaling me but I didn't know why.

I stepped past the doorway and approached the front desk, with the beauty queen. She was on the phone and ignoring me, providing me a moment to linger. I did my best impression of someone waiting patiently to ask a question, while my eyes scanned the desk around her until I found a list of phone extensions on a white piece of paper taped to her desk. I ran down the twenty-some list of last names opposite the extensions. Before I'd reached the bottom, my eyes popped back to a familiar name.

Espinoza.

Right. The woman in the office was Lorena Espinoza, wife of Joey Espinoza, the principal witness against Hector Almundo. She was in court every day that Joey was on the stand, always wearing a defiant expression and ready with a scowl for any lawyer.

We'd looked hard at Joey as we prepared for trial, and looking hard at someone includes looking at his family. Lorena, if memory served, was a stay-at-home mother of three whose education was limited to high school. As far as we could tell—and we looked closely at Joey Espinoza's finances for evidence of bribes—Lorena had not worked or contributed any income to her family for a decade.

But now here she was, sitting in an expansive, elaborately appointed office, hired by one Ciriaco Cimino.

Life, it seemed, was full of coincidences.

21 THE NEXT DAY, AT THE STATE OFFICE, I WAS LOOKING over the Department of Corrections contract Charlie Cimino had mentioned when Patrick Lemke jumped through my doorway.

"You're looking at the DOC sanitation contract," he said. "The top two bidders." He dropped a couple of big files on my desk. "This is the background information. Looks like each of them has had some problems on jobs in the past. It probably won't be hard to find them not responsible."

Another term of art in this world. All bidders who won contracts had to be found "responsible." Otherwise, anyone could put in a lowball bid and win a lucrative contract, and then have no idea how to perform it.

I looked up at Lemke, though he was staring at the wall, that eye-contact problem he had. "Who said I was going to find them not responsible?"

"Well . . ." Patrick shifted his feet, stuffed his hands into his pockets. "I mean, why else would Mr. Cimino want you to—"

"So let me see if I have this right," I said. "Cimino wants to eighty-six the two lowest bidders. I take it, then, that Cimino has some reason that he wants the *third* lowest bidder to get the contract?" I flipped through some papers. "Higgins Sanitation is the third lowest. So Charlie wants to fix it so that Higgins gets the contract, and he wants me to make it happen?"

Patrick didn't seem to like my framing matters so on-the-nose. But it was clear that my summary was accurate.

"Patrick, what's with this guy, Cimino? I mean, how's he in charge of this?"

Patrick stood still and said, "He's an adviser to the governor. Unofficially. He offers guidance. Our direction is to follow it."

It felt like he'd said this before, like it came right after name, rank, and serial number.

Patrick pranced to the door again but put on the brakes so abruptly that I thought he might pull a muscle. "Jason?" he said to the wall, though I think he was talking to me.

"Yes, Patrick?"

"You should do what Mr. Cimino says," he advised me, before disappearing.

22 During Hector Almundo's trial, which centered around contributions to Hector's campaign fund, I became acquainted with the website administered by the State Board of Elections. Through its searchable database, you could track campaign contributions made by any particular person, as well as receipts by any particular campaign fund.

I did a search for the company Charlie Cimino was trying to help, Higgins Sanitation.

The database showed that, prior to this calendar year, Higgins had made a grand total of zero campaign contributions. Not a dime.

But in the past year, Higgins had become more generous in opening its wallet. In the last nine months, Higgins Sanitation had made two contributions to our new governor, Carlton Snow, to the tune of thirty thousand dollars.

Another coincidence, I'm sure.

Next I turned to the other fix that Charlie wanted from me—the school bus contract, which I was supposed to say was so unique that only a single company in the entire state could perform it. The company Charlie wanted for the job was Swift Transportation.

I searched the database and got no hits for Swift Transportation. No political contributions from that company.

But then I searched the campaign fund of Governor Carlton Snow. When I searched for "Swift," I didn't get that company, of course, but there were contributions from "Swift, Leonard J."

Turned out that Leonard J. Swift had also contributed thirty thousand dollars to Governor Snow. And it only took two minutes on Google to confirm that Leonard J. Swift was the founder and CEO of Swift Transportation.

Yet another coincidence. Companies contributing thirty thousand dollars to Governor Snow's campaign fund were becoming remarkably proficient at obtaining lucrative state contracts.

"Enough," I said aloud, though I was alone. I got the picture.

I thought again about Jon Soliday's words: *Cover yourself.*

Now it was time to do the work Charlie wanted me to do. I reviewed the prison sanitation contracts, the documents Patrick Lemke had left me, and some court decisions on the subject of what it meant to be a "responsible" bidder in this state. In the end, it wasn't a close call. Each of these bidders was more than amply qualified, and my two-page memorandum summarized it as follows:

Each of the two lowest bidders for this contract qualifies as a "responsible" bidder under the Code. Either of them is perfectly qualified to be awarded this sanitation contract.

Next it was the school bus contract. This one took even less time. How could anyone argue that driving kids in a school bus is a unique skill? My conclusion:

As multiple, qualified bidders could provide the busing services identified in this contract, the contract is subject to sealed competitive bidding. Swift Transportation, Inc., is by no means the only company capable of performing this contract.

I smiled when I printed out the two memos—no emails, I was told—and threw them into my bag. I just wished I could see the look on Cimino's face when he read them.

Sorry, Higgins Sanitation. Sorry, Leonard J. Swift.

Sorry, Charlie.

23 I WENT BACK TO THE STATE BUILDING AFTER REGULAR business hours. I was hungry and I longed for a burger and milkshake, but I was short on time. Charlie Cimino would be bouncing me from this job any day now, after I defied his orders. Before that happened, I wanted some private time with the PCB files. It took me a while to find the cabinets that held that "old" PCB files, from back when the board fell under the lieutenant governor's office, but eventually I got there.

Once I found the old files, it didn't take me long to navigate them. The scope of the PCB under then–Lieutenant Governor Snow was relatively small compared to its gargantuan reach under Snow as governor. It didn't take me long to find the contract for beverage supplies that Adalbert Wozniak's company, ABW Hospitality, had tried to secure.

I knew most of the facts from the lawsuit ABW had filed when it lost the contract. The contract had been let under sealed, competitive bidding, and ABW had been the lowest bidder. But the PCB had made the decision that ABW was not "responsible" because of some prior lawsuit that had been filed over a previous catering contract. Sound familiar?

The legal memorandum in the file disqualifying ABW was crap. Everyone sued everyone these days. It was just another part of doing business. I had no doubt that the lawyer who wrote this was doing so at the direction of Charlie Cimino or someone like him.

The next part of the file was even more interesting: It was a legal document prepared by the Office of the Inspector General—I didn't have great familiarity with that office—detailing an interview with Adalbert Wozniak over his concern with the bidding procedures for this beverage supply contract. Wozniak had apparently pleaded his case to the inspector general, who ultimately concluded, in typical bureaucratic/law enforcement jargon, that "no credible evidence existed" to indicate any impropriety in the sealed bidding process, and that the legal counsel's determination that ABW was not a responsible bidder appeared to be "sound and even-handed." The inspector general concluded that the matter would be "closed without referral."

Interesting. While preparing for Hector's corruption trial and poring over all the documents and digital records and appointment books we had reviewed from Adalbert Wozniak's office, I had never known that Wozniak had met with the state's inspector general. Maybe it was there and we just missed it, or maybe Joel Lightner had followed up on the lead without success. I would have to ask.

And maybe it didn't mean a thing. But it seemed like Ernesto Ramirez thought so. I now had the "IG" to complete the nebulous initials on Ernesto's note:

$$ABW \rightarrow PCB \rightarrow IG \rightarrow CC?$$

ABW Hospitality had bid on a contract before the PCB; it had been the lowest bidder, which normally would have meant it got the contract, but then it was denied when the PCB determined the company was not "responsible." Then Wozniak turned to the inspector general after being rejected. And the inspector general, if I was deciphering Ernesto's notes correctly, had turned to Charlie Cimino. And then somebody turned to Adalbert Wozniak and pumped seven bullets into him.

I wasn't surprised by any of this. After having spent just a few days with the Procurement and Construction Board, it was clear to me that this place was a cesspool. Adalbert Wozniak had smelled a rat and hadn't kept quiet. He went to the inspector general and made some kind of noise—what, exactly, he'd said, I couldn't be sure. This brief report from the inspector general, dismissing Wozniak's claims, looked like a whitewash.

I needed to know more. And with Charlie Cimino sure to can my ass any day now, I was running out of time.

24 THE REST OF THE WEEK PASSED WITHOUT MY EVEN thinking about the Procurement and Construction Board, or Charlie Cimino, or anyone else. I stayed home from work on Thursday, worked about a half-day on Friday, and had an uneventful weekend. Shauna and I went to a movie Saturday night, but I lost focus halfway through and then I didn't have an appetite for dinner afterward. I was finding it hard to be interested in much of anything; I didn't even think my disinterest was interesting. I was tired of the malaise but that probably made it even harder to shake.

I went to the state building on Monday morning, in preparation for the PCB meeting the following night. Patrick Lemke was bouncing around even more than usual. Strap a battery pack on his back and he could have been in commercials—*he keeps going and going . . .*

Three other lawyers, also working for the PCB, were also milling about. I was introduced to each of them and forgot each of their names instantly. "You should meet Greg," Patrick told me, meaning Greg Connolly, the chairman of the Procurement and Construction Board.

Connolly had a medium-sized office on the floor above me. Patrick knocked on the door and introduced me. The board chairman was a big guy with graying hair that he tried to tamp down with hair grease, with moderate success. He wore a nice suit but he looked like a guy who might be more comfortable at a ball game wearing a sweatshirt. He had blotchy skin and droopy eyes and was about twenty pounds overweight. "I hope Hector bought you a nice dinner afterward," he said. It shouldn't have surprised me that everyone around state government had taken note when the feds lost a case. It didn't happen often.

"It was an interesting case," I told him, because I never give an editorial on the outcome of a case to a stranger. Besides, I wasn't sure how easily words like *good* or *bad* applied to Hector's acquittal. I thought the feds and their stool pigeon, Joey Espinoza, had been overly ambitious, but that didn't mean that Hector had been a Boy Scout, either.

Connolly didn't speak for a while, preferring to nod his head and smile at me while he sized me up. "You've done good work so far," he said. "I've seen your work product. The memo on the DOC sanitation project—the two bidders who underbid Higgins Sanitation."

"Those bidders were well qualified," I said.

"Course they were." He chuckled. "Course they were. That's why I'm saying, good job."

Interesting that he would say that. I'd stood up to Charlie Cimino, and he seemed to be applauding me. And he was the chairman of the PCB. How did he rank compared to Cimino?

"Charlie talked to you about the bus contract, too. I saw that analysis you did."

"There's no way that's a sole-source," I said. "Providing a bus? A hundred companies could do it."

Connolly smiled with approval. I figured there must have been some kind of rift between Cimino and him, a turf battle. He tapped his fingers on his desk. "So, again, good job on that. You'll do very well here, Jason, if you want to."

It wasn't a question, as my former partner Paul Riley would have said, so I didn't answer.

But it was interesting. Greg Connolly had summoned me to his office to give me a pat on the back for defying Charlie Cimino.

Why, I wondered, would he do that?

*   *   *

I hustled back to my law office, where I had a one o'clock appointment, a client who had cold-called me yesterday about representation.

"Sorry to keep you waiting," I said to a man sitting in our small reception area. I took him back to my office. I probably should have offered him water or coffee but didn't. I grabbed Shauna, whom I had asked to attend the meeting, because I was told the conversation would include some transactional issues, and I only did trial work. I was hoping I could throw Shauna some work, as she had done for me several times since I moved into these digs.

"Jack Hauser," the man said, introducing himself to Shauna and me. I could see from his hands and the weathering on his face that he worked in the trades. "Hauser Construction," he said. "We're located out west but we do a lot of subcontract work on jobs here in the city. Flooring, mostly."

He gave me the skinny on why he was here. He had an airport job and the city was screwing him. Also, he wanted to form a joint venture with another company for a downstate stadium renovation— transactional work that was Shauna's domain.

I nodded along as he spoke, scribbling notes on my pad of paper. "How'd you get my name?" I asked.

He looked surprised. Most lawyers don't look a gift client in the mouth. "How did I—I thought you did trial work and things like this."

"I do, sure."

"You probably heard about that corruption case with that state senator?" Shauna said, pumping me up, and probably unhappy with the question I'd asked. It's not good business to seem surprised that a client has come to your door. "Jason defended the senator and won."

Hauser nodded, like that rang a bell. He still hadn't answered my question.

Shauna said, "The joint venture shouldn't be a problem. I did one last year for Ralph Reynolds. We'll just have to be careful with any local business preferences."

I didn't follow very much of what Shauna was saying, but it was clear that Jack Hauser did, and he seemed to like what he was hearing.

"Okay. Well, you're hired, obviously," he said.

I didn't understand what was so "obvious" about that, but I wasn't going to complain.

"So, what do you charge?" he asked, preparing himself for the bad news.

"Three hundred an hour," I said. If it was low enough for the state, why not Jack Hauser, too?

He didn't seem to see it that way. He winced like I'd stuck him with a hot needle. "Any chance we can work on that?" He held out his hands. "I mean, okay, fine, I'll hire you, but—any way to knock that number down?"

We settled on two-fifty, which was still a decent chunk of change. He showed me the complaint the city filed, left me a retainer, and gave me some basic information on the case. Before the end of the day, I had signed an appearance to enter the case as counsel for Hauser Construction, which Marie took to court to file.

Maybe, I thought, hanging a shingle in private practice wasn't as hard as I'd thought. Shauna, dutifully impressed, offered to take me out to dinner of my choosing. "Doubling your clientele in ten days is cause for celebration," she said. Actually, zero times two was still zero, but I didn't want to pass up the chance to pick the restaurant, where I ordered two racks of barbecue ribs with extra vinegar and sweet-potato fries.

I had three glasses of their homemade brew—a red ale—and then Shauna and I had the wonderful idea of staying out a bit longer. We found a tavern down the street, I switched to vodka, and sometime around midnight, I found myself staggering out of a cab. I was bloated and dizzy and thinking about Talia, but otherwise I felt great.

Great, that is, until I saw the car parked in the driveway of my townhouse.

They got out of the sedan in tandem, all four of them, moving in sync, smoothing out their coats, heads darting side to side—all they were lacking were the trademark sunglasses, as it was midnight.

"Jason Kolarich?" One of the four men, from the driver's-side rear door, approached me. He didn't need to bother with the credentials. I'd made them before I had two feet out of the cab. "Special Agent Lee Tucker, FBI."

"How nice for you." I kept walking to my door, trying to mentally steel myself through my intoxication.

"We'll need a minute of your time, sir."

"Not now. I promised my hamster a bath."

"It'll have to be now," said the man behind him. I recognized the voice, and as he approached, his soft Irish features came into focus. It was Christopher Moody, lead prosecutor on *U.S. v. Hector Almundo*. These were serious customers, all four of them, most of all the humorless Moody, but I swore I saw the seeds of a smile cross his face.

THE FEDERAL GOVERNMENT HAD DESCENDED ON MY living room. Four agents, all of them straight-faced with faux solemnity, when underneath it all this was what they loved most about the job. A standard deployment, two to the right, two to the left, as I sat on the couch, staring at a laptop computer resting on an ottoman in the center of the room.

When Chris Moody hit "play" on the computer, dialing up the disk drive, the volume popped too loudly, and he quickly adjusted it. The first voice I heard was easy enough to recognize. It was Charlie Cimino, coming in loud and clear in a conversation that had been intercepted by the FBI:

"Okay, what's next . . . oh, the bus contract. Board of Education. That's the one for Lenny Swift. Okay, here's the problem with that one. The kid—the new guy, Hector's lawyer—he says there's no way to say this is a sole-source and just give it to Lenny's company. No

way to claim there's something unique about buses. So what he says is, the only way to get around the requirement of competitive bids is to break the contract into pieces, so each piece is small enough to stay below the ten-thousand-dollar threshold."

"Very creative," Chris Moody commented as the tape continued.

I didn't answer. My internal thermometer was rising, but I wanted to see Moody's entire hand before I said anything.

"*How do you do that?*" came a second voice over the recording. "*How do you take a hundred-thousand-dollar contract and break it down to increments of ten thousand?*"

"That voice is Greg Connolly," said Chris Moody. "The man you met today," he added, letting me understand how deeply the feds had sunk their fingers.

Cimino's voice again:

"*Break it up by school, the kid says. Give each school a separate bus contract, instead of going through the Board of Ed.*"

I shook my head. Cimino was trying to reassure Connolly by invoking my name—the lawyer had said it was okay. The thing was, I hadn't.

"*Yeah, we could do it by school. That would work.*" It was a third voice, and it was unmistakable. It was Patrick Lemke. "*It would be, like, a dozen contracts, all under ten thousand.*"

"*Then we'll do it that way, by school,*" said Cimino. "*And Lenny gets all of them.*"

"He's talking about Leonard Swift," said Chris Moody. "Swift Transportation. The same Leonard Swift who's donated more than thirty thousand dollars to Governor Snow in the last twelve months."

"I didn't give Cimino that advice," I said. "I never said anything about breaking the contract up to circumvent the law." I was at the boiling point, and without a clear head—I knew better than to be talking to the feds without a sober brain, or a lawyer. My mouth had gone painfully dry, and the buzz I had been enjoying was now an annoying migraine that prevented me from fully focusing on the problem at hand.

Chris Moody, who was now leaning casually against the book-case, looked at me with amusement. The other agents sat stone-faced on the couch.

Moody nodded to the agent who was now manning the laptop. One click and we were listening to the second installment of my nightmare.

"Next is this thing with Marymount. The prison contract." Cimino's voice started the second tape as well.

"Yeah, the, uh, what's it—sanitation?" said Greg Connolly. *"Jani-tor work?"*

"Right, right. Bobby Higgins's company," said Cimino.

"Yeah, and what was the deal there? Someone outbid him?"

"Two companies were lower," said Patrick Lemke.

"Right, but the kid, Kola—what's it, Kolarich, right?" Cimino asked.

"Jason Kolarich," said Lemke.

"Yeah, Kolarich." Cimino coughed loudly, a prolonged, phlegmy gag. *"Yeah, the kid did a number on 'em. DQ'd both of 'em."*

Bullshit again. I didn't disqualify either of those bidders. I wrote a memo doing just the opposite, for God's sake. It was all I could do to sit silently, fists clenched, struggling to keep my legs still.

"This Kolarich is the one—this was Hector's lawyer?" Connolly asked.

"Right, right. Sent the G packin'," said Cimino. *"Why?"*

"No, I'm just saying," said Connolly. *"This is a pretty smart kid, right? He did a good job on this thing for Higgins. I mean, he could be useful, is all I'm saying."*

"Remains to be seen. Smart enough, yeah, sure. I mean, he pulled Hector's head out of his ass, and we know how hard that can be."

Everyone on the tape got a good chuckle out of that. Moody nodded to one of the agents, who turned off the tape. He could have turned off the tape a few sentences earlier, but he wanted me to hear Charlie Cimino diss Hector, as if, being Hector's former counsel, I would be offended. Under the circumstances, it didn't even hit the top ten list of things bothering me.

Chris Moody, for his part, was absolutely enjoying this entire affair. He must have been bouncing around all day, awaiting this visit, thinking of all the smart one-liners he'd throw my way.

"My word against Cimino's," I said. "And I've got paper to back it up."

"Paper? You mean *this* paper?" Moody nodded to one of the agents, who handed me a document. It was a memorandum about the school bus contract that bore my name and looked a heck of a lot like the one I wrote. But a few paragraphs had been inserted at the end, with this conclusion:

Thus, provided that the Board of Education contract were reduced to smaller contracts of ten thousand dollars in value or less, the competitive bidding law would not apply, and the contract could be awarded to whatever company the PCB desired.

"I didn't write that memo," I said, realizing I should probably keep my mouth shut.

"I see," said Moody with mock sympathy. "You probably didn't write this one, either."

On Moody's cue, an agent handed me a second document, this one a legal memorandum bearing my name on the prison sanitation contract—once again different in its conclusion:

Neither of the two lowest bidders on the Marymount Penitentiary sanitation contract should be considered "responsible" bidders. Accordingly, the contract should be awarded to the next lowest bidder, Higgins Sanitation.

It was like Cimino had said on the tape. *DQ'd both of 'em.* But I hadn't, of course.

"These have been doctored," I said.

"You've been framed?" Moody asked, the question dripping with sarcasm. "Railroaded?"

I didn't answer. I wouldn't give him the satisfaction of baiting me. I didn't know if "frame-up" was the right phrase here. More likely, Cimino was just using me as legal cover to justify what he wanted to do.

But to the federal government listening in, it sure looked like I was playing right along with Charlie.

"Oh, we're not done, Jason." Moody nodded to the agent manning the computer. "Play the next one," he said.

CHRIS MOODY KEPT HIS EYES ON ME AS THE FBI AGENT played the next intercepted conversation.

"You've done good work so far. I've seen your work product. The memo on the DOC sanitation project— the two bidders who underbid Higgins Sanitation."

I did a slow burn. It was the voice of Greg Connolly, speaking to me in his office earlier today.

"Those bidders were well qualified," I said in response.

"Course they were," Connolly said. *"Course they were. That's why I'm saying, good job."*

It was pretty clear how this was lining up now. From Moody's perspective, I was admitting to Greg Connolly that I knew those bidders were well qualified, and yet there was a memo with my name on it saying the exact opposite. I was admitting, that is, to deliberately giving a false legal opinion to further a crime—directing state business to an undeserving company that had given campaign contributions to Governor Snow.

And the recording wasn't finished, either.

"Charlie talked to you about the buses, too," Connolly went on. *"I saw that analysis you did."*

"There's no way that's a sole-source," I said. *"Providing a bus? A hundred companies could do it."*

"*So, again, good job on that. You'll do very well here, Jason, if you want to.*"

The tape shut off. That was all they had, but it was more than enough, if they chose to believe that I had authored those memos in the form they now appeared. And they were definitely choosing to believe that.

"I didn't write either of those memos," I repeated. "Someone took those memos and changed them. Connolly may have been talking about the doctored memo when he was telling me 'good job,' but I didn't know that. I thought he approved the memo that *I* wrote."

Moody raised an eyebrow. "Is that what you'd believe, if you were me, Counselor?" He strolled around my living room. "It sounds to me like you impressed the chairman with your creative ways to get the favored companies their contracts, and it also sounds to me like you admitted that your legal conclusions were bogus. And that, Mr. Kolarich, sure sounds like fraud and conspiracy to me."

"And why would I do that?" I added. "Even if I were inclined to do that, what would I get out of it?"

"Why would you do that . . . why would you do that . . ." Moody looked around the room at the other agents, like everyone was in on the joke except for me.

"I see you filed an appearance in the Hauser Construction case today," he said to me.

My jaw did a few rotations. I couldn't see it, not yet, but I had an idea.

"Jack Hauser," he said. "The guy who hired you today? Minority partner in Higgins Sanitation? His other business, the construction company, needs a lawyer and suddenly turns to a guy with absolutely no experience in construction law? And, lo and behold, the lawyer he picks is the same lawyer who just helped him bypass two lower bidders to get a sweetheart prison sanitation contract."

I was overcome with anger—at Cimino and at myself. Looking back, Hauser had seemed to be coming to me as if I were his only option. What had he said, when I'd quoted him three hundred an hour?

Well, you're hired, obviously, he'd said. *I mean, okay, fine, I'll hire you, but—any way to knock that number down?* It was like he knew he had no choice, and he was pleading for mercy on the hourly rate.

And when I'd asked him how he got my name, he looked at me like we both knew that answer, like he couldn't understand why I'd be asking.

Jack Hauser, it was now clear, had been sent to me. Cimino had told him that there would be a price to getting that prison contract—besides a campaign contribution to the governor—and that price was legal business for me, the lawyer who supposedly had made it happen. Cimino was cutting me in. This was how it worked. Everyone got a piece. Apparently, I was supposed to understand that.

I'd just taken a kickback without even knowing it.

Moody took the only remaining empty seat, nearest me, and leaned forward on his knees. "This is a criminal enterprise that makes Hector Almundo and the Cannibals look like the Girl Scouts of America. Connolly and Cimino are steering state contracts away from deserving companies to people who contribute to the governor's campaign fund. I know it, Kolarich. I fucking *know* it. And I'm going to prove it. And you're going to help me. Because if you don't, you'll be sitting next to all of them at trial. You can try to convince the jury that you're the only honest one of the bunch of scumbags. You, the one who *asked* to be part of this—who used Hector Almundo to get you inside. Maybe you'll be the one guy at the table who walks. But I wouldn't like your chances, Counselor."

I watched Moody, thinking through my options.

"What's Cimino going to say at trial?" Moody went on. "And Connolly. 'Advice of counsel,' that's what they're going to say. They're going to say they relied in good faith on you, their lawyer, for the actions they took. Everyone at that defense table is going to take a big dump on Jason Kolarich."

He was right, of course. I'd be lined up at trial with a ring of criminals, all of whom would be busy pointing the finger at me.

"Chris," I said, "you missed a spot on your face."

He drew back. He fought every instinct to wipe at his face. "What?"

"You still have a little egg on your face from blowing the Almundo case. I mean, that's what this is all about, right? You've had a hard-on for me ever since the not-guilty."

Moody didn't crack, not for a second; he had way too much of an upper hand here. Instead, he smiled. "If it eases the pain, Kolarich, go ahead and fantasize. But I wouldn't want to be you right now."

I looked away, my mind racing. I found a picture of my wife and child on the bookcase and stared it a long time.

"Looks like I'm going to have to beat your ass in court," I said. "Again."

Moody's eyes did that rapid-blink thing I remembered. He thought for a moment and nodded. "Hope you can say the same for that partner of yours—what's her name, Agent Tucker?"

"Tasker," said the FBI agent. "Shauna Tasker."

"Right, Shauna Tasker. Sounds like she got a taste of that Hauser Construction work, too." He scratched his chin in mock contemplation. "What do you think, Jason? Does that make her a co-conspirator?"

I steeled myself, kept my voice low and even. "Keep her out of this. She has nothing to do with this."

"She does now."

We locked eyes. This was the highlight of Christopher Moody's year, putting the screws to me. He wasn't even trying to hide it.

Shauna. I thought I was paying her back, for once, by including her in some legal work I had drummed up. Instead, she was possibly in the soup along with me. I wasn't sure of that, and neither was Moody, but that wasn't the point. The point was that he could dirty her up without even prosecuting her. The same day he slapped the PCB with a federal subpoena, he'd hit Shauna with one and make sure the newspapers didn't miss the connection. And if he had any kind of a good-faith basis to do so, he'd indict her and effectively ruin her career. Whether she was guilty or innocent would be a lost detail. He knew all of this, and he knew I knew, too.

"Keep her out of this, Chris," I said.

He shrugged. "That decision isn't mine. It's yours." He looked at the other agents in the room. "Let's give Jason some time to think about this, guys." He pushed himself out of the chair. The lot of them moved toward the front door. Moody stopped at the edge of the living room and flipped a business card in my direction. "But I better be hearing from you tomorrow, Jason," he said. "Or you and your girlfriend will be hearing from us."

27 I DIDN'T EVEN TRY TO SLEEP THAT NIGHT. I DID LAPS around my townhouse, pacing everywhere, even taking a long walk outside in the below-freezing temps. Throughout it, I kept telling myself that I should be afraid. Afraid of prison. Afraid of losing my law license. But I wasn't. With each passing hour, I only grew angrier. Angry at myself, for dipping a toe into that cesspool and then being surprised when it came out dirty. But most of all, angry at Charlie Cimino. He had given me instructions to do things I shouldn't do, and when I refused, he'd doctored documents and misrepresented my words.

The federal government wasn't flying blind here; this was no bluff. Clearly, they'd placed eavesdropping devices in Greg Connolly's office and on someone's phone—either his or Charlie Cimino's. They were Title III intercepts, meaning the government was intercepting these conversations without the knowledge of any of the participants. That's hard to do. It's an easier task when one of the parties to the conversation consents to wearing a wire, but when the feds want to eavesdrop without anyone's knowledge, they have to go under Title III and get the approval of the chief federal judge as well as the top levels at the Department of Justice. They have to clear about ten different hurdles. They have to already have a pretty solid case.

And I was their gift-wrapped package, the insect that walked right into the spiderweb.

Maybe you'll be the one guy at the table who walks. Those words from Christopher Moody, more than anything else he'd said or shown me, were the essence of my problem. The evidence he had on me, at this point, wasn't that great. And if he really thought I was dirty, he would have waited for more. He could have waited weeks, months, to catch me deeper in the soup. But he didn't do that, because he knew I wasn't part of this thing. Maybe he even knew I was on the verge of quitting, after getting a sniff of the stench. Maybe that's why he was here tonight, before I got out. He was scooping me up before I left the sandbox.

But none of that changed the fact that he had a basis for charging me, and that I would be one of several defendants sitting at the defense table, when the prosecution tried a multiple-defendant case featuring scumbags like Charlie Cimino and Gregory Connolly. I'd be part of the conspiracy. And I'd be trying, probably in vain, to separate myself from these other pieces of garbage, trying to persuade the jury not to flush me down the toilet with the lot of them. By the time the jury got down to me on the verdict form, they'd be so disgusted that they'd just check "guilty" and hand the slip to the bailiff.

The one guy at the table who walks. It was possible, sure. But guilt by association is a cliché for a reason. It happens all the time, which is why the prosecution likes to try defendants together in these cases. And this is to say nothing of the very real possibility that some of these assholes would plead out and, in exchange for a lenient sentence, point the fingers at everyone they could. Cimino surely would swear that I advised him on how to evade the public-bidding requirements for the bus contract. He and Connolly and Patrick Lemke would be happy to swear that I wrote up a memo disqualifying the obviously qualified bidders who beat out Higgins Sanitation, and they would probably throw in a little bonus fabrication—like how I demanded getting outside legal work from Higgins's partner, Jack Hauser, in exchange. I would tell the jury that I had no idea that Jack Hauser came to me as part of a kickback, but after hearing months of testimony about sordid dealings from the likes of Charlie Cimino and Greg Connolly, would a disgusted jury believe me?

Advice of counsel. It's what all of them would say. We're not lawyers; we relied on Kolarich to tell us what to do.

And even if I did manage to beat the rap, I was looking at a good twelve, eighteen months under the federal spotlight, my reputation ruined, my career shattered. People don't equate "not guilty" with "innocent." The burn heals with time, but it leaves a real nasty scar that I would wear forever. I would just be the guy who got away with it.

And then, for the kicker, there was Shauna. Would Chris Moody go after her, just to hook me in? I had no doubt that he would. When the government wants you, they get you, whatever it takes. She would get hauled in for questioning, her one-person law firm hit with a federal subpoena, and I couldn't rule out the possibility of an indictment. All because she gave an office down the hall to an old friend, and I just happened to invite her to that meeting with Jack Hauser.

I couldn't let that happen. I just couldn't.

Moody had me, and we both knew it.

 I MET PAUL RILEY AT THE MARITIME CLUB, WHERE only about a week ago I'd had lunch with Jon Soliday, who had warned me not to go near the Procurement and Construction Board. I longed for a do-over where I took Jon's advice and tried a different angle for discovering who killed Adalbert Wozniak and Ernesto Ramirez. But I hadn't, and now I was dealing with the mess.

"Anyplace but the law firm," I'd said to Paul. I had not walked into Shaker, Riley since the day Talia and Emily died. I couldn't stomach the pity or the awkward small talk. Someone there, at some point, had gathered together all my personal items from my office and delivered them to my house. I couldn't even remember who it was. My memory of that entire stint with Shaker, Riley was much of a blur at this point.

When he showed up at the Maritime Club, Paul looked the same as I remembered him, fit, tan, well-dressed, comfortable in his own skin, quick with the self-deprecation when I asked about his nomination to the federal bench, pending before the Senate Judiciary Committee. "They've been trying to find people to say something nice about me," he said, when I asked him about the delay. Closer to the truth was a hostile senate, slow-footing the judicial nominations of a president from the opposing party.

"You know you have a standing invite to return," Paul told me, when we took our seats for lunch. "I won't belabor it, but it's there for the taking."

My laugh was uneasy. Surely, Paul would rethink that invitation after this conversation.

In his lengthy career as a lawyer, Paul had done a lot, and there was very little he hadn't seen. I don't know where my plight fell on the spectrum, but as I began to explain it to him, I sensed it was personal to him, particularly as I mentioned characters from our trial together, not the least of whom was the prosecutor, Chris Moody. His face went tellingly blank when I told him I'd gotten involved with the PCB—he held his tongue-lashing, I suspect, because he knew it was going to get worse—and he was white as a sheet when I recounted my conversation last night with federal agents. I ran through everything while Paul listened silently. It was clear that he felt sorry for me, which was the last thing I wanted. I would have preferred a glass of cold water in the face, which I probably deserved.

"Well, we could fight it," he said, after I'd rehashed everything. I appreciated the use of the word "we." I had no doubt that Paul would step in to help me if asked. But I wouldn't ask.

"This guy Cimino has made you the fall guy, Jason. My guess is, the feds know that, and if Chris had an ounce of decency, he'd let this go. You could tell him to go scratch his ass and see what happens. If he charges you, you fight it."

That was certainly a possibility. "You think Moody would let it go?"

"Probably not," said Paul, with his characteristic frankness. "He'd want everyone pointing fingers. They blame the lawyer, you blame them, and everyone goes down looking dirty."

My thought exactly.

"Well." Paul sighed, examined his fingernails. "You could get immunity and see what that costs you."

"You know what it'll cost me," I said. "The supreme court would be very interested, too." The state bar is controlled by our state supreme court, which handles lawyer misconduct. Even if I got immunity from prosecution, it wouldn't be immunity from them. "I'd probably lose my license, Paul."

"Oh, Jason, Jason." He shook his head. Paul Riley was the best lawyer I'd ever worked with. It was like disappointing a parent. He looked up at the ceiling and sighed. "You could agree to immunity without stipulating to the charge—"

"Which gets me the same thing," I said. "I'd still have to plead my case to the supremes."

He didn't have a rejoinder. I was right. We both knew it. If I took an immunity deal, I'd probably lose my law license, at least for a while.

Paul shrugged his shoulders. "Okay, so you won't take immunity. You just sit back and hope they decide against charging you? I mean, that doesn't sound—"

"Oh, I'm not going to just sit back," I said. "I'm going to work for them."

Paul chewed on that, drumming his fingers on the table. Someone told a joke a few tables away that left everyone in stitches. How I wished for that kind of frivolity right now.

"So you cooperate without a deal and hope for leniency later?"

"Fuck leniency," I said. "I am never, ever going to plead guilty. Never."

"Then I'm missing something. Why work for the G? Why go undercover? What does that buy you with them?"

Nothing. That's what it would buy me. Absolutely nothing.

"You don't want immunity or leniency," he said. "So what do you want?"

I wasn't sure what I wanted for myself. I knew what Talia would say, were she here. This would be one of her patient commentaries, with phrases like "hard-headed" finding their way in there.

"Oh," Paul said. "You're just pissed off. You want payback."

I shrugged. "These assholes dragged me into their swamp. I should let them get away with it?"

"Jason. Jason." Paul reached out a hand toward me. "Don't do what you're thinking. You're mad at those guys—Cimino and the others. I get that. I would be, too. They made you an unwitting accomplice. But you have to look at the bigger picture. You have to think of yourself. Take immunity. Because otherwise, Chris Moody will let you do his bidding as a CI and then fuck you afterward. He will, Jason. You know he will."

Paul was making sense. I suppose I was the one who wasn't. I would work as a confidential informant for the federal government without any promises from them.

"They screwed me, Paul. And they're screwing the public, if I needed any further motivation. I'm not going to take that."

"Fine, then work for the feds, but take the damn immunity, Jason. Don't be a hero. Because I'm telling you, son, no one will be standing in line afterward to say 'thank you.'"

But I didn't need a thank-you. I just needed to stick to my principles. I didn't do anything wrong. Taking immunity meant I did. No, if Chris Moody and his thugs wanted to chase after me on a bogus charge, then I'd have to deal with that when the time came. But I couldn't let Charlie Cimino and the rest of them—whoever they were—walk away from this.

If I was going to lose everything, at least I was going to do it on my terms.

Paul grimaced as we stood at the doorway of the Maritime Club. "I don't know how much help I was, my friend. I think you already had your mind made up."

"I needed your input. And you gave it to me. You told me I'm completely nuts."

"You're standing on principle, Jason. I admire that. I do." He offered a hand. "But admirable can still be foolish. Please take my advice and cut a deal. And please let me represent you."

"I hope I'm calling you Your Honor sometime soon, Paul." I shook his hand and pushed through the door, into a wind that was colder than I'd expected.

And I hope, I thought to myself, *I'm not doing it from a prison cell.*

AT THREE O'CLOCK SHARP THAT DAY, I WALKED INTO the U.S. attorney's office in the federal building downtown. I was shown directly into a conference room. Chris Moody, looking fresh and relaxed, walked in with his government-issue white shirt and red-and-blue checked tie and sat across from me. He was wearing bright blue braces strapped over his narrow shoulders that let everyone know he was a hungry prosecutor. He seemed surprised that I wasn't bringing a lawyer, but so much the better, for him.

He pushed a document in front of me. I took a quick look at it and shook my head.

"I'm not doing a letter agreement," I said.

"Sure, you are."

"Sure, I'm not."

Moody wanted me to sign a letter agreement, in which the government agreed to immunize me from prosecution in exchange for my cooperation, without us ever appearing in court on formal charges. It was standard stuff for people the feds flipped—like Joey Espinoza, for example. They couldn't very well unseal an indictment and arraign a guy in open court if they wanted him to work undercover. This was how they did it outside the public view.

"Get one thing clear, Chris. I will never admit that I did anything wrong. This is voluntary or it isn't happening."

Moody's initial reaction was a smirk, but it faded after a moment.

"This is what's happened so far," I said. "You guys showed up at my door last night, you played me the overhears, it stoked my sense of outrage, and I agreed to help you ferret out this corruption on a purely voluntary basis. You never specifically told me I was being charged with a crime. You never said anything, one way or the other, about what the future might hold. You didn't make any promises to me; I didn't make any promises to you."

This was unconventional, no doubt. Most people jump at the chance to get immunity, a get-out-of-jail-free card. But there was some merit to this arrangement, from Moody's perspective. Every government informant, when testifying at trial, gets cross-examined on the deal he cut with the G. It's standard fare for a defense attorney—you were looking at a severe prison sentence so you cut a deal, and you'd say *anything* to make those prosecutors happy; therefore, your testimony should be discredited. But what I was proposing to Moody would avoid that problem. I wasn't getting a deal at all. I wasn't getting immunity or a promise of any kind. The United States would be free to prosecute me if it so chose.

But the problem Moody would have with my proposal was the same reason I wanted it in the first place: He couldn't control me. I wouldn't march to his command. If I wanted to shut this thing down, I could, at any time. I'd be risking the prosecutor's ire, and a federal indictment, but the decision would be mine.

"Too risky," Moody said. "You sign this agreement or I convene a grand jury."

"No, you don't," I said. "I'll be your CI, but it will be voluntary. No plea agreement. No admission of wrongdoing. I'm just an ordinary citizen volunteering to help expose government corruption." I leaned forward. "And risky? You want to hear risky? I go do whatever it is you want me to do, and I know that at any time, you can start thinking back to how you got your ass kicked in *Almundo,* and you can decide to take out your humiliation on one of his defense attorneys. I do all this work for you, you get a hundred-count indictment, and then you are perfectly free to throw in one or two more counts with my name on them. Just because you can, Chris. Just because you can. So don't you talk to *me* about risky."

"Sign the letter agreement, Kolarich." He pushed it in front of me. "It's the only way."

"It's the only way you control me. And that's never going to happen." I got out of my chair. "You want to indict me now, indict me. And Charlie Cimino, and Greg Connolly, and all those other scumbags? It will take them about one-tenth of one second to realize that they should probably fold up their tents and go home. Your big undercover investigation is halted in its tracks. You're stuck with whatever you have on them as of right now, which I'm guessing is not all that much, or you wouldn't be yanking my chain so hard for my cooperation. Stop me when I'm wrong, Chris."

Moody rubbed his hand over his face. As much as he longed for the day that I'd be behind bars in a federal prison, he clearly had preferred the immunity route. It gave him power over me. But from his perspective, he pretty much had the same power, anyway. If I didn't jump high enough for his liking, he could always turn the screws on me. And if I messed around with his investigation, he could always hit me with obstruction of justice, in addition to the underlying case he might pursue against me. He was a federal prosecutor, after all. He had twenty different ways to fuck me.

I figured this would all come into focus for him, eventually, but either Moody was too cautious to say yes immediately or, more likely, he didn't want to readily agree to something that wasn't his idea. More quickly than I'd anticipated, he let out a small, bitter laugh.

"These guys you decided to lay down with?" he said evenly. "They're scum. They make a joke out of the idea of honest government. And I'm going to take them down, Kolarich. Anyone who gets in my way will be sorry." He got out of his chair and leaned over the table. His voice lowered to a controlled whisper, as our faces were only a few feet apart. "I'll have a chain around your neck so tight it'll hurt when you swallow. And after you're done dancing for me?" He gave me his best Machiavellian smile. "Well, like you said, no promises, right? I guess we'll see what the future holds."

Moody's taunt felt like an appropriate note on which to exit. I was tempted to make another comment about his courtroom skills, should he decide to prosecute me, but it wouldn't make me feel any better and it would only increase the odds that he'd come after me at some point. Like it or not, I was going to have to behave myself around this guy. A little, at least.

I walked outside into a cold, gray dusk, inhaling the frigid air and feeling my head clear, my perspective broaden. I stifled the instinct to second-guess my decision. I felt like I did after I filed a document in court, or turned in a paper in law school, afraid to review my work after I'd turned it in, sure that I would find an error that countless attempts at proofreading somehow failed to catch. I didn't want to think about what I'd just done. I didn't want to reevaluate. I didn't want to think about Paul Riley, the best lawyer I know, who was sure I was making the wrong decision.

You make your own bed, as they say. I'd gone into this with good intentions, hoping to find some clue to the murder of a man I hardly knew, and instead found myself in the middle of a budding political corruption scandal that already had tarnished me, as well. I had to find a way to come out of this intact. I had to find a way to clear my own name, avoid the same fate that befell Ernesto Ramirez and Adalbert Wozniak, and stop these thugs from selling out the state.

And I had to keep my promise to Esmeralda Ramirez to find out who killed her husband.

As I walked, I wondered if I would have to settle for some, not all, of the above.

30

"THE PROBLEM IS THAT IT'S NOT A FEDERAL OFFENSE TO get around competitive-bidding statutes." Special Agent Lee Tucker looked comfortable in his white button-down shirt, blue jeans, and loafers. He had a wiry frame, a bad complexion, deep-set eyes, a grassy mop of dirty-blond hair. A tin of Skoal tobacco rested in his front shirt pocket. "Or to contribute money to the governor."

"And there's plausible deniability," said Chris Moody. These two people would be my contacts, Tucker, the handling agent from the FBI, and Moody, the assistant U.S. attorney. We were sitting in Moody's office in the federal building, the following day.

The problem, they were explaining, was that to prosecute the things Cimino and the PCB were doing, prosecutors had to show a quid pro quo—that people were buying their way into these state contracts, that the awarding of the state job was directly and intentionally tied to the campaign contribution. Was it suspicious that a company landed a lucrative contract with the state, only to turn around the following week and give the governor twenty-five or fifty thousand? Sure. Red flags everywhere. But illegal? Only if you could read minds, or if you could get them on tape admitting that there was a direct relationship between the two. And that was very, very hard to do.

"Cimino's no idiot," said Tucker. "You guys at the PCB—you can't even call him on the phone. Or email or fax or text him. Everything's in person. Right?"

I nodded. Cimino was avoiding all the ways that the feds like to catch people these days. The wire-fraud statute—committing any kind of fraud by way of telephone or electronic communication—was their bread-and-butter nowadays. It was how the feds were able to grab any number of state crimes or other wrongdoing and get federal jurisdiction.

"Christ, he's not even a state employee." Tucker shook his head. "He does everything out of a private office. A guy who's not even on the state payroll is directing traffic."

"Then what's his angle here?" I asked. "He must be getting a cut somehow."

"Oh, yeah." Tucker nodded. In one fell swoop, he scooped tobacco out of the tin in his pocket and deposited it inside his cheek. It seemed to cheer him up. "He has all kinds of companies set up for consulting, things like that. Some company gets a big fat contract from the state, you can bet that company will suddenly hire one of Cimino's companies for some bogus consulting work. It adds up quick. He could make over a million a year this way."

"Let me guess," I said. "On paper, all of those side contracts with Cimino's companies are legit. Actual work is performed. Grossly overpaid work, but work nonetheless."

I could see from their expressions that I'd hit the nail on the head. That would be the smart way to play it. If Cimino were shaking down contract bidders to shoot some consulting work his way, he'd make sure that the contracts held up to superficial scrutiny—that he provided at least some minimal consulting work, albeit for an exorbitant fee.

"Look, we think Cimino is all over the place in the Snow administration," Tucker said. "We think he has a say in almost every significant decision they make. But it's hard to prove."

That explained why they needed me. The tapes they played for me were probably enough to warrant an indictment against Cimino. But they wanted to play the string out. They were expecting, hoping that they could put a lot more on Cimino. And they were betting that I could deliver it.

"He sees you as a potential asset," Tucker told me. "You're not just the everyday lawyer they get. You have a lot more experience. You come from a major law firm. And most of all, you got Hector out of a huge jam. You navigated Almundo through the very same kind of stuff these guys are doing, and Hector never spent a day in prison. You're valuable."

Tucker only seemed to realize after the fact that Hector's prosecutor was sitting in the room while he glorified Hector's acquittal. I like the impolitic, bull-in-a-china-shop types myself. Tucker might not be so bad to work with.

"You heard Greg Connolly on the tape," Moody added. "He said you could be 'useful.' These guys like to keep their circle small and tight, but you could penetrate it, Kolarich. We're counting on your well-earned reputation as a bullshit artist."

I didn't get the sense that Moody meant it as a compliment. But that didn't make him wrong. If there is one thing I learned when Talia died, it's that I am my father's son—I can become another person altogether. I can pretend. I can smile at you and keep my hand steady while I am doing somersaults internally.

I was, in many ways, the perfect person for this job.

And then, over the space of a handful of days, it all came together. Chris Moody and I met with the state supreme court's Division of Attorney Discipline—DAD—to get their blessing for my undercover role as a corrupt lawyer, a necessary protection given that I was going to be breaking laws right and left and didn't want to lose my law license for doing so. For Moody's part, he didn't want my cross-examination at trial to begin with an assault on my professional ethics. And even more fundamentally, Moody needed to be sure that my testimony would be admissible. The first thing any defense attorney would do is try to exclude every recording made by me as a flagrant breach of the attorney-client privilege. We wanted to be sure that my role was clearly defined, limited as much as possible to committing fraudulent acts with Charlie Cimino, Greg Connolly, etc.—which would allow us to invoke the crime-fraud exception to the attorney-client privilege.

"Well, Kolarich, I guess you're out of excuses," said Moody, his way of telling me the supreme court had signed off on my undercover role.

And he was right. The federal government and I had agreed that I'd cooperate with them without an immunity deal, and the state supreme court had given the green light. The idea hit me as if it were a fresh notion, despite having dominated my thoughts for the last four days: I was actually going to do this. I was going to be a snitch for the federal government.

THE NEXT MORNING, I MET SPECIAL AGENT LEE Tucker in an "employees only" lounge at a hotel that was midway between my office and Charlie Cimino's. Tucker was dressed pretty much the same as I'd last seen him, a white button-down under a blue sport coat and blue jeans. I'd told him I typically wore a suit when I went to work, and he said that would work fine, so that's what I was wearing.

Tucker looked at his watch. "You're late," he said. "It's almost eight-thirty. Okay." He sized me up. "How you doing?"

How was I doing? I was about to wear a wire for the federal government. These guys were sinking their hooks in me and threatening me and my best friend if I didn't play ball. Whether his question was small talk or sincere, it deserved a sincere response.

"Fuck you," I said.

He looked at me for a moment. He was appraising me, the entire situation. What kind of a witness would I be? I didn't doubt my importance to the operation. A lawyer could take them places they couldn't otherwise infiltrate. He had two choices: Come on strong, with continued threats, or go easy. I figured he'd choose the latter.

Tucker opened his palm and showed me the recording device, which looked like one of those pagers people used to wear, before everyone had cell phones, only it was even thinner; it was about the size of three AA batteries strapped together with black tape. "This is an F-Bird," he said. "Put it inside your suit pocket."

It was even lighter than the weight of three batteries. I dropped it inside my suit pocket and didn't even know it was there.

"This is audio only?" I asked.

He nodded. "A simple recording device. No eyes. No transmission signal."

I didn't know what that meant.

"I won't be listening in, real time," he explained. "It's not transmitting any signal to me. I won't know what's said until you bring it back when you're done."

"And then you'll grade my performance."

"Don't think of it as a performance, Jason. Just be yourself. Act like the recorder isn't even there."

I shot him a look.

"I'm serious. If you think about it, it'll make you edgy. Just relax. Don't force the conversation. Let him come to you. It might take a long time, Jason. That's okay."

"How do I turn it on?"

"You don't."

"How do I turn it off?"

"You don't. We do those things. We start letting CI's turn those things on and off—"

"Right." The government couldn't trust the cooperator to turn the recorder on and off; it would lead to claims of selective editing by defense lawyers at trial: *You turned it off when my client said something that exonerated him; you turned it on, out of context, to capture something damning.* It made sense. Better to have the thing running all the time.

Tucker looked at his watch again. "Now you better get going. And next time we're supposed to meet at eight, make it eight you show up."

Tucker was worried about my showing up late to the meeting

with Cimino, but that was already my intention. I'd been late every time I'd visited him, and I didn't want to stray from character.

I arrived at his posh offices at a quarter past nine. One of the supermodel receptionists made me wait a good twenty minutes before she showed me back. As I followed behind her, I thought that Tucker should regret not wiring me for video.

Cimino, as always, was pacing in his airplane hangar of an office and talking on the phone. He pointed to a chair when I walked in, and I planted myself. The tiny recorder felt like a hundred pounds in my jacket pocket. I felt like a siren was going off. Every word that he and I were about to say would become part of a record. It was like having your mother in the room with you.

"When I say I'm tired of excuses, do you think I'm speaking another fucking language?" he said, as always abusing whoever was on the other end of the call. "What's this thing you have with tardiness? I say eight-thirty, you be here at eight-thirty."

It took me a minute to realize that he had segued from rebuking some poor building contractor to scolding me. He snapped his fingers at me. "Hey, am I talking to you?"

"Are you?"

"Yeah, I'm—okay, listen, Arthur. Are you listening? No . . . more . . . excuses. Get it done by the end of the week or I find someone else." He tore off his earpiece and sat down behind his desk. "And you," he said. "You're very aggravating, kid, you know that? People say you're fucking smart, but you can't tell time so good, can you?"

I had a few responses in mind, but none of them seemed appropriate.

"And I tell you to do something, you fucking do it. Are you working for me or are you working for me?"

He was referring, I thought, to my refusal to write that memo disqualifying the two bidders on the prison contract, but he hadn't said so explicitly. I was hoping he'd elaborate. I'd love to have Charlie Cimino admit, on tape, that he'd had someone doctor the memo I had written.

I handed him the document I'd worked on yesterday at the state office. It was a memo on the prison contract with the conclusion Cimino wanted, but written by me.

He looked at it for two seconds. "What's this?" he asked.

"That," I said, "is a memorandum I wrote yesterday, detailing why the two bidders who beat out Higgins Sanitation for the prison contract were not 'responsible' bidders, and therefore Higgins should get the contract."

"We already have one—"

"Yeah, you already had one, whoever wrote it. Who did write it, by the way?"

Cimino just stared at me, looking annoyed. Strike two for me. He wasn't going to help me out. Listening to this tape later, Tucker and Chris Moody would probably have a nice chuckle as I flailed away.

"Well, whoever did it—it was crap," I said. "It wasn't convincing. You want to disqualify the bidders, *that* is how you do it. *That's* the memo you want."

He stared a hole through me for a while. I admit it occurred to me, a flash of panic—*he knows*—but there was nothing I could do but sit still, and eventually his eyes moved down to the document. He read it over, skipping to the good part. "Okay. Yeah. Yeah, this is better." He looked up at me. "This looks better."

"Jack Hauser came by the other day," I said. "I signed him up on a lawsuit with the city."

He looked at me, his eyes narrowing. "Yeah?"

"I think maybe you and I have had a communication breakdown," I said.

We were dancing around it. I couldn't imagine another way to do it. I couldn't rush in here and be direct. I had to let him know that we were on the same page without saying so explicitly. And he needed to see that there was a reason for my sudden change of heart, a reason why my stubborn refusal to do what he wanted was suddenly replaced with eager compliance. That reason was his referral of Hauser Construction to my law office. A guy like Cimino, I figured, would willingly believe that I'd want in, that I'd do what he asked, if there were sweeteners involved. It's how he operated, so it was psychologically soothing for him to believe it motivated others, too. He'd sent me that legal business to get me on board, and I was telling him that it had worked.

"Yeah?" he said. He was being noncommittal, which was smart of him.

I pointed to the document. "There are a couple of companies there that might not be so happy, losing out on that prison contract. They might sue. They might make a lot of noise. They might talk to other people. Reporters. Politicians. Maybe—shit, maybe law enforcement. People will want to know, what's the reason?"

He was stoic, listening to me. "You telling me something I don't know?"

"No, I think you know. But that other memo—the one bearing my name, that I didn't write—that memo's garbage. It wouldn't hold up. Look," I said, leaning forward, "if an action of the PCB comes under scrutiny of any kind, you need to be able to say you relied on advice of counsel. But the advice of counsel has to be somewhat convincing, Charlie. That other memo—it wasn't persuasive. I think this one I prepared, on the other hand, is."

He looked back down at the memo, but he wasn't reading it. He was thinking.

"You need an advocate," I said. "Someone who argues for a living. Someone who can take facts that smell like shit and convince everyone they're perfume. Or at least, someone who can muddy up the water enough to make our position plausible."

He made a thoughtful noise. "And I suppose that's you?"

"Ask Hector Almundo if that's me."

Judging from the taped conversations the feds had played for me, these guys already seemed to have a favorable opinion of my skills. It was probably why I had lasted this long on the job, despite my stubbornness—Hector, and what I had done for him.

"Or not," I said. "I don't care. But I'm not a transactional lawyer,

Charlie. You want someone who will read a thirty-page document and robotically apply the law—honestly, you don't want me. I'm not interested. But the good stuff—where you need someone to make an argument, a convincing one—I'm your man."

He slowly nodded his head.

"And I still have a full-service law firm," I said. "Open for business, if the occasional customer wants to drop by. I'm always grateful for new clients."

His expression seemed to soften. This, I thought, was making sense to him. I was presenting the world in exactly the way he, himself, viewed it. And I was being as tactful as I could. I wasn't using words like "fraud" and "collusion." But I was telling him, in so many words, that I now understood the rules, and I liked the game.

Cimino reached into a candy dish on his desk and threw a couple of jelly beans into his mouth. He cupped a few more, like he was guessing their weight, and considered me. "What was it with Hector?" he asked. "How'd you pull that off?"

"Plausible deniability," I said, without hesitation. "But with Hector, it was tougher, because the feds had him on tape. We had to work after-the-fact. We had to dissect every sentence uttered by him and by Espinoza and show that Hector didn't take Espinoza seriously. The jury thought it was plausible."

He kept nodding his head. I thought it was nervous energy more than agreement.

"Now, hypothetically, if I have the luxury of counseling a client beforehand, not after the other shoe has dropped," I said, "it's easier. I make a convincing case for a particular position, and all the client has to do is say, 'Okay, I accept your advice.' The client can always utter the three magical words—'advice of counsel'—and me, I can just say that I stand by my legal reasoning. That's the great thing about the law, right? There's no concrete answer. It's all about opinions."

"It's all bullshit, if you ask me."

I didn't respond to that. I wasn't going to convince Charlie

Cimino that he should respect the legal profession, much less the law itself.

"Okay. Well." I got out of my chair. "If this is the last time we talk, then—that Hauser Construction case? Thank you. I hadn't expected that. I think I understand the world a little better now. If you want me for the—for the more complicated issues, let's say, I'll be around."

Cimino was still playing with the jelly beans in his hand when I showed myself out. I got into the elevator and waited for the doors to close. Then I let out a long exhale, what felt like twenty minutes' worth of breath.

32 I STOPPED AT A COFFEE SHOP A FEW BLOCKS FROM MY office. I ordered a large coffee, black, and left the small recording device—the F-Bird—on a paper napkin as I paid the guy. The next guy in line, Lee Tucker, snatched up the recording device as I walked away. I felt instant relief when that thing was out of my possession.

I went back to my office and collapsed in my chair, feeling utterly exhausted from the affair. I'd never done anything like this before, and I underestimated how draining it would be to perform on camera, so to speak. The conversation with Cimino was no more than twenty minutes, but I felt like I'd lost five pounds in the process.

Late in the afternoon, Shauna walked into my office and dropped down on the couch in the corner. We actually had pretty spacious offices, and my brother had given me the couch, which I thought added something to the space, though I wasn't sure what. Early-nineties-college-slacker, maybe.

"I have a date," she said. "A guy named Roger. Opposing counsel on a breach-of-contract thing. We settled it last week. Now he wants to take me to dinner."

I felt something swim around inside me. I wasn't sure what it was, but it seemed like I wasn't happy to hear this news.

"Coolio," I said, like an absolute moron. *Coolio?* I'd never said that word in my life.

"You think I should go?"

I busied myself with some papers and made a face. "Sure, if you want to."

I avoided her eye contact and felt a bit of tension form between us. Then I was saved by the bell—by the phone, actually. Marie, our assistant, on the intercom.

"David Hamlin for you?"

"Put him through."

"Who's David Hamlin?" Shauna asked.

"David Hamlin" was Lee Tucker.

I picked up the receiver. "David," I said. "Long time, no talk. How'd the circumcision go?"

"Are you able to talk?" Tucker was on his cell phone in crowd noise, walking while he talked. "Let's meet in ten minutes. Suite 410?"

"A friend of a friend," I said to Shauna, which wasn't terribly convincing, since we shared most of the same friends, and we went to college and law school together. But her mind was on her steamy date with *Roger* and she let it go.

Suite 410 in our building had been vacant until today, when a bogus company called Hamlin Consulting rented the space on a month-to-month lease. I opened the frosted-glass door and found an empty reception area and what appeared to be two offices on each flank.

"Honey, I'm home!" I called out.

I heard Tucker clearing his throat down the hallway to my left. I found him in an office with a chaw of tobacco protruding from his cheek and an empty Coke can on a desk.

"What the fuck are you doing?" he said. "I told you to go slow, to let Cimino come to you. You remember me saying that?"

"That rings a bell."

"That meant, go in there, keep your trap shut, and let him give you assignments, and fucking do the assignments," he said. "That didn't mean going in there and propositioning the fucking guy."

I didn't feel the need to respond. I thought it had gone fine.

"Well?" he asked. "You have some great reason why you didn't follow my directions?" Lee Tucker was a generally easygoing guy, I gathered, but not at this moment. His eyes were on fire.

"You were trying to clear your own name in there," he said, annoyed that I wasn't responding. "And in the process, you might have fucked the whole thing up."

"Is that what you think?" I asked. "That I fucked this thing up?"

"It's sure as hell possible you did, yeah. Maybe you seemed too eager to him."

"Maybe," I agreed, which only made him angrier. I admit, I was enjoying this.

"You do what I tell you," he said, directing a finger at me. "You run it past me first. There's a certain amount of ad-lib we can't control, but you don't walk in there with an agenda like that without passing it by me first. Are we clear?"

He was right, but I couldn't acknowledge it. He didn't know that I had an agenda that differed from the federal government's. They were trying to catch some swindlers. I was trying to solve a murder. Okay, and I was pissed off at Cimino and his people for dragging me into the mud with them. I was letting the feds use me for both reasons. But in the end, when all was said and done, for me this was about Ernesto Ramirez, not some public corruption case. I wanted to gain Cimino's trust so I could get inside, so I could find out more about who killed Ernesto. If Cimino went down because he had his hand in the public coffers, so be it.

"You wanted me to hook Cimino," I said. "I think I did that."

"You better hope you did."

I shook my head, like he was a nuisance. "Think like Cimino," I said. "I refuse to do these bullshit memos he wants. But he doesn't bitch me out. He doesn't say a word to me. He just has someone rewrite them, still using my name. He fucks me, basically. Then he sends this Hauser guy to hire me for some legal work. This is how he says 'sorry' and 'thank you.' That's his world. He's made me an offer, Lee, and he's waiting to see if I'll accept. He's betting I will. So what did I just do in there? I just said 'yes.' I made him think he's the smartest guy in the world. You think I just made him suspicious? I think I just stroked his ego."

Tucker stared at me for a long time. One eye closed to a wink, but he definitely wasn't exhibiting affection toward me. "I've handled a hundred of you," he said. "Guys who think they're suddenly experts in how to do this."

"Did they all have clean, fresh breath like me?"

He laughed, a humorless grunt. "Well, you are one fucking hot-shot, aren't you, Kolarich?"

My cell phone rang. Didn't recognize the number. Lee seemed annoyed that I would take the call while we were in the midst of a conversation, which was why I did it.

"Mr. Kolarich? This is Janine from Ciriaco Properties. Mr. Cimino would like you at his office tomorrow morning at nine. He said he'd like to discuss your business offer."

"Certainly, Janine," I said with mock sweetness for Lee's benefit. "I'll see Mr. Cimino tomorrow at nine."

I closed my cell phone and thought for a moment. Replayed the call in my mind.

"Go ahead, hotshot," said Tucker. "Pat yourself on the—what is it?"

Something was rubbing me wrong. I shook my head. I related the call verbatim to Tucker.

"So?" he said. "I'll meet you at eight-thirty for the hand-off."

I paced in a circle and stopped. "No," I said.

Tucker thought about that a moment. "No?" he asked, but he wasn't putting up much of a fight. He may have been having a similar thought.

"Something about the way she framed it. 'He wants to discuss your business offer?' It's like Cimino was telegraphing it."

"Hmph. Maybe. He wants to make sure, if you'd ever wear a wire, that you'll wear it tomorrow?"

"Let's leave it off," I said.

"That creates problems for me, you know that."

Of course I did. I was a defense attorney. When a government cooperator only wears a wire some of the time, it leaves the other conversations open to cross-examination. A good lawyer will claim that the government informant entrapped the defendant during the non-recorded conversations and then turned on the wire when it suited his purposes. Prosecutors prefer their cooperators all wired, all the time. But these things are fluid. Every situation is different.

I stated the obvious: "It'll create more problems if he makes me."

Tucker relented, more easily than I would have expected. "Okay," he said. "I have to trust you on this."

33   I MADE IT TO CIMINO'S BUILDING BY TEN MINUTES TO nine. For some reason, it seemed to make sense to me to be punctual for once.

"How are you?" I said to the Amazon princess at the reception desk. I didn't know where Cimino found these women.

"You're actually on time." Cimino appeared from the hallway, looking immaculate as always in his slick Italian suit and bright tie. He kept walking, past me. "Come on."

"We're going somewhere?"

"We're going somewhere. Sweetheart, tell them to have my car out front?"

I followed Cimino to the elevator. He kept his thoughts to himself. He stared at the doors of the elevator, rocking on the balls of his feet, breathing with some congestion. He probably expected me to break the silence with nervous conversation. He probably also expected that his silence was unnerving me. It wasn't, other than a fleeting notion, maybe one-in-a-hundred chance, that he was taking me somewhere to be executed. Okay, maybe one in fifty. I'd just make sure that Charlie went first through any door.

We joined a few people on the elevator and took it down to the main floor. Cimino took me out a side door, where a bright yellow Porsche 911 awaited us with an attendant standing sentry.

Cimino handed him a tip and got in. I jumped in the other side. The car was immaculate, with a black leather interior and a top-of-the-line stereo.

"Nice ride," I said.

Cimino threw the stick into first and turned out onto the street with the fluid precision you'd expect from a Porsche. My first time riding in one of these, and I hoped it wouldn't be my last.

"Not so great in the winter," said Cimino. "When it gets slick, I don't even bother."

"Where are we going?" I asked.

"You play racquetball?"

Did I play racquetball? "Yeah, I guess."

"Good."

"Not well," I said.

"Even better." It was a ten-minute ride, and I would have been happy with ten hours in this thing. The leather was so soft, and the ride so smooth, I could have dozed off if I weren't enjoying myself so much. An air freshener shaped like an evergreen tree, hanging from the rearview mirror, bobbed around as Cimino navigated the car through traffic, injuring a few traffic ordinances in the process. The air freshener seemed a little out of place, a little tacky in a hundred-thousand-dollar sports car, but that seemed appropriate for Charlie Cimino: first-class with a touch of vulgar.

We pulled up to the Gold Coast Athletic Club and got out. "Good morning, Mr. Cimino," a man in a blue jacket greeted him.

"I don't have any workout clothes," I said.

It didn't seem to trouble Charlie. We took an elevator to the third floor and walked through a well-appointed room with a buffet of fruits and coffee and a sitting area. We entered the men's locker room and Cimino told an attendant, "My friend needs clothes for racquetball, Jamie."

"Sure, Mr. Cimino. Shoe size?" he asked me.

"Um, probably thirteen," I said.

We walked through a few aisles of lockers, the smell of aftershave and soap in the air. By the time Cimino had taken off his shoes, the attendant had arrived with a gray t-shirt, black running shorts, socks and a pair of gym shoes.

I opened a locker and undressed. I threw my shirt and tie on one hook, my suit coat and pants on the other, my shoes and dress socks on the bottom of the locker. I put my wallet, keys, and cell phone on the top rack. The clothes fit pretty well; the shoes were a little snug but it wasn't worth complaining.

"Size thirteen," Cimino said. "What are you—six-three? Six-four?"

"Somewhere in there." Six-three, two hundred thirty in college, when measurements mattered. I hadn't weighed myself in years.

"You were an athlete?"

"Played some ball in college."

"What college?"

"State."

"What position?"

"Wide-out."

"No shit?"

I closed my locker. "Is there a lock or something?"

He shook his head. "This is the Gold Coast Athletic Club." Apparently, that was supposed to mean that no locks were necessary. Rich people don't steal? In my experience, they do it more than anyone.

I was handed a racquet, and I followed Cimino onto a court. It was clear from the outset that he knew how to play the game—he was rather adept at hitting the ball low against the front wall so it bounced twice before I could reach it—but he was pushing fifty years old and he was overweight and, it appeared, was not very athletic even during his heyday. It wasn't really a challenge. I didn't hit with the same strategic precision, but I could chase down most balls and force him to run a lot, which he didn't like doing. It occurred to me that if I worked him hard enough, I could induce cardiac arrest, kill him, and get the feds off my back.

It also occurred to me that Lee Tucker, were he here, would have counseled me to let Cimino win. Keep me on his good side, that kind of thing. But I wasn't wired that way. Put me in a competitive sport, and you better keep your hands away from the cage.

It felt good. I used to be a workout fanatic, but I had dropped off after everything happened with Talia and Emily. I hadn't gained weight—if anything, I'd lost some—but my muscles felt loose and flabby and I didn't have much wind.

"Enough. Fuck. Enough." Cimino's gray shirt was plastered to his chest with sweat. He ran a hand towel over his face and then wrapped it around his neck. I followed him back to that reception area, where we drank orange juice and Cimino ate a plate of cantaloupe.

"That was fun," I said, putting the cool glass against my forehead.

"For you, fuckin'-A it was."

A man in a sport coat and slacks approached him. "Mr. Cimino, hello."

"Hey, Rick, how are you?" He shifted upright, with some discomfort, and shook hands.

"Very well," the man said. He gave Cimino a knowing nod. "Everything's great."

"Great, Rick. Good to see you."

The man left us, and Cimino seemed to focus on me awhile. He finished off his plate of cantaloupe, devouring them with the same enthusiasm he probably brought to any moneymaking scheme he could get his hands on.

"All right, Jason Kolarich," he said. "Now it's time we talk."

34

"So you were a prosecutor," Cimino said. "Why'd you quit?"

I rubbed my thumb with my index and middle fingers, the universal sign for money. "Tired of struggling to make ends meet."

He watched me. I thought of this as an audition. I wasn't completely lying about my reason for leaving the county attorney's office, but this was the answer he wanted to hear.

"Okay, so you hit it big at a fancy law firm, and then you left. Now you're all by yourself at a rinky-dink law firm and you want to work for a state procurement board?"

I thought about that for a moment. "I wanted more flexibility," I said. "Being my own boss, I can do whatever I want. Nobody's looking over my shoulder."

He nodded. But I had only given half an answer.

"But you know something?" I went on. "They don't knock down your door quite as much when you're not working alongside Paul Riley and those other lawyers. They want someone with gray hair. They want experience. So I figured, I needed to branch out more. Make some connections, meet the right people, show them what I'm capable of. I'm betting that when I show what I can do, people will notice. Maybe one day, I'll have one of those 911s in my garage."

I was feeding him red meat. He'd done the same, after all, probably after working under other people. My law firm was nothing compared to Ciriaco Properties, but the concept was no different.

Work hard and the money you make goes into your pocket, not the guy's above you. And I didn't have to take anyone's shit. I worked as hard as I wished. It was hard to imagine any other way now. It would feel like a small defeat to go back to working for someone else.

"You got family?" he asked.

"My mother died a few years back from cancer. My old man's in prison."

"For what?"

I had a feeling Cimino already knew all of this. "Fraud," I said. "He's a grifter. A con artist. And a shitty one. A drunk."

"You get along with him?"

"No."

"Why not? He offended your moral sensibilities?"

Actually, he did. I was always ashamed of my father's chosen profession, to the point that I repeated his lie—that he worked in "sales"—to everyone at school and quickly tired of trying to justify his actions to myself. But I didn't think it made sense to show Cimino my sense of moral outrage. It wasn't exactly a job requirement here.

"No, it wasn't that." I took a drink of orange juice. "I had two problems with him. One, he didn't do it well. He was lazy. You know how he got caught the first time? He scammed some old guy on some bogus time-share thing, got a nice down payment from the guy, but it turns out this guy's brother was retired FBI. So the brother gets the G to follow my dad around, and it took all of about two days to pinch him. He was too damn lazy to scout out his target."

Cimino seemed to find this interesting, maybe even surprising. "And what was the other reason?" he asked me. "You said two things."

"The worst part was that he didn't look out for us. He didn't provide. We were dirt poor, and he spent half of his loot on booze. He ignored my mother, and he took swats at my brother and me. You know, the beatings, I could've handled, if he put food on the table. If he took care of Mom. You take care of your own, or you can't look at yourself in the mirror."

Now this part was coming from the heart, but I wouldn't normally have shared all of this. I was trying to create an image for Cimino, an image that reminded him of himself. I didn't know the details of Cimino's life, but I assumed from the wedding band that he was married and he probably had kids. And no doubt, guys like him, they tell themselves they're doing it for their family. They wrap themselves around the dual justifications of familial obligations and past difficulties—a poor childhood, perceived inequities—to rationalize their criminal behavior. There are all sorts of players in their little game, but the bad guy is never them.

At his behest, I elaborated, telling him about my brother, Pete, who was still trying to get a grip on himself. We briefly touched on my wife and daughter—"Hector told me," Cimino said, sparing us both the morbid details. He was probably wondering how the loss of Talia and Emily factored into everything. Did it make me more reckless? Would I be unsteady? Unpredictable?

I was wondering some of those things myself.

Some time passed. Cimino got another glass of juice and some more fruit. A couple of old guys, one of whom was a judge I once tried a case in front of as a prosecutor, wandered in and out.

Cimino bit at a cuticle on his thumb. "You know, kid, you're right about one thing. There's a lot of opportunity out there. This thing here. This thing, there's a lot of room for everyone to make money. This could be one big happy fucking family. But you know what the catch is?"

I shook my head. "What's the catch?"

"The catch is that this *isn't* one big happy fucking family. There's risk everywhere. And I don't like risk, kid. I do not like it." He popped a slice of orange in his mouth. "I need a guy like you. I've been looking for a guy like you. Hector says you're as good a lawyer as he knows. Me, I haven't seen anything that tells me different. So that part, we're okay."

So far, so good. Cimino shifted in his chair and turned to me. "You're with me or you're against me. There's nothing in between. You understand that?"

"Yes," I said.

"You remember that, I'll make you rich. But you cross me, kid, you'll be sorry you ever met me. I take care of the people around me and everyone else—everyone else—" He made a noise. A smile crept across his face. He looked over his shoulder and then leaned into me. "A guy named Dick Baroni. B-A-R-O-N-I. He could tell you something about being with me and then against me. He *could* tell you, but he won't. You could cut off his dick, he wouldn't tell you about Charlie Cimino. Not anymore."

He gave me a moment to think about that. He'd even spelled the guy's name out for me, so he obviously wanted me to follow up, to look into it.

"What I'm doing right now," he continued, "I'm taking a risk. I'm taking a risk on you. I'm letting you in. So here's your chance to walk away, kid. You're having second thoughts, go have 'em on someone else's time. No hard feelings. But you work for me, you work for me. Are we clear?"

I don't think he could have possibly been clearer. "We understand each other," I said.

"Okay, then." He dropped his hand flat on the table. "Your job isn't to tell me what I can do. Your job is to make sure I can do what I wanna do. You see the difference?"

I chewed on that a moment. "If you want something," I said, "then my job is to want it, too. My job is to see if there is any conceivable way to get you what you want. And I'm aggressive. I'm competitive. Ninety-nine times out of a hundred, I'll find a way to argue that what you want is legal. But that one time out of a hundred—you'll have to listen to me. We have to make sure that what we do survives an audit."

"An *audit*."

I gave him a look. I leaned in closer. "We both know what I mean. Neither of us is worried about someone filing a lawsuit over what the PCB does. We're worried about those cocksuckers with trench coats and sunglasses and grand jury subpoenas. The ones who put my father in prison."

The mere mention of the federal government eliminated some of the color from Cimino's face. But all I did was say out loud what was already on his mind. Charlie Cimino didn't avoid cell phones and faxes and emails because he was opposed to twenty-first-century technology.

"And you're going to steer me clear of those cocksuckers," he said.

"I am. You're relying on my advice, Charlie. If something the PCB does gets a hard look, who do you think gets the *hardest* look? I'm the one with his ass on the line here. So if I say it can't happen, Charlie, you're going to say, 'Thank you, Jason, for making sure I can sleep well at night, knowing that you've got my back.'" I drilled a finger into the table. "And Charlie, no fuckin' foolin', you tell me right now if you see it differently. I'm giving *you* the chance to walk away."

I thought it helped to show a little spine here. That's what he needed, even if he didn't like it, and I was counting on him realizing that. It wasn't until a short laugh burst out of him that I knew he had.

35

AFTER MY WORKOUT AT THE GOLD COAST ATHLETIC Club, I returned to my law office. I knew it was only a matter of time before "David Hamlin" would be ringing me to pump me for information. I spent the time on Google, looking up "Dick Baroni," the guy Cimino had mentioned—someone who supposedly had learned the difference between being "with" Cimino and "against" him.

It didn't take me long to find that Richard Baroni was a real estate developer who had had a few balls in the air during the housing bubble in the late nineties. I didn't see anything that mentioned Charlie Cimino, but there were plenty of mentions of Mr. Baroni's office going up in flames, with him in it, in 1995. He'd managed to escape with a severely broken leg, a few superficial burns, and surprisingly no idea who might be responsible for the fire.

How nice of Cimino to relate that quaint little anecdote.

Tucker called me on my direct line, avoiding my receptionist, Marie, because we figured repeated phone calls from "David Hamlin" would prompt too many inquiries from the ladies in my office. He said he was going to order food from the downstairs diner and to meet him at Hamlin Consulting in Suite 410.

When I knocked on the frosted glass door, a little late, Tucker showed me in. He had a cheese omelet open in a styrofoam container and, across from him at his desk, a Reuben and hash browns with a sweaty bottle of water for me.

"So how did it go?"

"How it went," I said, settling in, "is I'm glad I wasn't wearing a wire. We got in his car and went to his club for racquetball."

"Yeah." Tucker shook out a bad thought. "Okay, good, then. He was probably checking you."

"Probably? I left my clothes, wallet, phone, everything in an unlocked locker. We play racquetball for an hour, then we're hanging out in a lounge area, and he doesn't say shit to me until some 'acquaintance' of his walks up to him and says, 'Everything's great, Mr. Cimino,' and suddenly Cimino opens up to me."

Tucker's head fell back against the cushion. "They went through your stuff."

"Give the man a prize."

"Could you identify the man? The one who searched your locker?"

"I don't know. Probably. And you're sure you've never called my cell from an official line?"

"I'm sure—"

"Because I'll bet Charlie's friend has my entire call log, Tucker."

"Relax, Jason. What, we've never done this before? There's nothing that could come back to me. Don't worry about that. You're good."

"I'm good? Easy for you to say." I let out a long sigh. "Well, I don't know if I'm good, but I'm definitely in. He gave me a big speech about me not fucking him. He even dropped a name, some guy who apparently didn't learn the lesson so well. I just Googled the guy and it turns out, life took a bad turn for him."

"Yeah? What's the name?" Tucker pulled a small notebook out of his back pocket.

"Richard Baroni. Real estate developer. His office was torched in ninety-five, and he almost went down with it. I can only guess it was a deal gone south or something."

Tucker scribbled a note. I looked at my sandwich and the burned hash browns, just how I like them, but I had suddenly lost my appetite. I pushed the food around and took a couple of bites but couldn't taste it. Tucker had no trouble downing his meal.

"So you passed the test," he said, wiping his mouth.

So far, I had passed. I had a feeling there would be some pop quizzes along the way.

"Tell me about his car. Was there anything unusual in the interior? Like, anything that he stuck to the dashboard or anything that looked out of place. Maybe a clock stuck—"

"An air freshener," I suddenly realized. "We're in this souped-up Porsche 911 with this beautiful leather interior and he's got this cheesy air freshener—"

"Okay." Tucker nodded. "Okay. It was a detector. It detects transmitter signals."

"Great." I pushed my food away. "That's just great."

"It just means we can't use a transmitter, Jason. All you're wearing is a simple recording device. A small tape recorder. You're not sending a signal back to us. No detector can pick up a tape recorder. It's only when you're transmitting a signal." He shook his head. "And now we know it's not even an option."

"And now we know," I said, "that *he* knows he's being watched."

"No." Tucker pursed his lips. "He knows he's a corrupt mother-fucker. And corrupt motherfuckers are paranoid."

"That makes two of us." I waved a hand. "I mean, this guy, without notice, takes me somewhere where I have to give up all my clothes, everything on me, and stick it all in a locker that he's going to search. That can happen at any time, Lee. Or he could just come right out and pat me down."

"So we need to be careful."

"That training from Quantico really paid off, Lee." I got out of my seat. Apparently, it wasn't registering with this FBI agent that, had it not been for a gut call on my part, I'd be burned right now. Cimino's thug would have found my recording device, and I might have a piece of concrete tied to my ankle right now, thirty feet under water.

When I pointed this out, Tucker said, "Quit with the drama. You were overly aggressive in your approach with this guy—against my advice—and it's natural that he'd come back with a check on you."

"If it's so natural, why didn't you think of it?"

Tucker worked a toothpick in his mouth. I thought it was less about removing food from between his teeth, and more about show-ing me his cool. "Jason, what do you think? You think you told me something I didn't know? There was no friggin' way I was going to let you go back there with a wire today. I was just curious if you'd figure it out yourself. And to your credit, you did." He chuckled.

Tucker reached into a bag at his feet and, with a dramatic flour-ish, produced a CD. He dropped it into the laptop on the corner of the desk. "From yesterday afternoon," he said.

"*Hello?*" It was Greg Connolly, answering the phone.

"*Greg, it's Charlie.*"

"*Yeah, Charlie. Look, I talked to Hector. He says this kid is the best. He says he hates the feds with a passion because they put his dad away. He says this kid isn't afraid of nuthin'.*"

"*Okay.*" Cimino seemed to be mumbling to himself. "*I mean, listen, I want someone like him as much as anybody. I hear you. But I hardly know this kid."*

"He's a kid looking for an opportunity, you ask me," Connolly said. "He's down on his luck after what happened to his wife and kid, right? Now he's thinkin', life owes me a thing or two. Maybe it's time I take what's mine. I mean, if he makes you uneasy—"

"No, I'm not saying—"

"—then let's just try him out, real safe or something. I mean, fucking pat the kid down, if that's what you're really afraid of. I mean, here, Charlie. Here it is. I wanna be as careful as you. But this kid, he's not fresh out of school like these other lawyers we got. The kid has some talent. Sometimes I wonder, if anyone ever took a hard look at us—"

"No, I know—"

"I'm just sayin', Charlie, a good lawyer can make this look a lot cleaner. I mean, whatever. I'll do whatever. But just—just think about it. I wouldn't mind having someone good watching my rear end."

"Yeah. Yeah, maybe. Maybe what you said about testing him. Patting him down. All right, I gotta go."

"Yeah, just let me know, Charlie. Whatever you say."

Tucker smiled at me.

"Thanks for sharing that," I said, "after the fact."

He smiled at me. "Better you didn't know." He kicked up his feet on the desk. "Now just put your head down and do the work, like I told you in the first place," he said. "Make him some money, and he'll fall into his comfort zone. You can handle that. I heard you on that first tape. You're good at this. Better than most, you wanna know the truth."

"Oh, gosh, Lee, I'll bet you say that to all the informants."

Tucker seemed to be getting a kick out of this. That made one of us. He had withheld information from me and didn't bat an eye in the process. He would tell me only what he wanted me to know. He would manipulate me and hide the ball and watch me fall when he was done squeezing every last drop of usefulness out of me.

"Maybe I just walk away from this whole thing and roll the dice," I said.

He gave me a yeah-right smirk.

"Hey, you want to be a cowboy, go for it. But just remember," he said, "you're making that decision for Shauna, too."

THAT FRIDAY NIGHT, SHAUNA AND I WENT TO DINNER and a movie. I made the mistake of picking the food (steak house), which allowed her to choose the flick (romantic comedy). I was shocked to discover that the two beautiful leads, after quarrelling throughout an agonizing ninety minutes of cinematic torture, realized that the true love they'd been looking for had been right there in front of them, all along! Fade to credits with a Top 40 adult contemporary love song.

We shared a cab and dropped her off first. I watched her until she was inside her condo building. She gave me a small wave and I nodded back.

She was my responsibility. The feds had her in their sights, however unfairly, because of me. I had to solve that problem. And I thought I knew how.

*   *   *

"PENSIONS," CIMINO SAID TO ME, as we hummed along in his Porsche the next morning. "State employees have pensions," Cimino went on. "Pensions have a lot of money to invest. Everyone wants a piece of that. Next month, the PCB's going to put out a solicitation for three hundred million."

"Someone's going to get three hundred million to invest?" I was wearing a sweater and a black jacket Talia had bought me last Christmas. The F-Bird was resting in my shirt pocket underneath my sweater, courtesy of Lee Tucker, who had come by my house at half past eight this morning through my back gate.

"I've got someone in mind. That's where we're going now. The commissions on this thing—they're unbelievable. We can get a hundred thousand for the governor and something for us, too." He looked over at me, noticing my lack of enthusiasm. "What?"

"Charlie, we can't just pick whatever investment banker we want. I mean, there are all sorts of criteria in the statute that the board will have to consider. We're locked down pretty tight on this."

"What are you telling me, kid? You telling me we can't handpick someone? You can't come up with some fancy legal argument?"

I sighed for Charlie's benefit. "I'm telling you, one, I can't make a *good* argument. And two, with this kind of money at stake, the spotlight on this, if we fuck around, will be huge. Every major player's going to go after this kind of money. They're not going to let us waltz in and fix this thing."

Charlie went radio silent. He looked like he was going to crush the steering wheel with his grip.

"I have a better idea," I said.

He looked over at me.

"Look," I said, "the way you're doing this now—it's hard. It's hard and it's risky. I mean, you have to comb through all the contracts that will be issued soon, and you have to recruit companies that are willing to contribute to Governor Snow's campaign in exchange for getting the contract and maybe even throw in a little side business to you or me or whomever. So you have to spend a lot of time looking for people who end up saying no, and you run the risk that one of them might do more than just say no—they might decide to report what they know to a news reporter or, even worse, the trench coats. And even if nobody talks, you got some bidder who thinks he should've gotten the contract instead of our handpicked guy, and then there's a lawsuit. Which means they shine a light on what we're doing. It means people testifying under oath. I mean, do I have this right so far, Charlie?"

Cimino had been nodding along with me. "That about sums it up."

"So at best, it's inefficient. And at worst, it's risky. I can live with inefficient, but not with risky."

"Okay, and you got a better idea."

"I do," I said. "Let's stick with current state contracts."

"Current ones." He looked at me. "Contracts already in place?"

"Right. Instead of looking all over the place for people bidding on *new* contracts, we just go to the people right in front of us—the people feeding at the public trough right now."

"And why would someone pay us squat if they already *have* a contract with the state?"

"Because," I said, "they want to keep it."

Cimino was silent for a moment, his eyes in a squint. "They want to *keep* it."

"The principle's the same, Charlie. We tell them the same thing: It's time to pony up. Only instead of offering them a contract with the state, we threaten to *take away* the one they already have, if they don't pay up."

"Huh." Cimino thought about that. "A stick instead of a carrot."

"Exactly," I said. "Every contract has some kind of termination clause. The state always has some reason why it can fire a contractor. I'll be able to find something to threaten them with. And here's the best part, Charlie: It's all under the radar. There's no disgruntled bidder who lost out on the contract. There's no bending and twisting of the Purchasing Code. There are no losing bidders. The people we'd be approaching already have contracts. Hell, we don't even *need* the PCB. We narrow the number of players to you and me."

"Right," Cimino said equivocally. "And if they tell us no?"

"Some might. But most won't. This is their livelihood. They have a state contract, probably worth hundreds of thousands, if not millions. They won't say no to a thirty-thousand-dollar contribution. And even those that do say no—they're not going to run to the feds over this. Why piss off the new governor and jeopardize their prized contract?"

Cimino kept thinking, but I could see that my idea was finding a warm landing. It made all kinds of sense from his perspective.

"They won't say no," I said.

"No, they won't." Cimino broke into laughter. "Brilliant." He slapped the steering wheel. "Fucking brilliant, Jason." He reached over and grabbed my arm. "You done good, kid."

I've never been one to shy away from praise, but this was a new one for me. I was being lauded for coming up with a new and improved criminal scheme, congratulated by someone whom I distrusted and disliked, whom I was screwing over in the biggest way. But it wasn't lost on me that I had accomplished my goal, which was to add value, to prove my worth, to further cement Cimino's trust in me. I wasn't going to have to worry about Cimino checking me for a recording device any time soon.

Famous last words.

AFTER THAT DAY WITH CIMINO, I SPENT THE WEEKEND before Christmas alone. Shauna's family had come into town on Saturday so she was occupied, and I resisted her invitation to join in any number of things they had planned. She'd pushed me hard to be a part of Christmas dinner, but so far I'd refused, and I figured once they were staying with her, she'd get caught up in all things family and leave me alone.

That was fine. I wasn't in the mood for a crowd. I did okay with loneliness, which is to say that I didn't pine for the company of others. Racquetball with Cimino had whetted my appetite for sweat, and I fell back into my bachelor routine of intense workouts, which included long runs in the frigid outdoors, my way of proving to myself how tough I was. My diet that weekend consisted of pizza and potato chips. Workouts and junk food, the staples of a contradictory bachelor lifestyle. I threw in a couple of crime novels and movies, though I didn't enjoy the sidelong glances from people when I went to a movie alone. I never really got why moviegoing had to be a shared experience. You go into a dark theater and watch something on a screen; why do you have to know the person sitting next to you?

On Monday, Christmas Eve, I got it into my head that I was going to dismantle Emily Jane's room—remove the crib and the custom rocking chair and changing table, tear down the Beatrix Potter wallpaper, repaint the walls something neutral, and move on with my life. I got as far as walking into the room before my blood went cold and the breath was whisked from my lungs.

It was odd to me how it all worked. On a daily basis, it was Talia who came into my mind more frequently. We'd spent so much time together, so many memories and experiences. Emily came in just at the end, a last, brief chapter in the book—three short months, most of which I spent tied up in the Almundo trial. I didn't remember her face like Talia's. Little things didn't remind me of Emily like they constantly did of my wife.

And yet, if I thought of Emily less often, it was more jarring when I did. It's easy to say the obvious thing, the absolute grotesqueness of a life lost after only three months. Barbaric enough to shake your faith, as it had mine. Sure. Of course. But there was more to it. We hadn't connected enough, Emily and me. Not yet. I can say all the right things—my love for her, my utter devotion—but the truth, I think, is that that kind of bond develops over time, and I simply hadn't had the time. I didn't love Emily Jane in the same way I loved Talia, or as much as I would have loved her over time. That, I had come to realize, is what bothered me as much as anything: I didn't get the chance to love my daughter as much as I was supposed to.

When the doorbell rang, I lifted my face out of the comforter on my bed. It was dark outside my window, which meant it was probably five in the evening, at least. I didn't know how long I'd been asleep, or if I'd even been technically asleep at all. I went to the mirror and saw hair standing in every direction, swollen eyes, and a line running south to southwest across my cheek from the pillow. But I made up for it with a fashionably wrinkled t-shirt and cut-off sweats. The doorbell rang again, and then I heard my cell phone buzzing where I had left it apparently, on the floor of Emily's bedroom. Whatever. I figured the phone caller was the impatient person at the front door, and it took me one second to narrow the candidates down to one.

I was wrong. It wasn't Shauna. It was Charlie.

"Jesus, kid," he said when I opened the door. "Did I wake you?"

He was in an expensive coffee-colored coat and cream scarf. A bit more nattily attired than I.

"I was giving myself a pedicure." It fell flat. Shauna would have laughed.

"Merry Christmas," he said. He handed me a package in silver wrapping. A shoe box.

I shook it. "And here I didn't get you anything. You want to come in?"

"No. Wife's waiting in the car." He nodded at me. "Go ahead. Open it."

I did. It was a shoe box. But it didn't contain shoes.

It was cash. Crisp, clean hundred-dollar bills wrapped neatly in bands.

Five thousand dollars in cash.

"Charlie, I—I—"

"You're doing great, kid. That's a thank-you. We're gonna have a great 2008."

"Charlie—"

"Get something for your lady friend," he said. "Shauna, right? The one you went to the movies with Friday night?"

Our eyes met. This wasn't a casual remark. He wanted me to know.

"You two close? Share each other's secrets? That kind of thing?"

"Charlie," I said, "are you *tailing* me?"

He made a compromising noise from his throat, like I was over-reacting. "I'm protecting my investment."

"Don't," I said.

"What do you tell her about us?" he asked.

"I don't. I don't tell her anything about what we're doing."

"You're sure."

"I'm *sure* that you better stop tailing me, Charlie."

"Listen, kid." He spoke out of the side of his mouth. "I know she's a great piece of ass, and I know you want to show her what a swell guy you are. But I'm telling you, women? They come and go. What's a secret today is something she'll tell all her friends tomorrow. And who knows? It ends badly? Maybe she calls a reporter or a cop or something."

"Charlie, I don't want you—"

He waved me off. "You want me paranoid, kid. You need me that way. And I need *you* that way. Just make sure Shauna doesn't have any idea what goes on between you and me. Don't make her a liability."

He clapped his hand on my shoulder. "Hey, all this seriousness. I really just wanted to give you that present. You deserve it. There's gonna be a lot more where that came from."

He headed for the door.

"Don't go near Shauna, Charlie," I said.

He waved as he walked out the door.

"Don't give me a reason to, kid," he said.

38

THE WEATHER OUTSIDE WAS DELIGHTFUL, BUT MY mood was rather frightful. Christmas Day. The air was crisp and the temperatures low. The sun was making an occasional appearance that lit up the light blanket of snow. All in all, it was a nice day outside, which sort of pissed me off. I went for a pretty good run through the quiet neighborhood streets of the city. When I got back, spent and sweaty, I had nothing else to do with my day.

So I got in my car and went for a drive. Talia and I used to do that on weekends. We'd drive around the various neighborhoods and check out their vibe, look at homes for sale and even walk through their open-house tours. Thinking about our next place to live, something I couldn't afford on an assistant county attorney's salary at the time, but it was fun to dream.

I thought of Charlie's friendly visit last night, letting me know he was watching me. I checked my rearview mirror but there was pretty much nobody driving. I wasn't being followed.

I drove in a different direction than usual this time. I drove to the southwest side. It was exceptionally quiet, almost barren, on Christmas Day. The area was overwhelmingly Latino and, therefore, overwhelmingly Catholic. Nothing was open. The housing was humble. Small and packed tightly together. I drove past Liberty Park, the scene of Ernesto Ramirez's death, a shiver passing through me. Then I turned left—south—and drove a couple of blocks, then west for another couple, then south again and looked for the signs for 6114 South Hastings.

Ernesto Ramirez's family lived on the bottom floor of a three-story brick building. Beyond a waist-high fence and a very tiny garden, dormant this time of year, was a concrete walk-up and side-by-side red doors, one for the Ramirez family and the other for the staircase leading to the upper floors.

From my view in my car, I could see a Christmas tree in the window of the Ramirez apartment. A tiny figure passed by, a head full of dark hair and pigtails. Presumably the daughter, the six-year-old, Mercedes. I got out of the car, went through the gate, and took the walk-up to the front door. I could hear them from my perch, the muffled sounds of children shouting and adults laughing inside the apartment. I was glad, almost relieved to hear it. This couldn't have been a good holiday for the Ramirez family. I poised my finger over the button for RAMIREZ but decided against it. I left the shopping bag on the stoop and walked back down. I was walking around to the driver's side of the car when I heard her voice.

"Hello."

I turned around. Essie Ramirez was standing where I'd just stood, her arms folded to keep warm. She was wearing a forest-green turtleneck and blue jeans. Her breath lingered in the frigid air outside.

I waved to her. "Merry Christmas."

"Same to you." She looked down into the shopping bag. "Presents?"

"For your kids," I said.

"Come in," she said.

"I shouldn't."

"Come in."

I hesitated, then shook my head. It wasn't that I didn't want to intrude. I just didn't want to do the family-at-Christmas thing, especially with someone else's family. "Another time," I said.

She paused, watching me, rubbing the arms of her sweater for warmth. Her dark hair hung past her shoulders. If memory served, she was in her early thirties, but she looked more like early twenties.

"How are they doing?" I asked.

She bobbed her head around. "Kids are better than adults," she said. "Good days, bad days. Today is a good day for them."

"For them," I repeated. "Not for you."

She paused. "Holidays are the hardest. It's supposed to be the best time of the year but that makes it even—well, it's hard. Are you married?"

I didn't know how to answer that. "No," I said.

I looked through the window again. I could see the boy now, too—Ernesto, Jr. He looked like a miniature version of his father, a stocky build and proud chin.

"Come in," she said again.

"I have to go. I just wanted to—just wanted to drop those off."

She watched me for a moment. Then she said, "I got a call from my landlord last week."

I nodded. "Wishing you a merry Christmas?"

"In a manner of speaking, yes." She smiled briefly. "I'd been getting calls from him for some time now. We've fallen behind on our rent here. Usually when he calls, he threatens me. But not this time."

I could see where the conversation was going.

"It was you, wasn't it?" she asked. "He wouldn't tell me. He said he was sworn to secrecy."

I thought about denying it but didn't.

"Why did you do that?" she asked.

I shrugged my shoulders. "I made a lot of money at my old law firm. I didn't have anything else to spend it on."

That was partly true, partly false. I was getting low on the residual money from when I was raking it in at Shaker, Riley. But it was true that I didn't have anything else to spend it on.

"And?" she said.

"And, nothing."

"And you feel responsible for Ernesto," she said. "And therefore, his family."

I didn't answer.

"So you paid for his family's rent for a year and it made you feel better?"

"A little, yeah."

"Why keep it a secret?"

"Because you wouldn't have accepted it," I said.

She couldn't disagree with that. "I can't pay you back. Not now, at least."

"Not necessary. Ever."

She thought for a bit. "All right then. I'll accept it because my kids need a roof over their heads. It was a very nice gesture. Thank you." She took a long breath. "But I am not a charity case. And you are not responsible for what happened to my husband. The people who killed him are."

"And I'm going to find them."

"I didn't ask you to do that."

"I know you didn't."

"If they killed him, they could kill you."

"Then I'll have to be careful, won't I?"

Her eyes narrowed. She wasn't going to win this argument. "Don't do this for me."

"How about I do it for Ernesto?"

The mention of his name moved her. I hadn't intended to upset her. But whatever it was passed quickly; she snapped out of it with a curt shake of her head. "He wouldn't want you to get hurt because of him."

But he got *killed* because of me. He lost everything because of my pursuit of him.

Essie Ramirez uncrossed her arms and walked down the stairs toward me. I wasn't entirely sure what she was doing, but I walked around to the curb side of my car. She put her hands on my arms, reached up, and kissed me on the cheek. "You're a good person," she said. "Don't lose your way." She went back inside, leaving me in the freezing cold with the fruity scent of her shampoo and something weird floating through my chest.

39

I WAS SUMMONED TO THE U.S. ATTORNEY'S OFFICE THE day after Christmas. That was somewhat unusual for this stage of the investigation. I'd have expected a covert meet at a diner or the offices they were renting in my building—Suite 410. But not this time. They wanted me on their turf.

Not a friendly discussion planned, I assumed.

I knew I was right when I saw the look on Lee Tucker's face when he met me at the elevator. He acknowledged me but didn't make much eye contact, and I could feel his anger coming off him like heat. The place was largely deserted. A day off for most, maybe for the whole office.

But not for Lee Tucker. And not for Christopher Moody, who was sitting in the conference room with a sour look on his face.

Tucker was in jeans and a sweatshirt, which wasn't all that different than I'd seen from him. But I'd never seen Moody out of uniform. He had a button-down checkered shirt and khakis. It almost made him look human.

"Why the long faces?" I said. "You guys didn't get what you wanted for Christmas?" I took a seat and kicked up my feet on the table. They'd brought me here, home territory, to establish power. I wanted to take some air out of them.

"Boys," I said, after a long silence, "I thought you'd be singing my praises. I just made your lives easier. I just—"

"What the hell are you doing, Jason?" said Lee Tucker. I was his responsibility, so he would handle the conversation. He was still standing, pacing in anger. "This audible you called with Cimino?"

He meant the new idea I'd proposed, which Cimino had accepted. We wouldn't go after companies seeking new contracts before the PCB. Instead, we'd extort the companies that already had state contracts and would want to keep them. Higher probability of success, lower risk, and far more efficient.

I opened my hands. "A better way to shake down companies for campaign donations."

"A different way," Tucker replied. "A *different* way. A way that doesn't include the PCB."

That was true enough.

"We build this case the way we want to build it," said Tucker. "Not the way *you* want to."

I held a stare on him and slowly shook my head. "We're improving our efficiency, Lee. Cimino will commit more crimes. More counts to the indictment."

"But you're keeping the board out of it," he replied. "The PCB doesn't have a say in this. And we want those guys. All five of them. Greg Connolly and the bunch. You're turning this into a two-man operation. Now it's the Charlie and Jason Show."

I laughed. "You should listen to yourself," I said. "You're disappointed that more people don't get to participate in the crimes. Like the whole goal is simply to rack up as many scalps as possible. That's your problem, you know that?"

"Oh, now I have a problem?" Tucker took a moment to contain himself. He preferred the image of the cool FBI agent. And it fit his personality. He didn't like balling me out, I could tell. It wasn't his way, plus it meant he wasn't controlling his operative. "You don't know everything, and you don't need to know everything. You are part of an operation, Kolarich. Okay? Just one part. That's why we tell you what to do, and how to do it. So everything stays consistent." He dropped into his seat and stared up at the ceiling. "I mean, first you go off and do a hard sell on Cimino—"

"Which worked."

"—and now you change the entire game plan—"

"Which will also work."

Tucker watched me for a long time, running his tongue over his cheek. He removed his tin of tobacco and dumped a pinch in his mouth.

From my take, Tucker wasn't prone to anger. He was a relatively easygoing guy. And more than that, I was his project. He had to work me. He seemed to have made the calculation that I was a bit harder to tame than most people in my position, and he had to take his subjects as he found them. But he was pissed. And I wasn't sure why.

On the other side of the room, Christopher Moody stared at me, his expression intense. He was supposed to intimidate me. Maybe he forgot how that Almundo case turned out.

Tucker said, "You're messing up, my friend, I shit you not. You're calling audibles you aren't allowed to call. You want to get yourself in more trouble than you already are?"

A long stalemate followed. It was true that I had cut down the players in this scheme, for the most part, to Cimino and me. Others would probably get caught up, as well, but for the moment at least, this was going to be a two-man operation.

"You've hindered our investigation," Tucker went on. "You've closed doors to us."

"You've obstructed justice." So the great Christopher Moody finally spoke. He delivered it with an even tone, meant again to intimidate. "We gave you instructions to work as an attorney with the PCB and you just shut them out completely. You are a lawyer for the board, not for Charlie Cimino. Cimino isn't even a government employee. And now we've lost part of our case. You've fucked up royally, Kolarich."

"Careful, Chris. Don't threaten me. You don't want Cimino's defense lawyer to—"

"Oh, it's no threat, superstar. I'm telling you square. I *will* charge you with obstruction when this case is over. One count, so far. You want to keep going? You want to keep disobeying us? Conspiracy and obstruction aren't enough? Then keep doing what you're doing, and the indictment will get thicker. I'm done fucking around with you, Kolarich. I am fucking done."

I waited to be sure he was finished. Then I nodded to Tucker. "Your turn, Lee. Good cop."

He snorted out a laugh, but it wasn't merriment. He made a show of shaking his head and flapping his arms. "You got any more surprises for us? Any other brilliant ideas that you might want to share with us?"

This might have been a good time to tell them that the reason I got involved with the PCB in the first place—and the reason I was still involved—was my attempt to solve the murder of Ernesto Ramirez. I didn't know if my search would conflict with their operation. It might have been wise to clear this with them. But I didn't.

I raised my hand. "Point of order, if I could. I have just completely gained the trust of the target of your investigation. This guy loves me right now. I'm serving up Charlie Cimino on a silver platter. We're going to be a two-man crime syndicate, and you'll have a front-row seat. My little 'audible' has just guaranteed you a conviction in federal court. So instead of ambushing me, maybe it's time you started playing a little nicer."

Chris Moody's head jerked up, like something had just occurred to him. Whatever else I may think of him, he isn't dumb. That last line of mine wasn't lost on him. He mumbled something to himself, shook his head, and pushed himself hard out of the chair. He walked over to the window looking out over the east side of the commercial district.

"I think you got it backwards," said Tucker. "You're working off a good deal of criminal liability right now. You've got a lot of working off to do."

I looked over at Moody. "Chris, why don't you help Lee out here? He's fallen behind."

Tucker didn't get it. But Moody did. He remained silent for a long time before speaking into the window. He probably didn't want me to see his face.

"Our good friend here Mr. Kolarich," said Moody, "has made himself indispensable. The Charlie and Jason Show? That was no spontaneous audible. Jason planned this out very carefully, Agent Tucker."

"Obviously, I deny that," I said. "I was merely doing my best to help gain the target's trust. But let's assume for argument's sake that Chris is right. Why would I want to make myself indispensable?"

Tucker was lost. Moody was pissed.

"Anyone," I said. "Just shout it out."

"Just get it over with, whatever it is," said Moody.

I turned to look at Tucker. "Lee, here's what's gonna happen next. Chris over here is going to exonerate Shauna Tasker of all wrongdoing."

Tucker paused a beat. "Bullshit."

"Oh, but it's true," I said, wagging a finger. "It's true. And there are two reasons why. The first is that he knows damn well that my friend Shauna had nothing to do with this. She just sat in on a meeting with that construction guy. She had no idea the client was sent over by Charlie Cimino. She didn't know anything about shakedowns of state contractors. She's completely innocent, and everyone in this room knows it. Right, Chris?"

Moody was still stewing in the corner.

"And the second reason?" Tucker said, but I think he'd caught on by now.

"The second reason is that the Charlie and Jason Show doesn't work so well without Jason. Right, Lee? Charlie, he likes me. I provide legal cover for him, or so he thinks. I make Charlie feel safe. I've had some swell ideas so far. And I've penetrated that very tight inner circle. It would only take you, what, another year or so to find someone who's gotten as close as I have."

"We don't do that," said Moody. "We don't give out clean bills of health to potential defendants."

"You do now." I got up and walked past Tucker to the door. "You have twenty-four hours," I said. "You walk Shauna Tasker or I do some walking of my own."

I pushed through the glass door and headed to the elevator. One of them—not hard to guess which one—had caught the door and was following close behind me. I pushed the elevator button and started whistling. Chris Moody stood close to me and spoke to my profile.

"Score one for you," he said. "Your girlfriend gets a pass. But I meant what I said in there. I'm going to indict you with Cimino and everyone else. You've now guaranteed that. You hear that, rock star? It's a guaran-fucking-tee. Everything I have on you so far and anything else I can think of.

"Now, you give me one hundred percent cooperation from here on out—I mean one *hundred* percent, Kolarich, not ninety-nine—and I'll think about a reduction. But you'll still spend time inside. Maybe two years, maybe three. All you did in there was dig yourself a deeper hole. You, my friend, are going to prison. It's just a question of how long."

His face was a bright crimson. He'd just been served his lunch, but he'd given as much as he'd taken. I'd lost all hope of good faith with him now. I would be standing trial with Charlie Cimino and Greg Connolly and whomever else they would charge.

I'd freed up Shauna, but at considerable cost.

Hell hath no fury like a prosecutor scorned.

DEEPER

February 2008

40 "WE'VE ALWAYS APPRECIATED THE CHANCE TO WORK for the department." Mitchell DeSantis eyed Charlie Cimino and me with some trepidation as we ate seafood. He was talking about the Department of Revenue, with whom DeSantis's company had a four-million-dollar contract annually to print tickets for the state lottery. "I think we've done everything Revenue's ever asked of us."

"Well, obviously there's a new administration," said Cimino, a standard opening for us over these last two weeks. With a new administration—albeit a year old—came changes, especially with a different political party in charge. It was, at least, superficial cover. "We're conducting audits and we have some concerns."

"Concerns. What concerns? I haven't heard any concerns." DeSantis was a lanky, nervous man. His chin and nose gave him an academic, almost birdlike quality.

Cimino shot a look of annoyance and boredom—which really meant power. "You're hearing them now," he said.

It was my turn. By now, Cimino didn't even have to look in my direction. We had this down to a formula. "Mr. DeSantis," I said, "the contract allows the department to terminate the contract without notice, if the termination is for cause. And if it's without cause, you have as long as it takes the department to rebid the contract, which is about ninety days."

"What is it?" he asked. "We've always kept up our stock. We had one issue once with the new ink—which we fixed right away, and without charge to the state."

"What my lawyer here is saying, Mitch, is that we don't need a reason. In which case you have about ninety days left. And if Jason informs the department that cause exists, your contract could be terminated tomorrow. Mitch," he went on, changing his tone, as if he were now dispensing friendly advice, "I can see a situation where your company finishes out the governor's term. That's about a year from today. January 2009. And I can also see your company re-upping for another four years, if Governor Snow is reelected."

DeSantis seized on that. "Obviously, we'd be very grateful, if Governor Snow—"

"If, Mitch. 'If' is the operative word here. You realize he's running in a contested primary. And then the general election." Cimino shook his head. "These are expensive things, these elections. Did you know that candidates for governor are budgeting twenty million for the race?"

DeSantis sat back, as if flabbergasted at what was occurring. "No, I didn't know—"

"So Friends of Snow is looking for friends, right, Mitch? You follow me."

DeSantis pushed his thick glasses back up his nose. "I don't know that I do."

"Sure you do. Mitch, I know you got your contract under the Trotter administration. But now you're working for the Snow administration. So we want to know if you're willing to help."

DeSantis's face colored, as had the faces of several others, sitting in his spot, after hearing our pitch, over the last few weeks. "And if I don't, I lose my contract?"

"Did you hear me say that?" Cimino delivered the line with a cool glare, no trace of a smile. "You didn't hear me say that. Did you, Mitch?"

The man deflated. Cimino removed a piece of paper from his pocket and slid it over. The number on it was "25,000." DeSantis looked at Cimino, who raised his eyebrows. It was clear that certain things would remain unspoken. He took the paper back and said, "And obviously, with Willie Bryant running against Governor Snow in the primary, and Lang Trotter's son, Edgar, running in the Republican primary, there would be the question of whether you intend to support anyone else. We'll be sure to keep tabs on any contributions being made to other campaigns, as well. Jason, you check the semi-annual reports, right?"

"Like clockwork," I said. This was part of the routine, too, every time. Governor Snow had a serious challenger in the primary, the current secretary of state, a guy named Willie Bryant. And the Republicans were another concern, obviously; the smart money seemed to be on Langdon Trotter's kid, Edgar. Charlie was not only shaking down companies for contributions; he was threatening them if they contributed to anyone else.

"Look, Mr. Cimino," DeSantis said.

"Charlie. It's Charlie."

"Charlie." DeSantis sighed. "Look, Charlie, I have a small company—"

"Mitch, I want to thank you for lunch," Cimino said, which was probably news to DeSantis, who hadn't realized he was buying. "I suppose"—he looked at me—"I suppose the decision on the contract could be delayed for a week or so. That would give both of us time to think about our next step. One," he repeated, "week."

It was a script we'd worked out. We would start with an idle threat of terminating a contract, and nine times out of ten, that was all it took—a check to Friends of Snow was cut within the next twenty-four hours. On the two occasions, thus far, that anyone had pushed back, I had followed up by meeting with the contractor and

showing him a "preliminary" report demonstrating a basis for terminating the contract—basically showing him that we weren't kidding when we said we were going to shit-can them. At Charlie's
insistence, I never left a copy of that report with the contractor; I
always kept it with me. Charlie was extremely careful about leaving
bread crumbs.

But he wasn't being careful with me. I had gained his trust; it was
I who had come up with the idea to extort existing state contractors, and I who helped him orchestrate the entire pitch we made.
All of this was done under the guise of shielding our scheme from
unwanted scrutiny, and Cimino thought of me as the most risk-averse
person he'd ever met, which in turn further cemented my credibility
with him. I'd even gone so far as to insist that we not move on one
particular contractor who seemed more than a little nervous about
the whole thing; I told Cimino that the guy just didn't feel right, and
he decided to trust my gut, albeit with a patronizing laugh. It didn't
matter; the point was that he put me down as having as much to lose
as he did, which put me squarely beyond the realm of suspicion.

It became clear, quickly after our scheme began, that we'd need
to rely on some sort of technology to communicate with each other.
Charlie had always avoided emails, cell phones—anything that could
be captured by the feds. He'd always preferred face-to-face conversations. But we were working too quickly to pull that off anymore. So
we settled on text messages. And we came up with a plan. Charlie
had a master list of all companies that had contracts with one of the
governor's agencies in excess of a hundred thousand a year. Charlie
figured a hundred thousand was a good break-off, sufficiently large
that a company would be willing to make a campaign contribution,
and/or throw Charlie or me some side business, in order to keep it.

Charlie put that list in order, from bigger contracts to smaller,
and assigned a number to each one. When he had a company in
mind to target, he would send me a text message that contained that
number somewhere within the body of the message. A text saying
It must be 25 degrees outside meant the next target was contractor

number 25. *Did you see that article in the paper on page 11?* meant contractor number 11 was next up. That gave me the contractor's name and the contract itself. I would study it to look for ways that we could break the contract and dump the company. And after our meetings like the one we just had with Mitch DeSantis, I would be responsible for any follow-up. If the contractor balked in any way or if they reached out to me at all, I would text Charlie back, again using the coded number to indicate the company.

All of that was acceptable, from Charlie's perspective. He wasn't thrilled about the text messages but the messages themselves were indecipherable without a translator. The only person who could translate them, besides him, was me. And he trusted me.

The two of us were making out okay on these deals, as well. Cimino picked and chose among our targets—the ones with the larger contracts and, therefore, more to lose if we pulled the plug on them—and made sure consulting contracts went to his sham companies. Some legal work was sent my way, as well. My plate was beginning to swell at the office. Even Shauna was impressed, though still skeptical. The feds and I had to figure out how to handle the issue of the legal business. On the one hand, it was ill-gotten legal work, the product of extortion. On the other hand, I *was* performing legitimate legal work for these clients, however they arrived at my doorstep, and I couldn't be expected to do it for nothing. So the arrangement that I made with the U.S. attorney's office was that I would receive the hourly fee for private attorneys who are referred cases from the federal defender. Every private lawyer who was a member of the federal bar was eligible to be referred such a case and was required to handle it for a paltry hourly fee as part of our duty to provide legal services to the indigent; in my case, it wasn't the indigent but the extorted.

Lee Tucker could hardly complain. He met with me daily and marveled at our proficiency—and the case he was building against Charlie Cimino. As the evidence came in, the government had been documenting it with fancy color charts detailing each meeting with a state contractor; the date of the corresponding contribution to Governor Snow's campaign fund; any other perks, such as consulting work to one of Charlie's side companies or legal work to me; and the cell-phone communications about these things.

Every instance of extortion was a crime, and the feds were very good at taking a single act and multiplying it into about twelve crimes, throwing in counts for conspiracy and wire fraud, that kind of thing. The key to federal jurisdiction was the use of interstate communication. That meant phone calls, faxes, emails. That, of course, is why I came up with the elaborate text-messaging scheme between Charlie and me. Each of the text messages was a separate use of the wires in interstate commerce for the purpose of executing the criminal scheme.

I'd expected, at some point, for Charlie to delegate this work to me and not involve himself in the day-to-day affairs of the extortion. But he hadn't. He loved it, the raw power of holding the fates of these contractors in his hands, the thrill of the shakedown itself. The guy was a bully at heart. What he was doing was the adult version of stealing milk money from the weaker kids.

"I don't care," he said into his earpiece as we rode in his Porsche from the DeSantis meeting. "Just get them sold. I'm just carrying these fuckin' things. They're killing me. Sell them or I'll find someone who will."

He clicked off his phone and murmured to himself. "What a market. What a goddamn market."

It was not the greatest time to be a real estate developer, I gathered.

"Fifty thousand square feet of commercial space I got," he went on. "Tenants, I don't."

That was the life of a developer. Buy the land, build on it, and hope the buyers will come. But the market had crashed. Charlie was property rich but, for all I knew, cash poor.

His cell phone buzzed, and he looked at the phone for the caller ID. "Greg Connolly," he said with disdain. "That jerk-off can wait."

He looked over at me for a reaction but did not receive one. "Greg's feeling lonely these days."

Lonely, that is, because our new plan didn't include the PCB much at all. The "Charlie and Jason Show" didn't require Greg Connolly.

"Is that a problem?" I asked.

"Hard to say. It's a problem if he runs to Carl."

The mention of the governor's name gave me a jolt. Cimino was saying that the governor knew what was going on. There would be no point in Greg Connolly running to his childhood friend, Governor Snow, unless the governor had some idea about the scheme.

It was what we figured, the feds and I, but it was the first time Cimino had invoked the governor's name in this way. I hadn't brought it up. It would seem too forced. Sooner or later, the topic was going to come up, and now was that time. I'm sure Chris Moody would be scrutinizing today's recording from my F-Bird with particular care.

"And how plugged in is the governor to all of this?" I asked, going for it, because that had been the request from the federal government. If the topic came up, pursue it.

Cimino made a face but then changed topics. "That reminds me. He's having a funder tonight. You should go."

"To a fundraiser."

"You should meet him, kid. Fuck. Fuck!" he said, looking at his buzzing cell phone. "Connolly again. This guy calls me twice in five minutes. Anyway, yeah, you should go tonight. You got a tux? Or get one. I'll leave your name at the door. After all you've done for him," he said, looking over at me, "they oughta let you in for free."

41 BETWEEN MY CRIMINAL ENTERPRISE WITH CHARLIE Cimino and the new clients and cases I had as bonus prizes, January and February had been quite busy for me. That was good. I needed busy. Because I tended to keep my head on straighter when my thoughts were occupied. I didn't pass an hour of the day without thinking of my wife and daughter, but it wasn't dominating me as much. Part of that was the mere passage of time, I realized, but the constant demands of litigation were a welcome distraction.

The bad part was that I hadn't had much time to do what I'd originally set out to do when I joined up with the Procurement and Construction Board: find Ernesto Ramirez's killer. There was a very good chance that the person responsible for his death was my partner in our criminal scheme. But even if I knew that, I didn't have any proof. I couldn't very well ask him. It would make for an awkward conversation, and there weren't a lot of workable segues, either. *Hey, speaking of murder, Charlie, by chance did you have a guy named Ernesto Ramirez whacked?*

I didn't have much to go on, other than my gut. Ernesto's wife, Essie, didn't know anything. Ernesto's scribbling on the back of my business card wasn't any kind of proof. The only thing I had to go on was that lawsuit that Wozniak's company had filed when they lost that beverage contract. It could lead to something, but I didn't have the resources to follow up. I didn't want to use Joel Lightner; I didn't want to get him anywhere near this thing. Christopher Moody was just looking for ways to fuck my friends, and I'd been lucky to get Shauna out of it with a nice letter from the U.S. attorney's office, acknowledging that Shauna Tasker was not suspected of having any role in this thing whatsoever and was not a target of the investigation. I wouldn't get another one of those.

So I couldn't use Lightner, and I didn't have a whole lot of spare money to hire an investigator, anyway. Once the money from some of this legal work started coming, maybe. But not at the moment.

But then I caught a break. Charlie had sent me a text message that included a number, which I then matched with the list he'd written up of major state contractors. My job would be to pull the contract and look for ways to terminate it, should the contractor refuse to pay the ransom. As my eyes wandered over the list, I noticed that virtually all of the biggest state contractors had already been paid a visit from Charlie and me.

But one very significant one had not. And even more important, Charlie hadn't even assigned it a number. That company would not be receiving one of our visits.

The company was Starlight Catering, the very same company that had won the beverage contract after Adalbert Wozniak's company had been disqualified.

Life's full of coincidences.

And now I had an opening.

I went to my office at the state building and pulled the contracts currently held by Starlight Catering. Then I returned to my law offices and got a motion on file in one of my new cases. At five o'clock, I went down to Suite 410 and used the key I'd been given to walk in.

Special Agent Lee Tucker, who had documents spread out all over the office he was using, seemed pleased to learn of my invitation to the fundraiser. From his perspective, it suggested potential. It could open new doors for me. But he didn't ask me to wear a wire and I didn't volunteer.

"Hey," I said. "I have a question."

"Wow. Usually you're the guy with all the answers." Tucker and I got along okay. We'd had a rocky start, but I was eligible for a gold star after these last two months. The government had solid evidence of twenty-three separate shakedowns by Charlie Cimino and me. That kind of success seemed to smooth over any differences. Plus it was part of Tucker's job to manage me, and he'd come to realize that I didn't respond to threats.

I dropped Cimino's master list of major state contractors on the desk in front of him, a copy of which he'd had ever since I got mine. "Page two," I said. "You see there, about a third of the way down. Starlight Catering. They don't have a number assigned. Like they're not one of the targets. Any idea why they get a pass?"

I watched Tucker's eyes. If he didn't really look, it meant that he'd already noticed it. If he did, it meant he hadn't.

Tucker's eyes followed down the page and stopped, presumably, at Starlight. So that probably meant he didn't know. It could also make him a good bullshit artist.

"Why?" he asked.

"I'm asking *you* why."

"But why do you care?"

"Why do you guys always answer questions with questions? I'm just curious."

"Why don't you ask Cimino?" Tucker was pleased with himself. Another question.

"You've been a font of information, Agent Tucker."

He got a chuckle out of the whole thing. "That company— Starlight—is an MBE," he said. "A minority-owned business. There are laws covering them, right? So even Cimino's not dumb enough to start shit-canning the MBEs."

That made sense, I guess. But Cimino wasn't really planning to shit-can any of these companies. He wanted to strong-arm these contractors and was willing to push it to the brink if necessary, using me to threaten termination of their contracts, but I didn't think Cimino was sold on the idea of actually pulling the trigger. Too messy. The threat, alone, had been enough so far.

Starlight Catering might have been a minority-owned business, but that wasn't why Cimino had held off targeting them. There was something else there. I had to figure out what that was.

And the federal government wasn't going to be any help. And I couldn't use Joel Lightner to help, or any other private investigator.

So I would have to go to the source.

42

THE FUNDRAISER WAS HELD IN A DOWNTOWN HOTEL in one of their extravagant ballrooms. A nice enough setting. Too nice, for my taste. I never really understood why things had to be so opulent. It always struck me as a waste of money and little more than a jerk-off to people's egos. Couldn't we all agree on less humble homes, hotels, offices, whatever—and just give the extra money to starving people in Africa or something?

Altruistic and philanthropically minded was I, in my tuxedo, nursing a martini.

I was more than a fish out of water. I was a fish who didn't know any of the other fish. The place held about a thousand and it was near capacity, and I doubted that I had made the acquaintance of any of them.

I engaged in people watching for a while, but it wasn't all that interesting. Everyone there was the same. They all wanted something. A job. A piece of legislation signed. If nothing else, to be seen. After about half an hour, I was working on a decent buzz from the martinis when the room seemed to shift. Nearly everyone turned in the same direction, something out of a Hitchcock movie, and then broke into applause.

So I looked, too, because I knew it meant the guest of honor had arrived, and if somebody from the crowd assassinated him, the FBI would review the tapes afterward and see that I was the one person who didn't turn—like that guy who opened the umbrella on a sunny day before JFK was shot—and I'd be a suspect.

This is how my mind works when I'm bored and getting drunk.

He had entered through the main doors and was now inching along the crowd, shaking hands and waving. His security detail followed close by, several men in dark suits with earpieces attached to cords disappearing into their suits, which added to the overall effect.

From a short distance, I could say this much about Carlton Snow: He looked the part. He was rather tall and fit, with a nice head of hair and one of those robotically sincere smiles. He had all the movements down. He'd clearly been doing his politician's exercises. Wave, thumbs-up, point at someone, shake a hand. Wave, thumbs-up, point, shake. Sometimes he overlapped his left hand so he could shake two hands at once. He mixed in different facial expressions, too. Pleasant surprise to see you. Familiar grin for the "old friend." I wasn't a lip reader but he seemed to have the phrases down, too. Hey-how-are-you-great-to-see-you-thanks-for-coming.

"Jason, there you are."

I turned to see Greg Connolly, the chairman of the Procurement and Construction Board. A man who didn't have as much going on these days, at least not of an illicit nature, thanks to me. Someday— like when the indictments came down, and he saw himself included in far less counts than Charlie—he'd thank me.

But, I suspected, not now.

"Greg," I said, with some equivocation, like I wasn't sure who he was, given that we'd only met once. We shook hands. He looked like me, in a penguin suit, but shorter and with a much thicker midsection. His bow tie was crooked but I didn't point it out. Mine probably was, too.

"We miss you," he said.

"Right back atcha."

"Yeah. Yeah."

Yeah. Small talk. I don't like it.

"Charlie's keeping you to himself these days."

I had to play the role of the cautious confidant to Cimino, so I just said, "He's a good man."

"Sure. Sure."

Sure. Greg didn't seem too happy about my arrangement with Charlie. Charlie had mentioned it could be a problem, should Connolly run to the governor to complain. I didn't really care if that happened. My reason for proposing the new and improved scheme to Charlie was to gain leverage and get Shauna off the hook. I'd already accomplished that. Shauna would now be free.

Free to come visit me in prison.

Unless I pulled a rabbit out of my hat. I was still working on that.

"Maybe there's a way we could keep doing business?" he said to me. It was in the form of a question. I wasn't sure if he had an idea or was looking for one.

I smiled. "You're asking the wrong guy, Greg."

"Oh, I don't think so." He patted my shoulder. "I think you have Charlie's ear like nobody else."

I wondered if that was true. I'd only known Charlie for a short time. But he didn't seem to have a lot of people close to him, and I'd hatched a plan that was accomplishing his twin goals of enriching himself and getting the governor reelected, the latter purpose having the ultimate goal of enriching himself, too. I mean, it was all about money in the end. I was making him richer and more important to the governor, which in turn would make him richer still.

The governor ended up standing on a dais in the middle of the room that allowed him to see into and over the crowd. I didn't recall ever hearing him speak, though I must have, at some point, over the last year that he had served as governor.

"Thank you, everyone. Thank you. I don't want to—thank you. If I could just—I love you, too. Thank you."

It took the man a while to calm the crowd, to snap them out of their feigned adoration. He started and stopped a few times, as people shouted sweet nothings to him. Actually, he didn't try very hard to stop them. He was basking in the glow, standing in his crisp tuxedo, holding a microphone with one hand and raising a steadying hand to the crowd with the other like the pontiff in Rome.

"You go back with him," I said to Greg Connolly.

"Oh, sure. Grew up with him on George Street. Took every class together from kindergarten to graduating from State."

It sounded like a line Connolly had recited many times in the last year, his connection to the governor. This guy was a hanger-on if I ever saw one.

"I went to State, too," I said.

"Yeah? When did you—" He stopped on that. It dawned on him and he looked over at me. "Jason Kolarich. Wide receiver?"

I nodded.

"Huh. I remember you. And you, uh—you broke that guy—Karmeier, right?"

I nodded.

"Broke his nose, right?"

"Jaw," I said. "But he started it."

"Jeez." He chuckled. "He played a few years with the Steelers, y'know."

I knew. Tony Karmeier missed the rest of his senior year after our altercation in the locker room. But he still went in the second round of the NFL draft and made millions, while I was kicked off the team, lost my scholarship, and narrowly avoided expulsion from the university. All in all, I think Tony had the last laugh.

"We've done some good things," said Governor Carlton Snow to the crowd. "We've expanded health care for children. We've put a thousand more cops on the streets. And we're not done. We're just getting started. And that's why what you're doing tonight is so important."

"I think there's still a role for me," said Connolly, leaning in to me close. "You can figure something out, right?"

I shrugged my shoulders. It wasn't my problem. But all things being equal, I wasn't looking to draw more people into the federal government's spiderweb. Or, in Connolly's case, more than he already was. "Talk to Charlie," I said.

I was bored. I was going around in circles with a guy who, unbeknownst to him, was trying very hard to get himself into more trouble with the feds. And I had only come here at the behest of Charlie, who wasn't anywhere to be found and, anyway, why the hell did I need to see him? I saw him all the time. It was time to leave, I decided.

"Hey," said Connolly, "you want to meet some people?"

And then it got more interesting.

43

THE PARTY WENT ON ANOTHER TWO HOURS. I DRAINED several martinis and did the dreaded small-talk dance. Turned out, I knew some of the lawyers in the room, and a couple others knew of me from the Almundo trial. Greg Connolly stayed pretty close to me, which was sort of creepy. He'd promised me a meet with the governor when the place cleared out some, not that I had requested the meeting or even looked forward to it. In fact, I realized that I was probably the only person in the room who *didn't* want to meet Carlton Snow. But Connolly seemed to think it was a tantalizing prospect and he kept sight of me as the night drew on, as if to reassure me.

Greg was trying to curry my favor. He really seemed to think that I was pulling the strings. I didn't know enough about the players involved—Charlie included, who still, in many ways, remained a stranger to me—to know why Greg would think that, but I had been elevated to a prominent status in his mind.

I looked over the shoulder of one of the lawyers in our conversation circle and saw a woman standing with Connolly. I didn't recognize her, but she caught my attention. Greg eagerly waved me over and I excused myself.

"Jason Kolarich, Madison Koehler. Maddie's the governor's chief of staff."

"I've heard a lot about you," she said to me.

I extended a hand. "All of it good, I hope."

"All of it," she said. Her hand was warm. Hot, in fact.

Madison Koehler was well-packaged in a form-fitting cocktail dress, bleached-blond hair, and a healthy dose of makeup. I put her at a little north of forty, but she was clearly doing the best she could to keep her age a mystery. Her eyes were large, brown, and predatory; there was a severity to her overall look that told me two things—she didn't take any prisoners and she was good in bed. Take a photo of her and she wouldn't win too many contests. But there was something about her up close and personal, a confident, aggressive style that oozed sensuality.

Or maybe it was just that I hadn't been laid in a year. I was beginning to have romantic feelings for my mailbox.

"All of it," she repeated, keeping her eyes on me. Well, then.

"Maddie here directs the traffic, I like to say." Connolly was still talking. He kept on doing that and we both listened, but I was feeling something and I wasn't sure how to handle it. I hadn't been with a woman since Talia. I hadn't thought about a woman since Talia. I decided not to analyze it at all. I just listened to Greg Connolly sputter on about this woman's résumé while I followed the outline of that sequined cocktail dress and wondered what was under it. My eyes moved up until they made contact with hers. She didn't react, save a small fluttering of her eyebrows. She was telling me that she didn't mind the tour my eyes had taken.

"I told him I'd introduce him to Carl," said Connolly.

"The governor," she said. I took that as an admonishment for his informality. "Greg, I'd like a moment with Jason," she said, her eyes squarely on me.

"Sure, sure."

As Connolly excused himself, applause erupted again throughout the place. I wasn't sure why. I didn't care why.

"The governor's leaving," Madison said to me. Over her shoulder, I could see Governor Snow waving to the crowd. But not out the main exit. An exit that led further into the hotel's interior.

"Where to now?" I asked.

"We have a suite of rooms here. For more private discussions, away from the hordes."

Our eyes remained on each other.

"I wasn't talking about the governor," I said.

Her expression eased ever so subtly. "Neither was I."

I followed her through the room, fully charged, a loaded weapon. She said she wanted to use the ladies' room and left me in the main lobby with about a hundred people and my imagination. The governor and his state police entourage were nowhere to be found. Most of the people were filtering out.

She took her time. I imagined the point was to let the crowd dissipate. When she came back, she made eye contact with me and headed toward the elevator. I followed her in. About a dozen other people did, too. Shoulder to shoulder. I found myself in a corner as the elevator abruptly lurched upward. Madison was standing directly in front of me, and with the lift of the elevator, her body moved backward into mine. Her hair was directly beneath my chin, hints of dark roots to her bleached hair. Her perfume was something expensive. I looked around the elevator. All eyes forward. Some small talk about the weather, Barack Obama's surprise showing in the primaries thus far, the fundraiser tonight. But nary a word from my female companion or me. A certain part of my anatomy, standing at full attention, was thrust against the small of her back. She didn't seem to mind. Neither did her hand, which had curled behind her back to, shall we say, grip the microphone.

Moses's trek through the desert seemed like a sprint compared to this elevator ride. Every person on the elevator seemed to be getting off at different floors before us. I was bursting at the seams, and Madison wasn't doing anything to lessen my anticipation. If she'd moved that hand any faster, in fact, I might not even have made it to the room. But she knew exactly what she was doing, grooming her new acquaintance just enough to keep everyone in the proper frame of mind without spoiling the surprise.

As the group dissipated, and things were more conspicuous, she cleared some space between us. She looked through her purse for something, biding time. I kept my eyes appropriately down—or inappropriately, because all I was doing was looking at that dress. About twenty different pornographic scenarios bombarded my imagination, as I stood stoically on that elevator. Positions and role plays and sweaty bodies slapping and silk sheets and hair tugging and legs in the air—

The room was a suite itself, with a spacious front room and then a bedroom. She'd done well enough so far, so I thought I would let her take the lead, at least for now. She closed the door behind her and placed her purse carefully on a small table.

She appraised me with those voracious amber eyes. Then she approached, placing her hands delicately on my jacket. "These silly costumes," she said. She reached up and untied my bow tie.

"And I was so proud of how I tied that," I said.

She pulled the tie off my neck and slipped it around hers. "Then tie it again," she said.

So I did, best I could, anyway. I was having some trouble concentrating. She reached behind her and unzipped her dress. Before I'd put the finishing touches on the bow tie around her long, thin neck, her dress was at her ankles. A moment later her strapless bra and panties hit the carpet as well.

"We'll need some privacy," she said. I was only then aware of the window in the room, looking out over nothing but another hotel a couple blocks away. I watched her walk to the window, wearing nothing but high heels and the bow tie. She slowly pulled the curtains closed. Maybe a lucky someone got a nice peek. I was pretty sure that thought had crossed her mind.

Then she slowly walked back toward me, taunting me with each careful step of those high heels. She took my hand and led me into the bedroom. It was a queen-size bed, I thought, but it could have been a dirty tarp for all I cared. She put a knee on the bed, then another, and crawled to the center of the bed.

Still in the position, on her hands and knees, she looked back over her shoulder at me.

Maybe these fundraisers weren't so bad, after all.

44 Dear Penthouse Forum, I never thought this would happen to me. . . .

A knock at the door. I put on a robe from the bathroom and answered. We'd ordered champagne and some finger food. I brought it into the bedroom.

The bedroom had been through a rough two hours. One of the lamps was knocked over. The clock radio on the bedside table had somehow taken a spill as well, standing in a vertical position on the carpet. The bedspread was on the floor, as were the sheets. Only two pillows remained on the bed and they were propping up Madison Koehler, who was checking her BlackBerry, wearing only three things: her glasses, my tuxedo shirt and satin panties.

"Did you, like, read a book about male fantasies or something?" I asked.

"I wrote it." She seemed pleased with herself. She finished reading whatever email or text message was on her phone and looked up at me.

I poured the champagne into glasses, sat on the bed, and handed her one. "I hope this won't affect our friendship," I said.

She looked over her glasses at me and took the champagne. "Let's promise it won't."

By my estimate, I had known Madison Koehler for a hundred and forty minutes, and I'd spent a hundred and twenty of those ravishing her body. Or maybe more accurately, she had spent it ravishing mine. She knew what she wanted and hadn't been afraid to provide direction. And I was generally willing to accommodate, although I drew the line at the Russian accent.

"Am I your first?" she asked.

That question surprised me. I thought maybe I should be insulted.

"Since your wife, I mean."

That surprised me even more. She'd done her homework. But on me? I wouldn't have thought she'd even known who I was.

"Yes," I said.

She put down her BlackBerry, got off the bed, and took some strawberries from the room service tray. I enjoyed the view. I was enjoying myself, generally. Maybe a little conflicted, but this day had to come. I wasn't going to spend the rest of my life celibate. And this was probably the way it was destined to happen, an impulsive urge without the opportunity for deliberation and second thoughts. Regardless, the dam had broken. In a small but meaningful way, I had moved on.

"How do you like working for Charlie?" she asked, sitting in a chair, tucking one leg under herself.

"I don't."

"You don't like working for him?"

"I don't work for him. I work for myself."

"Oh, *I* see," she said playfully. She pushed a strawberry into her mouth, what I would have found to be a somewhat provocative gesture had I not been completely spent at this point. "You'd do well to be clear with him on that point."

I didn't comment on that. Charlie had made it clear to me that he didn't have a sense of humor about disloyalty. *You fuck me, I'll fuck you harder,* he'd said. He'd even made a point of mentioning that guy Dick Baroni, someone who apparently had crossed him in some way and who wound up with broken bones and a torched office as a result.

Madison walked into the anteroom and returned fully dressed. She tossed my tuxedo shirt on the bed. "Carlton Snow is going to win this November," she informed me. "He has the money and the incumbency label."

"He's not an incumbent. He fell backwards into the job."

"Doesn't matter. Everyone calls him Governor. Same difference." She primped in front of the bedroom mirror, fixing her hair and her makeup. "We have enough money that we can win the primary without emptying our bank account. Edgar Trotter doesn't have that luxury in his primary. He has to spend a lot. We'll have a two-to-one advantage in money, and we'll win."

"Okay, so why are you convincing me of this?"

She finished with the mirror and grabbed another strawberry. "Charlie says you're as sharp as they come. Hector thinks you walk on water."

"And you listen to them?"

She thought about that. "The governor does. Absolutely."

That seemed to be true. Hector had gotten me an interview for the job with the PCB in the time it would take me to blow my nose. I figured what Hector did for the governor was all about race. The governor needed the Latinos, and Hector was a celebrity for the time being.

"Do you?" I asked.

She angled her head. "What you did for Hector was plain for all to see. And Charlie, whatever else you might say about him, is cautious. He is very slow to trust. The fact that he trusts you tells me a lot."

"Okay, so the governor's going to win and I get a gold star."

She still hadn't reached her point. But I sensed she was about to, and I thought I knew what it was.

"I want you to work for me," she said.

I didn't know what that meant. My job was with the Procurement and Construction Board and, in a very real sense, with Charlie Cimino. It was a role that suited the FBI's purposes. What would I be doing working for the governor's chief of staff?

"Carlton Snow didn't hire me to be his chief of staff," she said. "He hired me to get elected to a full term. Everything I do is about that. I'm his chief of staff, but I'm also running the campaign. Do you—do you know anything about campaigns?"

"No," I conceded.

She sighed. "I'm chief of staff to make sure that Carl doesn't step on himself. I don't do anything unless it involves the campaign in some way. I don't worry about personnel issues or anything technical. I just make sure his policies are right. Otherwise, I'm on the campaign."

"Okay, and I just told you I don't know anything about campaigns."

She shook her head. "I don't need you for that. I need you to make sure that everything we do receives a lawyer's blessing."

Receives a lawyer's blessing. Lovely, how she put that. Not *legal*.

"You must have people who do that," I said.

She made a face. "We have campaign lawyers, obviously. People who can navigate the campaign finance laws. But on the state side? Government work? No, it hasn't been a priority. Half the people in the office are from Governor Trotter's staff. Republicans. Remember, Carl got thrown into this job on a week's notice."

I hadn't thought about that. You have an entire staff for the governor, and then mid-term, the governor resigns and the lieutenant governor jumps in. He hadn't been in office even a full year yet. He was probably stuck with a lot of Langdon Trotter's people.

"Besides," she said, "I need someone more . . . talented."

More creative, she meant. More ethically flexible. Better able to take something illegal and give it the appearance of legality. Apparently, I'd come highly recommended in that regard. Quite the name I was making for myself.

"You and Charlie—you can still work with him, but I would take priority."

I threw her words back at her. "You'd do well to be clear with him on that point."

"Don't worry about what I tell Charlie Cimino," she snapped. "You worry about what I tell you."

Sometimes I smile when I'm not pleased. This was one of those times. "I don't recall accepting the offer to work for you. So you might want to take caution in your tone."

She raised her chin and stared long and hard at me. "Charlie mentioned the attitude."

"Did he? Good."

"How long do I have to wait before you say yes?"

Now I was smiling because I admired her brass. "And why am I going to say yes, Madison?"

"You're going to say yes," she said, gathering her purse, "because Governor Carlton Snow will make you rich and powerful."

She had no idea what she was doing. She didn't know what I represented. She didn't realize that she was inviting the federal government into the inner circle of the governor's office.

She slipped a card out of her purse and left it on the bed. "Oh, and one more thing," she said on her way out. "What happened here tonight? That doesn't leave this room. Nobody can know about this."

She didn't want anyone to know about the sex? Fair enough. Wasn't my style to kiss and tell, anyway. And since I wasn't wearing a wire to this event tonight, not only would the feds not know what we did between the sheets, but they also wouldn't know that she just asked me to work for her, either.

Not unless I decided to accept her offer. That one would require some thought.

45

I GOT BACK HOME AFTER MIDNIGHT. I COULDN'T SLEEP. My limbs were tingling from the reintroduction to sexual intercourse. I wasn't interested in television. I wasn't sure what to do with myself.

I didn't know what to think about Madison Koehler's offer, either. I'd gone after the PCB to learn about Ernesto Ramirez's murder, and I worked with Charlie initially for the same reason. I was trying to catch a killer. And then Charlie and Connolly and the rest of them screwed me over with the doctored memos and handed

Chris Moody a golden opportunity to pinch me, so my conscience didn't bother me one bit in helping the government make a case against them.

But neither reason—solving a murder or payback—had anything to do with Madison Koehler, at least as far as I could tell. I didn't know her. I had no agenda with her. If I accepted her offer, and the job was anything like what she'd subtly suggested, she was going to get into trouble as well.

I decided I would hold on to the idea for the time being.

Nothing better to do, I took a look at the documents I had taken from the state office regarding Starlight Catering. I figured I might as well make myself productive.

I knew two things about the company: They'd won a major contract with the state after Adalbert Wozniak's company was disqualified, and Charlie Cimino had left them off the list of companies we were targeting. There was no chance it was a coincidence.

After I went through the documents, I knew a third thing about Starlight.

I knew the name of the owner.

Starlight Catering was a corporation whose sole principal officer was a man named Delroy Bailey. He had checked the box for "African American" in the form the state made you fill out to determine whether you qualified as a minority business enterprise. Sure enough, Agent Tucker had been right. Starlight Catering was an MBE.

But I didn't recognize the name Delroy Bailey. I looked up the name on my laptop's Internet and got a lot of hits, as the company had a website and had also catered some big events. There was a photo of him at one of the parties. He was a handsome, young, skinny black guy, which didn't help me one way or the other, but hooray for him.

Here was another hit: Delroy Bailey and his wife, Yolanda, at a fundraiser for some alderman named Diaz. Yolanda looked a little older than Delroy, and she was Latina, not African American. Again, that didn't really help me.

I froze. Wait. *Yolanda.*

I went to my bag and retrieved the computer that Paul Riley had lent me, with the database from the Almundo trial. The more I thought about it, the surer I was, but it took a few minutes to find the right spot on the computer, the background workup on the prosecution's star witness, Joey Espinoza.

"Will wonders never cease," I mumbled, something my mother used to say.

Joey Espinoza had a sister named Yolanda Espinoza Bailey.

Starlight Catering was run by Joey Espinoza's brother-in-law.

*   *   *

"So how'd it go last night?" Lee Tucker had a pinch of tobacco in his mouth and his feet up on the table. I'd barely walked through the door to Suite 410 in my office building before he was asking.

"It went." I took a chair across from him.

"Anything good?"

I made a face. "A roomful of greedy jerk-offs."

"You make any good contacts?"

"It was a pretty boring affair."

Tucker watched me for a moment. "That it? Nothing else?"

"The martinis were good."

He let that comment hang for a long time. Slowly, he nodded. "Okay, then."

"Okay, then."

His feet came off the table. "Today you have number sixteen."

"Right. Hoffman." Using our code, Charlie had identified the contractor denominated "16" on his master list, Hoffman Design and Supplies, as the next target on the list.

"Okay, and I've got the text," he said, checking a box. The feds were downloading all of the text messages Charlie sent me. The texts were their lifeblood. It was how your basic, stateside fraudulent scheme became a federal offense.

He looked up at me. "So, if that's it, then I guess you're good to go." He handed me the F-Bird recording device.

"Great. It's been dreamy." I pushed myself out of the chair. Sometimes these meetings took a while, but we were becoming much more efficient.

"Nothing at all from last night?" he asked me. "You meet the governor?"

"No."

"Learn any useful information?"

"No."

Tucker nodded for a long time. He looked disappointed. "Well, that's too bad," he said.

46

CHARLIE WAS IN A RARE GOOD MOOD TODAY. I DIDN'T know what market-driven event had lightened his capitalistic heart—maybe landing an anchor tenant on one of his commercial properties—but I thought it would be good to take advantage.

"Missed you last night," he said. The Porsche was humming down the interstate to the south side.

"I was there."

"Yeah? Well, that place was a mob house. So who are we doing today? Hoffman, right? Eric Hoffman?"

"Right," I said.

"We're blowing through that list."

It was true. Knowing Charlie, he had the whole thing charted out. Someday, he might want to compare his chart with the one on a conference room in the U.S. attorney's office.

"Hey, I was noticing," I said. "I saw on the list that one of the companies didn't have a number next to it."

"Yeah?"

"Yeah. Starlight Catering. Any particular reason we're leaving them alone? Or was it an oversight?"

He didn't answer right away. He was thinking about his response.

"Don't worry about that," he said.

"What does that mean?"

Charlie grew quiet. I had snapped him out of his uncharacteristically good mood back to the angry, aggressive one. That told me something right there.

Charlie made an aggressive move with the Porsche, switching into the right lane and then swerving onto the off-ramp.

"What are you doing?" I asked.

He didn't answer. We took a right after the ramp. He found the nearest gas station and parked at the far end, where we were alone.

"Get out," he said.

I paused, but too long a hesitation could be lethal. I got out and met him at the rear of the Porsche.

"Open your coat," he said.

My heart did some gymnastics. I had hit a nerve with Charlie.

And now he was going to search me.

I unbuttoned my winter coat. My suit coat, the left inner pocket of which was holding the F-Bird, was already unbuttoned. I raised my arms. Charlie put his palms on my shirt at the chest and then ran his hands down to my belt.

"Spread your legs."

"Jesus, Charlie."

"Spread your legs," he repeated.

I did. He did a quick pat on my thighs.

"You want me to empty my pockets, too?" I asked with indignation. I wasn't eager to do it, of course, but I knew that was his intention so it only made sense to appear willing. Better than unwilling. Indignant, insulted, offended was fine. But not unwilling.

I didn't try to stall or talk him out of it. I pulled my car keys out of my right overcoat pocket and then turned the pocket out. There was nothing in the left coat pocket and I turned it out, too.

Charlie didn't seem inclined to stop me. He threw my keys to the ground and put his hand out.

I didn't want to think about what might happen next. I couldn't seem the least bit apprehensive. I tried not to think about the fact that after my pants pockets, there was nothing left but my suit jacket and the F-Bird.

From my right pants pocket, I removed my cell phone and money clip before turning that pocket out. Charlie threw the money to the ground but held on to my cell phone.

One more pocket until we got to the suit coat and the F-Bird.

From my left pants pocket, I removed my wallet and a crumbled photograph I carry around of Talia and Emily. Charlie dropped the wallet but took a look at the photograph.

His expression relaxed. He struggled a moment.

"This is your wife and daughter," he said.

I nodded. "Please don't damage it," I said. "It's irreplaceable. It—means something to me."

Charlie let out a sigh and dropped his arms. As I hoped, the photo, combined with my clear willingness to comply with his search, had taken the wind out of his sails. "Okay, kid, sorry—sorry." He handed me the photo, then the cell phone. He bent down and retrieved my wallet and money and car keys. "Just—you with your questions. It makes me nervous."

"Charlie, I'm going to try real hard not to be offended."

He reached for my shoulder. He felt bad now. "Just being careful. The questions and all.

"Sorry," he said again, as he got back in the car.

47 LAST NIGHT, I'D ONLY KNOWN TWO THINGS—STARLIGHT had leapfrogged Bert Wozniak's company for a big project, and Starlight was being given a pass by Charlie in our shakedown scheme. Now I knew more. Joey Espinoza's brother-in-law was the owner of Starlight. And that brought back this little tidbit from the first time I visited Charlie's office back in December, when I passed by her office: Joey Espinoza's wife was on Charlie's payroll.

And now I knew how sensitive a thing it was for Charlie. Raising the topic with him almost cost me everything.

Here was how I figured it. Joey wanted his brother-in-law's company to get the sweetheart state contract. He talked to Charlie. They probably cut a deal. The PCB does what it does, manufacturing a reason why the lowest bidder—Adalbert Wozniak's company—isn't qualified. *Voilà*, Starlight gets the contract. Wozniak feels cheated. He starts making some noise. He even goes to the state's inspector general to complain. It comes back to Charlie. He and Joey decide that Wozniak has to be silenced. Especially because, at this point, Joey is already securely in the grasp of the federal government. They've already sunk their hooks into him. The absolute last thing Joey needs is more trouble. So Charlie handles the details. Wozniak is gunned down. It looks like one of those gang things that happen far too often. A tragic, senseless loss. An unsolved murder. Terrible, but not unusual, not in the part of town where Wozniak had his offices.

Only there's a problem: The murder is pinned on a teenage member of the Columbus Street Cannibals, the same gang that Joey Espinoza has been tied in to. The heat actually turns *up* on Joey. So Charlie does what he can to keep Joey from singing about the Wozniak shooting, and the Starlight Catering deal, to the feds. *I'll hire your wife while you're inside,* he tells him. Maybe he offers to cover Joey's mortgage, too. Maybe a job afterward. Joey won't lose his house or his wife while he's serving time. Probably other promises are made, too. Whatever it takes, to keep Joey quiet from his new federal friends.

Damage control.

Adalbert Wozniak wasn't murdered because he refused to pay the Cannibals' extortion demands. He was gunned down because he was about to expose a pay-to-play scheme involving Joey Espinoza, Charlie Cimino, and the Procurement and Construction Board.

I felt sure of it. But there were still things I was missing. I was missing the connection to Ernesto Ramirez.

And I was missing proof of any of this.

48   I MET ESMERALDA RAMIREZ FOR LUNCH AT A DINER near her home. I got there first. The place wasn't crowded. The economy was slipping further. People were worried.

The weather matched the mood of the country. Typical Midwest February, cold and wet and gloomy. No snow had fallen in several weeks, but sheets of ice lined the streets and sidewalks. I almost took a header walking into the place. Everything was harder to do this time of year.

I didn't recognize her when she walked in. She was wearing one of those puffy jackets, light blue, and a matching hat with a beanie on top. She looked like a little girl in many ways.

But she wasn't a little girl. She was a widow. A mother of two. And unemployed, last I checked.

"How are you?" I asked. I hate small-talk intros like that, but I really wanted to know.

From what I could tell of Essie Ramirez, she didn't like to play the pity card. She gave a bitter smile, like she was actually going to give me a substantive answer, but she quickly retreated. "I've had better days," she said. "And you? Have you succeeded in your quest?"

"Getting there."

We ordered coffee and took menus.

"I have questions," I told her.

She wrapped her hands around the coffee. Her youthful face was drawn, sleep-deprived, and lined along the eyes and forehead. She was tired and stressed. I wasn't having the time of my life these days, either, but I had some money and I didn't have two children to feed and care for.

She looked up at me.

"You said I'd made some progress with your husband," I said. "That I'd convinced him to tell me what he knew."

"Yes. That's what I thought."

"And then he came home one night and he said, 'The truth doesn't matter. It's not worth prison.' Words to that effect?"

"Yes."

"Why 'prison?' Why would he be worried about going to prison?"

She took a drink of coffee and savored it. It was actually a pretty good cup for a diner. Hot, dark, and smooth.

I liked Essie. She had very little going for her right now, but she carried herself with quiet dignity. She didn't complain or even raise her voice when she spoke. And I had to admit, she was attractive. Large, watery brown eyes, long lashes, a small curved face. Ernesto had done well for himself.

She stared at me for a moment. "Are you asking me if my husband was involved in something illegal?"

"Yes."

"Then ask me that."

That was another thing I liked about her. She was direct. From my limited conversations with her, she had absolutely zero capacity for bullshit.

"Was your husband involved in something illegal?"

"The answer is no."

"Do you think you would know? I mean, you said he was protective. Old-fashioned. He wouldn't talk to you about certain things."

"And I took all of that into account in giving you my answer. I knew him better than anyone. I would have known."

I believed her. I believed that she would know if her husband was up to no good, even if he tried to shield her from it. And that was saying something, because in my experience, the human capacity for deception knows no bounds.

"Did your husband ever talk about Joseph Espinoza? Or Joey Espinoza?"

"No."

"Hector Almundo?"

"No."

"Charlie Cimino?"

Third time was a charm. She held on that name. "That one," she said. "He owned housing, I believe. A slumlord."

That could be. Charlie was a developer. I thought he handled more commercial than anything, but sure, it was more than possible that Charlie did residential housing, too.

"My husband was part of a protest. He didn't lead it, but he was part of it. The conditions at the housing unit."

Interesting. A new connection, possibly. "Anything come of that? The protest?"

She shook her head. "I don't remember. It was a few years ago. I just don't remember. All I remember is that Ernesto did not like that man. He thought he took advantage of poor people."

I made a mental note. Okay, move on.

"Ernesto still had friends in the gangs," I said.

She nodded. "A fragile truce."

"Come again?"

"It's how he referred to his relationship with the gangs. The Lords and the Cannibals. He was trying to steal away their members. He was trying to give those children an alternative. He was a threat to the gangs, in a real way. But he managed to coexist with them. He knew them. He socialized with them. He liked them. He taught some of them."

I thought back to the day I confronted Ernesto in Liberty Park. The day he was killed. The two gangbangers standing with him. The tattoo of a tiny dagger on their upper arm, the sign of a Latin Lord.

"There was a guy I saw in Liberty Park with your husband," I said. "A little under six feet, broad-chested. He had a goatee. And a long scar across his forehead."

Nothing seemed to register, not surprisingly, until I got to the part about the scar on the forehead. Her eyes trailed off. She gave a presumptive nod. She knew whom I meant.

"I'd like to talk to him," I said.

After lunch, I went to the office. I drafted a couple of motions and prepared for a court appearance tomorrow. Most of the work I was handling was civil in nature, not criminal, as it had come courtesy of Charlie Cimino. Civil cases are different than criminal. The primary way they are different is that they are utterly boring. Pushing all kinds of paper. Preparing four to five years for trial. Not my style. But at least it was all litigation, and it was paying the bills for now.

For now. Until the U.S. attorney shut down its operation and swooped in with all kinds of indictments. Including one for me, as Christopher Moody had promised. It would be, for all practical purposes, the end of my legal career.

I brought some work home and reviewed some legal research. I also thought about Madison Koehler. More to the point, I thought about sex. The sleeping giant—figuratively speaking—had been awakened, and now I wanted more. I wasn't sure if it was the pure carnal gratification I craved or just the reminder that I was still alive.

I fell asleep on the love seat. I woke with a start somewhere in the middle of the night from a steamy dream. Silk sheets, sweaty bodies, soft moans, and naughty laughter. The woman in the dream, as it happened, was Ernesto Ramirez's wife.

49 Essie Ramirez called me the next morning with one piece of information: a place to meet the guy I had described, the forehead-scar-goateed Latin Lord. No name. Just a place.

The place was a restaurant called Su Casa, on the southwest side. I was relatively sure from the address that it fell comfortably within the territory claimed by the Latin Lords.

I got there at five-thirty, as directed. It was already dark outside, appropriate for what I assumed would be a clandestine meeting. I parked less than a block away and walked in right on time. Su Casa was a small establishment that smelled of grilled steak and sizzling onions. A soccer game played from a small television up in the corner. I scanned across the mustard-colored walls, but no one seemed to be paying me much attention. Finally a young woman, a teenager who looked like she worked there, approached me. "Mr. Kol-AR-ich?" she asked tentatively.

Not exactly. Emphasis on the first syllable. Kola, like the drink. Rich, like wealthy. "Kolarich," I corrected, but she wasn't concerned with pronunciation. She led me behind the counter, past a few pounds of *carne asada,* peppers, and onions cooking on a grill, into a back room filled with dry supplies, open boxes of napkins and straws and the like on cheap shelving, with a refrigerator off to the side. The woman kept walking, up to an exit door. She pointed to the door, which I took to mean I was supposed to go outside.

I pushed open the door and looked out before stepping out. It was an alley, with two large Dumpsters overflowing with garbage and, to my right, the outline of a single man, who fit the general build of the man I was supposed to meet. Behind him, about thirty yards or so, was the street.

Decision time. I realized that when I closed this door, it might not reopen. There was only one way out of this alley, and that was through this gangbanger. I didn't know what he had on him in terms of weapons, or whether he had some friends ready to join him. All I knew was there was no turning back, once I stepped into the alley.

On a list of good ideas, this one was pretty low. It was possible that this guy was Ernesto's friend, and he'd want to help me find his killer. But it was equally possible—maybe more so—that he was the reason Ernesto died. He was there when I did my thing with the subpoena, after all. He very well could have been the person who went back and got the word out: *Ernesto's going to talk.*

In fact, the more I thought about it, the more probable that prospect seemed.

I took the step down into the alley. The door slammed behind me.

He walked toward me. The lighting was for shit in the alley, but he got close enough so I could just barely make him out. It was him, all right, whatever his name was. The scowl, the idiotic goatee, the scar across his forehead. Scarface, I decided. Scarface was wearing a thick bomber jacket, pants that looked like he was warming up for a basketball game, and leather high-tops. Me, I was in a suit with a long coat. He had the advantage, if this turned nasty.

"You got balls," Scarface said.

"I have questions," I answered.

He stepped closer to me. Maybe ten feet. "Only reason I'm here is cuz Essie asked."

"Who killed Adalbert Wozniak?"

"Who?"

I paused. "You know who he is. What do you know about his murder?"

He didn't answer.

"I mean, that's why Ernesto was killed, right? Because of what he knew?"

"Don't say Nesto's name. You don't got the right."

I sighed. I put out my hands. "Okay. Fine. But he knew something. And he was going to tell me. I want to find out who killed him. And to do that, I need to find out who killed Bert Wozniak."

"Why do you care?"

"Because I think it's my fault."

"Damn right it's your fault," he spit.

"So help me figure out who did this."

Sixty seconds passed in what felt like sixty minutes. His hands were stuffed in his pockets, and I had a pretty good idea that those hands weren't empty.

The temperatures had fallen. I could see my breath. But my body wasn't cold in the slightest. Because I still wasn't sure whether this guy Scarface was on the right side or the wrong side. He hadn't told me anything yet. Could be, he was just letting me talk, to hear what I knew before he decided to *adios* me.

"They pinned Wozniak's murder on a kid," I went on. "A Cannibal. Eddie Vargas. They found his prints in the car and they found the gun at his apartment. But it wasn't him, was it?"

He didn't answer. I couldn't make out his facial expression, not in the dark.

"It wasn't the Cannibals at all," I said. "The kid was set up. It was you guys. It was the Lords. I mean, that's why we're in a dark alley, right? And why I don't know your name. Because you don't want to be seen with me. Because you want to give me a name, and you don't want it coming back to you."

Scarface didn't say anything. He shuffled his feet. Kept his hands in his pockets.

"So give me the name," I said.

Instead of producing a name, he produced a gun, from his right pocket, and pointed it at me. Had it done any good to try to evade him, I would have done so. But I was boxed in on each side and behind me. This guy was standing between me and my thirty-fifth birthday.

The best play, it seemed to me, was to stay perfectly still. It took some doing. It wasn't the first time I'd had a gun pointed at me, but it was close.

Scarface walked toward me, keeping the gun trained on me. He was comfortable holding it. Not his first time, either.

I slowly raised my hands, showing my palms, an unconscious reaction, trying to calm a situation. To an outsider, it would look like a stickup.

"Okay, listen. Hey," I said, as the gun's barrel pressed against my forehead. I leaned back slightly, another natural reaction, but it had the effect of putting me slightly off-balance. I didn't have much going for me at the moment, but the balance problem removed virtually any countermove I could possibly make, other than falling backward.

I could only assume that if he wanted me dead, I'd be toast already.

"There's only one reason you've been breathing for the last year," he said. "And that's Nesto. He wouldn't have wanted it. He'd say, 'Don't lose your way.' "

It was the same phrase Essie Ramirez had said to me.

"You fuckin' killed him, man. *You.*" He imprinted the barrel into my forehead. Now it was a struggle not to fall over. I wasn't in the mood for any sudden movements so this was becoming tricky. "Nesto, he was like my—he was—"

He choked up with emotion. The gun came off my forehead. He moved away from me, the gun at his side now. He put his hands on his knees, bending over like he was going to vomit, and started to cry.

He was like my father, he was going to say.

I didn't move. He was losing control of his emotions and holding a firearm. A smarter person might have started running. Or knocked him over. Or disarmed him. But I didn't move.

"I held his head. I held him. I said, 'Don't go, Nesto. You can't go, man.' "

He went on like that for a few minutes. I didn't realize he'd been there when Ernesto was gunned down. I'd never held a dying person in my arms. I couldn't imagine it.

I took a deep breath. The adrenaline, always lagging behind, rushed through my body. I wanted to tell him how sorry I was, but I couldn't speak. Neither could he, for a spell. I stood completely still. I could have gone for the gun but the drama had passed.

Finally, he raised himself. He caught his breath. Wiped at his face with his sleeve. Still holding the gun.

"The Polish guy," he said with no inflection, staring into the wall. "Kiko did that." He turned his head slightly in my direction. "You know Kiko?"

I did. Every prosecutor who ever worked in gang crimes knew Kiko.

I caught my breath and kept quiet, hoping he would tell me more. I was pretty sure that he knew more, and that he'd passed it on to Ernesto.

"Who told Kiko to kill Bert Wozniak?" I asked.

He shook his head. "Never said."

"Do you know why?" I tried.

His head stopped shaking. "Kiko and me—our families. Back when we was kids."

"You were close."

"Yeah. Not anymore. Not since this. But before." He took a deep breath. The emotion had drained away. "He was *borracho*. Drunk. He talks then. Kiko talks when he's drunk."

Okay. So far, so good. A drunken conversation with Kiko.

"He said, this better be it. This better be the only one, the Polish guy. I said, why? Why you gotta kill some Polish guy? Kiko said, the Polish guy's making noise. He said, they gonna start lookin' at Delroy. They start lookin' at Delroy, they gonna find out about the connection. Kiko said, I gotta cover up his connection to Delroy. He said, I'll do this one for him. This one time, cuz of his connection to Delroy and shit."

He was talking about Delroy Bailey. *A connection to Delroy.* He was talking, I assumed, about Joey Espinoza, Delroy's brother-in-law. But I wanted him to say it, not me.

"Someone had a connection to Delroy," I said. "And that someone was afraid that people would find out about the connection. So that someone asked Kiko to kill the Polish guy."

"Ain't that what I just said?" That was his way, I guess, of agreeing with my summary.

"Did Kiko say who that someone was? Did he say who had the connection to Delroy?"

He exhaled loudly. "No, man. Not even *borracho,* Kiko wouldn't say that."

He didn't move. I didn't either. We stood in the freezing temperatures, silent, for a long time. I needed this guy to say it, not me.

"But you know who it was," I said. "Even if Kiko didn't say it. You know who had the connection to Delroy."

Scarface slowly turned his eyes toward me. "You know Delroy?"

"I know who he is," I admitted. I'd been playing dumb, but I wasn't going to lie.

"So you know who he used to be married to," he said.

Used to be. So Delroy Bailey was now divorced from Yolanda Espinoza?

"He used to be married to Joey's sister," I said.

"Fuckin' Joey." Scarface spit on the ground.

"Joey Espinoza got Delroy a big contract with the state," I said. "Wozniak thought he got cheated out of it, and he was making noise. He was saying Joey used his influence to get his ex-brother-in-law Delroy the contract. And Joey wanted to keep his connection to Delroy a secret. So he had Wozniak killed. Is that pretty much how you see it?"

He looked down. "Gotta be."

"You and Ernesto both thought that."

He nodded.

Right. That's what Ernesto was going to tell me. Adalbert Wozniak wasn't killed because he refused to pay the Cannibals' extortion. It was about Joey Espinoza trying to cover up his connection to Starlight Catering and its owner, Delroy Bailey.

I tried again, because I needed him to say it. "Did Kiko actually *say* that Joey ordered the hit on Wozniak?"

"Man, I told you, no."

It was obvious enough. But I wanted the words to come from him, not me. Right now, I had supposition stacked on hearsay. Kiko said something, and we assumed he was referring to Joey Espinoza. Speculation and hearsay.

Not admissible proof in court.

I wasn't going to get that proof from this guy. We both knew it was Joey Espinoza who had the connection to Delroy. And we both knew he was a part of the decision to kill Wozniak, but this guy couldn't swear to that. He had led me all the way to the door, but he couldn't ring the bell.

And there had to be someone else. Joey Espinoza, at the time of Wozniak's murder, was already working undercover for the feds. There was no way that Joey would be plotting a murder with a notorious gangbanger while he was answering to the feds.

Joey had a partner. Someone else must have delivered the order to Kiko.

But who? Charlie Cimino? Maybe Greg Connolly? Someone involved with the PCB. Someone working in cahoots with Joey Espinoza. But I didn't know who, and this guy couldn't move that ball forward even one inch for me.

So I would have to go to the source. I would have to get the information from Federico Hurtado, the Latin Lords' top enforcer, their most feared, cold-blooded assassin.

Also known as Kiko.

SCARFACE WAS WORN DOWN, I THOUGHT, SPENT FROM the emotion and from unloading everything. I'd seen that as a prosecutor, the effect of purging information, especially revelations that triggered guilt. The release of the burden was palpable across their faces. I once had a suspect fall asleep in the interrogation room after confessing to stabbing his pregnant girlfriend.

"One more thing," I said. I had regained my balance. The adrenaline surge had passed. I was relatively sure now that this guy was not going to put a bullet in my head. "Essie Ramirez said that Ernesto was going to do something about this. She said I'd convinced him to talk. Do you know if he did? If he talked to anyone about this?"

I thought I saw him smile. But it wasn't one of those whimsical grins. It was a smile of pain. Bitterness. He was reliving the memory. And, I thought, he was deciding to share it with me, something he hadn't planned to give up. I saw that all the time in interrogations, too. The breakthrough. You get past that initial wall of denial and deception, and inside is a messy, gooey mix of truth and emotion. They end up telling you more than you even knew to ask.

"Man, *Nesto* didn't say nothin'."

I wasn't clear on his emphasis. It took me a minute. Finally, I got there.

"But you did," I said.

He nodded his head. "Nesto said it was the right thing to do."

"He convinced you to do something about this. So—what did you do?"

"We went to the cops, Nesto and me. That's what we did." He flapped his arms. The gun remained in his right hand. "I fuckin' told 'em. I told 'em, Kiko did the Polish guy, and Joey fuckin' Espinoza was the guy who called it."

"The cops—"

He burst out laughing, waving his arms and the gun, pacing around in a circle. "Oh, man, they fuckin' loved me. They was all in my face. They said, how do you know? What proof you got? How you know it was Joey? Just like you did, man. Kept askin', did Kiko *say* it was Joey? Did he *say* Joey? Just like you."

Cops not believing a gang member when he offered information? Not hard to believe.

"They said I was a liar, *ese*. They told me, liars go to prison. We gonna lock you up. One-thousand-one, they kept sayin'. The fuckin' brownies, they pull out my sheet, they tell me, who'd believe you, convict? They tell me, ten years, man. Ten years for lying to us, the priors *you* got." He looked at me. "You like that? They gonna lock me up for that. For doing somethin' good. Nesto, he grabbed me, he said, forget it. Forget it. Not worth it."

Not worth prison, Ernesto had told his wife. Ernesto hadn't been talking about himself. He'd been talking about his friend here, Scarface.

Scarface kicked an empty cardboard box into the air, almost falling down in the process. He was drunk with rage and despair, which wouldn't have bothered me so much if he wasn't holding a gun.

"Go home, lawyer-man," he said.

"Wait."

But he wasn't listening. He'd worked himself into a lather now, the pain and anger meshing together, making him about the last person who should be walking the city streets with a loaded weapon. But I wasn't going to be able to stop him. So I let him go.

I felt the cold wind, really felt it, for the first time that evening. But I stood alone in that alley for a long time. I'd learned three things tonight. The first was that Federico Hurtado—Kiko—had been the one who killed Adalbert Wozniak. Second, Kiko had all but named Joey Espinoza as the person behind the murder—to *cover up a connection to Delroy,* his former brother-in-law who was handed a beverage contract over Wozniak's company. And third, Ernesto

Ramirez and his friend here, Scarface, had tried to do the right thing and report the information they had to the authorities, and for their troubles had been threatened with perjury and sent packing.

I was getting closer. But there was someone else. Joey Espinoza couldn't have had a direct conversation with Kiko. He'd have to have balls the size of Jupiter to meet with someone like Kiko while he was also meeting on a daily basis with Christopher Moody and his federal agents, helping them nail Hector. Was it Charlie Cimino? Greg Connolly, the chair of the state board who gave Joey Espinoza's brother-in-law the contract over Wozniak's company?

I didn't know. There was someone else, and I had suspects but no facts.

I reached into my pocket and turned off the tape recorder. I hit rewind and played it to make sure I'd captured everything okay. Then I stuffed it back in my pocket and walked out of the alley.

WHEN I REACHED MY CAR, MY LIMBS WERE FULL OF electricity, my mind racing. I'd never really thought that Scarface was going to shoot me. He could have found twenty different ways to kill me anonymously, as opposed to a prearranged meeting orchestrated by Essie Ramirez. Still, having a gun against my forehead wasn't an everyday occurrence for me, and on top of that, I'd learned some new information that was getting me closer.

Sensory overload. I needed to burn off steam. When my cell phone rang, I thought of ignoring it but finally answered.

"I need to borrow you for an hour," said Madison Koehler.

She gave me an address. It was on the near west side, near the new lofts that had sprung up and the trendy restaurants and bars. Hot part of the city these days. I thought I was looking for a condo or house, but when I got close to the address she gave me, I realized it was zoned commercial. Then I found it. A small one-story with a large glass window in front, bearing the title FRIENDS OF SNOW. It was the governor's campaign office. I don't know why I was surprised.

I parked a block away and made the walk. It was close to nine o'clock. The block was quiet. The air was cold and wet. FRIENDS OF SNOW looked closed. It was dark up front, but there was some light emanating from the back part of the establishment. I rang a buzzer and saw a figure approach.

"I'm here about a job," I quipped, but Madison hadn't called me to follow up on the offer. She locked the door behind me, and we walked in relative darkness. It was hard to see anything very clearly, but the walls were papered with charts and documents. There were several banks of telephones and dozens of computers, some of them still beeping on power-save mode.

Not sure where I was going, I stayed close behind my hostess. Out of an abundance of caution, lest I find myself lost, I kept my hands on the lower parts of her body as she walked. Midway down the hallway, she stopped. My momentum carried me against her, which I thought was the point. We remained there, pressed so hard against each other that you'd think I was trying to poke a hole through her. My hands did not remain still, however, clawing at the buttons on her blouse and slipping inside her skirt. For her part, she showed herself quite skillful at working blind with those hands, to the point that she had managed to unzip my pants and liberate a certain part of my anatomy before I realized it.

I'm not sure where she'd planned to take me—her office, presumably—but we didn't make it there. Her feet didn't touch ground for about thirty minutes. My adrenaline explosion from this evening's events had translated into a testosterone avalanche. We pawed and grabbed and squeezed and pulled and thrust at each other like wild animals.

We stopped for a few minutes, had a cup of water at the dispenser, cracked a joke or two, then calmly walked to her large office in the back for round two. I needed a few minutes to recharge but there were plenty of other ways to spend my time, and I tried to be economical. We still had half our clothes on, for starters, so that needed to change. There was a large conference table filled with documents that I thought would make a nice landing for us, so I cleared it off with all the precision I could muster. I let her be my guide, of course, because she always seemed to lead me to places I'd never visited and enjoyed quite a bit, though I drew the line at the megaphone.

"I'm serious about that job offer," she said to me as I left. Say this much for her: I was out of there in sixty minutes as promised.

*   *   *

FEDERICO "KIKO" HURTADO had been a member of the Latin Lords street gang, by our accounts, since the age of twelve. No known father. Mother deceased. One brother, whereabouts unknown to me at the moment, at least. No wife and no children that we knew of.

Kiko committed his first murder at the age of thirteen. He committed his second, we believe, at the age of sixteen. We liked him for about twenty kills, all told, over the years. He'd maimed and raped a lot of others along the way. He'd largely remained free during this time. Witnesses tended to have serious memory losses when Kiko was a suspect. Some of them had unfortunate accidents.

Kiko was productive. He was ruthless. And he was savvy. He'd made his way up the ladder by being all three of those things. It was believed, in fact, that he assumed the role he currently held, at the right hand of the leader, by murdering the guy who previously held the position. The lore was he decapitated his predecessor with an ordinary kitchen knife.

At the ripe age of twenty-seven, by my estimation—it had been a few years since my stint on the gang crimes task force as a prosecutor—Kiko was now firmly entrenched in the upper echelon of the Latin Lords. He was the muscle, the enforcer, whatever word necessary to convey that when someone got out of line, Kiko got them back in line, or he put them out of commission.

No wonder, if Kiko was involved, that the guy in the alley,

Scarface, was reticent about having his name associated with the matter. And no wonder he didn't come forward after Ernesto's death. It would be the same thing as putting a gun to his head.

But these days, if things held to form, it would be unusual for Kiko to do the wet work personally. It was routine for the gangs to use juveniles for the heavy crimes because they were harder to imprison. The state kept lowering the age for an automatic transfer from juvenile to criminal—trying minors as adults—and the gangs kept lowering the age of their assassins accordingly. If Kiko was ordered to kill someone, he'd more likely dispatch someone else to do it than do it himself.

So this had been exceptional. I suppose Joey Espinoza would merit such an honor. I didn't know that Espinoza knew Kiko, but it didn't surprise me. He was a lot closer to the ground than his boss, Hector. He knew the streets. He admitted knowing members of the Cannibals, including the supreme leader, Yo-Yo. Not a stretch at all that he'd also know a guy like Kiko.

"Lightner," I said into my office phone. It was bright and early the following morning. My lower back was tight and my calf muscles were sore as hell. But somehow I didn't mind.

"Kolarich." Joel Lightner was in his typically effusive mood.

"Favor."

"Shoot."

"Address."

"Who?"

"Federico Hurtado," I said. I spelled it for him. It had been a long time since Lightner had been a cop. He wasn't a stranger to gangs, but he wouldn't be as familiar as I with the current rosters. He wouldn't recognize the name "Kiko."

Technically, I was violating my own promise not to involve Lightner. But this was a discrete assignment, far removed from anything associated with the feds and their sting operation. At least I thought it was far removed. I wasn't sure of a whole lot right now.

"What do you know about him?"

"Latin Lord," I said. "Age twenty-seven."

"Oh, nobility. A higher-up. And why do you want to find this guy?" he asked.

"I want to invite him to a baby shower I'm hosting."

He paused to show his displeasure.

"C'mon, Joel, say yes. I'll buy you some breath mints."

It took him a while to come around. He was worried about me, which I found aggravating. Maybe it was the breath mints that put him over the edge. Or maybe he decided I was a big boy and I could take care of myself, thank you very little.

"So you want to know where Mr. Hurtado lives," he said, relenting.

I figured Kiko had a lot of money, being at the top of the organizational chart. And he wouldn't want wads of cash lying around. My bet was he owned more than one house.

"I want to know where he sleeps," I said.

*   *   *

"Hey." Shauna popped her head into my office, having been in court all morning. She was dressed accordingly, a snappy sand-colored suit and cream blouse. "Aren't you the busy beaver."

We hadn't seen much of each other lately. With my legal plate swelling over the last few months and time spent with Charlie Cimino, I was stretched pretty thin. But it was more than that. I found myself putting distance between us. I felt radioactive these days, and I didn't want any residue rubbing off on her. She couldn't know what I was doing, and if we spent too much time together, she would. She'd sense it. She'd ask. I'd lie. She'd know. I'd used up a pretty good chit with the U.S. attorney's office to free her from their clutches, and I didn't have any more.

"Turns out, this practicing law thing ain't so bad," I said. "Depositions. Interrogatories. Motions to compel discovery. I can't get enough of it."

"Mmm-hmmm." She peered at me through squinted eyes. "You're a chipper one today."

That wasn't quite right. I wasn't in good cheer so much as I was hyped up. I'd had a few volts of electricity injected into my veins over the last week. Mind-altering sex and a gun pointed at your head tend to clear your sinuses.

"So, what do you say, sport—dinner tonight?" I asked.

She made a face, like she had an answer but didn't want to give it. "I'm seeing Roger tonight," she finally admitted.

Ah, yes. Roger. *Roger.* I remembered the initial date and my reaction to it. But Shauna and I had lost touch. Apparently this *Roger* was a keeper?

"You should meet him some time," she suggested.

"I'll count the hours." My intercom buzzed. Marie, at the reception desk.

"Hang on," I said. "This might be Uma Thurman. I stood her up last night."

"You got laid," Shauna guessed.

I punched the button. "Marie, my love. Who's calling? If it's Halle Berry, tell her I'm not ready for a commitment."

"Close," she said. *"It's Hector Almundo. And he's here to see you."*

HECTOR LOOKED LIKE HE ALWAYS LOOKED, WHETHER he was on trial for his life or out on the town, always the colorful shirts and loud ties, the collar pin. He wasn't skimping on wardrobe, but then again, he didn't have a wife or kids to spend money on. He was divorced and his wife had remarried, taking him off the hook for alimony. It reminded me of Joel Lightner's speculation, back during Hector's trial, that our client was gay.

Hector made an attempt at complimenting my office, but it was painful and awkward for both of us. This place didn't exactly compare to Shaker, Riley's space. But I didn't mind it. It was starting to grow on me. It would be nice, in theory at least, to measure my progress in the legal profession by such things as the size and quality of my office space over time.

I say "in theory" because I knew a certain federal prosecutor who had other plans for my future, including a criminal indictment. But I was working on that.

"I only have a couple of minutes," I apologized to Hector. Charlie and I were meeting with a state contractor today. But I didn't tell Hector that, because he might want to walk me to Charlie's waiting car, and it would be slightly awkward when we had to take a detour to Suite 410 so that Special Agent Lee Tucker could hand me the F-Bird before I met Charlie.

"Things are working out with Charlie," he said, taking a seat. It was a statement, I thought, not a question. More than anything, it was Hector reminding me, in case I had forgotten, that he was the one who got me the gig. "Are you enjoying yourself?"

"It has its moments."

"You know I've recommended you for other things, as well. Maddie discussed it with you."

So Hector was following up on the offer that Madison Koehler pitched me in the hotel room. He was recruiting me. I'd deferred the idea for a while and wasn't seriously considering it. I wasn't interested in helping the government ensnare anyone else. It wasn't my style. Charlie was different, because he and his buddies were the reason I got caught up with the FBI in the first place, the memos they doctored, but I wasn't interested in going beyond him. Not to get Madison.

And certainly not to get Hector. I wasn't the president of his fan club, but he'd been my client. That bond was inviolable. Technically, we were no longer attorney and client, but it still felt wrong to me. You don't defend a guy in federal court one day and turn state's evidence on him the next. I could, as a purely formalistic matter, but I wouldn't.

"You should do it," he said. "We need you."

" 'We'?"

"Yes, 'we.' "

Madison had mentioned that Hector had the governor's ear. I'd heard the same from some stray comments Charlie had made. I didn't completely understand it. Hector wasn't the worst of the worst, but he sure wasn't the best of the best, either. The way I described him to Talia, in a moment of private candor, was that Hector Almundo was a political thug. He led with his chin and he didn't take prisoners.

My take was that, as is often the case in politics, it was a pure case of need. The governor needed the Latino vote, and Hector had been something of a cause célèbre in that community, the poster child for persecution at the hands of white federal prosecutors. And better still, Hector stood up to the G and beat them. To many, he was a hero.

"I like where I am now," I said.

"Jason, you're not seeing the big picture."

No, my friend, I was tempted to say. *I see the big picture a hell of a lot better than you.*

"You know how Charlie is, right?" he said. "All about loyalty? Well, the governor's cut from the same cloth. I mean, look at Greg Connolly. That guy can hardly spell his name, but he and Carl grew up together. So Carl gives him a nice title. A job that, as you know," he added, with a knowing nod, "can be advantageous in other ways as well."

I think Hector liked the fact that I had gotten down in the mud with him. However devoted we were to defending him, regardless of what the evidence showed, it had to be embarrassing to Hector on a personal level to have to explain himself to Paul and me. It was probably psychologically comforting for him to see me joining him in the cesspool now.

"The point being?" I asked.

"Well, you know the point. You can be right there with us. You'll be right there when he gets elected. You can get a lot out of that, Jason. A lot. The sky's the limit."

I nodded warmly enough, shrugged a shoulder.

"Oh, you're crazy." Hector fell back in his chair. "You're going to turn this down?"

"I am."

"Listen, you don't have to give up"—he gestured around my office, then remembered how unimpressive it was—"you can still be in private practice. You can do whatever you want."

"Including turning down your offer?"

He shook his head, exasperated. "Is this because of Charlie? We can talk to Charlie."

"Hector, I'm not doing it."

He thought for a moment. He was thinking of another angle. "You should meet Governor Snow."

"No."

"Yes." He started nodding, warming up to his brilliant idea. "Yes, you should meet him. He's a good guy. You'll like him. If you don't, then turn it down. But give him that chance. Can you give him that chance?"

"Not interested," I said.

He struggled with that for a long time. He couldn't believe I was turning down this opportunity.

"Y'know, you're not just passing on a great opportunity," he said.

"No? What else am I doing?"

"You're saying no to the governor." He pushed himself out of his seat. "Make sure that's what you want to do before you do it."

*   *   *

LEE TUCKER WAS ON his phone when I unlocked the door and entered Suite 410. He was at the end of the hallway, and he nodded at me when he saw me. He said something into his cell phone and closed it up. "Hey," he said. "You're late. What were you doing?"

I looked at my watch. "I'm two *minutes* late."

"Okay. So, what were you doing?"

I went into his office and picked up the F-Bird off the desk.

"Hey," he said. "What were you doing?"

"Hey," I said, slipping the F-Bird into my jacket pocket. I was hitting the limit with these feds. "What were *you* doing, Lee? Who were you talking to on the phone? About what? When was the last time you screwed your wife?"

Tucker gave me his best look of disapproval. "Doesn't work both ways, superstar. What were you just doing?"

"I was getting a bikini wax," I said. "What the hell do you care what I was doing?"

He thought for a minute and decided to let it go. "We're thinking maybe it's time for you to expand," he said. "To branch out. We've squeezed this rag with Cimino pretty dry. We think you should try to position yourself to move on. I mean, we know Cimino's working with others. But we don't see that side of it. We need you to get us there."

"I've got a great idea," I said. "Why don't you pay a late-night visit to Charlie and make him an offer he can't refuse? I'm sure he could take you places I couldn't."

"C'mon, Jason. You know you're doing a great job with Cimino. You've built up credibility. You've raised a ton of money for the governor. You're in a perfect position to climb the ladder. I'm surprised they haven't asked."

I didn't answer.

Tucker's eyes narrowed. "Have they? Has someone approached you?"

I looked at my watch. "I'm late."

"You'd have to tell us if they did. You understand that, right?"

"I understand that Charlie doesn't like it when I'm late."

Tucker seemed like he was out of ammunition. He jaw was tightly set. He had his hands on his hips. He shook his head slowly. "Jason, listen to me. The smartest thing you can do right now is say yes."

"Who said I was smart?" I walked over to the door. "I'll finish what I started with Cimino," I said. "But I'm not taking you on an undercover tour through state government."

I WAS IN MY OFFICE BY EIGHT THE NEXT MORNING. I HAD a full day scheduled without anything having to do with the undercover operation. No appointment with Charlie. No meetings with the federal overlords. I had two morning court appearances and a witness interview in the afternoon. In between, I had to get working on a response to a motion to dismiss that was due next week.

After court, I was back in my office beginning the draft of my response. My cell phone buzzed on my desk. The caller ID said it was Joel Lightner.

"That was fast, even for you," I said. It had been only twenty-four hours since I'd given Lightner the assignment.

"You didn't tell me this guy was Kiko."

"Didn't I?"

"No, fuckhead, you didn't. Tell me why you want his address."

"I'm throwing him a surprise birthday party."

"You don't know this guy."

"Then imagine how surprised he'll be."

"Hey, asshole? You don't know this guy."

I groaned. Lightner meant well. He and Riley—both of them—feeling sorry for me, looking out for me.

"Joel, I know about Kiko," I said. "My eyes are wide open."

"They won't be for long," he replied. "Not if you get on his wrong side. So what do you want him for? Surveillance? Or a face-to-face?"

Neither, actually, if I was answering his question literally. "Not sure yet," I said. "But speaking of surveillance?"

"Oh—another high-level gang assassin?"

"Close. A caterer," I said. "I want you to find a guy named Delroy Bailey. Starlight Catering is the company. Home address, please. And marital status. I think he's divorced."

It sounded like Lightner was scribbling a note. "What kind of a name is Delroy?"

"I don't know. And before you ask—because I know you will—it's a fishing expedition," I said. "Call it a hunch."

* * *

MY CELL RANG AGAIN ten minutes later. The caller ID read "David Hamlin," meaning Lee Tucker. I thought about avoiding the call. I was running out of patience with these guys. I was beginning to see an end in sight here. What Tucker had said to me yesterday was right—we'd drawn about all the blood we could out of Charlie Cimino. They had him cold. And I had no interest in implicating other people. I had come into this thing for one reason, to find Ernesto's killer. And I thought I was close to doing that. When that was done, so was I. Tucker would tell me to keep playing ball, to make Chris Moody as happy as possible, holding out hope he might take a pass on indicting me. But I knew Moody would never let me off the hook. He was going to prosecute me. And I would just have to fight the charges.

"Hello."

"Jason. We need to talk to you. Come to our office. Right now."

"I can't do it right now."

A pause. "It needs to be now."

I waited a moment myself. "Suite 410 or your real office?"

"The real one," he said.

I looked at my watch. It was just shy of eleven. "I'll be there at three," I said, and closed the phone.

* * *

I SHOWED UP AT FOUR. I did it the way I typically did. I went to the twenty-second floor of the building, where Judge Graves had her courtroom, carrying a legal-sized envelope. I walked into her chambers, stuffed the envelope in my briefcase, and walked back out. Then I took an interior elevator to the floor of the U.S. attorney's office. If anyone was keeping tabs on me, I could always say the reason I was in the federal building was to file something in regard to the case I had before Judge Graves.

"Hey." Lee Tucker waved me into the conference room, where my good friend Christopher Moody was standing by the window, looking out over the cityscape.

"Okay, I'm here. And I don't have all day."

Moody turned and looked at me. His mouth was set in what I could only describe as a mild scowl. His eyes were fiery with anticipation.

"The day after the governor's fundraiser," he said in an even, icy tone, "Agent Tucker asked you if you made any contacts with any of the governor's people. You told him no. He asked if you had gathered any useful information. You told him no. And yesterday, he asked you if any of the governor's people had approached you about working with them."

He stared at me.

I stared back.

"Somehow, you forgot to mention that on the night of the fundraiser, Madison Koehler offered you a job."

"Says who?"

That surprised him. "You're denying it?"

"I just asked for the source, Chris. A question is not a denial."

A smile slowly crept about the corners of his mouth. "One thousand one," he said.

He was citing the federal criminal statute for making a false statement to a federal agent. He was saying I had lied to Lee Tucker.

"The hole you're in keeps getting deeper," he said. "You need to cooperate now more than ever."

I looked over at Tucker, to see if he wanted to chime in. He didn't. Then I turned back to Moody. "You want me to go to work for Madison Koehler?"

"That's right," he said, enjoying it.

"The answer is no. Anything else?"

Moody's smile got broader. He burst into laughter. "Well, you just ain't afraid of nobody, is that it? You want to show us how big your cock is?"

"I'm not showing you anything," I answered. "I'm just not going to help you troll for potential defendants so you can pad your résumé."

It wasn't like I hadn't seen this coming. Prosecutors always want to move up the chain. Charlie Cimino was their foothold. They wanted bigger fish.

They wanted the governor.

Moody's expression slowly deteriorated, as he realized that I was serious. He thought there was no way I'd turn him down. He'd expected capitulation at the mere mention of another criminal charge on which he could indict me. These guys were accustomed to getting what they wanted, when they wanted it. He hadn't planned this out any further.

"These innocent people you're so worried about?" he said. "They're scum. They're all a part of this. Cimino's just one of the messengers. These guys are filthy to the core, and I'm going to nail them. And you're going to help me. You're going to help me make a case against Governor Snow, Madison Koehler, Greg Connolly— anyone and everyone."

I didn't answer. I'd said enough stupid things.

"Including Hector Almundo," he said.

I waited to make sure he was finished. I looked at each of them, then shrugged my shoulders. "The answer's no. I'll see you tomorrow," I said to Tucker. I had an appointment with Charlie tomorrow evening, so Lee would have to hand off the F-Bird.

"Wait," said Moody, as I was pushing open the door to the conference room.

I turned back to him.

"I'm going to offer you the gift of a lifetime," he said. "Immunity. For everything. Conspiracy. Obstruction. The one thousand one."

"Several years in prison, you avoid," Tucker chimed in.

"You know I've got you," Moody said. "You know you're going

to prison. This is your one chance to avoid it. Your one chance. You walk out the door, the offer goes away."

Tucker said, "Take it, Jason. Don't be a cowboy."

Immunity. I'd turned it down initially, but things had gotten worse for me. It was true that I'd lied to Tucker about Madison Koehler. It was stupid of me. And maybe they had an obstruction case against me. Plus the doctored memos, which everyone at the defense table—Cimino, Connolly, everyone—would swear weren't doctored at all, but were, in fact, written by me.

I'd have an uphill climb in court. These guys were offering me a free pass. I knew what Talia would say. I knew what Paul Riley would say.

But in the end, it was something primitive, something very simple that drove me. I didn't like snitches. I used them, myself, as a prosecutor, but there was always a part of me that didn't respect them. It was something ingrained in me from my childhood. You don't rat on your friends.

Maybe I was splitting hairs and rationalizing, but I had told myself that what I'd done, thus far with the feds, wasn't the same thing. I'd gone in on my own terms to catch a murderer, and I was getting close to succeeding now. There was residual damage to Cimino, of course, but it wasn't something I'd initiated. Those guys at the PCB had screwed me with those doctored memos. So I was screwing them back. It was retaliation as much as anything. And it was finding a killer.

What they wanted from me now felt different. I didn't know any of these people. I had no beef with them. They very well might be criminals. I had no trouble entertaining that possibility. And if so, I hoped they got their due. But it wasn't going to be through me.

"I'll see you tomorrow, Lee." I walked out the door and caught an elevator going down.

54 AT SIX FORTY-FIVE THE NEXT EVENING, I UNLOCKED the door to Suite 410. Lee Tucker was reading something on his cell phone. He looked up and held a stare on me.

"Hey." I nodded to the F-Bird.

"Number twenty-two today," he said, his voice flat. "Kinion Consulting."

"Right. You got the text messages?"

"Yeah." He handed me the F-Bird. "I'll be here when you get back."

I grabbed the recording device, slipped it into my suit pocket, and started for the door. Then I stopped and turned back. "Listen, Lee. I realize what you did yesterday. When it was you and me in here. When you asked me if any of the governor's people had approached me."

He nodded.

"You were giving me a chance to correct my earlier statement. I'm sure Moody didn't want you to give me that chance. So, that was nice of you."

Tucker looked up at the ceiling. "I can get that offer back," he said. "I know what Chris said, but—I can talk to him. Just say the word."

I didn't say any words at all. I just left.

*   *   *

OUTSIDE, IT WAS ALREADY DARK. The temperatures had fallen below freezing again. Charlie was waiting for me curbside in the Porsche. It was just a minute or two after seven.

"Hey," I said. "Try not to get us killed on the way there." With the ice this time of the year, riding in the 911 was an adventure.

Charlie didn't answer. His eyes remained forward. His jaw was set tight. He put the car in gear and motored forward.

"So this is Kinion," I said. I ran through the details on the guy with whom we were going to have dinner tonight, as well as our plans for tomorrow. "And after tomorrow we're down to—"

"Why'd you ask me about Starlight the other day?" Charlie kept his eyes forward as he spoke.

"What? Who—who's Starlight?"

Charlie didn't respond. His eyes were locked in the forward position. His right hand was in a fist. His left gripped the steering wheel so hard his knuckles were pure ivory.

"Charlie, what—"

"You asked me, the other day. Why they weren't on our list. Starlight Catering."

"Oh. Oh, right," I said. "The company you skipped over on the list. It just stood out. I was just wondering why we were talking to all these other companies but not them."

We came up to a red light. Charlie didn't move. "Why so curious all of a sudden?"

"I just told you why." My internal thermometer had kicked up a few degrees.

The light changed to green. The car moved forward again.

"What's the problem?" I asked.

"Problem?" Charlie drummed his fingers on the steering wheel. "Why would I have a problem? I don't have a problem."

"Whatever," I said, like I didn't have a care in the world. But this was going badly. My antennae for all things dangerous and scary were at full attention. But I couldn't see any sense in pursuing it, in protesting. At least, not yet. I tried to think down the road to what might lie ahead. Maybe this was just a stray comment. Maybe he was just in a bad mood.

I sneezed. It wasn't a real sneeze but I thought I faked it pretty well. Illness can be helpful in a situation like this. Charlie was having his doubts about me. If so, he'd try to read me. And it's always harder to read someone when they're sick. I once interrogated someone on a sexual assault who had the flu. The way the guy was sweating and bobbing his head, I thought I was minutes away from a full confession. Instead, the only thing I got from him was the contents of his lunch all over the table in front of me. Turned out he wasn't our guy. I'd been wrong, and I wasn't wrong often.

I couldn't manufacture vomit, but I could manufacture a sneeze and a head cold. I could fake being sick. It would provide cover.

I sneezed again. I pulled a handkerchief out of my pants pocket. Talia bought me monogrammed handkerchiefs a couple of years ago. During the hay fever season that gave me fits, she got tired of finding tiny balls of Kleenex on the nightstand or in my pants pockets.

I blew my nose with the handkerchief and stuck it into my suit coat pocket next to the F-Bird. "Christ, this cold," I said, adding some nasal to my voice.

Up ahead on the right was the turn for the interstate heading north. We were still in the left lane. "That's our turn," I reminded him.

He stayed in the left lane and drove through the intersection. We'd missed the turn. It was clearly no oversight on Charlie's part.

Not good.

"Change of plans?" I asked.

"Change of plans. They want us to meet down here."

He kept driving due west, as the traffic filtered out. He was driving well over the speed limit, taking us past the gentrified loft housing into an area that was heavily industrial.

I faked a sneeze. And another.

"Where are we going?" I asked.

"It's not far."

He made a hard left turn down a street I didn't know. I didn't know this area at all. It wasn't residential. No bars or boutiques or coffee shops. It was the old-line factories. Many of them abandoned now. Desolate and dark, this time of night. It was a good location for a private conversation. It was a good location for a lot of things.

Charlie was driving recklessly. The city plows didn't come through here, and there was thick ice. His car wasn't cut out for it. The rear of the car was fishtailing, the wheels spinning, but he didn't care. His anger seemed to grow the longer we drove.

"This is where they want to meet?" I said, unsure of the final destination, but wherever it was, it was in a dark, remote pocket of the city if it was in this neighborhood. It made sense to continue to play innocent, as if I really expected that the president of Kinion Consulting would be making this meeting.

He hit the brakes. The Porsche fishtailed a bit. He turned the car into an open space, a garage with a high ceiling that housed a few larger vehicles, construction equipment. Vehicles that hadn't been in use recently. Charlie killed the engine to the Porsche and sat quietly.

"We're just going to sit here?" I asked.

He didn't answer. A few minutes passed. Then I heard the sound of another vehicle crunching over the ice. It drew closer. The next thing I knew, headlights were hitting the wall in front of us and a black SUV pulled up next to us. The driver got out. He didn't look friendly. He was wearing a long coat, so I couldn't make out his build; I couldn't tell if he was fat or muscular or both, but he wasn't small, and he wasn't nice.

A door opened, off on one side of the garage. A man in a black leather jacket and jeans stepped out. I recognized him. He was the guy from Charlie's club the first time I was there. That was back when they tested me. I'd left my clothes in an unlocked locker, and Leather Jacket here walked up to Charlie after we'd played racquetball and told him "everything was fine." It had been a signal to Charlie that he'd searched my locker, my clothes and possessions, and I was clean. I wasn't wearing a wire.

But I was wearing one now.

Charlie pushed open his door. "Let's start that meeting," he said.

55

WHEN YOU'RE IN A ROLE, YOU STAY IN THAT ROLE TO the end. You focus on it to the exclusion of all else. You try to avoid bluffing, but if you have to, you bluff, without fear of your bluff being called. If you're going to go down, go down in role. Even if you're caught, totally and completely. Because even then, there's always a tiny chance at succeeding, and you're no worse for trying.

I am the son of a con artist. My father didn't teach me much in the way of ethics or set any kind of an example for me. But I learned a lot about deception. I learned by watching him, by listening to him, and by surviving around him. I learned it because, in many ways, I was playing a role my entire childhood.

You're good at this, Lee Tucker had said to me more than once.

I had very limited options. I could run. I could open the car door and take off through the open garage. I didn't know if Leather Jacket or the guys from the black SUV—or Charlie, for that matter—had weapons. I could wind up facedown, for good, with a few bullets in the back. But I could stay and meet that same fate.

I could do something similar to headlong flight—not run, but walk. I could pronounce this entire exercise offensive and insulting and walk away. The "real" me—Jason Kolarich, not wearing a wire—would do just that. But it could produce the same result as running. These goons would probably grab me, and I typically liked my chances when it came to physical confrontation, but it would be three on one, not counting Charlie. And not counting any weapons they might have.

Either way, if I left and survived doing so, the operation was over. Completely. No doubt. Charlie would close up shop and make every effort to cover his tracks. Presumably, the FBI would move in before he had that chance. The moment I got word to Lee Tucker, they'd probably arrest him. Surely, they had plenty of evidence against him. But I'd be looking over my shoulder, at least for a while.

And I wasn't done. I was close, I thought. But I wasn't fully satisfied I knew the truth behind Ernesto Ramirez's murder. The moment I left this undercover operation, my access to the truth was gone.

Balance that curiosity against the likelihood that I was about to be exposed.

Curiosity killed the cat, I believe I heard once.

It was probably dumb of me. Probably smarter to run and take my chances. But it was dumb of me to step into that alley with Ernesto's friend Scarface, and that turned out okay.

You're good at this. I'd better be now. Nerves and fear are very difficult to conceal. They affect your movements, your speech, your actions. I had to stay in role. I had nothing to hide. I had to forget about the F-Bird. I had to be willing to hand my suit coat over to someone, to turn that pocket inside out if requested, without a care in the world. In fact, I might even volunteer to hand it over.

I got out of the Porsche and closed the door. I looked over at Charlie, to give him a *hey-what's-with*-these-*guys* look, but the lighting was almost nonexistent in here, and anyway, he wasn't making eye contact with me.

"Charlie, what's the deal?" I said over the car to him. It was what an innocent person would say. Unfortunately for me, it's also what a guilty person would say. At this stage, those two points of view would converge. Even an innocent person would be anxious at what was happening. Even someone with nothing to hide would be nervous about being interrogated and maybe roughed up.

Charlie, I had to concede, had been pretty smart up until now. He'd clearly been planning to confront me. But he didn't come out and say that while we were driving. He slipped a little bit with the comment about Starlight, but otherwise he'd kept his powder dry. Smart, because I might have had an opportunity to escape. I could have made a move for him while he was driving. I could have jumped out of the car while it was stopped at a red light or, if necessary, while it was moving.

Instead, he'd waited until I was here, and three of his goons were basically surrounding me.

Leather Jacket was holding the door open over in the corner. One of the thugs was directly behind me, the other—the SUV's passenger—was coming around the front end, and Charlie was coming around the back of the Porsche.

I still had the chance to abort. I could make it past these morons. I didn't have to win a fight. I just had to make enough of a mess to get away.

"After you," said the guy directly behind me.

I turned around, not too abruptly but not slowly, either. I stepped right up, face-to-face with this guy. My coat brushed against his. He had probably fifty pounds on me, but he was two inches shorter than me and had to look slightly upward to make eye contact.

His partner, the passenger, hadn't made it around the SUV yet. Charlie was well back in the darkness. That gave me about two seconds alone with this ape in the relative darkness. Two seconds that might be the most important two seconds of my life. Almost nose-to-nose with the guy, I said, "Hey, Vito, you must have me confused with someone who takes orders from you."

The thug I had named Vito was momentarily thrown by my comment, but then a wide, sick smile crossed his face. I would have preferred a scowl.

"Go inside, Jason," Charlie said, pulling up the rear.

I paused. Then I stepped back from Vito, shook my head, trying to show indignation. "Let's get this over with."

I walked past Leather Jacket holding the door, into a facility that looked like abandoned office space, space that once had been open to the public. There was a large room with a coffeemaker and a small play area for children. There were several desk areas with chairs on each side. It reminded me of a showroom at a car dealership.

"I'll check the Porsche," Leather Jacket said to the others, but I thought he wanted me to hear it, too. He wanted me to know that if I had tried to dump off anything incriminating—say, an electronic bug—in the Porsche, he'd find it.

Vito took the lead. I was next, followed by the other moron and then Charlie. We were headed into interior offices, which was a smart move if you were concerned about people hearing what was transpiring.

Vito opened a door and walked into an otherwise empty room. It was about the size of two offices. There was a single chair in the center of the room. That was it. Floor, ceiling, walls, and a single chair.

"The Kinions aren't going to have anywhere to sit," I said.

Nobody thought I was funny. I found myself in the center of the room, near the single chair. The two goons, Vito and his pal, spread out at forty-five-degree angles. Charlie stood in the doorway.

"I'll give you this one chance to make it easy," Charlie said. "Just give it up and get it over with."

"Charlie," I said, "I don't know what the hell has gotten into you. You think *I'm* working against you? I'm the best thing that ever happened to you."

He remained stoic. "Take off your clothes. All of them."

"The fuck I will."

Vito's friend, to my left, began his approach toward me. Apparently, he was going to enforce Charlie's edict. "Charlie," I said, holding my hands out. "Seriously, what—"

In mid-sentence, I turned and swung at Vito's friend. Call him Brutus. Brutus wasn't expecting it because I was talking. You don't expect the punch when the other person isn't braced. But I was braced. I just masked it by looking in the other direction and by talking to Charlie. Misdirection will do wonders in a fight.

Brutus stumbled backward and fell to the floor. He put a protective hand over what was left of his nose. That had to hurt. It wasn't the hardest swing I'd ever thrown, but it was square on target, and he was completely unprepared for it.

I thought Vito might come at me, too, but he didn't. He took a couple of steps back and drew a gun.

"This is crazy," I said. "You think I'm wearing a wire, Charlie? Is that it? You want to check me out? Fine."

I took off my overcoat and tossed it toward him. Then I removed my suit coat and tossed it in the same direction. I undid my tie, unbuttoned my shirt, threw off my pants, kicked off my shoes and socks. I tossed my wallet, keys, and money clip to him and slid my cell phone across the floor. I was down to my undershirt and boxers. Every other part of my wardrobe was in a pile near Charlie's feet.

Brutus needed some medical attention. His face looked like a used tampon. He stumbled out of the room as Leather Jacket appeared and whispered something to Charlie Cimino. I had to assume his report was favorable, because the F-Bird was not in the Porsche.

Leather Jacket gathered up my clothes into a small laundry basket he'd brought for the occasion.

"Easy on the starch," I said.

Leather Jacket thought that was humorous. "Underwear, too, sweetheart."

"Like hell."

He walked toward me, but not too close. He wasn't here for the earlier fun, but he could see a pool of blood where Brutus had been lying and he probably had caught a look at Brutus, too. He reached into his pocket. For a split second, I thought he was going to produce a weapon. Vito already had one trained on me, but two is always better than one.

Instead, he pulled out a balled-up pair of cotton boxers.

"Trade ya," he said. "But you go first. Take it all off."

I didn't really have much of a choice. But I was in role, and in that role, I would be annoyed but ultimately willing to cooperate.

"Normally, you'd have to buy me dinner first," I said. I stripped off the remainder of my clothes and flung them at his feet. Leather Jacket took only a quick peek, thankfully, just to make sure I didn't have some wire wrapped around my nuts or something.

He tossed me the boxers, which I quickly put on.

"Sit in the chair," Leather Jacket said. I was going to do that, anyway, because I figured they were going to need time to search my clothes.

Once I was seated, Leather Jacket showed me handcuffs and walked behind me. "Don't give me trouble," he said. "Give me your hands."

"This is ridiculous," I said, but I complied. He cuffed my hands behind the chair, through one of the bars, so if I tried to stand, I'd have to pick up the chair, too. Score one for them.

"Now what?" I asked.

"Now, you wait."

Charlie walked out of the room. Leather Jacket followed, holding a basket full of my clothes.

Vito kept the gun on me all the way to the door. "Cheap shot," he said to me.

"Sorry about his face," I said. "If I realized you two were boyfriend-girlfriend, I would have hit him in the stomach."

He gave me that same creepy grin, just like the one he flashed when we were nose-to-nose in the garage.

"See you soon," he said. He closed the door behind him and locked it.

 THERE WAS NO WORKING CLOCK IN THIS ROOM, BUT by my estimate I spent the next ninety minutes wearing only boxers in an unheated room in the dead of winter. I did my best to stay in role, both because you always stay in role—you never know when they might be watching—and because if I let my imagination run wild here, I might come to the conclusion that I was royally fucked.

Either way, I was royally cold, and an uncontrollable shiver was working its way through my body. If they were trying to determine whether I was working undercover against them, they would have been smart not to subject me to these conditions. The kinds of tells, the giveaways you look for in a liar are harder to detect when the subject is already trembling from the cold.

But it occurred to me that maybe they had passed that stage. Maybe they were convinced that I had joined the other side, and now they just wanted to know how much the G knew before they put a bullet in my brain. In that state of affairs, putting me through this was a smart move.

Or maybe I was just overthinking this, but I didn't have a lot else to do right now.

Except to stay in role. Above all else. No matter what.

The door opened slowly. Vito peeked in, confirmed I was still handcuffed to the chair, and walked in, still in that long coat, still smiling broadly and still pointing a gun at me. I thought, for a beat, that this was it, that all the forks in the road I'd tried to forecast, all the potential drama, was a fantasy; he was just going to shoot me and be done with it.

I think that's what he wanted me to think. He didn't like the way I chested up to him in the garage, or the number I did on his partner. But he wasn't in charge, and he hadn't had authorization to retaliate. He didn't have authorization to shoot me, either, at least not yet, but he enjoyed the chance to make me think otherwise.

Vito handed the gun to Leather Jacket and squatted down, so we were face-to-face. "That wasn't very nice, what you did to my friend."

"He wasn't paying attention. Tell him next—"

Before I could finish, Vito's right forearm clocked me in the kisser. My head snapped backward. Stars danced inside my eyelids. Everything went black for a count of one, two, before I opened my eyes and saw the floor below me.

"You mean like that, he wasn't paying attention?"

I spit blood. My teeth felt like they'd been rocked from their roots. My jaw was intact, thankfully, but not by much. My head was ringing. A sharp pain radiated down my neck.

"Who said you could do that?" It was Charlie's voice. It hurt to move my head, but my eyes peeked up at him. He was watching me. It was hard, in my state, to read his face. He looked unsure, I thought, which I took as a good sign.

"We'll handle this," said Leather Jacket.

"Fuck you," I said. "Uncuff me and let me go."

He didn't speak, but he slowly shook his head.

"I'm freezing," I said.

"Give him a coat," Charlie said.

"No, pretty boy's doing just fine," said Leather Jacket. Then, to me: "Why were you at the federal building yesterday? Four o'clock."

"Yester— I had a motion to compel that I filed yesterday. I delivered a copy to Judge Graves's office. She likes courtesy copies."

I answered quickly, no equivocation. Charlie had put a tail on me. I was followed. He'd been wondering about me. I didn't know why.

"What's the name of the case?" asked Leather Jacket.

"*United States v. Guevarra*. Illegal possession of firearms."

"What's the docket number?"

I spit more blood. "I don't have the fucking docket number committed to memory, dumbshit. Show me any lawyer who does. Look up the damn case. It's public record."

"Why did you want to know about Starlight Catering?" he asked.

"I already answered that."

"Not to me, you didn't."

I looked up. Charlie had left the room. It was just me, Leather Jacket to my left, and Vito to my right.

I spit again, a thick mixture of blood and saliva.

Another blow, harder than the last one, to the right temple. A soft, vulnerable part of the skull. It was Vito's forearm again. My neck hurt more than anything. It was being knocked around like a pinball.

"Answer," said Leather Jacket.

"We're shaking down the whole field of state contractors," I said, "and we give this one a pass. I was just asking. I don't give a flying fuck about Starlight whatever."

He was quiet a minute. All eyes were on me. I thought I was doing okay. Relatively speaking. I'd rather be sipping margaritas on a beach. I'd rather be giving myself an enema.

"What the hell is this? I work my ass off for Charlie and we've got a good thing going here. What happened?"

I said it to the floor. My head was hanging. I was woozy and struggling to maintain not just consciousness but clarity of thought.

"Dick Baroni is what happened." It was Charlie's voice again.

Dick Baroni. The guy Charlie told me about—even spelled his name for me so I could Google it. The guy who crossed him and got his office torched, with him in it. He lived to tell but apparently didn't tell. I was supposed to take a lesson from that.

"Dick tells me the feds were asking him questions about me," said Charlie. "Why, after so many years, would they be doing that?"

Lee Tucker. What the hell was he doing? They interviewed Baroni after I gave him the name? They might as well have painted a target on my chest. It had been a plant. Charlie had thrown out the name to see if it would spawn any interest from law enforcement. If it did, that meant the person he told—yours truly—was working with them.

"Okay," I said, like I was awaiting the punch line. "And who the hell is Dick Baroni?"

Charlie watched me for a long time. He hadn't expected that answer. "You know who he is."

"I have no idea who he is."

"I told you about him."

"When did you do that?"

"You're lying to me."

"When, Charlie?" I shook my head, exasperated. "Just answer me that. When did you ever tell me about him?"

He paused. "First time we talked. Really talked. At my club."

"Like, three months ago? I can't remember what I had for lunch yesterday."

I thought it was a plausible enough position to take.

"Three months ago," I said, "when—"

I cut off the sentence. I tried to summon emotion that I'd tried hard so hard to suppress. It wasn't all that hard. It was never very far from the surface.

"When I was just getting back—when I was just getting over what happened. I mean, I was a fucking mess when I met you. And you think—what—I remember that conversation so well that some name you dropped would stick in my mind?"

I had a head of steam now, and I let the anger release.

"And by the way, why would I do any of this, Charlie? Why the hell would I team up with the feds? Do I have some reason that I don't know about? I just woke up one day and decided that I wanted to work undercover for the feds to help nail somebody I'd never *met*?"

I had Charlie thinking. It was working. Maybe Tucker was right. Maybe I was a natural.

Charlie walked over to me. He put his hands on his knees and looked into my eyes.

"Tell me you're not working for them," he whispered. "Look me in the eye and—"

"I'm not working for those assholes," I said.

He slapped me hard across the face. "Again."

"I'm not a snitch," I said.

He reached around and grabbed the back of my hair, showed me his teeth. "Again."

"I wouldn't do that. I'm not a fucking rat."

The adrenaline was racing through me. He was buying it. I could taste freedom. I realized, only then, how much I'd expected this whole thing to go south.

"I put you on the map," he said, his face twisted into a snarl. He was still gripping the shorthairs on my neck. "I pulled your head out of your ass. And this is the thanks you give me?"

He opened his other hand. Resting on his palm was an F-Bird.

Charlie tossed the F-Bird to Leather Jacket. "Your turn," he said.

57 "**WHAT IS THIS?**" **LEATHER JACKET ASKED, DISPLAYING** the F-Bird right before my eyes.

"I don't know. What *is* that? A pager? A battery pack?"

"We *found* this, asshole. You can't lie your way out of this. You think we're fucking stupid?"

"I have no—"

"It's a fucking *recording device*!" he shouted into my face. "When did you start working for them?"

Stay in role. No matter what. I had no other options. I only had one bet left. It was a long shot, but it was all I had, and I was staking my life on it.

Vito hit me with the brunt of his hand, slamming against my temple again.

"When?" Leather Jacket asked. *"When?"*

"I'm not working for anybody but myself," I said. "I'm not a snitch. I've never seen that pager before."

Leather Jacket slammed his fist into my chest, just below my windpipe. I wasn't a moving target, so he was able to put a lot behind it. It drove the wind from me. It hurt a lot, too.

These guys were going to a lot of trouble to beat the shit out of me without leaving a lot of visible bruises. That had to mean something, but I wasn't sure what. I was having a little trouble with critical reasoning at the moment.

Stay . . . in . . . role.

"Paulie," Leather Jacket said, looking to his left, to Vito.

Vito—Paulie, apparently—walked behind me and grabbed hold of one of my hands through the handcuffs. I felt the edge of a sharp blade against the little finger on my right hand.

"Every time I have to ask the question without getting an answer, you lose another finger," Leather Jacket said. "So, that gives us ten tries. Here's try number one."

"I'm not a snitch!" I spit.

"When did you start working for them?"

"You can ask me ten *thousand* times," I said. "You might as well cut off my entire hand right now, you lousy piece of shit, because *I'm not a fucking rat*."

Leather Jacket watched me a long time, my heaving, quivering self. "Hey, tough guy? If I was you, I'd give me a straight answer. You're not gonna get that finger back once we slice it off."

"Stop," said Charlie. "That's enough."

"Nah." Leather Jacket shook his head. "It's not enough yet. After a few fingers are gone—he still denies it then, maybe I'll believe him. Go ahead, Paulie. Let's see how tough he is with nine fingers."

I closed my eyes and braced myself. I couldn't protest any longer. I'd done everything I could. I felt the blade's edge wedge into the skin of my smallest finger at the base. I held my breath and gritted my teeth.

The knife didn't move any farther. Then it came off my skin. Paulie released the hand. I wiggled my hand, all five glorious fingers in tandem.

"Give him your coat, for Christ's sake," said Charlie.

A coat fell over my shoulders.

I froze, catching my breath. Paulie walked out of the room, without the long coat that was now over my shoulders. Leather Jacket left, too. It took me a moment to catch up with the turn of events. Unless I was hallucinating, I had just passed the test.

Neither Charlie nor I was in the mood to speak right away. Certainly not me. Fear and stress and, ultimately, disbelief had converged to render me speechless. And my mind wasn't working much better than my mouth. I wasn't sure I trusted what I might say.

I'd stayed in role until the bitter end and it had paid off. He'd confronted me with the F-Bird and I'd done the only thing I could do, short of confessing: I'd feigned complete and total ignorance. I'd been prepared to elaborate if necessary, to explain that I had no idea what the thing was or how it got wherever it was they found it.

But I didn't have to elaborate. They had accepted my denial. They were willing to bluff, just to make sure, but in the end, they didn't do any permanent damage to me. They believed me. That could only mean one thing.

They hadn't found my F-Bird.

They'd searched my clothes and come up empty. They'd searched the Porsche, thinking I might have tried to dispose of it before getting out, and struck out again. Part of me was sure they would find it, but it was clear to me now that they hadn't.

They had an F-Bird, but it hadn't come from me. They'd taken it off someone else.

"So, I'm sorry about all that," Charlie said, as if he'd accidentally spilled some coffee on my pants or something. "They had to be sure. We just—had to make sure. You understand."

I needed time to gather myself here, but I probably didn't have that luxury. Staying in role was as important now as before.

"Say something, kid," he said.

"Fuck . . . you," I managed.

He liked that. "Say something else."

"Is that thing," I said between breaths, "really a recording device?"

"Yeah, it is."

"Someone's . . . wearing a wire?"

"Someone *was*," he said. "Not anymore."

"Great. That's . . . just great."

"I think we're okay, kid. I'm gonna uncuff you now." He showed me the key. Under the circumstances, he probably figured I would be reticent about anyone approaching me.

He came around behind me with the key. He took the coat—Paulie's coat—off my shoulders.

"Don't take the coat," I snapped. "I'm freezing. Put it back on."

I wasn't freezing, actually. The events of the last half-hour had elevated my temperature considerably.

"Okay, take it easy." He unlocked my handcuffs and then threw Paulie's coat over my shoulders again.

My hands were free again. I savored it. I rubbed my wrists.

"So, listen. I've got a few things I gotta take care of. My guy here, he's going to drive you home. Don't talk to anyone about anything until I get back in touch with you. You hear me, kid? Not a fucking word to anybody."

"Charlie . . . whatever you do . . . whoever it is . . . don't kill anybody. Keeping someone quiet . . . isn't worth . . . a murder charge. Trust me."

I thought it made sense to cast my appeal in terms of attorney-client advice as opposed to a plea to his morality.

"I'm going to get you your clothes," he said.

"You don't just . . . kill a federal witness, Charlie."

"I'm not going to kill anybody." He walked out, leaving me alone. He came back only a few moments later with my clothes, a little worse for wear but all there, in the laundry basket.

"Paulie's gonna need his coat back," said Charlie. "You know his buddy Sal had to go to the hospital? You shattered the guy's nose." He thought that was funny.

I handed Paulie's coat to Charlie. I didn't need it any longer. I just needed that brief interval of time, while Charlie left the room, to fetch my F-Bird out of Paulie's front coat pocket.

58 I SAT SILENT IN THE BACKSEAT OF LEATHER JACKET'S SUV. I didn't know what Charlie had in store for the snitch he'd caught with the F-Bird. I assumed the penalty for betrayal would be death, Charlie's denial notwithstanding. Either way, everything had changed now. The G had targeted Charlie Cimino, and now he knew it.

My F-Bird was once again resting comfortably in the pocket of my suit jacket. I'd removed it during the drive to this place with Charlie, once the warning bells went off with his questions about Starlight Catering. I'd faked a sneeze and removed my handkerchief from my pants pocket. Charlie hadn't noticed that I then placed the handkerchief in the inner pocket of my suit coat, which allowed me to snag the F-Bird and palm it for the remainder of the ride in my right hand. I'd thought about dumping it somewhere in the Porsche, but I figured if they were going to search me, they'd be bright enough to search the car, too. Lucky for me, the F-Bird was light as a feather, so Paulie didn't feel it when I dropped it in his coat pocket while we were squaring off in the garage.

It was a gamble, sure. Paulie could have discovered it, and I would have been toast. But I didn't have a better idea. And it didn't seem likely these guys would ever think to search each other for the device.

I got lucky when Paulie threw his coat over me at the end of the interrogation, allowing me to retrieve it. Otherwise, I'd have had a problem. Sooner or later, Paulie would have found it in the bottom of his pocket. I would have had to intervene before that time. But it would have been a bridge to cross later; the more immediate problem was surviving that room. And now, thanks to sweet Irish luck, I had survived and retrieved the F-Bird in the same sitting.

I paid attention to the route Leather Jacket was taking back to my house. I'd had some vague notion that his job might be to drive me to a remote location and put a bullet between my eyes. But if they wanted me dead, I would have died in that room.

I got out of the SUV without a word to Leather Jacket. When I got inside my townhouse and saw that the SUV had driven away, I pulled out my cell phone. It had been turned off. I powered it up. My plan was to call Lee Tucker. But my phone was already ringing. The caller ID showed "David Hamlin," meaning Tucker.

"Jesus Christ," he said. "You're okay?"

"In one piece."

"Thank God." He took a breath. "Okay, listen—"

"You better find Greg Connolly," I said. "Because Cimino has him and he's going to kill him. If he hasn't already."

Silence on the other end of the phone.

"There's another CI," I said.

"Jason—"

"Charlie knows that. He showed me his F-Bird—"

"Jason."

"I assume it was Greg Connolly—"

"*Jason.*"

I stopped. "What?"

"Greg Connolly is dead," he said.

I let out a breath. "Shit."

"Yeah, shit. Go to your back door," he said.

"Why?"

"Because I'm about to knock on it."

I went through the kitchen to my back door and opened it up. Lee Tucker was coming up the walk. "They killed him," I said.

He nodded. He walked past me and closed the door. "Found his body at Seagram Hill almost an hour ago."

I looked at my kitchen clock. I'd lost all sense of time. It was almost midnight. He threw his coat on the kitchen table and started pacing.

"A car just dropped me off," I said. "An SUV. Plate number is—"

"We're on it," Tucker said. "And we've got agents watching your house right now, from all sides. In case someone decides to stop by unannounced." He looked me over. "They did a number on you. You okay?"

I waved him off. I was anything but okay. My head and neck would be sore for days. I had a permanent chill that would last a long while, too. Even my right hand ached, from punching the one guy in the nose.

"Fuck," said Tucker. "Fuck, fuck, *fuck*."

I thought that was an accurate summary of tonight's events.

*   *   *

Two in the morning. Chris Moody had joined us. We were sitting in the kitchen. Tucker and Moody had listened to the contents of my F-Bird several times already on a laptop computer Moody had brought.

Charlie Cimino had returned home shortly after I did, near midnight, and was still there. They'd tailed Leather Jacket's SUV to some location, though Moody and Tucker didn't elaborate on where or what had transpired. All was quiet now. Greg Connolly was dead. I was alive and secure. Cimino and his cronies were home in their beds, hopeful that their crime had gone undetected.

Greg Connolly had been found facedown, with his pants at his ankles, in an area of the city called Seagram Hill but more typically known as "Semen Hill." The Hill was a notorious west-side locale for prostitutes, many of the male variety. Found in the condition he was, the story would be obvious enough: Greg Connolly was jumped and murdered while looking for a ten-dollar blowjob.

Tucker looked at me. "So you slipped the F-Bird out of your pocket in the car, then you dropped it in the goon's pocket?"

I nodded.

"So they're searching through your clothes, and meanwhile it's sitting in the goon's pocket." He shook his head. "Ballsy, Jason. I mean, seriously."

"Desperation is the mother of invention."

"No, ballsy is right," Moody said. It was as close as he could come to a compliment.

Tucker said to me, "Cimino never mentioned Connolly by name. How'd you figure?"

It had to be Connolly. There weren't that many options. And he'd been upset about being pushed out of the loop when I'd hatched this new plan with Charlie. It also explained why Tucker and Moody were so pissed off when I'd called that audible. *You cut out the board*, they'd complained. Sure. They'd flipped the chairman of the PCB to be their eyes and ears, and I waltzed in and cut him out of the action.

I explained all of that to him. Moody said, "Connolly wasn't good at this. He never was."

"Greg knew about me, didn't he?" I asked. "I didn't know about him, but he knew about me."

Moody nodded. I wasn't sure if he'd let me in on that piece of information. He probably figured it didn't matter at this point. "Yeah, he knew."

That stood to reason. Connolly recorded the conversation with me that the feds used against me, when they first confronted me. I had thought, at the time, that the feds had to go through the extraordinary procedure of bugging his office and tapping his phone without his consent. I'd been wrong. Greg had been working with them all along.

That was a significant point for me, in particular, but now wasn't the time to raise it.

"Where was Greg headed today?" I asked. "With the F-Bird?"

"He had an assignment," Moody said.

"Obviously. But where? With who?"

Moody didn't answer right away. He looked so unusual, wearing a sweatshirt and jeans, like a totally different person tonight. "I can't reveal that," he finally said. There was a trace of apology in his voice, which was uncharacteristic. But this was an unusual situation, to say the least. Everyone was tired and strung out. The operation had crash-landed over the last several hours.

I got out of my chair. I had two blankets draped over me and I was chugging coffee, not for the caffeine or the taste but the warmth. I'd spent the better part of two hours, wearing nothing but boxers, in temperatures that were probably just above freezing. It was hard to imagine that there would be a time when I would feel warm again.

I filled another cup, held it in my hands, and watched Tucker and Moody roll their necks and mumble to themselves.

"What's the verdict?" I asked. "You going to pick up Charlie and his crew?"

Moody shrugged. "Connolly's dead, so there's no urgency. Unless we think he's coming after you."

"He's not," I said. "He had his chance tonight."

The prosecutor stretched his arms, working out the anxiety. "I don't know yet."

"How do you vote?" Tucker asked me. "You're the big hero tonight. Do we roust Cimino tonight? Do we wait?"

I'd been thinking about that for a long time. I thought about what had happened tonight.

Who said you could do that? Charlie had said, when he walked into the room and saw that Paulie had thrown his first forearm into my face.

We'll handle this, Leather Jacket had replied.

Give him a coat, Charlie had said.

No, pretty boy's doing just fine.

"I think we hold off," I said to Tucker and Moody. "I don't think we're done yet."

And when Leather Jacket and Paulie had turned up the heat at the end, putting the knife against my hand. *Stop, that's enough,* Charlie had said.

Nah, Leather Jacket had said. *It's not enough yet.*

"The cover's blown," said Tucker. "Cimino knows we're onto him."

"Maybe yes, maybe no," I said.

And Charlie's words when the interrogation was over. *Sorry about that. They had to be sure.*

I paced around the kitchen, into the living room, my neck stiff and sore, my head throbbing, the eternal chill throughout my body.

Who said you could do that?

We'll handle this.

Give him a coat.

No, pretty boy's doing just fine.

"We might be able to put Charlie's mind at ease," I said. "If we can do that, we can keep the operation going."

"What operation?" Tucker said. "Cimino's been spooked, at the very least. He's not going to keep up that scheme of yours."

"He's not talking about Cimino," Moody said. "You're talking about moving up the ladder. You're talking about accepting Madison Koehler's offer to work for the governor."

"Chris wins the prize," I said.

"Wait a second," Tucker chimed in. "You tell us no, over and over again, when we want you to go inside the governor's inner circle. Now, tonight, you come this close to getting your ass killed, and *now* you want to do this?"

"Lee has a point," Moody said. "We know for certain that Cimino would kill you if you were ever burned. We have a federal witness lying facedown in the mud on Seagram Hill to tell us that much. And you can figure you'll be watched more closely than ever. So why now?"

It was a valid question. Like many things, there was more than one answer. Moody was right. We couldn't be sure what Charlie knew. He definitely knew the federal government was sniffing around, at a minimum. And now we knew, firsthand, that Charlie Cimino did not have a high tolerance for risk. I'd have to watch my back, more than ever. But I thought it was worth the risk. And I was the only person who could do this.

And I still had a murder to solve. I still wasn't sure I had the answer to that one. Charlie Cimino was looking pretty good as the puppet master behind the murder, but I wasn't totally convinced. Not after tonight.

Who said you could do that?

We'll handle this.

Give him a coat.

No, pretty boy's doing just fine.

Stop. That's enough.

Nah. It's not enough yet.

"So?" Tucker asked again. "Why now, all of a sudden, you're willing to go work for the governor?"

Sorry about that, Charlie had apologized to me. *They just needed to be sure.*

They.

I looked out the window in the kitchen. Somewhere out there, FBI agents were guarding every exit to my house. This would be risky, no doubt.

"Because Charlie wasn't calling the shots tonight," I said. "And I'm going to find out who was."

I WAS IN MY OFFICE THE NEXT MORNING AT NINE. MY back, shoulders, and neck were faring the worst after last night. I couldn't turn my head in any direction— hell, I couldn't cough without feeling a searing pain all the way down to my ass. My jaw was sore as hell from Paulie's forearm, and the side of my head was swollen and tender.

I had a deposition scheduled for eleven on one of the cases that had been handed to me courtesy of Charlie's and my extortion scheme. I was neither prepared nor interested. I would have shoveled it off to Shauna, but I didn't want to involve her in any way in the stuff I was dealing with.

The city's newspaper was on my desk. Greg's death wasn't on the front page; it was reserved for another obituary, the death of Warren Palendech, one of the justices on the state supreme court. Justice Palendech was dead of a heart attack? It was an article that would typically captivate me, but I had more pressing concerns.

There it was, across the headline of the metro section, the story of one of Governor Carlton Snow's top aides and oldest friends, Gregory Connolly, found dead near Seagram Hill from a gunshot wound. The reporter was not afraid to speculate on what Mr. Connolly had been up to in that neighborhood, what most people are up to in that neighborhood. She didn't directly attribute sexual folly to Greg, but anonymous police sources believed that Mr. Connolly's reason for being in that area was not original.

Good. Not good for Greg's wife, who would now be coping not only with her husband's death but with the notion that he'd been late coming home because he stopped off for a hummer from a teen-aged prostitute. But good from our perspective. Charlie's thugs had dumped Greg at Seagram Hill to give this precise impression, and the morning papers were announcing that their plan had worked. And spending much more time on a dead supreme court justice, at that.

Marie buzzed my phone a few minutes after I arrived. *"Charlie Cimino,"* she said.

I took a breath and said, "Put him through."

"Jason, it's Charlie."

"Yeah, Charlie—"

"Did you see the paper today? About Greg Connolly?"

I felt a bitter smile on my face. Charlie was playing to anyone who might be listening. He was being careful. Did he still suspect me? Tucker and Moody had both mentioned it to me last night, as we kicked ideas around my kitchen table. Their concern was well founded. Connolly knew that I was working for the government. Had he given up that information under duress? The smart money said no, he didn't, or else Charlie would have killed me last night.

But the smart money doesn't always win. The truth was, nobody knew what Charlie knew and didn't know.

"I was just reading about it," I said.

"Yeah, God, that's terrible," Charlie said. "Hey, listen, want to grab a cup of coffee?"

"Sure, Charlie."

"How's one o'clock look for you? In the lobby?"

"Great," I said. I might have to leave the deposition early, but that was hardly my concern at the moment.

I went down to the fourth floor of my building and opened Suite 410. Lee Tucker was there. We'd expected Charlie would be contacting me soon, and we couldn't be sure what he'd been doing in terms of surveillance on me, so the plan had been that Tucker would park himself in this office until we heard from him. We knew for certain that nobody was watching me last night, as the feds had been covering every side of my house, and presumably everyone working for Charlie had been busy disposing of Greg Connolly's body. But today was a different story. Charlie had put someone on me two days ago and for who-knows-how-long before that. He could do it again.

"You look like shit," Tucker pronounced. "Does it hurt?"

"Only when I breathe."

Tucker tossed me my cell phone. "Phone's clean," he said. Overnight, federal agents had looked over my cell phone to be sure Charlie hadn't planted a recording device of his own in my phone.

"Charlie called. Coffee at one o'clock," I said.

Tucker nodded slowly. "How'd he sound?"

"Cautious. 'Did you hear about Greg,' that sort of thing."

"So he's still worried," Lee said.

"Worried about you. Not necessarily about me."

Tucker seemed skeptical. "You willing to bet your life on 'not necessarily'?"

It was a legitimate question. "Charlie trusts me," I said.

"You realize, Kolarich—even if he doesn't think you're wearing a wire, he could think that Connolly gave us information about you.

Which means we might come to pay you a visit. Which makes you a liability. If Charlie's as cautious as we think, it would make sense to get rid of you."

"Of course I know that. That's why we have to set his mind at ease."

Tucker tossed me the F-Bird. It felt like a hundred pounds in my hand.

"You understand my limitations," said Tucker. "I can't cover you. I can't wire you up for real-time monitoring, and I can't follow you wherever you go."

"I understand," I said.

Tucker sighed. He started to say something but thought better of it.

"Talk," I said.

He struggled for a moment.

"Speak," I said.

He held up a hand. "Look, when they found Greg—the bullet to his brain? It wasn't the only . . . it wasn't the only . . . injury. You follow?"

I thought I did. Before the end of his life, before the bullet entered his brain, Greg Connolly endured things he probably considered worse than death.

Tucker leaned back in his chair. He wasn't accustomed to talking people down from taking risks. He'd spent far more time talking people into them. "I'm just saying, we've got Cimino on a lot. We can confront him, flip him—get to the higher-ups that way."

"You think that would work?" I said it like I was doubtful. Because I was. I couldn't imagine Charlie agreeing to cooperate with the feds. Nor could I imagine him being successful at it if he tried.

At one o'clock, I went down into the lobby. Charlie was there, on his phone. He gestured to me and started walking toward the exit. He liked a coffee shop down the street. I joined him outside, not braced for a cold, gusty wind. We headed due east, my head down against the wind, when he hit my arm. I looked up and saw his Porsche parked at a meter.

"C'mon," he said.

"Change of plans?"

He got around to the driver's side and looked at me. "That's right. Change of plans. That okay with you?"

Charlie trusts me.

"Whatever," I said. I got into his car.

 I WOULD FOLLOW CHARLIE'S LEAD. HE DIDN'T SPEAK, so neither did I. It wasn't hard to figure out where he was taking me. We were going to his club, presumably for another game of racquetball. For another chance to strip-search me without strip-searching me.

It hadn't been that hard to foresee. Tucker and I had discussed it. We'd gone back and forth in Suite 410 earlier today about the F-Bird. We finally decided against it. As much as we wanted Charlie on tape, confessing to the murder of Greg Connolly, there was too large a risk that Charlie would search me for a listening device. If he had even the tiniest lingering doubt about my loyalties, the day after Greg's murder would be the time to test me.

Charlie's expression was tight. Controlled. He had a lot of worries at the moment. He knew the feds had been looking at someone— presumably him included—and he didn't know what the shakeout of Greg Connolly's murder would be.

We went through the same routine as previously. An attendant gave me clothes and a racquet, and I left my clothes in an unlocked locker. Once again, I had dodged a bullet with the decision to leave the F-Bird at home.

"What the hell, Charlie?" I said to him when we were on the racquetball court. It was an isolated court, but my voice echoed. It hardly seemed the place for this conversation. And he hadn't received confirmation yet from whoever it was who was going through my clothes, searching for an F-Bird.

"Let's just play," he said. So play we did. Each of us, in different ways, had a lot of steam to vent, and this was the perfect setting. I was sore at first for obvious reasons, but the flow of adrenaline helped, and soon enough I was playing like my life depended on it. I felt sorry for the little blue racquetball and for Charlie, if he had any pride in how he played, because I showed him no mercy whatsoever. The first game was over in less than twenty minutes. The second, less than fifteen.

Charlie was grabbing his knees. His gray shirt was stuck to his body with perspiration. I had to admit, I wouldn't have minded if he'd keeled over right there, but justice wouldn't work that way. In the end, I think it was good for him, the workout. "Three out of five," he suggested.

I was just getting loose. I shut him out in the third game.

He grumbled about it, but he had weightier issues on his mind than a racquetball game. We retired to the same parlor area for juice. He excused himself, presumably to meet with the person who had searched my clothes in the locker, and who would give me a clean bill of health. Probably Leather Jacket was not that person this time, or if he was, he wouldn't want me to see him.

When Charlie returned, it seemed that his load had been lightened slightly. Once again, I had won his trust. I wondered how many more times I would need to do that.

"Christ, this thing," he said to me, considering a glass of grapefruit juice. "You understand, it wasn't something I enjoyed doing. I mean, can we get past this? You wanna punch me in the face to make us even or something?"

"What, this thing that happened?" I asked. Never say it outright. A code of the corrupt—say it out loud as little as possible.

"Not something I enjoyed," Charlie said again. "I wish it hadn't happened."

"Hey, Charlie," I said, tapping him on the shoulder. I leaned into him. "First of all, just to reiterate a thought from last night: Fuck you. Second thing: Fuck you again. You do that to me again, you better kill me. Okay, glad that's settled." I took a breath. "I don't give a shit about some snitch. Greg made his bed. I just want to know what he told them. Is someone going to be knocking on my door?"

Charlie didn't smile—it was hardly the occasion—but I sensed that he liked my remarks. He didn't want me playing ethical watchdog or getting cold feet. I had reassured him on both counts.

"I think it's okay." He said it so quietly that the F-Bird wouldn't have picked it up even had I been wearing it.

"Put my mind at ease," I said.

"What Greg could offer the feds would be earlier stuff." Our heads were almost touching. "Mostly before you showed up. And then that stuff you did with us, early on. Before you and I branched out. Those few contracts with the buses and the prisons, that stuff."

I pondered that for a moment, then nodded. "The stuff you did with me, you can say I signed off. The lawyer signed off. What about the stuff before I came aboard?"

Charlie paused. "Don't worry about what happened before you came aboard."

"I'm worrying," I said.

"Don't."

I didn't think I was going to get what I wanted, but I took a shot, anyway. "Who else knows about what happened to Greg?"

"Nobody," he said. "Nobody knows."

"I need to know, Charlie. I need to know who to worry about."

"Worry about yourself. We'll be fine." He evened a hand over the table. "We lay low for now. Slow down our operation."

That much made sense. He wasn't going to give me any more information. I wasn't in a position to bargain.

"Until we see where this is going," he added. "You hear anything, you let me know."

"Okay."

"Let's hope you don't," he said.

What he didn't know is that I'd be hearing from the U.S. attorney's office very soon.

I spent the rest of the afternoon in my office, eating aspirin and doing not much of anything. Joel Lightner called me near five with some news.

"I found your good friend Kiko," he said.

THE NEXT DAY, AFTER WORK, I MET JOEL LIGHTNER for drinks. Note my use of the plural. It's never just one with Joel. The stated purpose was that Joel claimed to have some information for me. I'd asked him for two things. One was to find where Federico Hurtado—Kiko—laid his head every night. And the other was to give me the home address and marital status of Delroy Bailey, the owner and operator of Starlight Catering.

But Joel had added one reason for the conversation. He wanted to know what the hell was going on. He wanted to know why I needed this information. He said he wouldn't give me the information until I did so. I'd kept Joel at a distance out of an abundance of caution, not wanting him to get on the federal government's radar. And I found his paternalism annoying, however well-intentioned. But I was growing weary of all the deception, and I thought I could use Joel's perspective. That's how I explained it to myself, at least. It was also fair to say that I needed someone on whom I could unload all of this information.

He ordered a Maker's Mark, and I ordered a dirty martini. And I talked. He listened. I went through the whole thing. We went through two rounds of drinks before I had finished.

"So the Cannibals had nothing to do with Wozniak's murder," he said. "It was the Latin Lords. It was this guy Kiko who you're so interested in."

"Yeah."

"And I was wrong about Ernesto Ramirez," Joel said. "You were right. He *did* have some information. He and this friend of his, you called him Scarface? They'd heard from Kiko that Wozniak got whacked to 'cover up a connection to Delroy.' And they took that to mean Joey Espinoza."

"Right," I agreed.

"Joey Espinoza pulled strings at this state board, and he got his ex-brother-in-law Delroy a beverage contract over Wozniak's company. Wozniak was making noise. And so Joey needed to cover the thing up by having Wozniak killed. Joey covered up his connection to Delroy."

"Correct."

"And you figure, since Joey was already under Chris Moody's thumb when Wozniak was taken out, he must have had a partner. Someone else talked to Kiko."

"Right. You disagree?"

"No," he said. "You're probably right. Especially because then Ernesto got whacked, too, and it's hard to believe that was Joey Espinoza, with the feds watching his every move. So, okay, there was someone else. And you like this guy Charlie Cimino?"

"He seems like the best fit," I said. "But I'm not sold."

"You're not sold because of what happened to you the other night. When Charlie's crew did a little Guantánamo Bay routine on you."

"Right. The point being, I don't think they were *Charlie's* crew. I think someone else was in charge. Someone higher than Charlie."

"But the other night was all about rooting out snitches," said Joel. "It wasn't about Adalbert Wozniak or Ernesto Ramirez. Why do you put those things together?"

I shook my head. "Something tells me they're all related, Joel. I mean, someone in that group is willing to kill. There can't be that many people who fit that description. Plus, everything seems to revolve around that state board, the PCB. Charlie Cimino was asking me about my interest in Starlight Catering. The goons who interrogated me asked the same thing. That's the company the PCB gave the contract to over Wozniak. And Ernesto, the information he had was about Starlight, about its owner Delroy. And Greg Connolly was the chair of that board, even back when Starlight got that contract. No," I decided, "they're related. All roads lead to the same place. Whoever killed Greg Connolly killed Ernesto and Wozniak."

"And it's someone higher than Charlie," Joel said.

"I think so."

"Okay," he said, "so who's higher than Charlie?"

That was the thing. I could only think of two people who outranked Charlie Cimino. One was the chief of staff, Madison Koehler. The other was Governor Carlton Snow.

Both of them made some sense, I guess. I didn't know much about how the governor did business, but the chief of staff—Madison—was typically in the loop on everything. And it was hard to believe that the people who murdered one of the governor's oldest friends, Greg Connolly, would have done so without the big guy's consent.

Still, all of this was hard to believe. We weren't talking about hardball politics here. We were talking about murder.

"Someone in the inner circle," I said, keeping it vague.

"And now you're going into that inner circle."

"Now I am."

"Knowing that someone in that group is a killer. Having narrowly escaped being killed once, already."

"Well—"

"And if you aren't taking enough risks," Joel said, growing angry, "you also want to have a nice, friendly chat with the most hard-core assassin from the most hard-core street gang in the city."

"Maybe he's misunderstood, Joel. Maybe behind that assassin's veneer there's a sweet, cuddly kid just dying for a hug."

"Yeah, maybe you two could go for ice cream." The third round of drinks arrived. Joel took a healthy swallow of his scotch. I was on my third martini, and I'd been out of practice. My head and neck were beginning to feel pretty good.

We didn't talk for a while. Joel, on some level, had to be feeling a little bad about all of this. He'd been the *Almundo* investigator and he'd missed some things. I couldn't really blame him. It would have been very hard to catch this stuff with the information we had. But that would be little consolation to him. He prided himself on catching everything.

"So," he said, "you're doing all this—what—for Adalbert Wozniak?"

"No, I'm doing this for Ernesto Ramirez. He's dead because I wouldn't take no for an answer. I made someone nervous and he paid the price. A very sweet woman is now a widow, and two little kids are without their father, because I tried to force information out of him and made him a threat to someone."

Joel shook his head.

"And maybe I'm doing this because whoever killed Greg Connolly should face the music. I mean, Greg knew about me. He knew I was a fellow informant. But he didn't give me up. They tortured him, and he didn't give me up. I owe him, Joel. And anyway, I'm not letting those assholes get away with it."

Joel played around with this before reaching his conclusion. "You," he pronounced, "are fucking nuts."

"You aren't the first to say that."

"Kiko is the worst of the worst, J."

"I worked gang crimes, Joel. I know all about the guy."

He downed the remainder of his Maker's Mark. "You're just going to knock on his door and introduce yourself and tell him, 'I know you killed two people, and I know Joey was a part of it, but could you please tell me who Joey's partner was?' Yeah, that's a helluva plan you got there. You'll be dead before you say hello."

"Life is full of risk."

"Life is full of risk? Life is full of risk," Joel said to the waitress, who had noticed Joel's empty glass and stopped by. "I think Riley and I are going to have to do an intervention on you."

"You're overreacting," I said.

"Maybe I am," he agreed. "But you know what I'm *not* doing? I'm not giving you Kiko's fucking address."

Not wanting Joel to feel awkward about outpacing me in the alcohol department, which would be rude of me, I made quick work of my martini.

"Joel, I have to make this right. This guy's death is on me."

"No, it's not. You were just doing your job."

"Give me Kiko's address, Lightner. Don't make me dance on your face."

Lightner went quiet. His eyes narrowed, evidence of critical appraisal. I'd seen that look before. I didn't like that look.

"Jason, I don't know how else to say this."

"How about you say it after I've left the bar? I just need an address, Joel. I don't need a lecture."

"Yes, you do, my friend. You're not right. Okay? Take it from me. You are not right. It's like you're looking for trouble. Like you're looking—" He didn't finish the thought. He didn't need to.

"Oh, I'm suicidal now?"

"You know what? Maybe you are. I mean, this shit you're doing— this is for law enforcement. This is for people with badges—"

"Still got my old one."

"—and guns—"

"Got one of those, too."

"—and bulletproof vests."

"Two out of three ain't bad."

"Hey, shit for brains? I'm not joking." Lightner looked like he was going to get up and leave. I think he was but changed his mind. "Be serious for a second," he went on. "You know what I'm saying is right. You're chasing down killers and you're talking about strong-arming the most dangerous assassin in the most dangerous street gang in the city. Like you're going to walk away from that unharmed? You'd—" He caught himself, then decided to continue. "You'd never do this if your wife and daughter were still alive. Sorry to bring that up, but you wouldn't."

"So maybe I wouldn't."

He threw up his hands. "So your life doesn't mean anything anymore?"

"My life is different, that's all. Yeah, I'd be more cautious if I had Tal and Emily. That doesn't mean what I'm doing is wrong."

"Yeah? And what *are* you doing?" he asked. "Say Kiko gives you a name. He won't, but say he does. What are you going to do? Kill that guy? I mean, even if you get Kiko to talk, it's not like he's going to testify in court. You're never going to have the evidence you need to convict whoever this is. So what's the plan, J? When you figure out who killed Ernesto? You going to kill that person?"

I removed some money from my pocket and threw it on the table. This conversation was going nowhere.

"Just—all I'm saying, J—take a breath, cool down, and get yourself some help. You need some professional help."

"Hey, you're a professional. I'm seeking your help."

"You know what I mean."

"Give me the damn address, Lightner."

I knew he'd give it up. He was concerned for me, which was sugar-sweet of him, but the better part of him was as contrarian and stubborn as I. He pushed the piece of paper in front of me. "Let me go with you," he said. "When you talk to this asshole."

I made a show of considering it, but I wasn't going to involve Joel. Better just the two of us, I thought, Kiko and me.

The more I thought about it, the surer I became: These murders were connected. Whoever had Adalbert Wozniak and Ernesto Ramirez killed was responsible for Greg Connolly's murder, too. Solving one murder would solve them all.

I had two possible sources of information. I had Federico

Hurtado, the notorious Kiko. And I had the people surrounding the governor, if I could penetrate that inner circle.

I'd made an inroad on the first front: I now had Kiko's address.

If things went as planned, I'd be good on the second front very soon.

 TWO DAYS LATER, I CALLED CHARLIE AND TOLD HIM we had to meet. We found a restaurant in between our offices and got an early lunch.

"I just got a call from the U.S. attorney's office," I said.

I couldn't deny, on some level, a sense of satisfaction at watching Charlie's face go bleach white. "And?" he asked.

"They want to talk to me about the Higgins Sanitation contract," I said. "You remember that one? There were two lower bidders who I disqual—"

"I remember, I remember. And that's it?" he asked. "That's all they mentioned?"

"That's all they mentioned."

He fell back against the seat cushion. "Shit."

"I can defend that," I said. "I can."

He was quiet for a long time. I'm sure all kinds of thoughts entered his head. I wasn't sure if one of those thoughts included getting rid of me, a potential witness against him. A liability, like Tucker had said.

"You're going to talk to them?" he asked.

"Sure. Why would I take Five? It would look wrong."

"You need a lawyer." Charlie opened his cell phone and worked it. "Norman Hudzik," he said. "You know him?"

"Heard the name. Charlie, I can get my own—"

"You want Norm."

It was what I expected. Charlie would want someone he could trust to handle my representation when the U.S. attorney interviewed me. He wanted eyes and ears in there.

"Don't worry about his fee," Charlie said. "Don't worry about that."

"I wasn't."

"Charlie Cimino for Norman," he said into his cell phone. "Tell him to call as soon as possible. He has my number." He closed his phone. "Don't worry about this."

"I'm not worried."

"Maybe you should be," he said.

"You're not making any sense, Charlie."

"Shit. Shit." He drummed his fingers on the table. "We'll get together and talk to Norm. We'll put our heads together."

"We'll be fine," I said.

"Norm's good," Charlie said. "Norm's good."

We skipped lunch. Charlie was in no mood to eat. I went back to my office.

But first, I stopped in at Suite 410.

"Norman Hudzik," I said to Lee Tucker. "Now try not to fuck this up."

NORMAN HUDZIK HAD SPENT THIRTY YEARS REPRESENTing criminals, mostly of the white-collar and organized-crime variety. He was large in every way: Tall, heavy, with a baritone voice and a charismatic confidence. His hair was a mess of gray and black, a swooping part and too long in the back.

Circumstances notwithstanding, I liked him. I found myself more inclined toward the defense bar these days, probably because I was now a member. Something about standing up to power and being a contrarian found a safe harbor in my soul.

I'd told Norman that the prosecutor who had phoned me was Brian Ridgeway, someone with whom I wasn't acquainted. Norm had lit up at the mention of the name. "I go back with Brian. We tried *Capparelli* together. Brian's a dear friend. I can handle Brian."

That's why Chris Moody had picked Brian. We wanted someone Hudzik knew, someone with whom he would feel comfortable. The way I'd heard it, Brian Ridgeway did not exactly consider Norm a "dear" friend, but the relationship was cordial. Good enough. It made Hudzik happy and it made Charlie happy, as the three of us had sat in Norm's office yesterday. We'd spent several hours, during which time Norm Hudzik had given me about twenty ways to say, "I don't recall."

Now we sat in the U.S. attorney's reception area, Norm and I, waiting for the meeting with Assistant U.S. Attorney Brian Ridgeway.

"I think I know this guy!" Norm bellowed, as Ridgeway appeared from a doorway.

"Norm! Good to see you. Good morning, Mr. Kolarich. Brian Ridgeway."

"Nice to meet you," I said.

We went back to a conference room, where prosecutor and defense attorney spent ten minutes catching up, while I bided my time. Norm did most of the talking, which was good, because I wasn't sure this guy Ridgeway was a very good bullshit artist.

"Jason and I were a little surprised by the call," Norm said, settling in. "What does Jason Kolarich have to tell you?"

"Well, it's just one of those things I gotta say I did." Ridgeway waved a conciliatory hand. "Well, here." He slid a document in front of me. It was the memo I had written for Charlie, disqualifying the two bidders who should have received the sanitation contract instead of Higgins. It was the final version, the one I rewrote to impress Charlie and gain his trust.

"Mr. Kolarich, did you write this memo?"

"Call me Jason."

"I'd prefer to call you Mr. Kolarich."

"I'd prefer you called me Jason."

Ridgeway looked over at Hudzik, like *What the hell?*

"The answer is yes," I said. "I gave this to the chairman of the PCB, my client. That makes this privileged, last I checked."

Ridgeway hemmed and hawed a moment for good measure. "Greg Connolly gave it to us. So don't worry about a privilege."

"Well, Brian, I'm a lawyer, so I'm going to worry about little things like attorney-client privilege, if it's okay with you."

Ridgeway paused, shooting another look at Hudzik.

"He told you that the client gave the document to him," Norm said, putting a hand on my arm. "So let's go ahead and answer."

I thought for a moment, or more accurately, I pretended to think. "Okay," I said. "Yes, I wrote it."

"Who told you to write it?"

I shrugged. "It would have been a normal part of my job. I was an outside counsel to the PCB."

"Did anyone—well, here. Did anyone talk to you about your conclusions?"

I shrugged again. "Not that I can remember. You mean, someone disagreeing with something I wrote?"

"Or discussing your conclusions before you made them?"

"*Before* I reached my conclusion?" I drew back. "You mean, like, telling me what to say?"

"That's what I mean."

"Absolutely not. Absolutely not. I would quit first." I explained to him, briefly, how it was my job to review the qualifications for winning bidders and to memorialize my conclusions in writing. I told him that we had a file on every bidder, including its history with the state, any previous lawsuits or other concerns related to their work, and the like.

"After reviewing everything," I said, "I reached my conclusion entirely on my own. One of the bidders that was DQ'd might disagree with it, but they always disagree, and they usually sue. But nobody whispered in my ear. Nobody told me to say this or that. I stand completely by what I've written here, and the decision was mine and only mine."

Ridgeway nodded, like that was what he expected me to say. "Okay, good enough. I appreciate you coming in."

I looked at my lawyer and back at Ridgeway. "That's it?" I asked.

Norm said, "This is why he came down here?"

"Oh, you know how it goes," said Ridgeway. "Gotta play out every string."

"What's the string?" I asked. "I don't like anyone questioning my integrity."

"No, no, it's nothing like—" Ridgeway raised his hands. He looked at both of us, like he wanted to say more.

"Any chance you can enlighten us?" Norm asked. "It doesn't sound like there's much to this."

Ridgeway let out a laugh. "That's an understatement."

"Oh, c'mon, Brian. You brought us all the way down here."

Ridgeway paused, then out of the corner of his mouth, he said to Norm, "Off the record?"

"Sure, of course."

"This guy who runs this state board—Connolly? Greg Connolly? You guys friends?"

"Hardly knew him," I said.

"Well, my take? He's one of these Johnny-come-lately crusaders. I mean, off the record."

"No problem," said Norm. "Completely off the record."

"I think he didn't like how he was treated over there, for some reason. So he comes to us and shows us this thing and tells us he wants to be a whistle-blower. He tells us there might be something screwy with this contract. What he *didn't* tell us is that an outside lawyer had performed a legal analysis of the whole thing and signed off." He nodded in my direction. "A lawyer who we know around here as being pretty good, even if some people are mad about the outcome of a particular case."

I thought he was laying it on a little thick. But as I thought about it, this guy was vouching for my credibility by referencing Hector's trial. The feds thought that my word counted for something, he was telling Norm Hudzik, which of course would get back to Charlie. It would make me more valuable still.

"Anyway," Ridgeway said, "this guy Connolly, he's something else. He wants to wear a wire and be the guy who shakes up the system. Meanwhile," he said, nodding toward me, because he figured I already heard the news, "on his way home from work, Mr. Crusader likes to go over to Seagram Hill and get yanked off for five dollars a pop. He gets jumped out there and killed."

Norm, who of course knew of Connolly's demise, feigned surprise.

"So," Ridgeway said, "not that there ever really was anything here, but with Connolly gone—I mean, I had to follow up. Now I have. Sorry for your troubles. You can keep the memo if you like. I won't be needing it."

Norm Hudzik, for his part, bought in all the way. He was laughing that gregarious laugh of his as soon as we walked out of the federal building. "Ridgeway's okay, like I told you," he said. "They've got nothing, my boy. It's a dead end. That memo you wrote locked it down, if there was any doubt. You want to tell Charlie, or should I? This will make his week."

"He'll want to hear it from you," I said.

"Sure." Hudzik eagerly agreed. Everyone likes delivering welcome news. It would give Hudzik the chance to embellish, to make himself the big hero in his version. "You're a real ballbuster, y'know that, kid? 'I'll worry about little things like the attorney-client privilege.' I love it." He slapped me on the shoulder. "Be well, son."

When I got back to my office, I went down to Suite 410. I opened the door and found Lee Tucker. I could see he'd already heard from Brian Ridgeway. He had a big smile on his face.

"They bought it," I said. "I'm in."

"Ridgeway said you acted like an asshole."

"It came naturally."

Tucker drummed his fingers on the table and shook his head. "Well, let's see what Mr. Cimino has to say."

*　　*　　*

WE DIDN'T HAVE TO wait long. I had dinner that night with Charlie. He was like a little kid, giddy with relief. As he now saw it, the murder of Greg Connolly was being chalked up as a garden-variety mugging in a very seedy part of town. The corruption probe, initiated by Greg Connolly, was a dead end. He would sleep well tonight.

The pair of three-hundred-dollar bottles of Cabernet would help him sleep, too.

"You were a real ballbuster, Norm said," Charlie told me. "He said you gave that prosecutor an earful." He winked at me. "I could learn to like you, kid."

I decided to say as little as possible, else I might screw something up with the mild buzz I was enjoying. It was becoming difficult to keep up with the layers of deception. The man with whom I was dining on New York strip steaks and expensive Cab was probably a killer. And he was now feeling at ease, courtesy of a fake interview with a federal prosecutor, in which my fake legal memorandum, used to perpetrate a fraud, was being used to exonerate the two of us.

I didn't know whom to trust. I just had to make sure I could keep trusting myself.

"You're the golden boy," he said, slurring his words. "Norm said, when these guys saw your name on the memo, they figured everything was on the up-and-up. You bought yourself some credibility with Hector's case."

I could see that our little charade in the U.S. attorney's office had worked perfectly.

"But this thing we have," Charlie went on, "better we stop it, all the same. No point in pushing our luck."

It's what I expected Charlie to say. The heat was off as far as he knew, but Charlie had been very close to the flame and hadn't enjoyed it. He'd be back someday, in his mind, but he was still feeling the aftereffects and would stay on the sidelines for the foreseeable future. If he hadn't suggested we abort our current scheme, I would have done so. But better that it was his idea.

"I told Maddie she can use you."

I looked at him. "Madison Koehler?"

"Yeah, that position she offered you, right?" He leaned into me with typical intoxicated bluntness. "Didn't think I knew about that? Well, I know you stiff-armed her, but go ahead and do it. It'll be good for you."

Translation: It would be good for *him*. He'd get the finder's credit on Jason Kolarich, I figured. *I told Maddie she can use you.* I was still his guy, but he was loaning me out.

"Help 'em work the system," Charlie said. "He gets elected to a full term, we can really make us some dough. There's a fuckin' sea of money out there for us, Jason. A sea of it."

Not where you're going, I wanted to say. I wanted to ask him if he felt the least bit bad about Greg Connolly's death. I wanted to reach over the table and smack the drunken grin off his face. But I was still in role. I could down a bottle of wine and stay in role. I could be tied up, with a gun pointed at me and a knife about to slice off my finger, and stay in role.

I had found my calling. I was a liar. A fake. A pretender. And now, for my final act, I was going to help take down a sitting governor.

THE GOVERNOR

March 2008

64 CHRIS MOODY STOOD BEFORE A POSTER BOARD THAT looked exactly like the kinds of flow charts the FBI used for organized crime, or we at the county attorney's office used to make for the street-gang hierarchy. In this case, the chart bore the heading KITCHEN CABINET, and it listed the people closest to Governor Carlton Snow.

"Madison Koehler, chief of staff," said Chris Moody. "You've already made her acquaintance. She's run several political campaigns around the country. Moved here to work on the mayor's last race. Governor Snow hired her when they took the 'lieutenant' off his title and he knew he'd be running for a full term. Divorced, one kid in college. She's tough. She doesn't suffer incompetence or disloyalty. She fires people all the time, in fact."

"Point being," Lee Tucker said, "play nice with her or you'll be out on your ass and no good to anybody."

They knew, presumably from Greg Connolly, that Madison had propositioned me for this job but they didn't know the breadth or scope of that encounter. They didn't know that I'd seen Madison Koehler perform feats of gymnastic agility that would make women half her age green with envy.

Below Madison, there were several people on the same level. "Brady MacAleer," said Moody, pointing to the name in the first square. "'Mac' or 'Brady Mac.' Chief of government administration. Grew up on the north side of the city. He ran a labor union and then went to work for the city clerk's office under Snow. Followed him to the lieutenant governor's office. Always a paid position, always hard to pin down what it was he did to earn that paycheck. He's one of the operators. Favors and fixes, they like to say."

I wasn't sure what that meant, specifically. Moody seemed to pick up on my reaction.

"Fundraising. Jobs for cronies. Side deals for contributors. Opposition research. Not a lot different from Cimino, except Cimino has outside wealth. Brady Mac is no financier. You'll probably deal with him a lot. Especially with Cimino cooling his heels a bit."

"Got it."

"Next: William Peshke. 'Pesh' to everybody. His title is 'special adviser to the governor.' That's just an excuse to get him a six-figure salary on the government's dime. He's the policy guy. He's known Governor Snow since college. He wanted to be running the campaign. He doesn't get along so well with Madison Koehler but the governor likes him. So there's a turf battle there."

"Okay."

After Brady MacAleer and William Peshke were three names I recognized. Greg Connolly, now deceased. Charlie Cimino. And Hector Almundo.

Moody paused only briefly over Connolly's name. "All respect to the dead, the way we saw it, Greg was just riding coattails. He didn't provide much value. He ran that board, but he just followed orders. Charlie, obviously—but we don't expect much from him, right?"

"Right," I agreed. "But you never know. I'm not sure he can help himself. I'm not sure he can stay away for long."

"Our thinking as well," Moody said. "Either way, we expect him to stay close to the action. You stay away too long, they forget about you, that kind of thing."

I fully concurred in that assessment. Charlie was looking at me as one of his guys, and that's why it was so important to him that I be near the action, if he couldn't be.

I looked at the final name. Hector Almundo.

"You and I would have different opinions on this one," said Moody.

I wasn't so sure about that. My take on Hector Almundo probably didn't vary all that much from the federal government's view. I assumed they were right when they alleged that Hector had orchestrated that shakedown by the Columbus Street Cannibals for campaign contributions. I was relatively sure, in fact, that Hector would shake down his own mother if it suited his purposes.

"Why's he a part of this inner circle?" I asked. I'd had my own thoughts on this question. But I wanted to hear Moody's.

He shook his head. "A Latino face for the Latino voters, I guess? Politics is not my game," he added, using a tone he might normally reserve for mass murderers.

"We don't know," said Lee Tucker. "Chris's guess is a pretty good one. He'll be out front getting out the vote in his community. He's not the brightest of the bunch."

"He's a political animal," said Moody. "But his utility to the governor? Not clear."

"Why does Snow need help with the Latino vote?" I asked. "I thought that was a reliable Democratic voting bloc."

Moody shrugged. "Couldn't tell you. But even if that's true, there's the primary."

Right. That was a good point. Carlton Snow still had to win a primary. The secretary of state, a Democrat named Willie Bryant, was seeking the nomination as well. He had some money and he had name recognition. But nobody had ever called him Governor.

"Do you know what they have in mind for me?" I asked.

Moody took a seat. I could see that the answer was no. "Greg Connolly—you can probably imagine—he wasn't the world's greatest informant. He let on like he knew every step the governor took, but we were pretty sure he was left out of some of the meetings. The truth is," he said, like it was a concession, "until you, we weren't making much headway."

I imagined that the federal government had entertained high hopes for Mr. Gregory Connolly, being one of the governor's oldest friends. Seems that what they got instead was a tag-along, a hanger-on. He was perfect for the role he served in the administration, a loyal follower who wielded power over the awarding of state contracts exactly in the manner he was dictated. But dictated by whom? Charlie Cimino, to be sure—but the feds were hoping the direction came from higher.

"Greg couldn't put the governor next to all those bogus contracts, could he?" I asked. "All the stuff the PCB and Charlie were doing. You can't link the governor to any of that, can you?"

Moody paused. He hadn't been particularly good about sharing. I understood his thinking to a point. I'd worked with undercovers. Sometimes, it's better they not know certain things. I would be cross-examined heavily at Charlie's trial. Everything that Chris Moody, Lee Tucker, and I discussed would be fair game. The less information I had from the feds, the better. But there were limits.

"Listen, guys," I said, "you're going to have to be a little more forthcoming with me. You didn't tell me Greg Connolly was your guy, and it could have cost me my life. You want me to do this, I'll do it, but I need to know what you know and what you have in terms of people and resources. I need to know that."

Moody looked over at Tucker, but this was Moody's call. Our relationship had defrosted a little over the last week. We'd lost an informant, and that wasn't something they took lightly. And now I was volunteering to keep going at considerable risk to my ability to continue breathing.

Moody nodded to Lee Tucker, who left the room. That made sense. Lee Tucker would be a witness at trial. He'd be an especially valuable witness if I somehow didn't survive through trial. So it was better that Lee not be a part of this conversation, on which he could be cross-examined.

"Start with informants," I said.

"Just you," Moody said. "You and Connolly. Now just you."

"Bugs," I said.

Moody shook his head. "We had a bug in Greg Connolly's office with his consent. He locked the door when he wasn't in there. We tapped his cell phone with his consent. He was the only one who used that phone. That's it, Counselor."

"Wires," I said.

"F-Birds," Moody answered. "You and Connolly."

"Tell me what you have on these guys so far."

Moody pushed himself out of his chair. "If Greg Connolly could put Governor Snow, or Madison Koehler, or any of those people next to those shady contract awards, you think I'd let you risk your life going in there?"

"Yes," I said.

He watched for a beat before a reluctant smile emerged on his face. "Greg was a talker. A blowhard. He answered to Cimino. Not the governor. Not the chief of staff. He talked a good game to us, but he couldn't give us anyone else. We had some decent stuff on Cimino before you arrived and now we have Cimino over a barrel, thanks to you. I still have half a mind to pinch him right now and see if he wants to deal. At least I won't lose another cooperator."

That cooperator being me. I was glad to see he was viewing me as a statistic on his scorecard, as opposed to, say, a living, breathing human being.

"I don't have them," he concluded, drawing circles on the desk with his finger. "Not the governor or anyone else. Just a gut call—which I'd take to my grave, by the way—that there was no way Charlie Cimino and Greg Connolly were doing all this stuff without the governor's knowledge." He looked up at me. "You don't think Cimino would deal with us?"

"No," I said. "Maybe eventually. I mean, most of them do eventually, right? But his initial reaction would be to tell you to go scratch, so you'd have to arrest him and make it public, and everyone would clam up. Down the road, looking over the charges and counting the number of months he'll spend in the pen, he might decide to cooperate and finger the governor, but you'd have no tapes, no anything but Cimino's word against the governor's. And they'd hire a lawyer like me and argue that Cimino and Connolly were doing this stuff for personal enrichment, getting side consulting contracts and hoping to curry favor with the governor without his direct knowledge of what they were doing. The governor would do the classic ostrich defense and even if you got an ostrich instruction—which I'm not sure a judge would give you here—the defense would have a strong argument. Cimino's damaged goods, looking at twenty years in the pen, versus the word of public officials who have no record. That, Christopher, is why you need me."

I wasn't telling Moody anything he didn't already know, that he hadn't already calculated twenty different ways. "That still doesn't mean it's a good idea that you do this."

"One of those people ordered Greg Connolly's murder," I said. "And mine, if I hadn't convinced them I was clean. As a general rule, I don't take kindly to people who try to kill me."

Moody still didn't seem convinced, but he'd obviously decided to move forward with our plan. Because what I'd said was true. He was out of options. I was his best, and possibly only, way to move beyond Charlie Cimino.

"The minute it gets too hot, you tell us," he said. "No foolin'."

"You'll be the first."

Moody walked over to me and extended a hand. It was a gesture typically reserved for friendly acquaintances, so I wasn't sure what to do. I decided to shake it.

"Don't get dead," he said.

65 THE FIRST DAY OF MY NEW JOB BEGAN WITH THE MIND-numbing rigmarole of filling out forms of every possible color. I was placed in an office that was standard government size, standard government décor. After an hour of providing the state a bunch of information I'd already provided when I signed up with the PCB, I was ready for a drink.

"There he is." Hector Almundo waltzed through the door, beaming. Hector looked better every time I'd seen him since the trial, as his reincarnation continued. He was back on a winning team, climbing a ladder again.

And he looked the part, as always. He was wearing an expensive coffee-colored suit with an orange tie and another of those tiepins he always wore, even during his trial when we told him to dress down. Hector didn't know how to dress down. Me, I was wearing my standard dark suit, white shirt, conservative tie. Expensive, admittedly, but not flashy. No tiepins or pocket squares or French cuffs, nothing extravagant, unless you counted the elaborate eavesdropping device I was wearing inside my coat pocket.

After we shook hands, he sat down next to me. "You're getting here just in time," he said. "Big things happening. We'll need you."

Because I couldn't think of anything better to say, I asked, "How's it going?"

Hector moved his head in virtually every direction, showing worry and excitement. "The thing with Greg. You heard about that?"

"Heard about it," I said, which was an understatement.

"Yeah, that put everyone on their heels for a few days."

I didn't know who knew the truth about what happened to Greg Connolly. There was no chance that Charlie Cimino would be generous with that kind of information. But my working theory was that someone was in on it with him from above. Hector didn't really qualify as "above" Charlie, as far as I knew. But the truth was, I didn't know. That's why I was here.

"But you can't slow down, y'know?" Hector went on. "Willie Bryant's been making some headway. He could hurt us downstate. He's getting some money now, too. He was a slow starter, but he's building steam. So it's like, you feel terrible about Greg, but you have to move on. Bryant sure as hell isn't going to slow down."

Until last night, when I looked him up on the Internet, I couldn't have picked Secretary of State Willie Bryant out of a lineup. Before his two terms as secretary of state, he'd been a state representative from a downstate county adjacent to the one where our last governor, Langdon Trotter, came from. He even looked a little like Trotter, the rugged hunter look, which probably shouldn't matter but obviously did. From what I could gather, he fell into the category of conservative Democrat, which meant he liked guns as much as trial lawyers.

I looked up some polling numbers online and saw that Carlton Snow seemed to have an edge over Willie Bryant, 37 percent to 29 percent, with a healthy undecided vote.

A young woman appeared in the doorway and knocked gently on the door. "Excuse me. Mr. Kolarich, the chief of staff would like to see you."

"I'll take him," Hector said.

The office of the chief of staff was at the corner of my hallway. The number of people filtering in and out of Madison Koehler's office, while we waited patiently outside, could have filled a small convention center. Most of the people were young and fresh and ambitious. I envied them not because I lacked ambition myself but because I'd once had it in vast supply. It went off the cliff with my wife and daughter. I had something akin to ambition now, a mission to be sure, but not one of personal advancement. It allowed me a detachment that would probably serve me well.

The assistant outside Madison's office called to me. "The chief will see you now."

The chief? You gotta be kidding me.

Hector stood up with me. "She likes being called Chief," he whispered.

Madison Koehler had a spacious corner office, sufficient for a conference table at one end and windows showing the north and east side of our commercial district. She was seated behind a steel desk she must have imported because it wasn't government-issue, or if it was, the taxpayers were spending too much money on such things and I might have to write a letter to my state senator. Or to my governor. Or to Charlie Cimino.

The desk was busy in terms of the sheer volume of paper but immaculate to a fault, everything neatly categorized and the stacks lined up with razor precision. I could live my whole life, and I'll never understand how people can be so tidy.

"How we doing, Chief?" Hector called out.

"Good . . . good." She looked up from whatever she'd been reading, wearing those glasses I had last seen when Madison was lying on a bed, wearing my shirt and her panties. "Jason," she said.

"Madison," I said.

"Sit, sit."

She returned to the document on her desk. If she was still busy with whatever that item was, she could have kept us waiting outside. But she'd invited me in so I could sit, compliantly, while she showed me I wasn't that important. I just love office politics.

"Senator, I'll just need Jason right now," she said. She momentarily looked up at Hector. "If that's all right."

Hector, no stranger to politics of any kind, looked a bit out of sorts, a clenched jaw and sullen expression. But he didn't put up a fight. "Sure thing," he said.

Having expelled Senator Almundo from the room in a probably unnecessary display of power, Madison kept working on the document in front of her for another few minutes. It was hard for me to look at her without recalling our last encounter. Nothing was going to happen in this office, but that didn't stop my mind from traveling down salacious corridors.

"Okay," she said, looking up. She appraised me for a moment, then slid a piece of paper across her desk. On a piece of stationery that reminded everyone she was the governor's chief of staff was written a list of names down one column, across from each of which were job titles and names of various administrative agencies. Nine names, nine different jobs.

"Those people need those jobs," she said.

I didn't know what to do with this, so I just waited. Madison had returned to writing something but, after a healthy spell, looked over her glasses at me. "Those people," she repeated, "need those jobs."

It was obvious that I required more information. I don't particularly enjoy being set up to look stupid. Call it a character flaw.

"Then hire them," I said.

She froze a stare on me, but when I said nothing further, she elaborated. "There are some people who would argue they have a superior right to those positions over the people on this list," she said. "Veterans, for one. We have a veterans' preference for most positions. Is any of this"—she rolled her hand—"sounding even vaguely familiar to you?"

"Not even vaguely," I said. "But I'll figure it out."

"Oh, *would* you?" She delivered it with mock sweetness, returning to the notes in front of her. I wasn't sure what she was writing. My money was on *I am not a pleasant person*. "It would be very helpful . . . if you could do your job . . . so I could do mine." She finished what she was writing, put down her pen, and looked at me. "Mac will give you details."

Mac, meaning Brady MacAleer, presumably.

"One other thing," Madison said, peering over her glasses at me. "Have you heard of Antwain Otis?"

I shook my head.

"He's on death row. He's scheduled to be executed in a few days. The governor's meeting with some people tomorrow seeking clemency. I want you there. The meeting's—it was supposed to be tomorrow but it might have moved back one day. My assistant has the file. She'll know."

"What did he do? Antwain Otis."

Madison spoke as she rearranged files on her desk. "He killed two people, eleven years ago. Now he's part of the prison ministry. He's made a name for himself. Too bad he hadn't found God before he killed a woman and her son. Read the file, handle the meeting, and then help Pesh with anything the press might want on this. We want everyone to know that the governor gave this careful consideration."

"Okay. You want me to evaluate the clemency petition?"

She stopped what she was doing and stared at me a moment, like she would a slow child. "Make sure the governor has all the support he needs for his decision. The IRRB already recommended denying the clemency petition. Some of our staff attorneys—leftovers from the Trotter administration—also reviewed it and recommended denial. There should be plenty there for you to choose from."

Ah. I understood now. If she wanted me to pull from the recommendations from the Inmate Review and Release Board, as well as our internal staff lawyers, both of which had recommended denying the petition, it wasn't hard to see which way she wanted me to fall.

"We're denying the petition," I said.

"Of course we are. He killed a mother and child. Oh, here it is." She found some document she was looking for and scribbled a note on it. "Thank you," she said.

I wasn't really sure why she was thanking me.

She looked over her glasses at me again. "Thank you. That's all."

Ah. I showed myself out. It was a slightly more polite excusal than Hector had received. I wasn't sure why Hector had to be excused at all, now that I thought about it, but I was glad for it. I was wearing a wire, after all, and I was hoping that I could spare Hector from the fun that would ensue. It seemed that Hector wasn't in on some of the things I would be asked to help out with—meaning the illegal stuff.

When I returned to my office, I had a message to call Charlie Cimino on his cell.

"The honeymoon's over," he told me. "Six o'clock for dinner."

66 I MET CHARLIE OUTSIDE THE STATE BUILDING. WE jumped in a cab and headed north.

"You're getting in just in time," Charlie said to me. "We've needed a lawyer for a long time."

"You guys are short on lawyers? They're not exactly hard to come by, Charlie."

"Not one of our own." He looked at me. "You've got to appreciate, Carl's only been the governor a year. And it flew by. Most of the people working for him, they're Lang Trotter's people."

"Republicans?" I asked.

"Well, that, yes—but more to the point, not Carl's guys. I mean, we had to hit the ground running. Trotter didn't give a lot of notice before he jumped ship to D.C. It took Carl two months to even find Madison—and until Maddie arrived, these guys didn't know their asses from their elbows. Remember, Carl was city clerk and then governor lite. He never had anything to do. All of a sudden he's governor. These guys"—Charlie chuckled at the memory—"these guys looked around at each other like, 'What do we do now?' I mean, they're *still* in catch-up mode. And now we have an election upon us," Charlie added. "He never hired a lawyer of his own—not at the top level, and definitely not someone with your talent."

All of this, I assumed, would be music to Chris Moody's ears, when he listened to the contents of the F-Bird in my coat pocket. The criminal schemes—whatever they were—were still in their infancy, waiting to happen right before the federal government's eyes.

We arrived ten minutes later at Travelers, an old-school steak house just over the river. The place was crazy busy with the professional set, but that didn't stop Charlie from parting the crowd and walking through the restaurant to a reserved area in the back, separated by space and a rope from the rest of the restaurant. There, a man was seated at a lone table, nursing a glass of scotch. I'd never met the guy, but I'd seen his photo stuck to a piece of poster board in Suite 410.

"Brady MacAleer, Jason Kolarich," Charlie said.

"Call me Mac." *Favors and fixes,* Moody had said about Brady MacAleer. He certainly looked the part of a fixer. Big through the chest, short legs, a weathered face that was square and flat and had been through some scrapes. He'd lost most of his hair to the north and cropped it to the east and west in a military buzz. His eyes were small and bloodshot and hostile in their appraisal. I was a new guy, an unknown, and guys like him didn't like unknowns.

I knew his story, more or less, before he'd said ten words. Drank his liquor straight, had a short fuse, viewed the world in an uncompromising fashion. You were with him or against him, nothing in between. The kind of guy you'd prefer to have on your side in a scrape. A pit bull. He reminded me of guys I played ball with. I didn't like most of the guys I played ball with.

Charlie talked me up to Mac but followed the felons' etiquette of keeping it vague. He imparted no material information to Mac but basically told him that I had proven myself useful in delicate matters. "He could walk up to you, pull out his dick, piss all over your leg, and convince you it was raining," Charlie said of me. I was supposed to be flattered. It wasn't lost on me that Charlie's description was almost exactly how I would describe my father.

"Yeah, I heard all about Jason." Mac took another swallow of his scotch. He wasn't returning the compliment. He liked his circle of friends small and airtight.

A plate of fried calamari arrived without warning. Charlie and I ordered drinks.

"So here it is," said Charlie. "This thing is coming down to the unions. Two—"

"We gotta wait for the queen," said Mac.

Charlie looked at him, annoyed at the interruption. "I'm giving him background."

"Queenie said to wait for her."

"I'm giving him background, so when she arrives, we can dive right in. That okay with you?" Charlie made it clear he wasn't talking to an equal, at least not in his mind. Charlie wasn't a government employee. He was a capitalist. A successful one. He'd made a calculation that money could be made by getting close to people in government, but that didn't make him a bootlicker. And that, I could see, was how he ultimately viewed Brady MacAleer, an unsophisticated lackey. Mac had the governor's trust, apparently, which bought him a seat at the table, but Charlie wasn't going to pretend they were on the same level.

MacAleer fished a stringy piece of the calamari off the plate, his silence indicating acquiescence.

"The race is tightening," said Charlie. "Willie Bryant's making headway. It's going to come down to media and organization. Media is all about having the cash to buy airtime. Organization is all about the unions."

Okay. I was following so far. A union endorsement bought a lot of votes from the rank-and-file members.

"But it buys more than that," Charlie said. "It buys workers. It buys foot soldiers on Election Day. We need people to get our voters to the polls. We need the union people."

"Got it."

Charlie made a peace sign with his fingers. "Two unions that matter in this state. The government employees and the laborers. The IBCL—the International Brotherhood of Commercial Laborers. And SLEU."

"Slew?" I asked.

"S-L-E-U. State and Local Employees United. The IBCL and SLEU haven't made endorsements yet. They haven't picked us or Bryant. We get the laborers and employees, and we win on organization. We already have more money than Bryant. If we have the organization, it's game over."

"Gardner goes back with Bryant," said Mac.

"Gary Gardner," Charlie explained to me. "He runs the IBCL."

"It's a wonder he hasn't already gone with Willie," said Mac.

"He hasn't gone with Willie because we've been begging him to hold off," said Charlie. "These guys—Gardner with the Laborers, Rick Harmoning with SLEU—they're playing kingmakers right now. They know it. See, here's the problem—"

Our drinks arrived. Mine was wrong; it was a straight martini without the splash of olive juice, but it still tasted good so I didn't complain.

"Nobody knows us, is the problem," Mac said, filling in for Charlie. "Willie Bryant was a state rep for ten years and secretary of state for eight. He's been around the block with all these guys. The governor's only had a year of being governor, compared to eighteen years in state government for Willie." He shrugged. "Nobody knows us, is the problem, you wanna hear it straight. Only thing keeping us in the game is the cash."

That sounded like an accurate assessment. Governor Snow was apparently outpacing Secretary of State Bryant in the fundraising department. It kept him viable and gave him credibility. The unions, presumably, would want to go with a winner. They pick a loser, then next time their endorsement is a little less important and, thus, so are they. That's how I would view it, if I were making the decisions.

"What about the politics?" I asked. "Does one have better policies than the other?"

Both of these guys smirked. I could see it was an irrelevant consideration. Charlie said, "The unions want a Democrat, but it probably wouldn't make much difference between the governor and Bryant."

"They're deciding next week," Mac said. "Both of 'em. And my intel says both of 'em are leaning towards Willie."

Chris Moody, back in Suite 410, had mentioned that Mac used to be a union official, before he joined up with Carlton Snow. Sounded like he still had his ear to the wall over there.

"So we're down to last options," said Charlie.

"So how does the governor win the unions' endorsement?" I asked.

"Hey, Chief." MacAleer got to his feet, addressing Madison Koehler, who was walking past the rope into our segregated spot in the back.

"Hey, Madison." Charlie nodded.

"Gentlemen." Madison set her purse on the floor next to her and took the seat opposite me, between Charlie and Mac. A waiter quickly came over. She ordered a glass of Cabernet. Then she looked right at me. "We already know how to win the unions' endorsement," she said. "We just need you to help us do it."

THE THREE MALE CARNIVORES AT THE TABLE ORDERED steaks of various sizes. Madison ordered a piece of fish. The Caesar salads and bottle of wine arrived as Madison laid out her game plan.

"The name Warren Palendech mean anything to you?" she asked me.

It did. I'd read about him the same day the papers covered Greg Connolly's death. Justice Palendech was a member of the state supreme court until he died from a heart attack, at roughly the same time Greg Connolly was found on Seagram Hill, facedown and pants down, about ten days ago.

Ever the quick learner, I noted, "The governor appoints a replacement until the next election."

"Exactly."

"But that's not much time," I said. "The general election is this November."

She looked at Charlie. "It seems our lawyer needs some schooling on the law."

Apparently she knew something I didn't, which wasn't surprising when it came to the laws governing our elections. But I didn't appreciate her comment and wasn't going to bite.

"It's too close in time to the next election," she explained. "Not enough time for a primary before the 2008 general election. So the law says the newly appointed justice gets to stay on until 2010. That's basically two years before he or she has to run in a primary. Two years of incumbency. Two years of fundraising as a sitting supreme court justice. That person is going to have a huge leg up."

Okay, so it was a valuable commodity. I still wasn't all the way there.

"The name George Ippolito mean anything to you?" she asked.

I laughed reflexively. Judge Ippolito sat in the trial court up in the city. I'd tried a couple of cases in front of him in my time, pleasant experiences none of them. He was what the ACAs called a "yeller." The moniker said it all. His judicial temperament fell somewhere on the spectrum between Joseph Stalin on a bad day and a wounded grizzly protecting her young.

Madison couldn't be thinking what I thought she was thinking.

"You know him," she said. She didn't show a trace of apology, or equivocation, in her expression.

"The governor's going to appoint George Ippolito to the supreme court?" I asked.

"He's considering it," said Madison. "The word we have back is that he's tough on crime. Does that sound right?"

I looked away, incredulous. I couldn't believe I was hearing this. George Ippolito was not the dimmest judge I had stood before, but he was far from the brightest. And that was to say nothing of our state appellate court, which held several excellent jurists.

"I suppose," I conceded. "Ippolito's tough on anyone who gets within fifty feet of him."

"No-nonsense," she said.

"Unstable," I answered.

"Independent."

"Okay, but there are plenty of judges who are tough on crime. Why George—"

Oh. The picture was filling in now. Dots connecting. One plus one equaling two.

"Ippolito's connected to one of these union guys," I gathered.

"George Ippolito is Gary Gardner's brother-in-law," said Mac.

I suddenly lost my appetite for the Caesar salad. So this was how it would work: Gary Gardner gives the governor the endorsement of the laborers' union, and the governor puts his brother-in-law on the state's highest court.

The governor was going to sell a seat on the state supreme court.

"Have we offended your delicate sensibilities?" Madison asked.

Yes, as a matter of fact, she had. I wasn't so naïve to think that advancement up the judicial ladder was tied, in a direct linear fashion, to merit. Judges were elected in our state, after all; it was impossible to separate out politics. But this—this was too much.

On the other hand, my job wasn't to talk Madison out of this. I wished it was, but in fact the opposite was true. I had to recover quickly here and get on board. If I started showing reluctance, they'd drop me like a bad habit.

"Look, I won't lie to you," I said, which felt ironic given my undercover role. "George Ippolito is a terrible choice for the supreme court. Terrible. But my point isn't that *I* think that. It's that everyone will think that. The bar associations will go ape-shit. Lawyers who practice before him do not hold him in high regard, let's put it that way. I think there'll be blowback."

"So?" Madison challenged. "Governor Snow doesn't need a bunch of lawyers to stop him from appointing a judge who's tough on crime."

It was a decent political response, I suppose. The public wasn't fawning over lawyers these days. Going against them might be a badge of honor. It sounded like Madison had done some homework here. My reaction hadn't really surprised her. She'd already begun formulating a response to any criticism.

"Aren't there other judges tied to this union guy Gardner?" I asked.

"She didn't ask you about other judges. She asked you about Ippolito," said MacAleer, ever the loyal soldier. I recall about five minutes ago, this guy was calling her Queenie behind her back, and now he was kissing her rear end.

I didn't have a rebuttal. And I had to continuously remind myself that it wasn't my place to *have* a rebuttal. It was my job to go along, the FBI riding sidesaddle, with whatever criminal enterprise these guys could conjure up.

"Okay, it's not my call," I said. "What do you need from me?"

I noted a slight softening in Madison's expression. "I need you to make the case for Ippolito," she said. "Conduct some interviews. Draft an analysis. Whatever you need to do. Just come to the right conclusion and make it look convincing. Do you think you can handle that? I mean, after everything I've heard about you, this should be a walk in the park."

"I can handle it," I told her.

"And do it fast," she said. "We want to appoint Ippolito next week."

"Before the laborers decide their endorsement," I said, ever mindful of the F-Bird and the need for a clear record.

"Very good, Counselor," she said. Madison poured herself some wine. She seemed pleased to have checked this meeting off her list.

When he listened to this evening's conversation, Christopher Moody would be checking off a box of his own. Madison Koehler would now be a codefendant at Charlie Cimino's trial.

"And what about this other guy? The guy who runs SLEU?" I asked. "Harmon-something."

"Rick Harmoning," said Mac. "You're already working on getting his endorsement."

"I am?"

"The list," he said.

The list of jobs, he meant. The people who wanted certain positions in the administration, positions that I was supposed to figure out a way to give them. Madison had told me to talk to Mac about them.

"You fit those people into those jobs, Rick'll come around," said Mac.

"I'll do my best," I said. "Am I going to run up against lawyers in the different agencies who say that I can't put these people into these jobs? I mean, that's why you need me, right? Because you've had resistance?"

"Yes," said Madison, "and yes."

"Just come up with an argument," said Charlie. "What you do best. Something plausible to get around whatever hurdles exist."

I nodded. "And can I overrule these lawyers in the agencies? I mean, if push comes to shove?"

Mac laughed. So did Charlie. Madison smiled and focused on her wine.

"Of course you can," said Mac, lightly pushing my arm. "We're the fucking governor."

68   I RETURNED TO MY OFFICE BUILDING AFTER DINNER and went to Suite 410, where Lee Tucker awaited me. The box of discarded chicken wings and Diet Pepsi told me that Lee had dined on more modest fare than my horseradish-crusted rib eye and salad and Cabernet. At least I was getting some good meals out of this gig.

"Wow. Fucking wow." That was a pretty accurate summation, I thought, after Lee had listened to my debriefing. Selling a seat on the supreme court and placing cronies on the payroll, all for precious union endorsements, would make nice headline charges in an ever-expanding indictment. I'd been on this new assignment for one day, and already Madison Koehler and Brady MacAleer had been snared.

"Time frame is one week?" he asked me.

That's what it had sounded like, based on my conversation with Madison and Mac. I wasn't sure what that meant for me. Would the federal government sit back and let George Ippolito take a seat on the supreme court? Or would they intervene before it happened? If it were the latter, it meant I didn't have much time left in solving my own private puzzle. I might have as little as one week to figure out who was behind the murder of Greg Connolly and, presumably, the others—Adalbert Wozniak and Ernesto Ramirez—as well.

I checked my watch. It was close to ten o'clock. I went home. I had a headache from the wine and my mouth was dry. I wasn't in a very good mood, either, but I wasn't sure why. I no longer held reservations about what I was doing. One or more of the governor's people—if not the governor himself—had ordered people murdered to cover up their crimes. They deserved everything they had coming.

When I got home, I didn't want to be there. There were times, like now, where the emptiness was so explosive, so maddening that I just couldn't stay in this townhouse. There had been nights since Talia's and Emily's deaths that I'd gone to a hotel, just for a different place to sleep.

I looked at Talia's picture on the bookshelves in the living room. College era. In the bigger photo that had been truncated, Talia was refusing a bite from a chocolate sundae that I'd offered her in jest, after she'd spilled half of it down her shirt. She'd thought it was funny, and my offer of another bite funnier still. She'd turned away from the spoon-ful of ice cream and shut her eyes, with a crooked smile on her face. I'd isolated the photo on her face and blown it up. I loved that expression. It showed the essential Talia, carefree and self-effacing and—

And beautiful.

"I'd give anything," I said.

I dialed up Shauna, with whom I hadn't spent much time over the last few weeks. I didn't know if our separation owed more to my involvement in this sordid criminal enterprise or to her involvement with her new beau.

"*Hey*, stranger danger," she said. In the background was music—the Counting Crows, one of her favorites—and a man's voice.

"Just seeing what's up," I said.

"We just went bowling, if you can believe it. It was actually a blast. You want—you want to come over? Roger's dying to meet you."

I did the retreating dance—tired, big day tomorrow, just calling to say hi. The last thing I wanted to be was a third wheel.

Roger must have said something funny because I heard Shauna laugh. She sounded good. She sounded happy. For a reason I couldn't quite pin down, that made me unhappy.

I hung up and put on some music, most of it from my college days, most of it dark and dreary. I fell asleep with the phone in my hand. I woke up when it rang.

"Hello?" I said, shaking the remnants of a dream. I lost the detail as soon as I opened my eyes. Something about exotic dancers and a car wash.

"Hello—Jason?"

"Mrs. Ramirez."

"Essie."

"Right, Essie. How are you? Everything okay?"

"I should have called earlier. My oldest was having trouble sleeping tonight. I hope it's not too late—"

"Not at all."

"I wanted to say thank you. Again. I got the job."

"With Paul?"

"Yes, with Mr. Riley. He seems like a nice man."

"He's the best."

"I don't know how to be a paralegal. I told him that."

I'm sure she did. Essie didn't pull punches. It was one of the things I liked about her. But it wasn't the only thing.

"You'll learn fast. Paul wouldn't have hired you if he didn't think you could handle it."

"I'm not sure that's true, Jason."

"All I told him was to interview you, give you a shot. All I got you was a foot in the door. You got that job on your own. Scout's honor."

She laughed. "Were you a Scout?"

"Nope. But I understand they're honorable."

"I want to buy you dinner one night. My treat. No arguments."

"That's not necessary."

"I know it's not necessary. I want to."

It occurred to me that Essie, since her husband's death, probably hadn't had a lot of fun, either. Me, I could disappear into a nightclub, or go hang with Shauna, or have a night of drunken debauchery with Madison Koehler. Essie was anchored at home with two children.

"Sounds great," I said.

Essie made me think of her dead husband, Ernesto. Ernesto made me think of his buddy, Scarface. Scarface made me think of the man who killed Adalbert Wozniak, and probably Ernesto, too: Federico Hurtado. Kiko.

I put on my coat and some gloves. I was still in my suit, which might come in handy. I drove to the southwest side of the city. The temperatures were near freezing and it was dark, so the activity level was low on the streets. There were a few bars over on this side of town that seemed to be doing good business, but this wasn't a trendy area, not yet. This was still a heavily Mexican neighborhood and generally poor. The condos were small and stacked atop each other, almost no yards of grass or driveways around the buildings. The cars were parked up and down the streets, mostly beaters taking punishment on a daily basis from these neglected roads, pockmarked with potholes.

It got a little nicer as I moved southward. The apartment buildings and stacked townhouses became single-family homes, even a few yards with gates and small gardens. I looked for street numbers along the way and found it easily enough. Kiko's house. It was nothing to write home about. It was on the same half-acre lot as the other homes, two stories, some brick and some siding. That's where these guys lived, same as the old-time Mafioso around here—housing that was facially modest, but with extravagant interiors and high-priced accessories.

I drove around the block a couple of times. I went down the alley twice. I thought I had a pretty good feel for the place. I knew how I would want to proceed—if I decided to exercise that option. A big if. Confronting this guy wasn't at the top of my list. I didn't want to make Kiko my enemy any more than I wanted to jump out of an airplane without a parachute. But I thought I was running out of time before the federal government closed in on Charlie Cimino and company, and when that happened, it would be too late.

So, not tonight. But maybe soon.

69   I MET BRADY MACALEER IN HIS OFFICE AT NINE THE next morning. It was hard to square the title on his door—CHIEF OF GOVERNMENT ADMINISTRATION—with the pug-nosed, knuckle-dragging thug sitting behind the desk. His shirt didn't fit him very well and the tie appeared to be an afterthought. His eyes were once again bloodshot, narrow, and still unfriendly.

"Charlie says you're stand-up," he informed me. He said it as if we'd never met, as if we hadn't talked shop all last night at dinner. He also said it as if, from his standpoint, the jury was still out.

"Me, I don't know you yet," he continued. "You see what I'm saying?"

"I think so. You don't know me yet."

"And I don't trust people I don't know. You see what I'm saying?"

We had two-thirds of a syllogism so far. Wait for it . . .

"So I don't trust you," he said.

"I'm glad we cleared that up," I said.

I didn't think his eyes could narrow any further, but they did. I think he had the vague notion that he was being insulted. Some people can be very sensitive.

As riveting as this conversation was, Mac segued into a brief discussion of office hierarchy. He held a hand, horizontal, in the air at face level. "This is the governor," he said. He lowered his hand a notch. "This is Queen Madison," he said. Then he lowered it again. "This is me." He lowered it more than a notch—maybe two or three of them, until his hand was almost down at the desk. "This is you," he said.

"That's pretty low," I observed.

"Yeah, and it's gonna stay like that." Then, for good measure, he actually repeated the whole idiotic thing. Governor. Madison. Mac. Kolarich.

It occurred to me that I should play nice with this guy, seeing as how I was supposed to get close with everyone in the inner circle and uncover secret truths.

"Could you diagram that on a piece of paper?" I asked. "In case I forget."

He didn't think much of that, but his phone rang before he could comment. He spent a lot of time listening and making various grunting noises. By the time he got off, he'd mentally moved on.

"Okay, mister smart guy. We've got these people that we want to put in these jobs to make Rick Harmoning happy, and we got these pain-in-the-ass lawyers coming in to tell us why we can't hire them. They're going to tell you about veterans' preferences and people scoring higher and all sorts of lawyer crap, and all of that comes down to, I can't do what I want. And I wanna do what I want. Right?"

"Sure."

"So these guys are going to come in, they're going to give you the lawyer rap, and then you're going to figure out how to get my guys those jobs. Right?"

"Right," I said. "You're the man."

*   *   *

AND MAC WAS ESSENTIALLY correct in his prediction. We met with a guy named Gordon. I couldn't remember if that was his first name or last, or maybe he just went by one name like Bono or Madonna. He was a pudgy guy with a shock of black hair on top and droopy cheeks. He was the deputy counsel to the Division of Personnel and Professional Services and Other Assorted Bureaucratic Quagmires, or something like that.

"You've got two problems with these jobs," he said. "First, the veterans' preferences are absolute. Each of the jobs you're seeking to fill with these people on this list of yours? They're right here in the city. There are dozens of veterans up here who are on a list for jobs like these. All of them would start with a preference. You have to consider them first and give them a weighted score."

"What's the other problem?" I asked.

"The other problem is that some of these positions, we've already taken applications and administered tests, and the people you want for these jobs will have to score higher on the tests."

I looked over at Mac, who shook his head. Not good. Apparently we weren't confident relying on the intellectual acuity of the people Harmoning wanted us to hire.

"Veterans are sorted by county?" I asked.

"That's right."

"Are there counties with no veterans applying?"

"Are there—well, probably," he said, thinking about it. "We have over a hundred counties in this state. There are probably counties that don't have any veteran applicants, yeah."

"And these five different agencies we're talking about here," I said. "Would any of them have offices in those counties without any veteran applicants?"

Gordon blinked at me. "You're talking about moving the jobs to counties with no veterans applying?"

"I am." I felt a small pain in my gut just saying it. But it was my role to do this, to fuck over the veterans to get the jobs for these people Madison and Mac wanted hired.

"Well, you can't—" Gordon looked at me and then at Mac. Gordon knew the law, meaning he knew that it was *against* the law to try to skirt the veterans' preferences. But he also knew that Brady Mac was his boss, and I came from the governor's office. Each of us outranked him.

"He's asking you to check," Mac said. "Check to see if these jobs can be moved."

Gordon's eyebrows arched and met in the middle. He looked at me for assistance. I looked away. I wasn't enjoying this, not one bit.

"By the end of the day," said Mac.

"And what if they can't?" Gordon asked.

"Well, let's talk about that," I said. "Suppose we wanted our people in these jobs and we couldn't locate the jobs in a county without veterans applying. Or suppose other people have already been interviewed and taken tests. How do we do it? How do we get our guys in?"

Gordon shrugged. He didn't know, or he didn't want to help us. A sheen of sweat appeared on his wrinkled forehead. The two people in this room who outranked him were asking him how to bend and twist the law. Gordon may have been a bit of a stiff, but he seemed like an honest guy.

"Aren't there jobs that don't require tests?" I asked.

"No," said Gordon. "I mean, other than internships."

"Internships. You mean, like, college kids?"

Gordon nodded.

"How does the law define an 'intern'?" I asked.

"It doesn't."

"An 'intern' is whatever we say it is?"

"Right."

"We can create an 'internship' whenever we want?"

"Well—I guess so. Sure."

"An 'intern' can hold the job indefinitely?"

"I—well, I suppose so. Yes."

I looked at Mac. He seemed to be following.

"We can pay an 'intern' whatever we want?" I asked.

"Yes."

"So if we turn a job into an internship, we can hire whomever we want and pay them whatever?"

Gordon leaned forward. "But these jobs aren't internships, Mr. Kolarich. I mean, here." He looked at the piece of paper. "Associate supervisor for administration in the Board of Education. That's not an internship."

"Maybe it is now," I answered. "I mean, it is if we *say* it is, no?"

Gordon looked like he'd swallowed a bug. By the time he left

Mac's office, he'd stained both of his armpits and probably lost about five pounds of water weight.

"What an asshole, that guy," Mac said to me. "This guy forget who he's working for?"

"He's just doing his job," I said.

"Yeah, well, let's see how long he *has* a job."

"You're not going to fire Gordon," I said.

Mac looked at me. I could see him mentally run through his diagram, himself up at the top, me several notches below. "And why aren't I going to fire him?"

"Because I said so. You fire him, you fire me." I opened my hands. "You want to fire me, Mac? Be my guest. I'll figure this out for you, but you're not going to run this guy Gordon out of the office. You're not."

I left the office on that note. Looked like I wasn't going to be counting Brady MacAleer as someone whose trust I would gain. But there was only so much I could tolerate. I began to wonder how long I could wade in the swamp with these assholes.

*   *   *

I found Gordon in his office an hour later. When he saw me, his posture went rigid. It wouldn't have surprised me if he'd peed his pants, too. Fortunately, he was behind his desk.

"Listen, Gordon," I said. "I understand that you were troubled by our conversation. Here's what I want you to do. I want you to write me a memo explaining that we can't deliberately avoid the veterans' preference laws. I want you to put it in writing and give it to me and me only."

He stared at me, a deer in the headlights. "And Mr. MacAleer fires me."

"No. That's not going to happen. He'll never see the memo. Just me. You need to cover yourself."

Gordon took a deep breath and nodded slowly. "Is he—really going to do that? Move the jobs around and create internships?"

"I don't know. Maybe. It won't be your decision, and I want you to be able to say that it wasn't your idea. Because it wasn't. Okay?"

He was off-balance. He didn't know me. And this kind of stuff, it clearly wasn't his game. He was a bureaucrat, an honest one.

"It didn't used to be like this," he said.

"I know." I patted the door and walked back to my office.

I SPENT THE REST OF THAT DAY AND EVENING RE- viewing all the state statutes on this stuff, most espe- cially the veterans' preferences. The next morning, I met with Brady Mac and Madison Koehler in her office.

"Good news and bad news," I said.

Madison rubbed her eyes. "The good news first," she said. I'd have gone the other way.

"The good news is that three of the agencies we need— Transportation, Education, and Corrections—have offices in at least one county where there are no veterans applying. So we could hire these people for jobs in those counties and not have to deal with veterans."

"What counties?" she asked.

"Two in Norfolk County and one in Summit County."

"Those are downstate," she said. "Rick Harmoning's people live up here. That's no good."

"So we hire them for jobs down there and then transfer them, almost immediately, up here. They'll already have the jobs so we don't have to deal with veterans' preferences. A job transfer doesn't count."

She looked at me, then Mac, and nodded. "Okay, so for three of the five agencies, we get them jobs by *moving* the jobs to counties without veterans waiting in line."

"Right. And then move them back, once the job is theirs."

She rolled her hand for me to continue. "What about the other two?"

"The other two agencies—Commerce and Community Affairs and Public Health—we're fucked," I said. "But we can hire those people as interns."

"*Interns?* That's not going to work. These people don't want minimum-wage contracts. They want full-time employment with a salary and benefits."

"It will work," I said. "We hire them as interns at the full salary they'd receive as full-time state employees. We can do that. There's nothing stopping us. We can pay them whatever we want. And the law says we can hire an intern into a full-time position if they successfully complete a six-month probation period. The veterans' preference doesn't apply to them."

Madison thought that through. "So they get the job now, with full salary, and after six months they become full-fledged state employees with benefits?"

"Exactly," I said.

She seemed okay with that. "And the bad news?"

"The bad news," I said, "is that everything we've just discussed is illegal. We aren't supposed to do any of this. The law says that we must give a veteran's preference to all of these jobs we're trying to fill. It says we must take 'every reasonable measure' to ensure veterans are given their rightful preference. We're doing the opposite. We're taking every measure to consciously *avoid* the veteran's preference."

Madison put down the pen she was twiddling between her fingers and sat back in her chair. "I don't want to hear that."

I'm sure she didn't. But it was essential that I say these things. It had to be clear that I was helping to orchestrate an illegal scheme. Otherwise, the crime-fraud exception to the attorney-client privilege didn't apply, and everything we were discussing might be deemed privileged and unusable to the prosecution in court. Plus it made the case airtight, when the jury listened to the recording of this conversation. Madison couldn't claim that she was relying on advice of counsel when her counsel was telling her, up front, that their plan was illegal.

It was one of many times when I took a moment for inventory. I was getting pretty good at this. And what a talent: I was opening doors for people who, if they chose to walk through them, would be rewarded with an indictment from a federal grand jury. I was, for all practical purposes, sending people to prison. I was a loaded weapon. I was like a roach motel for criminals.

"Well, my *job* is to make sure that you hear that," I answered Madison. "I'm a lawyer. I tell you what the law says. It just so happens I'm also telling you how to circumvent it."

Madison seemed unhappy now. "So what the hell does this mean?"

"It means," I said, "that if you're going to do what I suggest, be careful about it. Because it's illegal. Paper the file. Make a point of needing these people in those downstate counties. Something convincing. And then paper the file again, explaining that with the budget crunch, you have to consolidate or something, and move these people up here. Same thing with the internships. Just create a few internships and maybe—maybe don't start them at the full-blown salary, because it will be too obvious. Just make it something decent, and let them know, six months from now, they'll be getting full pay and benefits." I looked at each of them. "Bottom line, make sure that if anyone asks, they can't prove that we were doing this to fuck the veterans."

Madison made a face. She didn't like my stark description of what we were doing. Criminals never do. They rarely like to talk about what they're doing out loud. I mean, what I'd said was spot-on. The public policy of this state was to thank people who had risked their lives for this country in armed conflict by giving them a small bump in job preference; it was a mandatory state law, and here we were, doing everything we could to circumvent that policy. It made me sick. My only consolation was that I was nailing these people to the wall, courtesy of a recording device in my coat pocket.

"Give us a minute, Mac," said Madison.

"Sure, Chief." Like the dutiful soldier he was, Brady Mac dragged his knuckles out of the office.

Madison fixed her stare on me. "You don't like this," she said.

"It is what it is."

"That's exactly right. It is what it is. You don't win election to the highest office in the state by just hoping that good things will happen."

"A civics lesson."

"A life lesson," she said.

I didn't answer.

"I don't have time for consciences," she continued. "You want to be mother superior, do it on someone else's time. There's the door, any time you want to walk out."

"You firing me?" I asked.

"I'm telling you that I don't want to see that look on your face again. Get on board or leave. Is that clear enough, sport?"

"One thing I'll give you, Madison: You're always clear."

"Good, then." Her computer beeped, which I think meant an email message had arrived. She turned to it but kept talking. "Today's my last day in the office until after the primary. We're going all out now. Good work on those jobs. That's exactly the kind of creativity we need from you. Now I'll want to hear that you've wrapped everything up on that supreme court appointment."

"I've already set up some interviews with candidates," I said.

"But George Ippolito wins." She turned her head and looked over her glasses at me.

Yes, of course, one of the worst judges I'd ever stood before would be the winner of my faux interview process to select the next member of our state supreme court.

I walked back to my office and went to work on the supreme court appointment. I got a call at two-thirty.

"The governor's in the city today," a receptionist said. "He'd like to meet you."

THE GYMNASIUM, PACKED TO FULL CAPACITY OF ABOUT two thousand, simultaneously went up in a roar at the announcement of Governor Carlton Snow. The governor appeared from the hallway, doing his typical gubernatorial calisthenics—wave, thumbs-up, point, and repeat— as he moved toward the center of the basketball court, encircled in purple for the high school's nickname. He was wearing a button-down plaid shirt and blue jeans, which from what I had gathered from watching the news and reading the papers—I was paying more attention to such things of late—was the governor's trademark look on the campaign trail.

There were kids in the audience but it was mostly adults, the racial mix being approximately two-to-one, black to white. We were on the city's south side, at Duerson High School. The place was badly in need of refurbishing, but the gym was in pretty good shape. One of the guys I played ball with had come from Duerson, but it was my first time in the building.

"Thank you for the very nice greeting," said the governor. "Usually, this time of year, when you hear Snow's coming, it's bad news."

I sensed this was not the first time the governor had cracked that joke, but the audience liked it. In a corner not that far from me, where the reporters who were following the campaign were gathered, a couple of them traded glances that indicated they'd heard the line more than once.

I was standing next to Hector Almundo, dressed resplendently as always, who had actually arrived with the governor but came over to me. He'd given me a brief rundown. Today's theme was education, and the governor was unveiling a plan to add more teachers to the city schools by expanding gambling—adding a new casino just outside the city—and using some of the state's share of the gambling revenues for funding.

I was aware of the fact that we had some casinos in this state but I'd never visited one, nor had I stopped to consider the moral ramifications of legalizing gambling at all. I guess if I'd thought about it, I'd say, don't go if you don't want to play. But the point seemed to be that gambling carried with it some unsavory baggage like prostitution and addiction, and the people who seemed to play the most— the ones looking for the big score—tended to be the people who could afford it least.

"Well, these people seem to like his proposal," I said to Hector, leaning into his ear.

"These people are teachers," he said back. "That's who he's doing it for."

Ah. Rallying the base. "Why spend time courting people who are already voting for you?" I asked.

Hector looked at me and smiled. Oh, the naïve child was I. He leaned into me but had to speak up as the crowd erupted in applause. "This is just the setting, J. He's doing it for the cameras. These campaigns are mostly television these days. Or Internet. Same thing. Plus G-O-T-V."

I didn't know what the hell that meant. "That's different than regular TV?"

His smile turned to laughter. "Get out the vote," he shouted over the din. "The more excited they are, the more they make sure that they and their friends go to the polls. We need a big turnout in the city because Willie's doing well downstate."

The governor went on for more than thirty minutes. He was good at what he did. He knew how to punctuate his lines, and he knew how to connect with the audience. He had that ridiculous politician's smile but they all did, so it didn't strike me as a handicap.

When it was over, I followed Hector and became part of the entourage. There was the state police detail and Madison and some other people, including a guy whom I recognized from the photo

Chris Moody had showed me as William Peshke. We filtered into three stretch limousines that were part of a cavalcade, and before I knew it I was sitting next to Hector and this Peshke guy. And I was sitting across from Madison Koehler and Governor Carlton Snow.

The governor put out his hand. Madison squirted some sanitizer in his palm and he rubbed his hands together voraciously, like he was about to settle down to a big meal. Then he took a sweaty bottle of water from her and took a long swallow, smacking his lips with satisfaction when it was over.

"That was fun," he said. His adrenaline was still flowing from the event. He looked around the cabin for a response, and it didn't take him long to get it. *You were on. They love you. Let's see Willie Bryant work a room like* that.

"You're Jason," he said to me.

"Nice to meet you, Governor." And please say hello to my little recording device, which I had nicknamed FeeBee.

"You, too. Yeah." He nodded at me. "Like your tie."

"Just trying to keep up with Hector." My former client was into the monochromatic thing these days—today it was a tan shirt and mustard tie.

The governor looked at Hector and allowed a wry smile. Then to me, he said, "You played ball at State."

"Yes."

"I remember that game. Your last one. I was there. You went off on that linebacker after that crackback block."

I forgot that he'd gone to State as well. Greg Connolly had mentioned it.

"Then you punched out Karmeier the next day."

Jesus, does everybody remember that? Well, Tony was All-Conference and a captain. Apparently I'd carved out a place of infamy at my alma mater.

"You keeping us out of trouble?" he asked.

"Doing my best."

He drank from his bottle again. "Well, it's a full-time job if I ever heard one."

More appropriate laughter from the posse.

"You know everyone here?" he asked me.

Well, let's see. I'd fully explored your chief of staff's naked body a couple times now. I kept your buddy Hector from a stint in the federal penitentiary . . .

"Bill Peshke."

"Nice to meet you," I said.

"Call me Pesh."

I recalled what Chris Moody had said. Peshke was a special adviser to the governor but he was a campaign guy. The strategist. Moody had mentioned a turf battle with Madison Koehler. He was in his mid-forties, on the lean side, polished and plastic. His hair was sharply parted and well-sprayed. His clothes were pretty decent. His smile was robotic and his eyes moved about the limo, like he was looking for a better offer.

"I've heard nothing but good things about you," he said.

"Pesh is the one with the PhD," said Hector. "That means he's smarter than the rest of us."

The governor clapped his hands together. "Where to now?"

"Darling Theater," said Peshke.

I knew that place. It was a small auditorium on the near north side. I saw a concert there once. The Pogues, I think. Back when they had mosh pits. Do they still have those?

"Right, right. Okay, good, good." The governor looked at Madison. "What's Willie doing?"

"Marinaville," she said. "Talking about crime and tort reform."

"And we have that ad?"

She nodded as she checked her BlackBerry. "It's up tomorrow, unless he gives us something today to throw in. It's running in every major market downstate."

When we reached Darling Theater, we were escorted into a side room that I hadn't known existed. A spread of food lay across some long tables, cold cuts and pastas and fruit. Some others filtered in who were interested in chatting with the governor before he entered the auditorium. Hector and I held back. He seemed interested in being my guide, imparting his expertise to me, the young grasshopper. Also, it didn't seem like anyone else was particularly interested in conversing with him. The thought crossed my mind once again: What was Hector doing here? I kept falling back on the same conclusion. Window dressing. But it gave me a problem.

"Willie's playing to his base," Hector explained to me. "Downstate, conservative Democrats. He's been talking more about gun owner's rights and tort reform, the kinds of things you expect a Republican to talk about."

I thought I was supposed to ask, so I did. "Why?"

Hector shrugged. "He's made the calculation that it's how he wins. Moving to Carl's right is easier than to his left. He's running against an incumbent. He's the challenger."

"Snow isn't the incumbent," I said.

"Doesn't matter. Everyone calls him Governor. Same difference."

That was a popular line around here.

"Where's Charlie tonight?" I asked.

Hector shook his head. He didn't know. "You like working with him?"

I shrugged. "I guess so."

"But you still remember who got you here, right?" He said it with a hint of playfulness, an elbow in my side, but he meant it. He wanted the finder's credit, to the extent I turned out to be an asset to the governor. I wouldn't be, of course. When everything came down, the last thing anyone would want to do is claim credit for bringing me into the fold.

But Hector didn't know that, obviously, and in fact I was doing my level best to keep him at arm's length. I couldn't change the fact that he was here, that for some reason the governor kept him around the inner circle. Thankfully, he didn't seem to be a player in the illegal stuff. He hadn't been in on the conversations with Madison,

Mac, Charlie, and me about the supreme court appointment or about getting those jobs for the union guy's people. Window dressing, like I said. A good face to put forward, but not someone who would be counted on for the wet work.

"So what do we have you doing?" he asked, as if he were reading my mind, in tune with my concern.

"Nothing much, yet," I said.

He didn't seem to like that answer. "You and Madison and Mac—you had dinner the other night? You've been meeting?"

"We've talked about a few things," I said.

"And Charlie, too," he added. "What, but no one can tell *me*?"

"Nothing to tell," I assured him. I imagined that Chris Moody and Lee Tucker would be none too pleased with my response. I was walling off Hector. I knew what they'd say, what they'd already said about Hector: *He's not your client anymore. He's as fair game as anyone else.* But I just couldn't see it that way. They were technically correct, but this guy and I had shared his deepest, darkest secrets. I'd stood with him at the abyss, we'd been to war together—choose your metaphor—and no matter what I might have thought of him on a personal level, I couldn't just shrug off that coat.

Hector was clearly displeased and clearly trying not to reveal that emotion to me. He wanted in on the good stuff. He wanted to be involved. It was, in many ways, the same-old, same-old with Hector. He wanted respect.

"Let's do it!" Governor Snow said to someone. He was wearing a navy suit and red tie now. I hadn't noticed him changing clothes. Other than Peshke, the entourage held back in this adjoining room as the governor fixed his hair and walked on stage.

I poked my head into the auditorium and saw the governor doing his hey-nice-to-see-ya-how-ya-doing calisthenics before taking a microphone. I hardly knew the guy, and I wasn't sure how I was going to know him in the time I had. I was assuming, at this point, that ten days was all I had at the maximum, and possibly as little as a handful of days. How was I going to figure out who was behind the murders of Greg Connolly and Ernesto Ramirez and Adalbert Wozniak?

"Usually this time of year, when you hear Snow's coming, it's bad news," the governor quipped.

72

AFTERWARD, EVERYONE WENT TO A SUITE AT THE Ritz-Carlton downtown. I wasn't entirely sure why. We were in the city. These people lived here. The governor, as I understood it, had a wife and daughter and a house up here. But maybe they were staying in the mansion in the capital right now.

The governor put his arm on the couch and looked approvingly around the room. Heady stuff, no doubt, holding the highest office in the state, staying in these lush surroundings, having so much power at your fingertips. He seemed to be basking in it. His tie was pulled down, collar open. Downtime. But he never seemed very far removed from the battery being fully charged.

Someone set a bottle of scotch on the ornate coffee table and everyone took a glass. Not my first choice of drink, but this was good stuff, hot and silky.

"Tomorrow, health care," said Peshke. "Prescription drugs and universal care."

"Great," said the governor.

Peshke ran off an impressive agenda for tomorrow. He listed seven stops, mostly up north but some down south as well. Rallies and speeches. Press interviews. Two fundraisers, one at lunch and one in the evening in a wealthy suburb.

"Holly Majors is asking about House Bill 100," said Madison. "The abortion bill."

Peshke groaned. The governor seemed to slide down in the couch a notch or two.

"What's the drop date on that?" he asked.

"Three days from now."

The governor shook his head. "I'll have to send a thank-you note to Tully and Wermouth," he said.

Grant Tully, I assumed he meant by the reference. The senate majority leader. I remembered my talk with Jon Soliday, Tully's lawyer, who'd tried to talk me out of ever taking a position with the governor's administration—correctly so, as it happened. From what Jon had told me and from what I'd read recently, there seemed to be no love lost between the governor and the senate majority leader.

Wermouth, I didn't know, but I was guessing he was the guy who ran the House.

Hector, as always, enjoyed his role as my guide through this process. "The House is Republican. They pass a slate of abortion bills every year. This one is parental consent. Teenagers have to get consent for an abortion."

"Got it."

"And the senate passed it, too, even though they have a Democratic majority. Some people see it as a moderate compromise between the hard lines."

"*Some* people," said Peshke. "Personal PAC and some of the prochoice groups, they aren't 'some' people. And they're our biggest supporters." He looked at the governor. "Bryant came out again today and confirmed he'd sign the bill."

Hector leaned into me. "See, that works for Willie's base, the downstate vote. They're in the mushy middle. That puts Bryant on the same page with the Republicans."

"And that's where we should be, too," Peshke said to me, although I sensed he was really delivering the message to the governor. "The issue becomes a non-issue. Personal PAC has to be with us in the fall. We're still pro-choice, but with a moderate position. Anything's better than a pro-lifer in office. And for the people in the middle on this issue, it's a wash."

"But we don't run in the fall unless we win in March." Madison, who had been on her cell phone, sat down and joined the discussion. "I don't like the downstate numbers, Governor. We need the city turnout."

"We go to the left of Bryant on this, the downstate numbers will look even worse," Peshke rejoined.

"I disagree." Madison made no pretense of addressing Peshke. She was looking at Snow. "We're already left of Bryant. Guns? Gays? Forget it. The governor vetoes House Bill 100 and nothing changes down there—we're still the city liberals to them—but up here, we turn out more."

"No. No." Peshke was shaking his head. "It hurts us more in the general than it helps us in the primary."

"You can't win in the general unless you win the primary, Pesh."

"And you can't win in the general if you *sabotage* yourself in the primary, Maddie."

"All right." The governor pushed himself from the couch and moved to the window, glass of scotch in hand. "Y'know, it would make my life a whole lot easier if you two could agree on this."

Hector leaned into me. "This is exactly what the Republicans want. It's why they passed the bill so quickly this session. And the senate didn't do us any favors, either. The governor has to sign or veto this bill within sixty days of receiving it. They knew the deadline would fall in the heat of the primary. They're trying to put us in a box."

"They want us to veto," said Peshke. "It will make their week. Another lefty city liberal. Edgar Trotter courts the downstate Democrats on this issue in the fall."

"I have to win the primary, Pesh." The governor drained his scotch and breathed out.

"Governor." Peshke stood up. "Who even knows how much this will help? If you're a pro-choice voter, odds are you aren't a gun lover, anyway. You're not going to vote for Willie fucking Bryant. And you're sure as shit not going to vote for Edgar Trotter or whomever the GOP turns out."

"They'll stay home," Madison said.

"Bullshit. *Bullshit*." Peshke was getting red in the face now. Something about Madison seemed to work him up. The turf battle. There was more than strategy at stake here, I sensed. This was about pride of authorship. "Pro-choicers are some of the most politically active people in this state. They're not going to vote? Really? They're going to run the risk that Willie Bryant wins? Governor Snow is better than Willie Bryant to them any day."

"They'll stay home," Madison said again. "They'll stay home and hope that we lose. It will send a message. They're not fucking around. Every Democrat who runs in the future will have learned something. At our exp—"

"It matters to them that much?" asked the governor. "That much that they'd run the risk of electing the wrong person to prove a point?"

"I think it does, Governor, yes."

He looked back at the group, a gleam in his eyes. "Then let them prove it," he said. "Let them prove it."

"How do they—"

"What are there—four or five groups of them, Maddie? NOW, Personal PAC, Women for Choice . . ."

"Right. Freedom to Choose."

"Okay, four of them. They want me to take a position that could hurt me in the general? Okay, then they can help make sure I win the general. A hundred thousand from each of them. A hundred fucking thousand from each of them. No more of this staying-neutral-in-the-primary crap. A hundred thousand from each of them. Right now. And *then* I veto that damn bill."

The room was quiet for a moment. Peshke kept to himself, as he'd lost the argument. Madison was thinking through what he'd said. Slowly, she began to nod. "Okay," she said, with a confidence that felt forced.

My heart skipped a beat. The U.S. attorney's office's collective heartbeat would, too. The governor was now on tape, courtesy of FeeBee in my pocket, instructing his chief of staff to shake down some special-interest groups to purchase a veto.

"Yeah. Yeah." The governor's enthusiasm was growing. "They want me to stick my neck out for them like that? It doesn't come free. Why should it? Get right on that, Maddie, okay?"

"Yes, sir."

"What do you think?"

I was watching Madison, who looked tired and frustrated.

"Hey. Hello?"

Hector nudged me to let me know what I had just come to realize, that the governor was talking to me. "What do *I* think?" I asked. "I'm just a lawyer, Governor. And not for the campaign."

The governor looked at me, then at Madison.

"He's handling some issues on the state side, sir."

This was an important point to make. If I was a lawyer for the campaign, we might have a problem with the attorney-client privilege, and the conversation I was recording could not be admitted in court. I was just another guy in the room, not the lawyer. Not for this.

"Okay, well, I'm asking anyway." Snow looked at me.

"Okay," I said. I cleared my throat. "If you want my legal opinion, you can't make a quid pro quo, one for the other. You can't say you'll veto the bill, but only if they give you campaign contributions."

Another important point. Now I had made it clear that the issue they were discussing was illegal, and therefore not covered by the attorney-client privilege under the crime-fraud exception.

The governor stared at me. Nobody spoke. The silence, in this animated room, was deafening.

"Of course I can," the governor said. "People can't give money to candidates they support?" He looked at Madison. "What the hell's he talking about?"

I was talking about the difference between voluntary and compulsory contributions to a candidate's campaign. Interesting, how easily the governor was able to wrap a shakedown in the blanket of democracy and freedom of speech.

"We can work out the details later," Madison said.

The governor seemed okay with that. I had the sense that these were the words Madison often used to defuse issues. Snow didn't want to be bothered by minutiae.

Thankfully, the conversation segued. Soon, everyone was tired and began to filter out. Madison cast a look in my direction, but what could she say to me? I was right, and I'd been asked a direct question.

"Hold back, Jason," the governor said to me. So I did. Madison and Pesh had left, leaving Hector and me with the governor. Hector excused himself, I think to use the bathroom or make a call or something. It was just going to be me and the governor, I guess. A tongue-lashing? A warning to watch what I say? If I'd expected to have any kind of a future with this guy—which is presumably what he thought I wanted—I might have been nervous.

"Sit, sit." The governor took a chair and so did I. "Hey, I heard what happened to your family a while back," he said. "I'm sorry to hear about that. If there's anything I can do."

He'd thrown me, I admit. I'd long become used to such statements, though not recently, and not from a guy who I thought was going to chew my head off.

"I appreciate that."

"I've got a daughter myself," he said. "I can't even imagine. Anyway," he added, pointing a finger at me, "I've heard from Charlie that you're a great asset. I appreciate everything you've done. So keep up the good work, okay? We can do some really good things for you."

"Thank you, sir."

"Tomorrow afternoon, we have that thing, right? That death-row inmate?"

"Antwain Otis, yes, sir."

"Make me look good in there, okay?" He winked at me.

I got up to leave. I looked for Hector, who was talking on his cell in the other room. I wasn't sure if I was supposed to wait for him, but I didn't bother. I walked out of the suite and nodded to the security detail. I left the Ritz-Carlton and walked into the cool night air, not entirely sure how I was feeling.

*　*　*

SUITE 410 HAD SUDDENLY become a busy place. In the sole conference room, a transcriber was listening to the conversations captured
today by my F-Bird and typing it up. I'd given a debriefing to Chris
Moody and Lee Tucker. I could see Moody doing the calculations as
I went on.

"So the governor has to either sign or veto this abortion bill by
when?" Moody asked me.

"They said three days, I think."

"And he wants the money from those pro-choice groups before
then?"

"It wasn't clear. I'm sure he would."

Chris Moody absently scratched his cheek. "You'll follow up on
this?" he asked. "This will involve you?"

I really wasn't sure. I'd done a lot of "fundraising" with Charlie
but didn't know if I would have anything to do with the shakedown
of these abortion-rights' groups.

"Tell me again what he said about Cimino," said Tucker.

I didn't remember precisely. "'Charlie says you're a great asset,'
something like that. It's on the F-Bird."

Both Moody and Tucker would analyze that phrase over and
over. I could see them playing it to Charlie Cimino one day soon. *We
know you talked to the governor about your "fundraising." We have
the governor on tape saying so.* But other than using it on Charlie,
would it be enough on its own to get the governor? I didn't see how.
It was flirting with the line but not crossing it.

Tucker put his hand on my shoulder. "You're all set for tomorrow?"

My interviews with the supreme court candidates, he meant. My
instructions from Madison Koehler had been to make this look like
a legitimate evaluation and vetting process. So I'd chosen a handful of candidates—three men and two women; three white and two
black—in addition to the prohibitive favorite, by which I mean the
shoo-in, George Ippolito.

Chris Moody joined us. "You're careful in your choice of words," he said, not for the first time. "You don't directly confront the issue. But try to stick the branch out and see if Ippolito grabs for it."

"He probably won't," I said. "If he has any brains, he'll play dumb."

Moody nodded. "Does he have any brains?"

I laughed. George Ippolito didn't have many. But on matters political, I suspected he had a little more going for him than he did on questions of law.

Moody stretched his arms. It was coming up on one in the morning now. I knew he wouldn't be leaving until he'd listened to the F-Bird from today. He'd listen and relisten, read and reread, the words of Governor Snow today. The case was kicking into final gear now, and he wasn't going to lose another high-profile political corruption case.

73

THE NEXT MORNING, I MADE IT TO THE STATE OFFICE by seven. I had a packed day. In the morning, I was meeting with five of the six judges I was interviewing for the supreme court appointment. In the afternoon, I would finish with the guy who was going to win the beauty contest, George Ippolito. Then at two-thirty, the governor and I were going to sit down with a group of lawyers and clergymen seeking to spare Antwain Otis from execution a few days from now.

The judge interviews started at eight sharp, a half-hour each with fifteen minutes in between each one for some cushion. I'd be done by eleven-thirty.

I reviewed my list again. Four trial judges, two appellate. Had this been a real contest, I probably would have focused primarily on appellate court judges, as they are the closest in line to the supreme court, they have a set of published opinions to review, and they are

accustomed to considering pure questions of law. Also, had this
been a legitimate vetting process, I'd have talked to other lawyers—
Paul Riley, for example—to get recommendations.

But this wasn't a contest. This was a sham. And if the governor
were going to choose a judge from the trial-court level to sit on the
state's highest court, which would come as a surprise to many people,
I needed to lay the groundwork for it. Thus, the four trial judges on the
short list. I wanted the word to get out that the governor was thinking
outside the box, so to speak—he was looking beyond the ivory tower
of the appellate court to judges who had gotten their hands dirty, who
were on the front lines. So when Snow ultimately chose Ippolito, it
wouldn't look so odd that he'd picked a judge from the trial level.

It was with no shortage of dark humor that I observed my dual
role here, the layers of deception I was mired in. I was assigned by the
governor's office to throw up a curtain of legitimacy around an illegal appointment-for-endorsement deal while, at the same time, I was
assigned by the federal government to leave a little hole in said curtain
so they could peek through. Talk about the fox guarding the henhouse.

I'd written up a list of ten mostly softball questions, covering judicial philosophy and ethics and attorney discipline, for the interviews
this morning. If you were a fly on the wall, you would have found
the morning's interviews to be little different from the exchanges
you see in the Senate Judiciary Committee when questioning nomi-
nees to the U.S. Supreme Court. Just for the fun of it, I wanted to
ask them if they thought *Roe v. Wade* should be overruled.

But it wasn't fun. It was, at best, a waste of time for the "candidates" and me. At worst, I was raising the hopes of people who had
absolutely no chance of getting the appointment and who might be
tarnished by association once the feds closed in.

I scheduled George Ippolito as the only afternoon interview, figuring I should save the worst for last. Plus it made the most sense
from a practical standpoint. I needed to be wearing FeeBee for
Ippolito, but I wouldn't wear it for the other interviews. It had been
one condition I had laid down that the feds had accepted. It was

bad enough I was stringing along these other judges, bad enough that they might be tainted by this whole affair later. I wasn't going to record their conversations with me when there was no reason to believe they were corrupt.

So I placed a little separation in time between Ippolito and the others and I went down to the food court in the basement of the state building after the other five interviews, ostensibly for a quick lunch. I dropped my tray of pasta on a table in the foyer just as another customer—one Lee Tucker—was vacating said table, leaving behind the F-Bird.

Back at my office, FeeBee in tow, I felt a knot form in my stomach as the receptionist informed me that Judge George Ippolito was here to see me.

George Ippolito was somewhere in his mid- to late fifties, I gathered, from his weathered features. His wispy hair was the color of sandpaper, which I assumed came from a bottle. He had liquid eyes, a tight mouth, and a thick nose that owed to a few too many nights at Rusty's or Sidebar, one of the lawyer hangouts for the criminal bar. He was a reliable drinker, though no one was ever sure if that included daytime sauce. Judging from his temperament on the bench, it wouldn't be a stretch to think he added a little flavor to his morning coffee, but I can't say I ever heard him slur his words in the times I was before him. He was an asshole, but a sober one.

I could see from his expression when he walked in that he recognized my face, and he obviously knew my name, but he hadn't previously put the two together. I'm sure he'd had hundreds of prosecutors pass before him in his day and they blurred together.

"Jason Ko-LAR-ich!" he said to me, breaking into a broad smile when he saw me. So, I guess he was going to play like he remembered me. It would have helped if he'd checked on the pronunciation of my name before embarking on that plan. Kola, like the drink. Rich, like you have money. How hard is that?

"Great to see you again, Counsel," he said with a firm grip on my hand.

Somebody must have told him that I'd tried a case before him previously. I wondered if they also told him what I thought of him. Either way, no one bothered to give him the correct pronunciation of my name.

"Thanks for coming, Judge. This won't take long."

"Whatever you need, Jason. Whatever you need."

Great. Terrific. I started with my boilerplate. The governor was considering a wide range of candidates from diverse backgrounds; you've impressed a lot of people, you made the first cut, we're interested in speaking with you, blah blah blah.

"What kind of name is Ko-LAR-ich?" he asked, when I was finished.

"I'm three-quarters Irish," I said. "But my father's father was Hungarian."

"It sounds Polish."

It wasn't a question, so I didn't answer.

"You grew up on the south side?"

"Leland Park," I said. This guy was interviewing *me*.

"What was your parish?"

Ah, south-side geography. Identification by the Catholic church you attended.

"St. Pete's," I said.

"St. Agnes." He pointed at himself. "You went to, what, Bonaventure?"

"Right."

"You spend time at Louie's?"

"Best kraut dog in the city," I said. It was just down the way from Bonaventure, my high school.

"Got *that* right. I went to a ball game last summer, they put ketchup on my hot dog. *Ketchup.*"

Sacrilege for a city dog. A lot of people don't have a sense of humor about such things. Mustard is the only appropriate condiment for a sausage. Budweiser is the only beer at a ball game. On the other hand, I was supposed to be interviewing this guy for a seat on the supreme fucking court, so maybe we should talk about that for at least thirty seconds.

"How would you describe your judicial philosophy?" I asked him.

He watched me for a moment, then broke into a humorless smile. "My *judicial philosophy*? My judicial philosophy." He sat back in his chair, chin up, eyeing me. "You're interviewing me for this position?"

"Yes, I am."

"You're questioning whether I can handle this job?"

"I'm just questioning, period."

"And you're going to give a recommendation to the governor?"

"Correct."

"Mmm-hmm." He nodded at me. "How long have you been a lawyer?"

"Nine years."

His expression said it all: What was a kid like me doing evaluating judges? This guy was actually insulted that he'd have to answer questions from me. "I've been a judge for seventeen years. I've got a record and it speaks for itself."

Now we'd found common ground. His record definitely spoke for itself. And, if I was reading this idiot correctly, he wasn't going to be doing any other speaking on the subject.

"Please pass on to the governor how honored I would be to serve on the court."

"I'll do that, Judge."

"And when you write up that recommendation for me—that's something that will be disclosed publicly?"

"Not sure," I said.

"Well, if it's going to be—I'd like to take a look at it first. Make sure it works."

"I'll see what I can do."

"Good." The judge clapped his hands together. "And now we can say we met?"

"Now we can say that."

He got up and extended a hand. I took it and gave him my strongest grip, just a quick but hard squeeze. And then my vaunted interview with the honorable George Henry Ippolito was over.

74

HAVING JUST CONDUCTED A SERIES OF SHAM INTERviews to name the next justice of the state supreme court, I now moved on to a sham meeting to hear the pleas of a number of people looking to spare the life of Antwain Otis. Madison Koehler had already told me that my assignment was to support the governor's decision to deny clemency and let the state execute this inmate.

I'd read the considerable file on Antwain Otis twice now and drafted a one-page summary of its contents. His wasn't a particularly original story. Eleven years ago, while a high-school dropout and member of the Tenth Street Crew street gang, Otis held up a pawnshop on Mayfair Avenue in Marion Park, a south-side community not very far from where I grew up. The owner, after Otis had left the store, ran outside with a firearm that was stowed under his counter and shot at him. Otis sprayed return fire and missed, but his shots killed a woman and her son crossing the street. Clearly, the mother and child were not his intended targets, but the law didn't care about that. If you intended to fire the gun—which Otis clearly did—you were presumed to have intended to shoot whomever had the misfortune of being in the line of fire. In this case, the victims were Elisa Newberry, age thirty-two, and her five-year-old son Austin.

Otis was convicted of murder and sentenced to death. On direct appeal, the state supreme court upheld the conviction but vacated the death sentence because of improper argument by the prosecution. The high court sent the sentencing issue back to the trial court, where a new jury once again recommended death for Antwain Otis.

Otis couldn't claim that he lacked adequate representation, as his lawyers had actually beaten the death sentence on the first go-round. Plus, for several years now, Otis had openly admitted to the murders, so legalese aside, no one was claiming a miscarriage of justice. This was no innocent man.

That, of course, was significant. The horror stories involving death-row inmates, the examples most often cited by death penalty abolitionists—a shoddy lawyer who fell asleep at trial or failed to call any witnesses; a prosecutor who withheld exculpatory evidence; a cop who beat a wrongful confession out of an accused—were not present here. Antwain Otis was not denied due process of law. He had good lawyers and a fair trial. And he even now freely admitted he was guilty of the murders. He was not wrongly convicted; in fact, it was entirely fair to say that Antwain Otis was properly convicted and sentenced to death.

The clemency petition filed by Otis's lawyers did not claim that an innocent man was going to be executed. Their point was that Otis had been rehabilitated and had become a positive force within the prison system. Simply put, Antwain Otis had found God.

I heard that all the time when I was a prosecutor. People found God when their back was to the wall, after they'd lied through their teeth about horrific crimes they'd committed but now were facing a judge for sentencing. But I had to admit that Antwain Otis had a decent story.

With the assistance of local clergy, he started a new prison ministry called You Came to Me in June 2001. The file contained affidavits of twenty-four current and former inmates who'd served with Otis at Marymount Penitentiary, some on death row and others in general population, almost all of them violent offenders. The affidavits, predictably, attested to the impact that Otis and his ministry had made in their lives. Antwain Otis had brought them to God, had taught them the power of faith and forgiveness, had shown them a different path. Eleven of those twenty-four had since been released from prison, and none of them had been reincarcerated for subsequent offenses—a notable statistic, I had to say, given the high rate of recidivism, especially among violent offenders.

But none of that changed the fact that this was an election year, in which a Democratic governor would be sensitive to charges in the general election that he was soft on crime. None of that changed the fact that this man was undoubtedly guilty of the crimes of which he was convicted. None of that changed the fact that Antwain Otis was a black gangbanger who killed an attractive, young white woman and her young son.

The governor, while up in the city—which was most of the time, as far as I could tell; I wondered if he ever spent time at the mansion down in the state capital—had a number of offices at his disposal. I was directed to one of them, a long room with cheap furniture and mustard-yellow walls and uncomfortable chairs. Governor Carlton Snow and Bill Peshke were conferring quietly when I walked in. "Hi, Jason, sit by us," said the governor, before continuing his deliberations with his press guy, Peshke.

"Okay," he said, pounding the table and turning toward me. We formed a triangle, the governor at the head of the table and Peshke and I flanking him. "Antwain Otis. Did he do it?"

The question threw me for a moment. I thought it was a conversation starter but came to believe he was really asking me the question. He didn't know anything about this case?

"Yes, he's admitted to the crimes. He killed two people, a woman and her son, during a robbery."

Peshke, with the plastic hair and polished expression, took a note of that and asked for details, names and ages. He was the guy they put out front with the press. He'd need this stuff.

"So what's his deal?" said the governor. "Does he *have* a deal?"

"He's preaching the Christian faith to inmates. The argument is that he's making a difference, and we should let him stay in prison to keep doing it. A number of people have come forward who claim that this guy has changed their lives and given them hope for the first time."

The governor seemed to be waiting for more from me. Then he looked over at Peshke. The two of them made eye contact. I wasn't a mind reader but I didn't think either of them found this impressive.

I still couldn't believe these guys had no idea what was contained in the file.

"So, a double murder," said Peshke. "Young woman and her son?"

"Yes."

"No question of guilt?"

"None."

"Mmm-hmm." Peshke deliberated, jotted a few notes on a pad of paper. He held it up and cleared his throat before reading from it. "The governor's obviously sensitive to these issues on a case-by-case basis. He takes no joy in this task, but he recognizes his constitutional responsibility and he's given this case careful consideration. He's reviewed the file and the clemency petition, and he's listened at length to the people advocating clemency. There's no question about the defendant's guilt or about the fairness of the trial. Two innocent people were murdered, and the governor sees no reason to disturb the sentence imposed by the court."

The governor nodded along. "Good, I like that."

"Did I say anything in there that's wrong?" Peshke asked me.

Other than the part about giving this case careful consideration?

"No," I said.

"Great." The governor looked at each of us. "Then let's bring them in."

75

HAVING PREDETERMINED THE OUTCOME OF THE CLEMENCY hearing, we were now going to actually hold that hearing. I watched four people enter the room and immediately felt sorry for them, knowing their pleas would be in vain. Hey, I'm as cynical as the next guy. I know politics are going to dictate a lot of the governor's decisions. And I know that much of the time when I walk into a courtroom to argue some motion or legal issue, the judge has already made up his or her mind before hearing oral argument.

But this wasn't some routine, humdrum issue. The governor was deciding whether to spare someone's life, and other than hearing my thirty-second summary of the petition, the governor was denying this guy's plea for mercy without knowing anything about it at all.

A lawyer in a decent suit and bad haircut began the presentation. He made the intelligent decision to start by kissing as much ass as he possibly could—his admiration for the governor, his appreciation of the governor's willingness to keep an open mind and hear this out.

"We recognize we're asking you to do something that requires political courage," he said. "Antwain Otis is guilty of the crimes he's convicted of. He didn't mean to shoot those people, but he shot them nonetheless, and he's admitted his guilt. We are not asking you to set him free, Mr. Governor. We aren't seeking a pardon. But we *are* asking you to commute his sentence to life in prison without the possibility of parole. He'll never, ever leave prison."

The lawyer glanced at his notepad, resting on the table. He shouldn't need his notes this early on. His first minute should be the most powerful, and it should be eye-to-eye with the person he's trying to convince.

"Prison. For many, it's the end of the road. It's the last stop in life. But not for Antwain Otis. For Antwain, it was the beginning. The beginning of a new life. The Lord came to him in prison. He opened up doors beyond the tall cement walls topped with barbed wire. He showed Antwain a life full of love and hope and meaning. You've talked, Governor, about your faith many times. I know you know what I mean."

The governor perked up, nodding eagerly. I had no doubt he went to church every Sunday and waved to the cameras when he did so. But I had plenty of doubts about what it meant to him.

"But my point, Governor, is not that you should spare Antwain's life because *he's* rehabilitated. My point is that he's rehabilitated so many others. He's touched many, many people with his ministry. A good eighty percent of offenders become re-offenders. They don't learn much in prison. If anything, they regress. They become more resentful of a society that has discarded them. They learn few valuable skills. And they leave prison with a major stain on their record, a felony conviction. These people have little chance when they get out, so they ultimately resort to their old ways. They re-offend and go back inside. It's a revolving door of crime, prison, release; crime, prison, release."

The lawyer paused and glanced at his notes again. I wished he wouldn't do that. He should have been better prepared. You look at your notes and you lose some of the zing, some of the heartfelt sincerity, the connection to your audience.

"So what do we do? We build more prisons. We pass tougher laws. But do we rehabilitate? Well, maybe we try. We think we do, at least. We give money to the Department of Corrections for inmate programs. But we all know the kind of budget problems we have right now. What gets cut first? That's not hard to figure. And that, Governor, is why someone like Antwain Otis is so important.

"Antwain is rehabilitating people. He's offering inmates another path. Some of those inmates won't ever leave the system, that's true. They're on death row or serving life sentences. Does that mean they don't matter? Obviously not. We're not that kind of society. But Governor, even more importantly, a lot of the people Antwain has reached will get another shot at integration into society. And this time, they'll be prepared. We have affidavits from a number of former inmates who haven't re-offended. They may not be CEOs of Fortune 500 companies but they're working hard to make a life, and they're making a life with Jesus Christ as their savior. They're good, honest people. Let Antwain help more people, Governor. He'll serve his life in prison for the crime he committed. But he'll change the lives of so many more people if you let him live."

I thought maybe all four of the people were going to speak, but apparently there was only one other, an African American dressed in

black with a cleric's collar. He was elderly and appeared frail as he
stood up, but his voice was surprisingly commanding.

"Mr. Governor, I've spent my life counseling people and preaching the gospel. I've been involved in the correctional system for over
thirty years. And I've made a difference, I hope. I hope I have. I hope
so." He opened his hands. "These young men who I see every day
are haunted. They're haunted by what they've done and by what's
been done to them. And what they see in me is someone who hasn't
walked in their shoes. What they see in Antwain? They see themselves. Yes, sir, they see themselves. What Antwain says to them is,
'I've been there. Just like you. I've made the same mistakes. Maybe
worse ones. And look how I've changed my life.' Governor, there's
nothing more powerful to a young black man than to see someone
else just like himself, with as little as he has, who has made something out of it. Something positive. Now, I'm not gonna talk to you
about the Bible. I could. I could tell you that the death penalty is
immoral, that it isn't fair, that it's against God's will. I could cite
twenty verses from the good book about helping those in prison. But
I'll just tell you one thing I always tell these inmates. I always say to
them, 'Don't look backward. Look forward. You can't change yesterday, but you can make today and tomorrow better.' And that's what
I'm asking you to do, Governor. Look forward. I know Antwain—"

He paused, momentarily choked with emotion. The room was
utterly silent. The *tick* of the clock on the wall was like a chime.

The man raised his snow-colored head upward. "Governor, I
know this young man. I love him and I respect him as much as anyone I've ever met. And killing this young man? *Killing* him would
just be another . . . another *crime*."

Nobody spoke for a good minute. The lawyer put his hand on
the cleric's shoulder and whispered to him. Then he thanked us for
our time. The governor rose and shook their hands again, as he had
when they entered. "I have some hard thinking to do," he told them.

I shook hands, too, but didn't speak. I wasn't sure what would
come out if I did.

"I thought that was pretty good," Governor Snow said to Peshke, once the door had closed behind the people. "Hey." He turned to me. "What did the lawyer mean when he said he didn't mean to shoot those people?"

I explained to him the wife and child caught in the cross fire between Otis and the pawnshop owner, and how the law conclusively presumes intent to kill anyone hit by an intentionally fired weapon.

"Oh, okay. These guys are talking and I'm sitting here thinking, 'If the gun just accidentally went off or something, why would they give him the death penalty?' Okay." The governor pointed at Peshke. "I think what you have written is fine. What's next?"

"Fundraiser up in Highland Woods," said Peshke. "Jed Barker?"

"Right, right." He clapped his hands together. "Hey, Jason, come by tonight, when we're winding down."

He didn't wait for my answer. He was out the door, on to his fundraiser, not two minutes after the clemency hearing had ended.

76

AFTER THE CLEMENCY MEETING, I WENT BACK TO Suite 410. I was pretty stirred up about what had just happened, but it was the furthest thing from the minds of Lee Tucker and Christopher Moody. They wanted to know about my meeting with Judge George Ippolito. As eager as Tucker was to hear the news when I walked in, he made himself wait until he could locate Moody by phone. He spoke softly into the receiver and I got the hint: I wasn't supposed to know where Moody was. When Tucker got him on the phone, he hit the speakerphone button so we could all talk together.

"Ippolito didn't come out and say it," I told them. "But he might as well have. We didn't discuss a single substantive thing. We killed about ten minutes, and then Ippolito asked if he could see my written recommendation for him once it was finished. I mean, he clearly knows it's a fix for him. But there wasn't a direct admission."

Lee Tucker worked the plug of tobacco in his cheek and played the whole thing over in his mind. He was booting up the conversation from FeeBee on his computer.

"Pretty obvious, you think, in context?" Chris Moody asked me over the speakerphone.

"It was clearly a sham interview. I mean, he didn't even try to hide it."

"And you're back with them tonight?"

"Right. I'm meeting someone for dinner and then I'll hook up with them."

"And you'll talk about Ippolito?"

"I'll try."

"Try to talk about the other stuff, too. Cimino's stuff and the pro-choice groups paying up."

"I never would have thought of that, Chris. Your direction has been invaluable."

On one of the walls, Tucker had taped up makeshift diagrams of the various scandals and the players involved. One sheet of paper was entitled UNION JOBS, meaning our efforts to evade veterans' preference laws to get that union guy's cronies on the state payroll in exchange for one union's endorsement. Madison Koehler and Brady MacAleer were listed. Rick Harmoning, the head of SLEU, was listed with a question mark next to him. Presumably, they didn't have him on tape yet agreeing to the illegal deal. SUPREME COURT APPOINTMENT was another sheet of paper, involving Madison and Mac as well, with union boss Gary Gardner and Judge George Ippolito as question marks. HOUSE BILL 100 concerned the abortion bill and the governor's mention of payout money from the pro-choice groups in exchange for a veto. It was the one place where the name Governor Carlton Snow appeared. It was the only thing they had directly on Snow, and nothing had even happened yet.

I could almost smell the palpable hunger in Christopher Moody's gut. He wanted the governor. But he didn't have him. Not yet.

But I could sense what was happening now. They wouldn't tell me, but I had no doubt that the moment Christopher Moody heard that tape of the governor suggesting a shakedown of the pro-choice groups, he was drafting affidavits and preparing applications for Title III intercepts all over the place. It's not easy to place a bug in someone's office, or to tap their phones—to eavesdrop without anyone's knowledge. If one party consents—like me wearing FeeBee—it can be done quickly. But any time the overhear is done without anyone's knowledge, the process is rigorous. Chris Moody could very well be in Washington, D.C., right now, making his case at the various levels of the Department of Justice to allow him to tap the phones of the governor, Madison Koehler, Brady Mac, and others, and to bug the campaign headquarters and even their homes. Presumably, one day soon the U.S. attorney general himself—ironically, Carlton Snow's predecessor, former governor Lang Trotter—would be listening to the tape that I procured of the governor.

Things were moving fast. Probably they wanted to make arrests before George Ippolito could be seated on the supreme court. Possibly, out of some sense of conscience that I might attribute to people over Moody's head—but not to Moody himself—they wanted Governor Snow exposed before the primary, before the voters bestowed on him the nomination heading into the general election. Regardless, soon enough, they would have a lot more than me as weapons in their search. They would be listening in on all sorts of conversations to which I wasn't privy.

The question was whether "soon" was soon enough. If they had the primary election and the Ippolito appointment as deadlines, they were pushing it. I didn't know exactly how long this process took to secure the Title III warrants—through the various levels of the Justice Department and then to the chief federal district judge in our city. Five days? Twenty? They might not have enough time. I might be their only source of information.

"I'll do my best to raise the topics," I said. "Obviously I can't force it."

"I notice you're steering your former client, Senator Almundo, away from those topics," Moody said to me, static from the speaker-phone punctuating his words.

Right. I knew that conversation wouldn't be lost on Moody, when Hector asked what I'd been up to and I stiff-armed him.

"Emphasis on 'former' client," he continued. *"You don't owe him anything."*

"It's not just me," I noted. "No one seems to talk to Hector about this stuff. Besides, Chris, if you reindicted Hector, you'd look spiteful."

"Is that your problem or mine?"

"Hector's a hanger-on. The governor likes having him around but he's not the brains of the outfit. Hell, he wasn't even the brains of his own office, back when he was senator. Your good friend Joey Espinoza was the one who really called the shots in the senator's office. Remember?"

Lee Tucker made a face and slashed a finger across his throat. Abort. Bad idea.

He was probably right. And we were done, anyway. I didn't need Chris Moody to tell me that I should try to get incriminating statements on tape.

"Good luck," Tucker said to me, tossing me another F-Bird.

I tossed it back. "I have dinner first," I reminded him. "You don't get to listen to that."

That really made Lee's night. It meant he had to wait around for me until after dinner to hand off FeeBee.

I took the short elevator ride down, thinking about the dwindling number of days I had to solve three murders. I'd never considered fail-ure an option. I always figured I would sit tight and strike when the moment came. Now I was beginning to wonder if time would run out.

I also realized I was looking forward to seeing Essie Ramirez for dinner tonight.

And then the elevator door opened, and who was exiting another elevator but one Shauna Tasker. She was doubly surprised, first because we hadn't seen much of each other lately, and second because she obviously had come from our office, and I hadn't. She first raised her eyebrows in mock surprise and then wrinkled her brow in confusion.

"Hey," I said. Then, "Met with a new client."

"Oh? Who?"

It then occurred to me that I'd have to name someone in this building—not necessarily on the fourth floor, from where I'd come, but somewhere. And I had almost no idea who else was in this building. I can bob and weave with the best of them, but I didn't want to do it with Shauna.

I paused, made a face and waved off the question for a stall, hoping that she'd let it go. She can read me pretty well, but she blew it off. "We saw you on TV the other night," she said. "Governor Snow was speaking at some rally?"

"Oh. Right."

"Getting into politics now?" she asked.

"Oh, not really. Just thought it would be fun to see it. What are you up to tonight?"

Then I thought of what I was doing tonight, dinner with Essie Ramirez, and for some reason I didn't want to share that with her.

"Having dinner with Roger," she said. "Want to come?"

"I'll pass. But I need to meet him soon."

She seemed to find that statement odd, probably the lack of a sarcastic jab. We were becoming more formal, and it felt weird.

"Nice coat," I said. She was wearing a white winter coat that I hadn't seen before. I was losing track of this lady.

"Roger," she said.

"Ah, okay," I said, teasing. "And was there an occasion for such an extravagant gesture?"

"Oh. . . ." She seemed reluctant to answer. For a moment I thought she was going to tell me they'd gotten engaged or something. And then it hit me.

"Oh, shit," I said, smacking my palm against my head. "Oh, Shauna—"

"No worries."

Her birthday. Two days ago. I'd forgotten Shauna's birthday. Now I felt like a complete putz.

"You've been busy," she said. "And gone. We had to sweep your office for cobwebs."

I put my hand on her shoulder. "Jesus, Shauna, am I an asshole."

"I won't argue. But I forgive you."

"I'll make it up to you."

"I'll make sure of that." She winked at me and we walked through the doors, into the cool evening air. She stopped and appraised me. "You okay in there?" she asked.

"Just grand."

She still had those probing eyes that could see through whatever roadblocks I threw up. But she wasn't going to challenge me. She kissed my cheek and was off.

I suddenly felt hollow. I felt alone. I'd more or less completely lost touch with Shauna. It was excusable. Hell, it was necessary, I thought. I needed to keep her as far away from what I was doing as possible. And it was reparable, at least in theory—I'd make it up to her when this undercover gig was over. Problem was, this guy Roger was filling the void in the interim.

The other problem was, Shauna didn't appear to be as bothered about it as I was. She seemed to be moving on, with Roger's hand in hers.

*   *   *

ESSIE RAMIREZ WAS WAITING for me at the bar, nursing a glass of wine and studying the yuppie dinner crowd. I watched her for a moment before I made my approach. She looked the part of a young professional in the city—hair pulled back, blue suit, simple jewelry—but it occurred to me that Essie was out of her element. She'd been raising two kids and hadn't worked outside of the home for probably a decade. This could have been intimidating for her, but I got the sense that it was more exciting than anything.

She told me about her new job as a paralegal at my old firm, Paul Riley's shop. She told me about her kids. I thought she was rebounding, now with a reliable paycheck and some time passed since Ernesto's death. Then again, we were keeping it on fairly safe topics. She didn't talk about how much she missed her husband. I didn't talk about what I'd been up to.

She took the check from the waiter after we'd finished our coffee.

"You notice," she said, "that I didn't ask you about your search for the truth."

"I noticed." I smiled. "I'm going to figure it out. I'm getting close."

She nodded, appraising me with those dark, shiny eyes. "I want you to. I do. I might have sounded like I didn't before. I just don't want you to get hurt doing so. That's all."

"I understand."

"If I can ask," she said. "What do you plan to do when you figure it out?"

I told her the truth. "I don't know."

She accepted that. She was willingly staying in the dark, not asking for details. She probably assumed, correctly, that if I'd wanted to share, I'd have done so by now.

"Another question, if you don't mind," she said.

"Shoot."

"Why have you never told me that you lost your wife and daughter recently?"

It was true. I hadn't. And I'd forgotten that Essie was now working at my former law firm, where the first mention of my name would have elicited that information.

"Well, anyway, I'm very sorry," she said. "You've suffered. I had no idea. When you were standing outside my house on Christmas Day—"

"It's not a problem, Essie."

"This happened—near the time I lost Ernesto?" she asked.

"The same day, actually," I said. "The reason I didn't drive my wife and daughter to my in-laws' house is because I was waiting for Ernesto to call me. So she drove without me."

"Ah." I hate pity, and I was seeing it all over Essie's face. "So you put the two things together, don't you?"

I didn't answer.

"You blame yourself for—"

"Why don't we just drop it, Essie," I said, dropping my hands down on the table to indicate finality.

She placed a hand over her heart. "I have a knack for being direct."

I blew out a breath. "It's okay. I like that about you."

"Oh, Jason. Jason, you can't do that to yourself."

I didn't answer. An awkward span of time passed. Essie counted out cash and placed it with the check. She couldn't have very much money to her name, but she'd be insulted if I offered to pay. This was how she wanted it.

"Thanks for dinner," I said. "But you didn't owe me."

Her eyes flashed up at me. A strand of hair slipped out of her clip and curled around her cheek. She was debating whether to say something. She was searching me for a reaction, for a sign. I knew what I was thinking, but not what I was conveying. Something powerful was moving within me, a connection to Essie. Maybe it was just this joint tragedy we shared, like families who bond after losing their loved ones in a plane crash or something. I didn't know. All I knew for certain was that she was looking into my eyes, and I was looking back, and neither of us seemed inclined to retreat.

"Do you think I asked you to dinner because I thought I *owed* you?"

That sounded like a dangerous question for me to answer, so I didn't. There must have been a thousand love songs, and even more romantic comedies, built around this premise. Two people recovering from the loss of their spouses who find each other and rebuild their lives. Look, I couldn't deny an attraction to Essie, and it appeared that the feeling was mutual. And I felt like I'd crossed a bridge recently. I could swallow the idea of another woman in my life, at least in some fashion. But not this. I couldn't separate Essie from her husband, from guilt and anger. And I couldn't think of her in a casual way, a one-nighter or anything even close to that.

"Thanks for dinner," I said. "I have to go now."

She watched me a moment, still with those studious eyes. "Will you keep in touch with me?"

"I'll let you know when I figure this out," I said.

Her expression told me that I'd wounded her, that she'd had more in mind than merely the imparting of information. But I couldn't do anything about that. My thoughts and emotions were tangled up and I defaulted to the classic Kolarich option, retreat.

"It was fun seeing you again," I said, a comment which widely missed the mark in all directions. It seemed like an appropriately awkward note on which to exit.

77 I CALLED HECTOR'S CELL TO FIND OUT WHERE TO meet up. Then I hooked up with Lee Tucker for the hand-off of the F-Bird before taking a cab to a union rally over in Hector's district. When I pulled up there were about a half-dozen people picketing the place. They'd managed to gain the attention of at least one camera. They were protesting over Antwain Otis, the death-row inmate scheduled to be executed tomorrow night. I was still a little rattled from my dinner with Essie, thoughts of lust and passion and guilt and bitterness forming one hell of a knot in my chest. I never thought performing an under-cover role for the federal government and hearing about death-row inmates would serve as a welcome diversion from my thoughts.

I walked in through a side door protected by the governor's

security detail, one of these somber robots who had my name and even recognized me now. I stepped into an anteroom much like the one at the last rally. Madison Koehler was pacing while she barked into her earpiece at some poor subordinate. Brady MacAleer was eating chicken wings with some people I didn't know. I peeked into the main room and saw Hector Almundo warming up the crowd, mostly speaking Spanish to a group of blue-collar Latino workers, two hundred strong.

Carlton Snow took the microphone next, starting with his patented joke about snow and then working his magic for about twenty-five minutes. He introduced himself by talking about his parents and his family's struggles when he was a kid. No talented politician's bio is complete without tales of humble beginnings, say, a union-worker father who got laid off before he got cancer and had his leg amputated because the insurance company denied coverage, or some variation thereof. It was because of his upbringing that Carlton Snow was singularly qualified to relate to the common man, why he gets up every day wondering how he can improve the lot of working-class families in this state.

I watched the whole damn speech and found myself calming again. Snow was pretty good in a room, I suppose, and afterward in the adjoining room, Hector was jacked up, talking with some people in Spanish and beaming at the attention he was receiving, being so close to power again. I saw Charlie Cimino and waved to him and the others were there, too, Madison and Brady Mac and Peshke, all of them working their cell phones furiously.

As much as I disliked politics and in spite of my real purpose for being here, I had to concede that the power was enticing. Everyone wanted a photo with Governor Snow. Everyone wanted a few words or an autograph. He was the odds-on favorite to win the nomination and, in an election that was probably going to go to the Democrats nationally—either Hillary or Barack would be formidable—Snow would stand an excellent chance of being elected to a full term. And from there, certainly in his mind, there were no limits.

For some reason there was beer, and everyone started drinking, including me. I made eye contact briefly with Madison, and she gave me an important nod, like maybe I'd done something right. Or maybe she had plans to use me as a human jungle gym later, but I wasn't on that agenda at this point. I was fucking her plenty with the recording device inside my coat pocket.

"Tomorrow's the announcement." Charlie, liquored up himself, whispered harshly in my ear. "Both of them, SLEU and the Laborers. You did it, Jason. Those jobs for Rick Harmoning's people—Mac says there are some pissed-off people but you did it. It's done," he concluded. "It's fucking done."

Tomorrow was the announcement? Did that mean tomorrow George Ippolito would be named to the vacancy on the supreme court? And did that mean the feds were going to swoop in tomorrow, before it could happen? I felt a flutter of panic. I couldn't stomach the idea that Ippolito would be on the court, even for a day. But I didn't want Chris Moody, Lee Tucker, and company to make the arrests tomorrow, either. I wasn't done. I hadn't found my killer yet.

But I did find Madison Koehler, busy conferring with someone in one corner of the room. I stood an appropriate distance from them but made myself visible. When her subordinate looked sufficiently beaten down by Madison and skulked away, I moved in.

"The unions are announcing the endorsements tomorrow?" I asked.

She seemed annoyed with me. "Yes?"

"What about George Ippolito? Does he get appointed tomorrow?"

"And why is that your concern?" In Madison's world, it was all about control. She compartmentalized. The strategists did strategy. The lawyer did law. I'd done my part, conducting sham interviews and writing up a glowing recommendation for Judge George Ippolito. I didn't need to know anything beyond that.

"Ippolito had asked to see the recommendation," I said. "Plus I thought Pesh might want some help with the press conference."

She glared at me for a moment. You could almost see ice forming between us. "If you must know—no, we're not appointing George tomorrow. No need to be so obvious. We'll wait a few days. Maybe after the primary, maybe before. Does that address your concerns?"

"It does, and as always, Madison, it was a pleasure speaking with you."

I deflated with relief. I had a few more days, at least.

The outsiders slowly filtered out, and soon it was the same group, making a circle out of the folding chairs, a bucket of icy beers in the middle. The governor, Hector, Madison, Mac, Pesh, Charlie, and me. With the outsiders gone, there was a palpable sense of relief in the air. These people felt comfortable with one another. This was the team, against everybody else. I imagined that when you do these campaigns, these are the kinds of things you remember most fondly, the downtime, the drunken camaraderie. Boy, that really made me the fly in the ointment, didn't it?

The group was half conversing jointly and half broken up into whoever was sitting next to you, which for me meant Charlie and Hector. At one point Peshke cleared his throat and said, "Eleven-thirty tomorrow, Willie Bryant's going to lose his appetite for lunch."

Everyone clapped at the reference to the union endorsements tomorrow. Governor Snow, his sleeves rolled up and collar open, waved everyone down. "We don't slow down now, guys." He looked at Pesh. "Gardner and Harmoning are going to be there?"

"Joint presser outside your office," Peshke said.

"I love it. I love it!" Snow grabbed Peshke's shoulder. "Great job, everybody. And when do we leave?"

"Day after tomorrow," Madison said.

"We're going to take some digits from Willie downstate," said Brady Mac. He was probably taking a lot of the credit on this, along with Charlie. I didn't know where I fit in on that meter, nor did I care, under the circumstances.

"Let's go drink some good stuff," said the governor.

Everyone shuffled off to the waiting limos. Madison signaled me and said, "Ride with us."

Madison announced the seating arrangements as we approached the two vehicles, and no one seemed to question it. I ended up in a limo with the governor, Hector, and Madison.

I sat next to Hector and across from the governor and his chief of staff. Madison worked her BlackBerry for a moment. Hector and the governor started up a conversation, and Madison signaled me. I leaned forward on my knees.

"You'll have everything written up for Pesh on the Antwain Otis thing?"

I nodded. "I'll have it to him first thing in the morning."

"You'll hit the highlights? The victims' families, the senseless crime, that kind of thing."

I gave her a thumbs-up because I wasn't sure how it would sound if I answered verbally.

"You should be there when Pesh releases the statement to the press. In case they ask him something he can't answer."

"You mean, like, why would we execute someone who's turning lives around in the prison system? Questions like that?"

Madison's eyes narrowed. Otherwise, she didn't move a muscle or react in any way. That was her way, the steely resolve. "There it is again, that attitude. Did we not talk about that?"

I returned the stare. I wasn't going to debate her, and I wasn't going to back down. Nor was I going to win the argument.

"Next," she said. "This thing with the jobs."

"Rick Harmoning's people," I said, thinking that FeeBee in my pocket was now standing at attention.

"Mac says there's a hiccup with one of the jobs. Someone's complaining or something. I don't know the details, and I don't want to know them. All I want to know from you is that I won't be hearing about it anymore. Take care of the problem."

"What is this now?" the governor asked, breaking away from his chat with Hector.

"Just some details, sir," Madison said.

"Rick Harmoning's people?" he asked. "Oh, Rick. Oh, okay."

My heart skipped a beat. I could imagine Chris Moody and Lee Tucker poring over FeeBee's contents later with bated breath, as Governor Carlton Snow got his hand close to the stove and then pulled it away. *Oh, Rick. Oh, okay.* Were those statements enough to show, beyond a reasonable doubt, that he knew about this criminal scheme to trade jobs for a union endorsement? Or was he simply aware that Rick Harmoning had requested that certain people get jobs in the Snow administration? Moody would spend hours hashing over such questions. The better answer was that the words the Governor had just uttered were not, by themselves, enough.

The governor and Hector had resumed their side conversation as Madison gave me instructions. That seemed consistent with a governor who didn't sweat the details. I guess that's how it had to be. But it made me wonder how much Governor Snow knew about what was going on around him. Rick Harmoning, the union guy, for example. The governor seemed generally aware that Harmoning had put in a request for jobs for his friends in the Snow administration, but did he know that there had been a straight-up exchange of jobs for the union endorsement? I didn't know, and I didn't have proof of that yet.

And I wasn't sure how much I cared. I wasn't on the same program as my federal friends, Chris Moody and Lee Tucker. I wanted to know who was behind Greg Connolly's murder—and what was almost my own murder, had I not narrowly escaped during that fun-filled interrogation. That, in turn, would probably tell me who killed Ernesto Ramirez, too. Same people, I assumed, working with Charlie Cimino.

And yes, as much as I didn't relish being a snitch, I didn't mind having a hand in exposing corruption at the highest levels of state government. Putting an unqualified judge on our supreme court? Buying union endorsements with jobs and appointments? Shaking down pro-choice groups in exchange for a veto of an abortion bill? I could live with helping the federal government on that score.

But here, I thought, was the difference: I didn't care if the investigation netted Governor Snow. I wasn't counting heads, trying to rack up defendants for an indictment. I wanted to know who had me put in that room, naked down to my boxers, to interrogate me; who ordered the murder of Greg Connolly and left him with his pants down in a park; who had Adalbert Wozniak and Ernesto Ramirez taken out. If it was Snow, then so be it, I wanted him to fall. But Chris Moody wanted the governor for political ambition. I just wanted the truth.

"Governor," I said, "Judge Ippolito wanted me to tell you that he'd be honored to sit on the supreme court."

"Ippo—Ippolito." The governor gave me a blank stare initially. It was one I was seeing on him a lot. He looked at Madison. "Gary Gardner's guy?"

Madison nodded. "We can talk about that later," she said.

He took that comment under advisement, then nodded himself. It wasn't hard to see how this worked. Madison was protecting her boss. Everything was stopping at her. The governor would stay above the fray. I was back to my question: How much did Governor Snow really know? He hadn't even recognized George Ippolito's name.

The limos pulled up to the Ritz-Carlton. Again, we were in the city, where the governor's family lived, but he was staying in a hotel. The governor and Madison climbed out of the limo into the cold, fresh air.

Hector signaled to me. "We'll be right in," he said to the governor and Madison.

Then he turned to me. "I want a word with you," he said.

78

HECTOR WAS ON HIS SECOND SCOTCH IN THE LIMO, which, combined with a number of beers at the event, lent a rim of redness to his eyes and an easing of his posture. It seemed to put him in a bad mood, as well, if I was any good at reading people.

"What's this stuff you're talking about? Jobs for Rick Harmoning and this judge who says hello to the governor?"

Again with this dance. Hector, out of the loop and wanting in. Me, wanting to keep Hector out of the loop to protect him. "How come the governor stays at the Ritz instead of sleeping in his own bed?" I asked.

Hector seemed annoyed by the question, swatting at it like he would a buzzing fly. "He's in campaign mode. She knows he needs to focus. I doubt she misses him much. But hey," he said, returning to his subject, "what about all this stuff you're talking about?"

He swallowed the remainder of the scotch, refilled, and stared at me.

"Look, Hector, they tell me these things in secrecy. I'm just doing what I'm told."

"Secret from *me*? Who got you here, Counselor? You forget that?"

It was partly the booze talking, and Hector had had plenty. But alcohol typically lays bare true emotions, deep insecurities. Hector wanted to be a player again, and he took any secrets as the ultimate sign of disrespect.

"I do what I'm told," I repeated, which felt like a cop-out, especially coming from me. I tended to be something of a contrarian, and Hector knew that.

Hector held out his hands, like he was displaying himself to me. "You think I'm just some peon? You know I'm going to be the first Latino lieutenant governor?"

I drew back. "You're not running for lieutenant governor."

"I'm not *running*." He looked away in disgust. Then he leaned into me. "Mickey Diedman's going to win guv lite, and when Barack or Hillary becomes president, Carl's going to get Mickey on the federal bench and appoint me as the replacement."

All of this was news to me. Having become more attuned to politics of late, I was certainly aware that a downstate county prosecutor, Michael Diedman, was running for lieutenant governor as a Democrat and appeared to be the favorite. It was not exactly an unusual path from county attorney to federal judge. Had some deal been struck?

"Wow, that's great," I said, only because Hector's ego seemed to be suffering and I thought it was what he wanted to hear.

"Yeah, so tell *that* to all those assholes in there. Madison, Peshke, Mac—you think any of them have ever been elected to *anything*? No, they don't have the balls. They just stay behind the scenes while we go out there and take the fucking hits. Then they look at me like I'm some fucking puppy dog they have to pat on the head." He squirmed in his seat, really working himself up now. "Who do you think Carl listens to more than anybody? They think I'm just a fly on the wall but who does Carl listen to the most? Who tells him what to do?"

"You," I gathered.

"Me. Fuckin-a right, me." He patted his chest. "You see me tonight? You think I can't work up a crowd like he can? I'm going to be the first Latino lieutenant governor and then I'm going to be the first Latino *governor*. They think I'm just some brown face they can parade in front of the Mexicans? Fuck them. Fuck all of them."

"Hector—"

"Look at what *I* got for my public service. I got fucking indicted, that's what I got. I didn't do anything different from anyone else. But me? The Latino politician? No, the Latino, they can't have *him* in power. They have to take *him* down."

He took another long sip of his fresh drink, his hand trembling.

I'd heard this angle from Hector on occasion, this racial thing. I had my doubts; I thought federal prosecutors were equal-opportunity hunters when it came to politicians. But then again, I was a white Catholic boy. I'd never walked in his shoes. And the persecution complex is a natural reaction when the government comes after you, justly or otherwise. It stops being about what you did to get their attention; it becomes how bloodthirsty they are in their quest to catch you.

"Joey Espinoza fucked you," I said again, letting him gain momentum, because I sensed something here.

"Joey Espinoza." He had a physical reaction to the name, spilling some of his drink. "Let me tell you something about Joey Espinoza. I mean, now that it's over."

I steeled myself. I didn't know what was coming next. And I couldn't control it. I had a recorder in my pocket that would pick up this entire thing. I'd been trying to protect Hector from the feds out of a sense of loyalty to a former client. But I had a number of puzzle pieces that I hadn't fit together yet, and one of the biggest was Joey Espinoza. FeeBee or not, I needed to hear this.

"I mean, you're not my lawyer anymore, but you're still my guy. I mean, am I right or am I wrong? Are you my guy?"

That, of course, was how someone like Hector saw the world. It was like a damn *Godfather* movie, kissing the ring, pledging fealty to a master. Hector didn't need to know that our conversation would be protected by the attorney-client privilege. In fact, he was going to tell me something that he *wouldn't* tell me when I was sworn to professional secrecy. No, where he sat, being his "guy" was a more sacred bond than being his attorney. He just needed to hear me say it.

"Of course, I'm your guy," I said.

79

"YEAH, YOU PROBABLY ALWAYS WANTED TO KNOW." Hector chuckled, drained his drink, and reached for the decanter for another refill. He was pretty far in the tank by now, and it had loosened his tongue considerably.

"This fucking guy, Joey," he said. "You think that guy could spell his name without me?"

Actually, I did. Espinoza had always seemed like a smooth operator. That didn't necessarily require a high IQ, but he seemed intelligent enough from my observation.

"He couldn't come up with an idea like the Cannibals. You think he could figure out something like that?"

"It was your idea," I said.

Hector took a drink and licked his lips, took a breath. "I didn't think they were going to muscle people. I figured they wouldn't have to. Just them asking would be enough."

That stood to reason, I guess. A gangbanger wouldn't have to come out and explain the consequences of noncompliance. A simple request for a monthly street tax—or political contribution to Hector—followed by a sinister grin, would probably get the job done.

"And if anything ever blew back, you could just deny it," I said. "Chalk it up to the Columbus Street Cannibals exercising some street advocacy, without your knowledge."

He smiled at the summary. He wasn't going to come out and say it. "And all I asked was that Joey set it up. He couldn't even do that." He wagged his finger at me. "I gave that kid everything. Shit, I'm *still* giving to that cocksucker, even after what he did to me."

I wasn't sure what he meant, but I had an idea. "You mean Charlie giving Joey's wife a job. I saw her at Charlie's office once."

Hector nodded. "Six figures," he said. "Six figures and all Lorena does is show up and polish those long fucking nails of hers. The job is hers until Joey gets out."

"But why?" I asked. "Why do that for Joey?"

"Because Joey sticks his nose—hold on." Hector reached into his pocket and looked at his cell phone. "Ah, shit. Hang on." He opened his phone and lowered his voice. *"Dame un minuto, querido. Te veré pronto."*

Hector closed the phone and placed it in his suit pocket. "Ah, I'm drunk." The momentum had broken. I just had him on the verge of an explanation.

"Don't leave me hanging, Hector," I said, as he began to move toward the limo door.

"I don't want to talk about that anymore," he said, grunting as he bent down to step out into the cool night air. Since I was his "guy," that meant I was supposed to accept that decision without comment. "C'mon, Carl wants us up there."

Dame un minuto, querido, he'd said to whoever had called him. *Te veré pronto.* My summer studying in Seville hadn't gone for naught. *Give me a minute, dear. I'll see you soon.* Hector had been talking to someone he cared about.

"Vámonos," Hector called to me.

I pulled up alongside him and we got in the elevator. I didn't get what I wanted, but at least now, I'd have an opening in the future to raise the topic again.

Peshke answered the door to the suite when we knocked, talking in his earpiece to someone and holding a glass of champagne in the other. The governor was out of his suit, wearing an oxford and blue jeans. The governor pointed at me when I walked in. "Jason, quick—the center fielder for the 'seventy-six Yankees?"

"Mickey Rivers," I said.

The governor waved a hand toward Brady Mac. "That's one of the easiest questions ever. I mean, that was before free agency changed everything, Mac."

In one corner of the suite, Madison Koehler and Charlie Cimino were having a more serious conversation. Madison seemed to be dishing out and Charlie receiving. I couldn't imagine about what; Charlie had largely relegated himself to the sidelines since his brush with law enforcement. He saw me out of the corner of his eye and motioned me toward him.

"Madison and I were just discussing that some of the contractors we contacted about contributions haven't ponied up yet," he said. "We were thinking another phone call from you would be in order. Remind them of their commitment and their nice fat state contract that they want to keep."

It was true—some of the contractors still hadn't paid the extortion money to preserve their current contractual relationship with the governor's office. But the vast majority of them had, and given how spooked Charlie had become after learning that Greg Connolly was wearing a federal wire, and his subsequent decision to lie low, I figured we would let those few stragglers go.

I guess the little charade that we'd orchestrated with my visit to the U.S. attorney's office with Charlie's handpicked lawyer, Norm Hudzik, had convinced Charlie that the feds had no idea what he and I had been up to. That, and his overall greed and desire for maximum credit with Governor Snow, made him eager to squeeze every single dollar of campaign contributions out of his schemes.

"You want me to call them and remind them we can pull their contracts if they don't pony up?" I asked. It was a bit on the nose, I thought, once it came out of my mouth.

"If it's not too much trouble," said Madison with her typical sweetness. "Or do you have a moral objection again?"

Close enough, I figured, for Chris Moody's purposes. Madison Koehler had just directed me to use interstate wires for the purpose of coercing campaign contributions, which probably made her a co-conspirator in the shakedowns Charlie and I had performed for the last two months.

And now I had an opening to raise a subject I'd been wanting to tap, the whole reason I was doing this damned undercover work.

"Not a moral objection," I said. "It's just that, after Greg Connolly, I wasn't sure if we wanted to keep a lower prof—"

"What *about* Greg Connolly?" Madison's head snapped in my direction. "What does he have to do with this?"

"Nothing, it's nothing," said Charlie. "He just means, after Greg died, we—we were worried—y'know, that maybe they might investigate him or something."

"For getting a blowjob on Seagram Hill and then getting jumped? What does that have to do with us?" Madison looked alternatively at Charlie and me. She seemed genuinely puzzled.

Genuinely so. I like to think I can read a lie, and she wasn't lying. She didn't know, I decided. She didn't know the truth about Greg Connolly. She didn't know how he'd really died, and she didn't know that he'd been wearing a wire for the feds.

Wow.

"Forget about Greg," said Charlie. "He has nothing to do with this."

Madison wasn't following, but she also didn't care. "Collect on that money," she said.

Madison stalked off, and Charlie shot me a look. "The fuck are you doing?" he whispered.

"I thought she knew," I said. "The thing with Greg?"

"She knows what I fucking *let* her know," he said. He was whispering but also drawing in close to me, practically speaking into Fee-Bee. "*No*, she doesn't know."

"Well, maybe if you'd tell me who *does* know, I could avoid putting my foot in my mouth."

"Another way is you just don't mention it, period, smart guy."

Charlie broke away. He was angry. I was surprised. Madison Koehler didn't know that Greg Connolly had been exposed as an undercover informant? She didn't know that he'd been murdered? I hadn't thought that was possible. I'd thought everything went through her. I'd been working under the assumption that she was a part of this whole thing.

"Hey, all the secret stuff in the corner!" Governor Snow was calling out to us. "How about you join the party already?"

I returned to the fold, to the group sitting in the main area of the suite. Hector and Peshke and Madison were arguing about what to do with the abortion bill, the thing about parental notification for teenagers. The governor would have to sign it or veto it in the next forty-eight hours.

"I'm with Maddie," said Hector. "Veto it. You're pro-choice, Carl. Act like it."

"You can be *moderately* pro-choice." Peshke was sounding like a broken record. "Sign it and neutralize the topic during the primary. You still own the abortion issue in the general."

The governor looked bored with the discussion. He nodded at Charlie, who was now joining us. "Hey, Ciriaco," he said, using his formal name, "what's with your guys not paying? Maddie says we're still short about a hundred and fifty thousand from your people?"

"Working on it, Governor."

"Well, can you work on it some more?"

"Yes, sir."

I channeled Christopher Moody, wondering if these statements got him anything. By themselves, I thought, they didn't. This was the second time they'd have the governor on tape talking about what Charlie and I had done. The first time, the governor had just told me that he'd heard I did a good job. And this second reference just now, a little closer to the fire but still not on the nose. Still no admission. Neither of his statements indicated that he knew precisely the nature of what we'd been doing—the illegality, the extortion. For all anyone would know, the governor was just talking to a fundraiser about fundraising.

It would produce more than one clenched jaw in the U.S. attorney's office. The governor, without knowing it, was walking on a tightrope and constantly threatening a misstep, but thus far had managed to stay upright. He'd referenced a few of our schemes—George Ippolito; the jobs in his administration; and Charlie's and my shakedown—but never with any admission that he knew we were doing something illegal.

The only thing he'd come out and said that would be illegal, as I thought about it, was his suggestion the other day that we shake down the pro-choice groups for a hundred thousand each in exchange for his veto of the parental-notification abortion bill. And I hadn't heard him mention it again. I had no idea if that was even a "go."

Someone pulled a television front and center. We started watching campaign commercials the governor was planning to air in the last days of the primary. Some of them were the stars-and-stripes positive ones; more of them were negative ads that showed unflattering photos of Secretary of State Willie Bryant with sinister background music and assorted innuendo and spin.

After debating the merits of various ads and strategizing over the amount of ad buys in the various television markets over the coming days, the group was flattened and drunk, with much to do tomorrow. Everyone got up to retire, either to the hotel suites or to home.

I looked over at Madison, who'd been sitting next to me and was now preparing to exit. I was still rattled by the realization that she didn't know about Greg Connolly. She'd seemed like the puppet master behind everything. I'd been sure she was a part of the decision to eliminate Greg, that something like this wouldn't have happened without her sign-off.

Now, to my continued amazement, I had to cross her off my list. I'd have to reevaluate everything. Because my operating premise was that the person ordering the murder of Greg Connolly was higher on the food chain than Charlie Cimino, and after eliminating Madison, there was only one person left who fit that description.

I looked at him, Governor Snow, who it so happens was looking at me. "Stick around," he mouthed to me.

Sounded like a good idea to me. "Sure," I said.

"Hey," Hector said to me, turning me and walking me toward the door. "If you're tired, just take off. You don't need to stick around if you don't want."

Interesting that Hector would say that. Maybe he liked keeping tabs on me—his "guy," after all—and didn't want me getting one-on-one face time with the governor.

"No, it's okay," I said. I thought a little one-on-one was just what I needed right now. With his defenses down thanks to the liquor, this might be the best chance I'd have to find out what the governor knew, and when he knew it.

 THE ROOM FELT EMPTY AND LARGE WITH EVERYONE gone, all the aggressive banter evaporated. The governor poured himself another glass of champagne and offered me one, which I accepted. Anything to encourage dialogue.

"Sometimes it's nice just to talk with regular people," the governor said. "You strike me as regular. I mean, nonpolitical."

"That I am." I sat on the couch. He took the chair across from me. His face was flush and his eyes were bloodshot. He was drunk. Drunk but content. He loved everything about being governor.

"Let me ask you something," he said. He nodded toward the television. "That ad—the one about Willie Bryant, that supervisor in his office who was caught taking bribes? What did you think of that?"

I knew what I thought, but I didn't want to rock the boat. "He'd do the same to you," I said. "Rough-and-tumble politics."

He sipped his champagne and eyed me. "Give me the honest dope."

"I don't like negative ads," I said. "I mean, if everyone under Bryant is committing crimes, then okay, it's a relevant point." I stopped for one moment to consider the irony of that statement.

"But," I went on, "I take it from this ad that it was just one bad egg in his office. So I wouldn't read much into this, other than Willie Bryant's opponent is running a negative ad, trying to blame him for one rogue employee."

Governor Snow smiled. "Y'know, I pay these people a lot to think like a regular voter. But the truth is, they're so close to this—I mean, these guys hate Willie—I'm not sure they see things right. I think I agree with you."

"They get people elected," I said. "I don't."

"Right." He drained his drink and poured himself another. He rolled his neck, seemed to be unwinding after a day of being on camera. "How come you quit playing football?" he asked.

"I was kicked off the team after that fight."

"Right, but—why didn't you go somewhere else? You could have gone anywhere."

I shrugged. "Inertia, I guess. I was an idiot."

"Okay, then, why are you here?"

I wasn't sure how to answer that. He seemed to respond well to the no-bullshit, regular-guy talk, so I didn't want to light him up with sweet nothings. On the other hand, you can never underestimate the human ego, the capacity to believe favorable things about yourself.

"You seem like a winner," I said, stifling the gag reflex. "I like to go with the winner."

He watched me, maybe trying to decode what I was saying.

"You have to understand the rules before you play a game," I went on. "I think you're a guy who understands what he has to do to win. I want to be with the guy who brings a gun, not a knife, to the gunfight. I mean, you can't be a good governor unless you're governor, right?" I'd heard someone else say that. Carlton Snow probably said that to himself every day.

God, I hoped this was working, because it was all I could do not to laugh. I was trying to get him comfortable enough to talk about the things happening under him that fell somewhere outside the legal boundaries. I wanted it to be a source of pride, an emblem of his ambition.

"So, why are you here?" he asked me again.

I thought I caught his meaning, but I didn't have a clever response. "Why does anyone want to be with a winner?"

The governor moved from the chair to the large window overlooking the north side of the city. The commercial district had gone dark but the area to the north was scattered with lights, the yuppie crowds enjoying late-night dining, theater, the bar scene. Profiled against the cityscape, and notwithstanding the oxford and blue jeans, Carlton Snow looked more like a governor than at any time I'd seen him.

"It's hard to find people I trust," he said. "Everyone wants something. Everyone has their own agenda. Mac, I trust him from going back, but he just needs someone to follow, y'know? Maddie and Pesh and Charlie—I trust them because their interests intersect with mine. They only get what they want if I get what I want." He drank from his glass and looked out over the city.

He was a personable guy. I'd seen that in him from the start. It might have been practiced, but I didn't think so. That, in fact, seemed to be his chief attribute. I didn't see anything in him that particularly demonstrated superior intelligence, and certainly no great command of policy, but he could probably enjoy the company of just about anyone. That quality, in some ways, made him perfect for the job of governor, but in other ways made him wrong for it. If I was reading him correctly, he was longing for real relationships and not just lackeys who whisper sweet nothings.

But why was he sharing this with me?

"What about Greg Connolly?" I asked. It was a risk, of course, a cymbal crashing during the mellow music. But what the hell, the booze was making me impatient.

The governor did a quick turn in my direction before returning his gaze to the window. "Greg. Greg, he surprised me. He surprised me."

"How so?"

"I didn't know. None of us did."

Know what? I wanted to say. But I held my tongue, because the governor was already preparing to elaborate.

"I knew that guy my whole life, Greg. He had a great family. He loved his wife. He had this other side to him, and it made him do things like—like skulk around in a park after dark?" He blew out a sigh. "Christ, what a way to go. I looked at Jorie later that day—she wouldn't even talk to me. I mean, what is she supposed to think? What is she supposed to tell her boys?"

The governor seemed to be getting a bit emotional. And I was getting more and more confused.

After a moment, the governor cleared his throat. "He could have told me. I wouldn't have cared. I mean, it's one thing if you're an elected official, right? But Greg? He was behind the scenes. He could be whatever he wanted, I wouldn't have cared. He had a job with me for life. I wouldn't have cared about his damn sex life."

I didn't know what to say. I surely wasn't going to get an admission from him about Greg Connolly's undercover role with the federal government. And it was becoming awfully damn clear to me that he had no idea about it. I mean, this guy was a politician, a bullshit artist, but he couldn't fake what he was doing here. Not when he was half in the bag, at least, and not with me watching everything about him to look for signs of a lie.

Jesus Christ. Unless I had lost all ability to read people, neither Governor Snow nor Madison Koehler knew anything about Greg being a snitch. They couldn't have been behind his murder. Where the hell did that leave me?

"Now Hector," the governor said, turning to me. His voice had regained something, I wasn't sure what. "Hector, I trust. He understands me. I can tell that guy anything. That's a powerful thing, y'know? To know you can trust someone with a secret?"

I nodded. I was still a little flustered here.

He walked up toward the couch and stared at me. He seemed far removed from the guy mourning the loss of his friend only two minutes ago. Some people can turn on and off like that. "So, can I trust you, Jason? Like I can trust Hector?"

I felt some internal detector queue up. This wasn't a throwaway question, but I didn't quite get the drift. Regardless, there was no reason not to play along. Besides, I was still playing to a recording device in my pocket, and the feds would expect the same answer from me.

"Of course you can," I said.

He sat down next to me and turned to me. "Like Hector?"

"You can trust me," I said, getting annoyed now and more confused.

"So tell me what you want," he said. "You want to be a judge? You want some director job or something?"

None of the above, but I wasn't going to rock the boat now, though I wasn't sure where that boat was heading. Someplace turbulent, I thought, but I was beginning to mistrust my instincts. Or I just was having trouble believing them.

"You just want to be with a winner," he said, his eyes locking with mine.

I didn't speak. Something told me I should say something. Or maybe hold up a stop sign. But I didn't. Not in time, at least.

Not before he put his hand on my thigh.

I WAS A WIDE RECEIVER IN FOOTBALL, NOT A DEFENSIVE back, despite the fact that I liked hitting people more than catching a ball, for one simple reason. I didn't like to backpedal. I didn't like the feeling of being off-balance as I pumped my arms and legs in reverse gear.

Maybe I'd missed my calling, because nobody, not an All-Pro cornerback in his prime, could have bounced off that couch and moved backward to the door of the hotel suite as quickly as I did.

Neither of us knew what to say. I thought that this was one of those actions-speak-louder-than-words moments. I'd made it pretty clear how I felt about what the governor had just done. I stood looking at the carpet. The governor, from what I could gather, had no idea how to proceed at this point.

"It seems to me, what we have here is a failure to communicate," he said with an accent, parroting the famous line, hoping to ease the tension. Or just ease his embarrassment. He tried to laugh at his line, but the whole thing had fallen flat. I was hoping a phone would ring or something.

"Listen," I finally said, "if I did something to make you—"

"No." He raised a hand. "No need. My fault. I'm just drunk, that's all. Let's just forget about this."

"That's not a problem."

The color had drained from his face. It seemed like the intoxication had drained from his body, too. He looked stone-cold sober and completely humiliated. The governor hadn't just been rebuffed; he'd just revealed something extremely personal about himself to me.

"I should go," I said, the understatement of the evening.

"Yeah, sure. We've got a big day tomorrow. The execution and all."

I didn't think I could subtract any more from the painful awkwardness, so I got my ass out of there. I kept a straight face as I passed by the governor's security detail and essentially held my breath until I made it to the elevator. I ran my hand through my hair a few times, as if that would somehow remove the memory from my brain, and propped myself against the side of the car.

I wanted nothing more than to go home and take a very hot shower and bury myself under my covers, but I had to deliver FeeBee to Lee Tucker, which made me think about how those last couple of minutes in the suite would sound on tape.

Given the lateness of the hour some of these evenings, Lee Tucker didn't tend to sit around Suite 410 in my building waiting for me. I knew that in advance and called his cell phone when I had a moment. We agreed to meet at my house, with Lee entering through the alley.

He was wearing a sweatshirt and torn jeans, a ripped green hat, and a plug of tobacco in his mouth. His eyes were puffy and his cheek bore the faint sign of a crease. He'd been roused from sleep recently—presumably when I called. He was catching his shut-eye when he could find it these days. His day wasn't ending here at midnight; it was just beginning. These days, as things were escalating in the campaign and the end of the investigation drew near, these guys were taking the F-Birds and immediately scrutinizing them.

"Anything good?" he asked.

I almost laughed. Tucker, I knew, would get a laugh out of the last few minutes of the recording.

"Not really," I said, trying to focus. "No great admissions. To listen to this, you'd think neither Madison Koehler nor the governor had any idea about Greg Connolly working for you or the real way he died. You'd think the governor hardly knew the name George Ippolito and only vaguely knew about Rick Harmoning getting jobs for his cronies in the administration."

"He's a slippery one," Tucker said.

"Yeah, but it's not so much that, Lee. This guy—it's not like he avoids the topic altogether, he just doesn't go into detail. And every time he gets near something hot, Madison's there for a roadblock."

"Right. Insulating the boss. Classic."

I wasn't as convinced as my FBI handler about the insulation Madison was giving Governor Snow. Tucker might be right; it was possible that Snow knew everything that was going on—that he directed it, in fact—and Madison was just making sure he didn't slip up in public. But I thought it was even money that Madison was the string puller, and she figured the governor didn't need to know the details. And Carlton Snow sure seemed like a guy who could live with that arrangement.

Tucker nodded. "Anything else?"

"Tomorrow, the unions are endorsing Snow. SLEU and the Laborers. I think eleven or eleven-thirty."

I saw the urgency in his eyes, the same thing I felt when I heard that news, so I was quick to tell him that the word I received was there would be no Ippolito appointment tomorrow. "Madison thought the timing would be too obvious."

"She said that? That it would be 'too obvious'?"

"Yeah, she did. That'll be a nice admission for you at trial."

He seemed pleased with that. He should be, from his perspective. Madison, from what anyone could tell, was the closest to the governor. She had the most goods to spill. They'd do the old hard-soft on her. They'd throw everything they had at her, trying to scare the shit out of her, and then offer her a decent plea bargain if she gave up everything she had on Governor Snow. She would likely be the star witness.

I knew that all along, of course, but it hadn't bothered me until now. I'd assumed that she had a role in Greg Connolly's murder, which eased my conscience considerably for helping record incriminating conversations about the Ippolito appointment and the jobs-for-endorsement thing with Rick Harmoning. But now I didn't like her for that murder, and it made the whole picture a little grayer for me.

"Anything else?" Tucker shook the F-Bird in his hand. He was impatient, eager to get back and dissect the contents of tonight's recordings.

"Nothing major," I said. I left out the part about Hector admitting to me tonight that he orchestrated the Columbus Street Cannibals' shakedown of local businesses for campaign contributions. Chris Moody was going to love that part when he listened to the F-Bird. It was like rubbing his face in his courtroom defeat. I didn't know Hector was going to say that. It wasn't my intention to rub it in Chris's face. But it was a nice fringe benefit.

"Okay, so—that's it?" Tucker asked.

I thought for a moment. "I might as well tell you, you're going to hear it, anyway," I said. "The governor made a pass at me tonight."

"He made a—" Lee Tucker stared at me with innocent, unassuming eyes. A burst of uncertain laughter escaped. "Seriously?" he asked. "What did he do?"

"He sidled up to me and put his hand on my knee."

Tucker put his hands on top of his head. He got a real rise out of that.

"My thigh, actually," I said. "The inside part. There was . . . no doubt."

That made him laugh harder. It was probably a combination of stress release and sleep deprivation, but soon he had to use the door to prop himself up. "You've gotta be . . . kidding me."

"I wish I was, believe me."

My cell phone buzzed. The caller ID said it was Hector Almundo. I could imagine why he was calling, but I wasn't in the mood. I was hoping Tucker would stop laughing sometime soon.

"Eight tomorrow?" Lee said to me, catching his breath, his face the color of a tomato.

"See you then."

I could hear his laughter as he walked down the alley. I allowed myself a brief chuckle, as well, more an acknowledgment of the bizarre than pure comedy. But the frivolity didn't last. I was getting close to the end of my run with the governor's people, and I had done a lot for the federal government, but I had completely struck out on my personal mission. I'd set my sights on two people—the governor and Madison—as the people behind Greg Connolly's murder, and I had turned up a goose egg.

Maybe I'd been wrong about Charlie not running the show that night when Greg and I were interrogated, with only one of us surviving. Maybe there wasn't someone above him. Maybe I was doing nothing more than serving as a good old-fashioned snitch without a higher purpose.

My cell phone rang again. Hector a second time. No doubt now—he'd heard from the governor. He was being called in to play intermediary, to damp down any brewing fire.

I watched the phone as it played out its four rings, then silence, then a slight quiver of the phone and a buzz telling me a second voicemail message had been left.

Then I decided to call Hector back.

HECTOR ANSWERED ON THE SECOND RING. "HEY," HE said, clearly relieved to hear from me. "I talked to Carl. I heard about, y'know, what happened."

"I figured."

"I told you that you didn't have to stick around, didn't I?"

"Yeah, a little more specificity would've been nice, Hector."

"Carl feels terrible. He's really embarrassed."

"It's fine, Hector."

"Listen—this is something you can keep to yourself, right? I mean, you can keep this a secret?"

That, clearly, was the purpose of the call, not the apology.

"Who would I tell?"

"I know," he said, "but Jason, I'm serious here. This kind of thing gets out, it's over for Carl. He's finished."

In this day and age? "Oh, come on," I said, but I was reconsidering my reaction before I'd finished speaking. In many contexts, it seemed like it had become downright fashionable to swing from the other side. But, now that I thought about it, what was true for movie stars or baristas at Starbucks might not be true for governors of large Midwestern states. There wasn't exactly a sea full of outwardly gay politicians anywhere, actually. There had been the governor out east, Jersey I think, who'd held that press conference to out himself, but that presser was quickly followed by a resignation. Maybe that old line was still true, the only things that will end your political career are being caught in bed with a dead girl or a live boy.

"You have to tell me that you understand what I'm saying," said Hector.

"I thought I already did."

Silence. Then, "Tell me what you want, J. You can have whatever you want. Seriously."

"I want the vacancy on the supreme court," I said.

"The sup—" He spent a moment with that, to my surprise. "I mean, that's pretty—could we talk about the appellate court maybe?"

"Hector, I'm kidding. A Porsche 944, yellow with black interior, will be more than enough."

"I can't tell if you're being serious or not."

"I can see that."

"Jason. Jason. You understand, you're holding his whole political future in your—"

"I understand you're serious, Hector. I'm not going to mention this to anybody, all right? I'm probably more embarrassed than he is."

"I seriously doubt that."

In the background on Hector's side of the phone call, there was the sound of something breaking, a glass it sounded like, followed by cussing. Hector covered the phone and said something I couldn't make out, save for the scolding tone. The voice of the person cussing was a man's voice.

Right. Those of us on Hector's defense team had always suspected; Lightner had been absolutely sure of Hector's sexual preference. And now I had a much more informed idea why Hector was so close to Governor Snow. I'd always thought it was window dressing for Latino voters. Instead, it seemed they shared a common trait. I wondered if there was any kind of relationship between the two of them, but it was hard to imagine. More than likely, they were just two very public men who bonded over a shared, very private personal predilection.

Yesterday, I thought maybe I knew one gay politician; now I was sure I knew two.

"Hector, no bullshit, I wouldn't—"

My throat closed involuntarily. I couldn't finish the sentence. My heart started racing, my instincts outpacing my brain.

I asked myself a simple question, and I thought I knew the answer.

"You still there?" Hector said. "Hello?"

I braced my arm on the kitchen counter and played it out in my head.

Hector said, "I told Carl, if there was anyone I knew who could keep a secret, it was you. So I'm not gonna be wrong about that, am I? Jason. Am I gonna be wrong?"

I couldn't speak, or at least I couldn't focus on what Hector was saying. My mind was spinning now, trying to build a story, layer one fact upon another.

"Let's talk first thing in the morning? Okay, Counselor? Sound like a plan? Let's have breakfast at Apple Jacks, eight-thirty. Carl's going to make this up to you, Jason, I'll make sure of it. Okay?"

I didn't reply. I killed the cell phone and paced the kitchen, playing a game of what-if in my mind, recognizing holes in my logic but feeling in my gut that I could plug them up with additional information.

I tried it from different angles, questioning myself, playing devil's advocate, but I kept coming to the same conclusions. I was short on a couple of facts but I knew they were true, even if I *didn't* know. I was sure of it.

I felt my senses slowing, my mind shifting to a dead-alert focus. My limbs were trembling with rage.

What do you plan to do when you figure it out? Essie Ramirez had asked me.

So what's the plan, J? Joel Lightner had said. *When you figure out who killed Ernesto? You going to kill that person?*

I felt everything break down, all of the walls I'd built up crumbling like a house of cards. Maybe that was a good analogy. Maybe I'd been kidding myself that I could get past this. I thought I'd done so. I thought I'd moved on. I missed my wife and daughter, but I was putting it behind me. I told myself the guilt I felt would ultimately harden, would become a permanent scar but one that would fade with each passing day.

I was backsliding and I didn't care. How familiar and comfortable it felt, the self-destructive rage and bitterness. *This is who you are.* The guy who picked fights on the schoolyard with guys twice your size. The guy who blew his ride at State, his career in football, just so he could prove to the team captain how tough he was. Wanting to lash out and hurt, fully knowing the hurt would be returned twice over, wanting that hurt, seeking it out.

This is who you are.

I went upstairs to my bedroom. In the closet, top shelf, I found my old badge from the county attorney's office. I'd thought I lost it once and had to put in for a replacement. I'd paid a heavy price for doing so—a week's pay—the prosecutor's office not having a sense of humor about official badges making their way into the public domain, and when I found it later, my replacement already in my wallet, I figured I'd already paid for the right to keep the original issue. So I did, even when I left my job as an ACA and turned in my replacement badge.

I had a gun, too, which I hardly knew how to use. I'd had the bare amount of training and even spent an afternoon at the FBI shooting range, a Friday perk for us low-paid, hard-working prosecutors, but I hadn't handled this thing for more than four years and I wasn't sure I could hit a mountain from a distance of two feet with this weapon at this point.

I didn't have a plan, either, except that I wasn't going to wait any longer.

Now I knew. I finally knew. The only remaining question was what I would do about it.

83

IT STARTED TO RAIN AS I DROVE, MASSIVE TEARDROPS splatting my windshield. Dark and stormy seemed appropriate. I was growing cold inside as I worked through everything I knew, feeling like it was all coming up in one direction, no matter how I played it; growing cold as I did math that I knew *didn't* add up: If it wasn't for Adalbert Wozniak's murder, there'd be no Ernesto Ramirez. If there hadn't been Ernesto Ramirez, I wouldn't have been waiting for him that night to call me. If Ernesto hadn't been murdered, my wife and child would not have traveled alone.

Alone on a night like this, I thought, not cold but rainy, slippery, poor visibility.

I was past the *why* questions I'd asked for so long afterward. *Why* didn't Talia scrap the trip when it started raining so hard? *Why* didn't she slow down at the curve? I was past it as a pure function of a time cushion, and I was past it because I knew I was just transferring, because I was bitter and angry and everyone was to blame, me included but not alone.

I took deep breaths as the blackness mounted, coloring everything around me. I was trembling, white-knuckled hands gripping the steering wheel, my teeth grinding so furiously that I was tasting blood on my tongue.

I'd never been to this place, this townhouse, but I had the address courtesy of Joel Lightner. It wasn't hard to find. The area had exploded in the last few years, before the housing bubble burst, but these were not the homeowners who defaulted on their loans and left their homes in disarray. This was the near-west side, the lofts and condos all new, purchased by the young professionals and artists.

I stood next to the mailbox, a cold shower of rain pelting me, forcing me to squint as I peered at the three-story home. At two in the morning, all the interior lights in the townhouse were out. I removed my cell phone from my pocket and dialed the number. It rang four times and went to voicemail.

I hung up. Then I dialed it again.

A light went on up on the third floor, presumably the bedroom. That's really all I needed to know.

"Yeah, hello? Jason?"

"Hey," I said into my cell phone. My voice was even and flat. "I think the reception was bad on the phone before. Just wanted to tell you, I'm not going to say anything to anybody."

I could hear Hector clearing his throat, shaking out the cobwebs. "Okay, good. That's good. Hey, breakfast tomorrow, eight-thirty? Apple Jacks?"

"Breakfast tomorrow." I punched out the cell phone.

Five seconds later, the light went out in the third-floor bedroom again.

Hector was down for the night, sleeping more peacefully now that I had reassured him that I would not divulge the secret held by Hector's political coattails, Governor Carlton Snow. I wondered how often Hector stayed out here at this townhouse. For a guy who liked to keep his private life private, I suppose it made more sense to stay at his partner's place, not the other way around. He probably parked his car in a garage, maybe slinked out in the early morning hours before anyone could see him. Or maybe he figured he was sufficiently anonymous out here in the artsy-yuppie near-west side, several miles from the legislative district he used to represent.

I looked at the mailbox marked D. BAILEY. According to Joel Lightner, Delroy Bailey had moved here after his divorce from Joey Espinoza's sister. Lightner, in his typical flair for completeness, had even noted the grounds for divorce in the petition filed by Joey's sister: irreconcilable differences. Yeah, I guess it's pretty irreconcilable when your husband is gay.

If it wasn't hard for me, it wouldn't have been hard for Adalbert Wozniak, either. He was claiming that he'd been treated unfairly by the Procurement and Construction Board when the beverage contract was given to Delroy's company over his own. Did he actually figure out that someone very close to the PCB, Hector, was sleeping with the contract award winner? My guess was no. If Wozniak had gotten that far, there would have been some documentation of his finding. But no doubt, in his lawsuit, he was going to seek depositions of the interested parties, including Delroy Bailey. Wozniak and his lawyers would be sniffing around, and Hector would be in jeopardy. The story, from Hector's viewpoint, would be devastating. Not merely allegations of influence peddling—politicians live with those accusations all the time—but something that would be far more controversial to someone who was, at the time, seeking the Democratic nomination for the office of attorney general. It would be hard enough to become the first Latino statewide officeholder; the first Latino *and gay* statewide officeholder would probably be too much.

What had Hector said tonight about Governor Snow? *He's finished,* if word got out about his sexual preferences. Hector would have thought the same thing about himself. He was looking at a revelation that would end his statewide political ambitions. He didn't know that was coming, anyway, thanks to a federal indictment. He didn't know the feds were all over him, that they had flipped Joey Espinoza and were investigating the Columbus Street Cannibals.

What to do with Adalbert Wozniak, the man who could ruin him? Hector didn't turn to the Cannibals. He didn't know them. He admitted as much to me last night in the limo. The Cannibals shakedown was his idea, but he needed Joey Espinoza to deliver the message, to orchestrate everything with the Cannibals. And Hector couldn't turn to Joey for the Wozniak problem. He couldn't very well tell Joey, *I'm sleeping with your ex-brother-in-law, and it's about to be exposed if we don't kill this Polish guy.*

So he turned to a different street gang, the one that didn't dominate his legislative district, that wouldn't be so easily connected to him. He went straight to the top. He went to Kiko, the top assassin for the Latin Lords. He needed Adalbert Wozniak dead to keep him quiet.

To cover up Hector's connection to Delroy.

Hector. Hidden in plain sight, right in front of me. I must have missed about fifty clues along the way. An attorney's instinct, I guess, for his own client.

The moments shot out at me now like asteroids from my subconscious: During Hector's trial, when I told Hector and Paul Riley about this witness I liked, Ernesto Ramirez, a guy who seemed to know something and who was close to the Latin Lords. *Maybe the Lords killed Wozniak,* I said. *Why would they do that?* Hector responded, doing a very good job of playing dumb. I might as well have signed Ernesto's death warrant at that moment.

And the night my world changed, as I waited impatiently in my office for a call from Ernesto Ramirez. The call from Paul Riley, asking me why I was still at the office, and my response—that I was waiting on this witness, this long-shot, Ernesto. Hector in the background with Paul, laughing, knowing that the call from Ernesto would never come, knowing that I'd sit there all night.

I reached into my trench coat pocket and felt the gun, caressed it, pondered it.

The rest made sense, too. Greg Connolly was the chair of the PCB. He'd been the one Hector turned to for the favor, skipping over Adalbert Wozniak's company to give the beverage contract to Delroy Bailey and Starlight Catering. Surely Greg was aware of the lawsuit filed by Wozniak's company. Surely it gave him some amount of unrest, at the very least, to know that a legal process was under way to sniff around this sordid affair. And surely, it caught his attention when the plaintiff in that lawsuit, Bert Wozniak, wound up dead from multiple gunshot wounds.

Did Greg know that Hector was behind the Wozniak murder? Hector wouldn't have had to say it outright, though he might have. Hector liked to flex his muscles. I wouldn't put it past him to tell Connolly straight up. Or just as likely, something vague enough for

Hector to take credit without making an admission— *Took care of that problem* or *Don't worry about that thing.*

Did Greg know about Ernesto Ramirez, too? Hard to say, but I assumed so. Probably when Hector first heard the name from me, he reached out to Greg to see if he knew anything. This was in the heat of a trial whose headline charge was the Wozniak murder. Hector would have panicked upon learning that someone knew the truth about that murder.

The irony is that Ernesto Ramirez didn't know that Hector was the bad guy. Ernesto and his friend Scarface assumed it was Delroy's former brother-in-law, Joey Espinoza, who got Delroy the contract. Ernesto had no idea about a gay relationship between Delroy and Hector. He thought the "connection to Delroy" that Bert Wozniak was going to expose was the ex-brother-in-law relationship between Delroy Bailey and Joey.

But Hector didn't know that. All he knew, thanks to me, was that there was a guy out there who seemed to know something about the murder of Bert Wozniak, which included—again, thanks to my speculation—the involvement of the Latin Lords street gang, Kiko's gang. Hector would have been desperate to silence Ernesto. And he used another person who would be just as desperate, Kiko, to carry it out.

Greg Connolly might not have known every detail but he would have known enough. If he had any brains, he'd know that Hector had Wozniak taken out. Same for Ernesto Ramirez. So what was Hector to think when, one day, he discovered that Mr. Gregory Connolly was wearing a wire for the federal government? I mean, killing an aide to the governor is no small thing, but murder to cover up two other murders is less of a leap. What did he have to lose at that point? If Greg was flapping his mouth about Adalbert Wozniak and Delroy Bailey and Ernesto Ramirez, then on a risk-reward calculation, the pros of killing Greg Connolly far outweighed the cons.

Charlie Cimino, of course, was all around the PCB back then, too. Surely he knew all about the Delroy Bailey contract. He and

Hector were two of the main pigs feeding at that trough. So one of them figured out about Greg wearing a wire—I don't know which—and told the other. Then they jumped Greg and did a little water boarding routine on him to find out what he'd told the federal government before they killed him and dumped him on Seagram Hill. Had Greg told the feds about Adalbert Wozniak and Ernesto Ramirez? I didn't know. But either way, Hector couldn't let Greg just walk away and carry on as a snitch for the government. Greg had to die.

One of them—again, I didn't know which—also decided that I might be a threat, and treated me to the same fun-filled question-and-answer session. Only I managed to pass and live another day. They'd have been far better off killing me that night.

Regardless, it was Hector calling the shots, not Charlie. That was clear to me now. I didn't know where he got those guys working me over, but they were his guys, not Charlie's.

I never thought of Hector as "above" Charlie, and in many senses he was not. But he had the ear of the governor, and even if he wasn't respected by anyone else in the inner circle, he was probably feared because the governor seemed to listen to him as much as anyone.

My fingers formed around the gun in my pocket. I looked up at the bedroom on the third floor, where Hector Almundo was sleeping peacefully next to Delroy Bailey. My entire body—every limb, every muscle—ached from the tension, the flowing rage.

"Have a nice sleep, Senator," I whispered. Doing this right now, it would let him off too easily.

I released the grip on the gun. I headed back to the car and drove off, mindful of the speed limit, focused now on the last stop I would make tonight.

To the home of the man who carried out Hector's wet work, who killed Adalbert Wozniak, Ernesto Ramirez, and Greg Connolly.

84 THE SKIES EASED UP AS I DROVE, THE PELTING RAIN turning to soft drops. The roads were empty and I was making good time, not that it mattered. I was doing math that didn't add up, logic that had no linear path. The law does not permit unlimited cause and effect. A guy commits a crime, you can't blame his mother for giving birth to him, even though if she hadn't, the crime wouldn't have been committed. The law talks about "proximate cause," meaning reasonably foreseeable cause and effect. But there was probably nothing reasonable about my thinking right now.

It was a song I'd been singing, I realized, since this whole thing started. If he hadn't killed Wozniak, Ernesto Ramirez wouldn't have mattered. And if he hadn't killed Ernesto, I would have taken that trip with my wife. Different parts of my brain were battling this out but it was clear who was winning, who had won in a knockout.

By the time I pulled up in the alley that ran behind a line of houses including Kiko's, the rain had stopped. My chest was heaving. Everything was dark. The rain in my hair, on my wet coat and collar, felt like ice water.

I got out and closed the car door, which made a recognizable noise but probably one so familiar as to be innocuous, even at two in the morning.

I moved down the alley, thinking about obstacles. Probably a guy at his rank in the Latin Lords had a security system. Probably a guy like Kiko had several weapons at his disposal, too.

I stopped when I was positioned in the alley so that I could see the back of Kiko's house. The light downstairs was on. Through a sliding glass door I could see him, sitting on the carpet, his back against the couch, alternating lights emanating from a television set. So, even if he had an alarm system, it probably wasn't armed. And he seemed to be alone, consistent with my intel from Joel Lightner that he lived by himself.

I didn't have a definitive plan, and nothing particularly effective. Misdirection always works. Ring his front doorbell, maybe have something outside his front door—a note or something, to make him actually leave the house, occupy his attention on the front porch—while running around to the back of the house and breaking in, ready to surprise him when he returns. There was a side window, as well, probably to a bedroom, as an alternative point of entry.

All of those made sense, until the calculator started tabulating in my head again, as I watched Federico "Kiko" Hurtado lazily stretched out on his floor watching something on the tube. The man who took everything from me, from Essie Ramirez, from Adalbert Wozniak's and Greg Connolly's families, was resting in the comfort of his own home watching some inane sitcom or infomercial or soft-core porn.

Those other ideas would work, the misdirection. But other ways were effective, as well, especially if you had nothing to lose.

My walk was steady, one deliberate step after the other, but I found myself picking up the pace as I crossed his backyard and removed the gun from my pocket. I took an angle head-on toward the sliding glass door, out of his sight line, seeing only his outstretched legs. I raised the gun as I approached. When I was within about ten, nine, now five yards, I started shooting.

The bullets splintered the glass in five spiderwebs, one of them wildly apart from the others but the other four close enough to compromise the glass's integrity. I lowered my shoulder and crashed through, just as Kiko's feet began to move. I kicked out my leg with everything I had to complete my entry, to get my legs inside. I had the gun trained on him before he'd had the chance to react.

He looked up at me. His matted hair and puffy, unfocused eyes told me he'd been asleep. The multiple beer bottles lying sideways and the odor of cannabis told me that it had been an intoxicated slumber. Good for me. A guy quick on his feet might have had the chance to at least get some headway toward another room and, at that point, a real chance at escape. But none of that mattered now.

He didn't speak, though his nonverbal communication—the widening stain in the crotch of his gray sweats—told me I had his attention. Here was the most notorious assassin on the city's streets, in a t-shirt and urine-stained sweats, frozen in place with both palms planted on the carpet and one leg bent, as if he were just on the verge of bouncing up.

I trained the gun on him and let it all consume me. This, I now realized, was why I'd been on this quest from the beginning. Someone had to pay for what had happened to Talia and Emily, and I was tired of it being me.

"Why?" he said.

"*Why?*" I nodded at him. "How many people you kill?"

He was watching the gun more than me. "Not one," he said, "that didn't have it comin'."

I moved closer. Then I lowered the gun and delivered a kick into the center of his chest. He didn't take it well, his mouth popping open, his hands off the floor, his body falling to his right side. Something unleashed in me and I tossed the gun on the couch, then dropped my knees down on him, swinging wildly with my fists, missing more than landing, hitting his hands as they shielded his skull. I was doing plenty of damage anyway, slamming his head into the floor from my blows. When I took a brief pause, he surprised me with a surge upward, trying with his legs and arms to toss me off-balance. For one brief moment he almost succeeded, then I brought my full force down on him. He was now turned over on his back, facing up at me. He swung at me with both hands but he had nothing behind the blows, lacking the advantages of gravity or momentum. It was all me, and now that I had him square on his back, I made his face pay. He tried to run interference but it was raining down on him. I landed about a dozen solid blows before his defenses subsided.

I caught my breath and reached for my gun, which luckily I was able to do without compromising my position. I didn't know what I was thinking, giving up that gun, except that I hadn't been thinking at all.

Kiko made a low burst of noise, blood coming from his mouth in the process. I didn't recognize the sound at first but then I got it. He was laughing.

"You gonna kill me, you'd a done it."

That would make it all the more satisfying. I placed the gun against his forehead. The cymbals clashed inside my head, the hatred and anger poisoning everything inside me. Everything about this made sense. This guy had killed so many people. Maybe some of them not so innocent, but I could count a number of them that didn't have it coming. I didn't really know my God anymore but I couldn't comprehend a world where taking this guy out wasn't a good thing.

"Don't, Jason."

I stifled the instinct to turn, because I knew the voice hadn't come from behind me. Or next to me or in front of me. I imprinted the barrel of my gun into Kiko's forehead. He started mumbling something in Spanish. I thought he was praying.

"Don't ask God for help," I said. Then I raised the gun off his forehead. I pushed myself off him and stood over him. He wasn't moving, the only sign of life his soft moans and a bubble of blood enlarging and contracting from his mouth.

I opened the glass door, rather than work my way through the jagged glass, and walked through the yard. A couple of lights were on in the neighborhood, maybe even some people looking out. They might be able to identify me but I doubted it. Some white guy in a suit and long coat, walking through a dark backyard. Anyone living close by knew who resided at this particular address, and odds were they wouldn't be in a hurry to involve themselves in this affair.

I made it to the car and drove through the alley. When I got onto a main thoroughfare, I let out a long breath. The post-event adrenaline flooded me; it was all I could do to keep my hands on the wheel. I was confused, or at least incapable of rational thought, so I focused on getting myself home, on getting the car in the garage and myself into bed.

I would sleep tonight, I decided, at least for the few remaining hours of night afforded me. Like the flip of a switch, I was utterly exhausted. I fell onto the bed and closed my eyes. It was true, I'd been blaming Ernesto's killer for the death of my family. Maybe I'd done so to transfer culpability from where I thought it really belonged, at my own feet. But I now realized it had been something different altogether.

Don't, Jason.

She'd meant so much more with those two words, I thought, than just sparing Kiko's life. I'd assigned blame for her death everywhere I could find—myself, Hector, Kiko, whomever—to avoid the more plausible and, therefore excruciating truth, that what happened to my wife and daughter was nobody's fault.

The next thing I remembered was her hand in mine, our fingers interlocked, gripped so tightly that one hand ceased being independent of the other. Then, slowly, a release, our fingers straightening, our palms separating, nothing but our fingertips in contact.

And then my hand reached for hers and there was nothing. I opened my eyes and it was morning.

85

I NEEDED SOME EXTRA TIME TO GET READY THIS morning, having discovered a number of cuts along my hairline from shards of glass last night. My hands were swollen and sore, but I didn't think I'd broken any fingers. I had plenty of reminders of what had happened last night but it still felt more like a dream than anything else.

Lee Tucker and Chris Moody were waiting for me when I walked into Suite 410 at eight in the morning. They'd been deliberating quietly and hadn't heard me enter. They popped to attention when I showed my face.

"Cut myself shaving," I said when Tucker asked.

"Shaving your forehead?"

"I wasn't paying attention."

Moody leaned back in his chair. He didn't look good. His eyes were set deeply and shaded dark. He usually had a bright-and-eager look about him, but these were long days he was spending.

"Do you think you'll be having more conversations with Snow?" Moody asked. "I mean, after the incident last night. Is he too embarrassed now? Or do you think you'll still be on the inside?"

"Hard to say," I said. "My guess, I'm still in."

"Good. Because we need more," he told me. "Snow's a slippery one."

The same word Tucker had used. *Slippery,* as in, we know he's guilty but he doesn't quite admit it.

"You mean, *you* need more," I said.

"You need to pin him down," he said. "When he gets on a topic, you have to keep pushing it. You just let him move on."

"It's not cross-examination," I said. "It's conversation. I can't force it."

"You're being too cautious, Jason. You already passed their test. You passed. Greg failed."

"Whose test? Charlie's test? Yeah, I passed *his* test."

"Oh, and what happened to 'Charlie wasn't calling the shots'? You think Snow doesn't know anything about what happened to you and Greg Connolly that night?"

These guys had listened to every word of the F-Bird from last night. They'd heard what both Madison and the governor had said about Greg Connolly. They'd heard Charlie Cimino say that he hadn't told Madison anything about it.

Chris Moody did one of his patented chuckles, filled not with humor but condescension. "You think because Madison Koehler and Governor Snow played dumb last night, it means they don't know anything?"

"You weren't there," I said.

"No, but I know these people. I know them and I know a hundred people like them. They aren't going to admit it to you, Jason. Don't be so damn naïve. These people are programmed to lie. They're smart enough not to admit anything out loud."

Their skepticism wasn't surprising, nor was it unfounded. I was as cynical as the next person. But I was there last night. I saw both of them, Madison and the governor, when they talked about Greg Connolly. I didn't trust anyone in this room or anyone working for the governor, but I trusted my instinct, and it told me that neither of them had anything to do with Greg's murder.

"I don't think either of them knows," I said. "And I'm not sure I want to do this anymore."

"You're not—" Lee Tucker's head snapped in my direction. "What, you're announcing your retirement?"

"Maybe I am."

"Kolarich, I'm really not in the mood for this." Chris Moody pushed himself out of his chair. This conversation was upsetting him terribly, not simply because I was resisting him but because I was going to be his star witness at trial, and if asked, I would testify that I believed what each of these people were saying about Greg Connolly.

"Okay." Lee Tucker, ever the peacemaker, raised a steady hand. "You think what you think; we think what we think. But keep pushing, Jason, okay? If you're right, then you'll just prove that to us. What's the harm in probing the subject a little harder?"

I didn't answer. I was running out of steam here. I'd found what I was looking for. I'd finally figured out who was behind the murders and why. And I'd done plenty for the feds. They had Charlie Cimino on countless felonies, including a pretty good case on the murder of Greg Connolly. They had Madison Koehler and Brady MacAleer on the illegal trades for union endorsements—both the appointment of George Ippolito to the supreme court and the jobs for the other union boss's people, for whom we'd had to bend and twist a number of laws. They had three of the main players in the governor's inner circle dead to rights. Moody could ask *those* people what the governor knew and when he knew it.

Moody was staring at me, chewing on his lip like he was debating something. "The governor's going to appoint George Ippolito to the supreme court tomorrow," he said.

I looked at him. "How do you know that?"

He gave me a look that told me I didn't need to know that information. Madison had made it sound like it might be a few days away. But if she'd changed her mind, she wouldn't have told me.

"Shit," I said. "Are you going to move before then?"

He shrugged. "It's being debated right now. A lot of it depends on you, Counselor."

Sure. Right now, they were playing offense. Every day brought more admissions from the governor's people. Every day without an arrest was a day that the federal government could build a stronger case. The spigot would shut off the moment the arrests were made.

And as of right now, from my tally, the main target of their investigation—Governor Carlton Snow—had made a grand total of one clearly incriminating statement, his suggestion about getting those pro-choice groups to cough up money to get him to veto that abortion bill. I hadn't heard anything else on that subject, and it was entirely possible that nothing was happening on that front. And beyond that, the governor had only made veiled references to the things going on under him.

Which meant that they had the governor's people, but not the governor. Would they dance on the people they had—Madison, Charlie, Brady—to get more? Sure. Of course. And they'd probably succeed. But there was nothing more damning than getting it from the governor's mouth.

"Jason, listen." Lee Tucker framed his hands. "We never expected you. We never expected to get this close inside. But you're here.

You've helped us expose corruption at the highest levels of government. Now we're *this close* to Snow. Jason, they're insulating him. It's how this always works. His top advisers filter everything. It all stops at them, and then when no one else is around, they whisper in his ear. They carry out this charade for the exact reason that we're having this conversation—so the governor can deny everything."

"Maybe they don't tell him," I said.

"Bullshit," said Chris Moody.

Tucker raised his hands higher, keeping the fragile detente. "Okay, okay—but let's see then. Maybe today's our last shot, Jason. Let's assume it is. Will you see what you can get from Snow? Tonight's the night Antwain Otis dies, right? You're going to be having discussions with him? You'll have some time with him. Will you at least try?"

I wasn't sure where my head was at this point. Having finally fulfilled my own personal mission, and feeling sure that the governor knew nothing about the murders, I was really doing nothing more than being a classic snitch in an undercover operation. It felt different. It felt like something that wasn't me.

"Lee," said Moody, "we're talking to Jason like it's a friendly request. I think he forgot that he's got criminal liability hanging over him. He's working for our gratitude and mercy."

Judging from Tucker's face, he wasn't pleased with this turn of events. Tucker was a guy who always liked to use honey to catch the bee.

"And the fact that I almost got killed while helping you isn't enough?" I said. "And that I continued to risk my life for you? We forget all that, I guess?"

Chris Moody shrugged. "You're the one who didn't want a deal. I offered you immunity more than once."

He was right. I'd rejected a plea bargain because I didn't want even a tacit admission of criminal wrongdoing. I didn't want the word *immunity* attached to my name, because no matter how you sliced it, it meant you were a criminal who caught a break.

And I'd wanted my freedom. I wanted to be able to stop working for them whenever I pleased. Like now. But I'd known the risks, and now they were staring at me square in the face.

"So I take one more shot at the governor, you spare me an indictment? And you move in before Ippolito gets appointed? I got that pretty much correct, Chris?"

"Hey, look." Now he was playing the slippery one. "I'm just saying, we'll take all of your cooperation, and lack thereof, under advisement. I never promised differently." He raised a finger, then reached for a folder behind him. He held up a thick document that was stamped DRAFT. It was an application for an arrest warrant, along with several affidavits to be signed by FBI agents.

I took it in my hands. The draft application requested arrest warrants for Governor Carlton Snow, Madison Koehler, Brady MacAleer, and Ciriaco "Charlie" Cimino.

"Is this the document we file?" he asked.

Then he removed a second document from his folder. "Or is *this* the one?" he said.

He handed me the second document. It looked largely the same as the first, but with one addition. The document requested a warrant to arrest Jason Kolarich.

I put my hand out. Lee Tucker handed me the F-Bird.

"I guess we'll find out," I said.

I WAS TEN MINUTES LATE TO APPLE JACKS, A POPULAR breakfast spot just north of the commercial district. A lot of lawyers have their pretrial eggs here before heading down for a day in court. It felt like ages since I'd been one of those people.

Hector already had a booth for us. He looked fresh and eager, his wardrobe matching his attitude—olive suit with olive shirt and brownish-red tie and that fucking tie clip.

"I ordered you some eggs," he told me, which was his way of reminding me I was late. I wanted to reach across the table and shove the tie clip into his windpipe, but instead I just acknowledged his power move and let it go.

"Today's the endorsements, don't forget," he said, as if I'd given him some reason to think I'd forgotten. "With SLEU and the Laborers, we're golden. It's our fucking election."

He was reminding me that Governor Snow was going to win, and that was all that was supposed to matter.

"So like I said last night, Carl feels terrible about what happened."

Our food arrived. Mine was eggs over easy with toast and bacon. My stomach was growling but the way I was feeling about Hector right now, I wouldn't hold down the meal if I ate it.

"He's very grateful that you can be discreet, Jason. And what you should be doing, right now, is thinking about what you want when Carl is elected to a full term. I was serious, what I said last night. The sky's the limit for a talented lawyer like you. You want to be on the bench? You want a boat full of legal work sent your way? You just need—"

"Hector, stop," I said reflexively, when I couldn't stand hearing his voice any longer. I took a breath, because this was the last thing I wanted to do, but I had to get through it.

"I want to clear the air here, Hector. You and I need to be square on a few things."

Hector didn't particularly enjoy being interrupted, but his curiosity was trumping his pride. Plus, his number one goal here was protecting the governor, so he was proceeding with caution.

"I got into this thing because of you. Not Charlie Cimino and not Carlton Snow. Charlie's a good guy and the governor's okay, but I'm loyal to you. You understand?"

I made a point of not looking at my food as I spoke, because I wasn't sure how much more of this crap I could spew without becoming physically ill. But Hector? Talk about my words finding a soft landing. I'd hit his sweet spot.

"Good," he said.

"I think you're going to be governor someday, and I want to be there with you. I think you're twenty times the person Carlton Snow is, and all the rest of them. But if I'm with you, if we're a team, then we have to be on the same page. You have to talk to me. You have to be more careful. *We* have to be more careful. Okay? Or I'm out. I'm out, as of now."

Hector shook his head. "What do you mean?"

"I mean—and listen, I'm not your lawyer anymore, okay? You understand that."

"Right," he said, more as a question. Didn't matter—he'd acknowledged my point. He'd just eviscerated any possible contention that this conversation was protected by attorney-client privilege.

"But that doesn't mean you can't trust me. For some reason, you think you can't. Why is that?" I leaned forward over the table. "You, of all people, wonder whether I can keep a secret? You? How many secrets of yours have I kept? How many? Adalbert Wozniak? Ernesto Ramirez? Greg fucking Connolly? Did I ever say a word?"

It was a risk, I knew, throwing out all these names at him, but it was the only way I knew how to work this conversation.

Hector watched me intently, his face coloring. He was thinking things over now and wasn't sure how he felt about the progression of this talk. His eyes darted toward the other tables to ensure maximum privacy. "I don't know what you're talking about," he said cautiously.

"See, if that's the way you play it, then I'm out," I said. "You're taking way too many risks and if you don't start talking to me before you do things, you're going to get into trouble. And I'll walk away before I get jammed up. Life's too short."

Hector was still debating this, but his instinct was to default to a denial. "I don't know what secrets you're talking about."

I looked around, as if I were concerned that others might be listening, and then leaned inward and spoke in a quiet but harsh voice. "You think I don't know why you came to me, after Talia died, and offered me a contract in state government? That lunch we had? You think I don't know it was because of Ernesto Ramirez?"

He squinted his eyes. "Ernesto . . . ?"

"Oh, like you don't know who he is." I threw my napkin on the table. "I'm done, Hector. I'm done with this."

Hector reached out toward me, all but grabbing my arm across the table. "Just hold on a second. Just—say what you're going to say."

I pretended to stew, which was easy because it wasn't hard to feign hostility toward Hector at this point.

"You and I both know who Ernesto Ramirez is," I said. "The guy who knew the real reason behind Bert Wozniak's murder? The guy who knew about you and Delroy Bailey? About Starlight Catering? I mean, really, Hector, you think I didn't know all of that? Did you hire good lawyers to defend you or shitty ones?"

Hector was speechless. I'd unloaded a lot there. I was acting as if it was something I'd known all along, as opposed to just putting it all together in the last twenty-four hours. That suited my purposes.

My heart was pounding but my hands were steady. "You felt bad about what happened," I said. "That weekend, when I was supposed to take Talia and Emily to her mother's? I mean, that's why you offered to give me some legal work through the state afterward, right? That was you trying to make it up to me. Trying to ease your guilt."

Hector winced. His eyes dropped. He ran his fingers over his coffee cup.

"For what's it worth," I said, "I don't blame you. You couldn't have known I'd be waiting for Ernesto to call." I was mustering all of my will to control myself and think of the bigger picture. It was not an easy task. Breathe in, breathe out.

Hector's chin rose up. He looked over my shoulder, scratched his cheek, cleared his throat. Delay tactics, all of them. Nervous responses. He nodded to the waiter, who refilled Hector's coffee. "The timing wasn't ideal," he said, after the waiter departed. "But I didn't have a choice. I wasn't thinking about your personal schedule,

Jason. You may remember that I was on trial for my *life*? Remember that part? And here you are, running this one-man crusade to find this guy and get him to talk. I was days away from the trial ending and you were about to open a very messy can of worms."

My eyes rose to his. He was having trouble keeping eye contact. This wasn't something he enjoyed recalling. I wasn't having a load of fun, myself.

"So, yeah, I'm sorry—okay?" That, alone, was a lot for a guy like Hector to say, and he seemed almost annoyed at the same time he was repentant. "Yeah, of course, I wish the timing—I wish it had been different with your wife and all. But I didn't have a choice. I couldn't have that guy Ramirez out there flapping his mouth. He was a threat, and I did what I had to do. I didn't have a choice."

There it was, the rationalization that helped Hector sleep at night: I didn't give him a choice. Ernesto Ramirez was my fault, not his. Therefore, Hector's subsequent reaction—having Ernesto killed—wasn't his fault, either. And the fact that it coincided with my waiting for Ernesto in my office instead of driving my family downstate? Well, even I would concede, I couldn't put that on him. I'd finally turned that page last night, and I wasn't going to flip back to an earlier part of that story.

Still, Hector felt bad enough about how things shook out to follow up with me and try to give me something, the only thing a guy like him *could* give me—a perk from his government position. Ironic, wasn't it? Had Hector not invited me to lunch and discussed the idea of getting some fat-cat contract with the governor's office, I would never have made my way into the Procurement and Construction Board or the governor's inner circle. The one thing that Hector did that was born of some goodwill was the thing that ultimately would result in his downfall.

And the one time he actually said something heartfelt would be the final nail in his coffin. Hector Almundo had just admitted on tape to the murder of Ernesto Ramirez.

One admission down, one to go.

My hands weren't so steady anymore. I was thinking about my family, about Essie Ramirez and her two kids. I was thinking about the F-Bird in my suit pocket, which now contained Hector's confession to Ernesto's murder. It was like a loaded gun. But I had to stay focused. I couldn't screw this up now. I still needed Greg Connolly. And this was my last chance.

"My point isn't to make you feel bad about what happened," I said. "My point is that you were reckless. We could have neutralized Ernesto Ramirez some other way, if you'd told me. For Christ's sake, you didn't have to have him *killed*."

Hector grimaced with that final word. He didn't like hearing it aloud.

"Spoken," he said, "like someone who wasn't staring at twenty years in prison."

"I know, Hector, but look what that got you. You cover up Adalbert Wozniak by killing Ernesto Ramirez. Then you have to cover up Ernesto Ramirez by killing Greg Connolly. Maybe you're okay on Wozniak now, since you were acquitted—but that still leaves two murders. And one of those two was one of the governor's best friends and top aides."

Hector was back to his standby denial mode. He drew his shoulders in.

"The last I checked," said Hector, his voice calm and even, "Greg Connolly's death was being chalked up as a mugging on Seagram Hill."

That was an answer that my federal friends would have described as slippery.

"Yeah, but tomorrow's another day," I said. "You thought you got away with Ernesto Ramirez, too, right? And then suddenly, Greg

Connolly's talking to the feds and you have exposure. Now you think you're okay on Greg Connolly but who knows who *else* might turn on you? I mean, who else knows about that?"

Hector worked his jaw, his eyes narrowed in thought.

I said, "Joey Espinoza knows. Maybe not about Greg. But he knows about the contract you got for Delroy, right? And the real reason Wozniak died? I'm sure he'd know about that. And he knows about your relationship with Delroy, too. I mean, that's why his wife is on Charlie's payroll."

Hector's expression went flat. "Joey knows how to use leverage."

"Right. You give his wife a cozy job while he's in prison and he'll forget to mention a couple of things to the feds. He'll give Christopher Moody information about the Columbus Street Cannibals, because they're already hot on that trail, but he dummies up about Adalbert Wozniak. And Delroy Bailey. He buys his wife some financial security while he goes to the slammer."

Hector raised his eyebrows without enthusiasm. I'd hit the nail on the head.

"But back to my question," I said. "Who else knows about Greg? Who do we have to be worried about?"

Hector, at this point, was beaten down. "I would have thought it was just me and our mutual friend," he said. "But apparently that mutual friend told you."

Actually, no, our *mutual friend* Charlie hadn't told me about Hector's participation in that night of fun and torture. If he had, this whole thing would have been over a long time ago. Still, Hector had given me an opening and I was going to use it.

I made a face. "Yeah, Charlie told me after your goons went medieval on me in some abandoned warehouse. I think I was owed some explanation after—"

"That was Charlie's idea." Hector pointed a finger at me. "Not mine. He was the one who wasn't sure he could trust you."

I leveled a stare on him.

"That's not the way Charlie tells it," I said, an extrapolation on my part, but I wasn't concerned with follow-up conversations with Charlie Cimino at this stage. "Charlie said he didn't want to do that to me. It was your idea."

"Fuck that. *Fuck* Charlie." Hector became aware of his surroundings and leaned forward, talking softly like I was, but blurting out the words through a snarl. "That asshole panicked. As soon as we figured out about Greg, he starts thinking about you. He wanted to get rid of you that night. Did you know that? I fucking kept you alive that night."

He punctuated that final point with his index finger drilled into the table. This was precisely what I expected; Hector would want to change the subject to taking credit for something again, to get me back in his corner. I thought it was bullshit, what he was saying. From my vantage point, Charlie hadn't been in charge in that room; he hadn't been the one running those goons who worked me over. Charlie was trying to protect me in that room. Maybe I was wrong about that. I'd probably never know.

And it didn't matter. Hector had admitted his participation, which was all that I needed. Hector was going down for Greg Connolly's murder. It was done now.

"And by the way, Counselor, while you're lecturing me on being careful? Keep in mind that what I did to Greg helped everyone. Imagine Connolly walking around with a fucking federal wire every day. I saved everyone. Carl, Maddie, Charlie, MacAleer—and *you.*"

Hector wasn't completely off the mark here; killing Greg Connolly did help everyone. Who knows what Greg could have helped the government uncover? But in the end, Hector didn't kill Greg for anyone but himself. Greg posed a direct threat to Hector because Greg, as chair of the PCB, had steered a contract to Hector's paramour, Delroy Bailey, and because Greg either knew, or had an informed opinion, that what had happened later to Adalbert Wozniak and Ernesto Ramirez was related to that sordid affair. Hector couldn't risk having Greg Connolly chatting away to the federal government.

"Not that anyone will give me any fucking credit for that," he went on, seething now. "These assholes running around Carl, they're cutting me out of shit and taking credit for everything, meanwhile I'm saving their asses by exterminating a rat. They're fucking oblivious. They don't even know I got their backs. I take all the risks and they get all the benefit."

I started nodding along with him, supplying Hector more and more rope with which to hang himself. "That doesn't seem right," I said. "They don't even know what you did for them?"

He sneered at me, took a quick look around, and leaned inward again. "Those pussies think they know what it takes? They don't know shit. They'd probably piss their expensive little pants if they knew what I've done for them. They've never had to get their hands dirty. They've had everything handed to them on a silver platter. They don't understand what it means to reach out and take something. I mean, really take something that isn't supposed to belong to you. Charlie, he understands. He gets it. Nobody gave him nothing. He took it. He gets it. The rest of them? The ones who hang on coattails?"

Still nodding my head, I was. Hector was just warming up.

"Peshke? This guy's dad was a congressman so that makes him smart? Maddie Koehler? She got some governor elected in Tennessee who could've won with his pants down and now she's a genius? MacAleer? His dad was an old union boss. He's just a dog who follows his master. And Carl? Carl's a good guy, but c'mon. This guy was handing out marriage licenses until I came along. Try being a Latino politician for one goddamned second. I mean, sure, you can run in your legislative district, but try running statewide. See how many people are going to line up to help you when you have brown skin. Do any of them have to go to a fucking street gang to get contributions? Do any of them have the federal government targeting *them* because they're successful?"

I had a nice comeback to that last question, but I'd let Christopher Moody handle that one. I was done. I really didn't want to listen to this guy rationalize his behavior anymore. He was the thug I'd always suspected, but it hadn't mattered to me, because he was *my* thug. He was my client. He bought the resources of the best law firm in the city and the best lawyer, Paul Riley, with me at his side, and we pulled it out for him. Hector was guilty of masterminding the Cannibals extortion and we'd gotten him off. He was guilty of killing Adalbert Wozniak—not precisely for the reason the feds thought, but guilty nonetheless—and we'd cleared him of that, too.

Just doing my job. It was true. I couldn't be sorry about providing a zealous defense to a client. But I could be happy that some justice was coming his way now. There would be attorneys, in the coming days, who would criticize me for turning against a former client, but I wouldn't lose a wink of sleep over it.

"I'm coming to you," I said into my cell phone to Lee Tucker.

"Now?"

"Now. Bring another Bird. Ten minutes."

"Why do I need to bring another Bird?"

I hung up the phone without answering. He didn't need to know why.

 I WALKED INTO SUITE 410 FIFTEEN MINUTES LATER. Lee Tucker had just shown up, still wearing his coat, his cheeks still pink from the cold outside. "What's the problem?" he asked. "The F-Bird didn't work?"

I handed it to him. "It worked just fine. I just thought you should have this right away."

It wasn't the real reason I was turning in the F-Bird early, but it sounded like a sensible explanation.

Tucker stared at the recording device I'd handed him. "This was your breakfast with Hector Almundo?"

I nodded. "Listen to that. You might be adding a name to that indictment."

"Well—c'mon. Give me a preview."

"Let's just say you're going to learn a few things about Hector Almundo. I sure did."

"C'mon, Counselor. Don't be a putz."

I smiled, which felt odd. I hadn't done a lot of that recently, and this surely wasn't a time for mirth. "Greg Connolly," I said. "It was Hector. Hector and Charlie."

Lee Tucker nodded at me, but hardly reacted. Nothing in his eyes, nothing in his movements. "Okay. Anything else?"

"You knew," I said. "You already knew."

Tucker wasn't going to say yes, but he didn't say no, either.

"The guys he hired?" I asked. "You traced them back to Hector? Forensics? What?"

It felt silly, but I'd been living in my own little world, working up a case for these guys. I hadn't considered the obvious—these guys were capable of some investigating of their own. They could have swept the place where I was interrogated for fingerprints or DNA— shit, the one goon spilled a pool of blood out of his nose after I clocked him. And they followed the car that dropped me off that night. They probably knew the names of both of those guys and had easily secured search warrants to access phone records and anything else they might need to trace those guys back to Hector.

"Well, now you have a confession, too," I said.

Tucker paused, debating what he could say to me. "That will help us a lot. Let's say it will confirm what we strongly suspected. Great job, Jason. Really."

I held out my hand. Tucker put a new F-Bird in my palm but didn't release it. "You'll take one more shot at Snow? You'll give it the old college try?"

I pried the new F-Bird from his hand. I looked him in the eye but didn't answer.

"Jason, don't be an idiot. You've done so much for this case. Hell, you risked your ass for us. Chris won't prosecute you. Not if you take this one last shot. Even if you fail. Just try."

Mom always said, if you don't have something to say, keep your mouth shut. So I did.

"But you tell Chris to fuck off now—Jason, c'mon, man, you know he'll go after you. Don't throw all your hard work away. Don't do that."

I thought Tucker's impassioned plea was not entirely self-interested. Yes, he wanted to be part of an historic investigation that took down the governor. And yes, he could dutifully play the good cop to Chris Moody's bad. But I thought Lee meant what he was saying. I'd earned something with him after everything I'd done. He was rooting for me, I thought. He wanted me to avoid prison. That sounded like an okay idea to me as well. But it wasn't Tucker's call.

It was Moody's call. And, as Moody had said to me earlier, it really was up to me.

 I DIDN'T GO DOWN TO THE PRESSROOM IN THE STATE building for the 11:30 media event. I couldn't stomach the idea of watching the heads of State and Local Employees United and the International Brotherhood of Commercial Laborers announce their endorsement of Governor Carlton Snow. It was covered over the Internet, however, so I flipped it on in spite of myself and half listened to it, which is to say that it was on in the background as I packed up some of the few personal items I had brought to this office.

Rick Harmoning praised Carlton Snow's commitment to the working class but forgot to mention how Snow got all of Rick's family and friends jobs in the administration, veterans and better-qualified candidates be damned. Gary Gardner cited the governor's support of the federal employee free choice law but not his soon-to-be-announced appointment of Gardner's brother-in-law to the state supreme court.

I tried to care enough to be mad but I was punch-drunk at this point, numb from overexposure. And I was exhausted. I had done what I'd come to do. I'd found my killer and, only a few hours ago, had taped him over breakfast admitting to the crimes. His co-conspirator, Charlie Cimino, was already in the soup plenty for his role that night—much of which had been captured by my F-Bird—as well as dozens of other felonies Charlie and I committed for months before that.

So in that regard, at least, all was right with the world. It was hard to stay motivated. I listened with only passing interest to the platitudes the governor and the two union leaders heaped upon each other. I removed the two AA batteries from my boom box stereo, threw them in my pocket, wrapped the cord around the stereo several times, and placed it in a gym bag I had brought with me today. Other than the stereo, the only other things I had brought to this office were a bunch of my own pens—I hated the cheap, government-supplied ones—and an oversized coffee cup I bought at the Fiesta Bowl a couple years ago when Talia and I went to Arizona for Christmas. I looked around the office and considered stealing the stapler, which was actually nicer than the one at my office, but stealing is wrong and I decided against it. I did think, however, that after the valuable public service I'd performed over the last four months, the taxpayers of this state could spot me a couple of rubber bands, so I stuffed those in my pocket and called us even.

The boom box and pens safely in my bag, I zipped it up and put it under my desk. It occurred to me that someone might notice that I appeared to vacating my office and might wonder why.

I still had the rest of the day, though. At least I thought I did. Tonight would be Antwain Otis's last night on this earth, and I was hoping to have at least one more conversation with the governor about it. I had my own thoughts about the outcome but, at a minimum, I wanted to make sure the issue was thoroughly vetted. I wanted to make sure that Carlton Snow actually thought about this. I thought Antwain Otis was owed that much.

And then there was the federal government. Moody wanted the governor so badly he probably tasted Carlton Snow when he belched. And like anyone in his position, he wanted a slam dunk. Yes, he could flip the governor's people and make them testify against their boss, but having someone on tape was always the best way to win a case, and he wanted Snow to incriminate himself to the F-Bird.

"Happy to take some questions," I heard the governor say through the computer. I turned to listen, only because it was such a rare occasion that they allowed the governor to speak to reporters.

"Governor, twelve hours from now, Antwain Otis is scheduled to be executed. Have you considered the petition for clemency and what can you tell us about your decision?"

"It's a fair question, Nancy, and I'm going to have an announcement later today on that."

"But, Gov—"

"I can tell you that it's one of the toughest parts of this job. I've been doing a lot of hard thinking about this."

Hard thinking. Right. I took a look at the information I'd put together for the governor and Pesh this morning. The woman Antwain Otis killed, Elisa Newberry, was a schoolteacher and mother of four, the youngest of whom was the other victim, five-year-old Austin. Her husband, Anthony Newberry, was a commercial pilot who had to quit his job after Elisa's death so he could be home more with his three surviving children; he took a lower-paying job as a flight instructor with a community college. The trial judge, in accepting the jury's recommendation for death at Antwain's trial, had indicated that Otis had shown "particularly cruel indifference" in spraying gunfire across a crowded thoroughfare; had "repeatedly failed to accept responsibility" for his crime despite "overwhelming" evidence of guilt; and had shown a "singular lack of remorse" during the sentencing phase. The Inmate Review and Release Board, in recommending that Otis's clemency petition be denied, acknowledged the inmate's laudable contributions to prison life since he founded his prison ministry but decided that the "utter depravity of his crime" outweighed the good deeds he'd performed "several years afterward."

I had no appetite for lunch. I spent that hour making phone calls to some of the state contractors Charlie and I had shaken down, the ones who had been dilatory in paying into the governor's campaign coffers. Madison Koehler was on tape the other night instructing me to call them, to once again threaten the loss of their state contracts if they didn't pony up. And now I was completing the act, using interstate wires—a cell phone given me by the U.S. attorney's office—to coerce these individuals to pay. The actions felt robotic, dialing the telephone, mentioning our "concern that the agreed contribution hadn't been made" and suggesting that a "review of the contract would be forthcoming," then hanging up and checking a name off a list. I hadn't even tried to sound convincing. I just needed to say the words. It was like dotting an *i* or crossing a *t*. I'd made seven calls. Seven counts of conspiracy to commit fraud through the use of interstate wires for Madison Koehler.

I didn't know if I was going to speak with the governor again before everything happened. But I decided I wanted to. The Antwain Otis issue was one reason. But that wasn't all. What Lee Tucker said to me had made some sense. I'd had my doubts about the governor. I didn't know if he was an ignorant figurehead whose minions were doing bad things without his knowledge; a *willfully* ignorant leader who simply chose not to know the details, who stuck his head in the sand like an ostrich but knew something illegal was afoot; or a guy who was truly selling out his office for political favors.

I thought everyone deserved to know. The governor's political career was about to end, regardless, and people staring at long prison terms were liable to say anything to reduce their sentences. All of them—Madison, Charlie, Mac, even Hector—would know the direction to point their finger, and that direction was up. The U.S. attorney's office would be cutting deals for dirt on the governor, and I wasn't confident that the truth was going to remain intact during those desperate interactions.

At four o'clock, my phone rang, and I knew I'd at least have a chance to figure all this out. The governor wanted to meet with me when he arrived back in the city at nine tonight.

THE F-BIRD FELT LIKE A PAPERWEIGHT IN MY SUIT pocket when I stepped into the elevator at the Ritz-Carlton. It reminded me of the first time I wore it in Charlie Cimino's office. It had felt odd then, like performing before a hidden camera; I was self-conscious, off-balance, even nervous. But after a while it had felt as natural as wearing a watch, just another accessory when I dressed for the morning. I'd become so good at pretending that it was sometimes hard to tell the difference when I was not.

I felt a flutter of nerves as the elevator opened on the top floor. I wasn't sure why. This was old hat to me. Maybe because this was finally ending. But I didn't think so. The difference was that I cared about the outcome of this evening.

I nodded to the security detail planted outside the governor's suite. Bill Peshke answered the door and handed me a document, a press release. "I want you to take a look at what I've written up. We're issuing this thing in a half-hour. And listen," he added, making sure we had eye contact now, "we don't need any drama on this one. Okay?"

I didn't really know what that meant, and my expression must have given me up.

"It means the decision's made, and nobody needs second-guessing now," Pesh went on. "The governor needs to be focusing on other things right now. We're less than a week from the primary and he needs to be sharp. I don't need him up all night agonizing over this."

I didn't really see the governor agonizing over anything, certainly not Antwain Otis. I did a quick read of the press statement and told him it was factually accurate, meaning he got the names and ages of Otis's victims correct and the like.

Inside the suite, some technicians were working in the corner on a phone. A man in a blue jumpsuit was explaining things to Madison Koehler and Governor Snow. "We're all set," he said. He gestured to a black phone sitting in the corner of the suite. "That phone is piped directly into the chamber. You pick it up and dial zero, Mr. Governor. Zero. The red phone in the chamber will ring. The warden will answer."

The technician placed a call on his cell phone. "Okay, ready for the check. Okay." He hung up the cell phone. He walked over to the black telephone, hit a button—presumably zero—and waited. "Okay, all clear? All clear from this end. Give me the time. Okay, nine-o-six and thirty-two seconds. Good. We're in sync. Thank you."

The technician placed a timepiece on the small table with the black phone. "That watch is synchronized with the execution chamber at Marymount Penitentiary. When it's twelve midnight on that watch, it's twelve midnight on the clock in the death chamber. Down to the second."

I checked my own watch. I had nine-o-seven, so I was about dead-on with the official time clock.

"Any questions, Governor? Ms. Koehler?"

"Can I order a pizza on that phone?" The governor patted the guy on the back. "Bad joke. No, we're clear. What's your name again?"

"Craig."

"Great job, Craig. Thanks for your good work."

All the regulars—Madison, Charlie, Hector, Mac, and Pesh— remained quiet as the technicians filtered out.

The governor walked in a circle, then moved toward the black phone, keeping his distance like it was quarantined or something. "I mean, Jesus Christ."

He looked at Madison. It was my first shot of him head-on tonight. He still had the blow-dried, polished campaign thing going on, but he looked somewhat out of sorts, a weight to his shoulders. The run of the day's campaign events over, the final hours now drawing near, it was now dawning on him, the awesome power he held in his hands.

It occurred to me that he'd probably never had such a moment during his one-year reign as governor. He was a backbencher, a lieutenant governor who didn't have much to do; then suddenly he was the supreme executive officer of the state in the space of a few weeks. It had probably felt like a whirlwind, like a dream. Suddenly his every action made the news, his public appearances were heavily attended, and he was in constant demand. No doubt, any governor of a Midwestern state, in his mid-forties with a full head of hair, was dreaming presidential aspirations.

Heady stuff. And surely he'd made consequential decisions before now, but most of them were filtered through professionals who would lay out the policy and, more important, political nuances for him. But this, this was different. You could tell him a hundred times over what the right political call was, but it didn't change the fact that a man would either live or die, depending on whether the governor picked up that black phone.

"We have a lot to do—let's get started," said Madison, who, like Peshke, was trying to move on from the topic that seemed to be dominating the governor's thoughts. She was right, I thought, as everyone settled into his or her position for the nightly post-campaigning strategy, and she was wrong. In all likelihood, tonight was going to the last night this group would meet. Other than Bill Peshke, who as far as I know hadn't done anything wrong, everybody in this room was probably going to be arrested tomorrow, with the possible exception of Carlton Snow.

Madison and Peshke laid out the polling numbers (Snow still held a six-point lead over Willie Bryant), the fundraising stats (Snow had 2.2 million in the till to Bryant's 1.3), and the projected television buys for the final days of the primary. Through it all, Governor Snow remained largely silent, offering only tepid words of encouragement as his eyes were glued over everyone's heads. The liquor was flowing as usual—these people were remarkably good at staying focused through booze—but the governor had abstained.

An hour passed quickly. When I checked my watch, I realized it was coming right up on ten P.M. Two hours left. If I was following Chris Moody's direction, I was supposed to be engaging the group, but primarily the governor, in discussions of the illegal things we were doing. But I stayed silent. I was watching the governor, trying to read him, hoping—I realized it now, hoping—that he wasn't the person the federal government thought he was.

"Tomorrow," said Madison. "Eight A.M. is the prayer breakfast at Newport Baptist. Nine-thirty is the domestic violence shelter over on Boughton. Ten-thirty's the signing ceremony for the autism insurance bill. At eleven-thirty we file the appointment for Judge Ippolito and issue the press release. Pesh has the release and he has the informational that Jason wrote up that Pesh played with a little."

So Chris Moody had been correct—the Ippolito appointment was happening tomorrow. That meant that Moody had managed to get in place some additional surveillance that didn't include me. He probably had numerous sources now. It must be killing him that he'd have to abort now and make the arrests. I wondered if that was really going to happen. Moody had indicated that tonight *might* be the last opportunity. I couldn't trust him. I couldn't trust anybody.

"Noon is the funder with Senator Loman," Madison continued. "Then we fly to Summit County for the ICBL rally—"

"Hang on," said the governor. He got out of his chair and began to pace. "I want to go over Antwain Otis one more time. One more time."

The governor's aides collectively deflated.

"Pesh, you first. Go ahead."

I assumed Peshke was distressed, judging from our prior conversation, but he was smooth as silk. "A violent crime. Senseless murders. Nothing in terms of mitigating what he did, Governor. He robbed a store and then fired into a crowded sidewalk and street. Senseless and brutal. Yes, he's got that ministry thing, but Governor, you know what everyone will say. That's a song everyone's heard before. You're caught dead to rights and so you find God."

"It seems like he's sincere," said the governor. "I mean, did you read those affidavits?"

"Yes, and I'm not—I'm not saying he's not sincere. Maybe he is. But I'm talking about the perception, sir. You're a Democrat. You're already soft on crime compared to the GOP challenger, no matter what you do. No matter what. Commuting his sentence will be a tremendous gift to Edgar Trotter in the general."

When it was clear that he was done, the governor nodded at Madison.

"You can't commute his sentence, sir," she said. "You might be able to get away with it if his guilt were in doubt. That's what the death penalty opponents always talk about. Unfair trials. Miscarriages of justice. Coerced confessions. None of that's present here. Everyone knows he's guilty. What he did was ruin a family. The turning-to-God stuff? Pesh is right. That's the same-old, same-old. Maybe if this wasn't an election year. Maybe. But if you commute his sentence, you might as well be saying that you're opposed to the death penalty. If you won't permit an execution when the guy is dead-to-rights guilty and his crime was a double murder of a pretty young mother and her toddler son, then you won't *ever* allow one. That's how it gets painted, sir. You don't want to run in the general as being opposed to the death penalty. But that's exactly what you'll do."

The governor nodded. I could see this was helping him. He seemed to be relieved. "Hector," he said.

Hector cleared his throat. "I pretty much agree with everything that's been said. But keep in mind, Carl, you still have a primary. Don't be so sure Willie Bryant doesn't run ads downstate of a pretty young white lady and her little white boy next to the mug shot of this tough-looking black guy that gunned them down."

I was glad that someone brought up the racial thing. Hector, being the only nonwhite in the room, probably felt most comfortable saying it.

"That's very true," Peshke agreed. "*Very* true."

"Mac?" the governor said.

"I'm just thinking of what Hector said, those ads. The union guys? Y'know, we got SLEU and ICBL—we're getting their money and their people on the ground. But those rank-and-file members? When they go into the polling booth, last I checked, it's still a secret how they vote. Those union boys, they're not so liberal on things like the death penalty. Those ads would work downstate. If Willie's polls are the same as ours and everyone else's, he'll have nothing to lose in the last few days."

"You pick up a grand total of zero votes if you cut this guy a break," said Madison. "But you'll lose votes. And not just downstate. You'll lose some in the city, too. It's a net loss. And for what? I mean, if you're going to have a death penalty, this guy deserves it."

The governor rubbed his hands together. "Charlie, you wanna say anything?"

Charlie shrugged his shoulders. "Sounds like a net loss. I can't disagree with anything I heard."

"Okay. Okay." The governor breathed a heavy sigh. It was clear that the governor had heard all of this before. He wasn't asking for a debate. He was asking for reassurance, for confirmation of a decision he'd already made. "That's all for tonight, everyone. I need some alone time."

Where there would normally be a quick reaction—*sure, Governor, see you bright and early*—there was a pause. But Madison stood up and then so did everyone else.

"Jason," said the governor, "I'd like you to stay."

91 THE GOVERNOR GRABBED A BOTTLE OF WATER FROM the refrigerator and offered me one, which I declined. He kept his distance from both me and the black telephone in the corner of the room, preferring the safety of the picture window.

"Lang Trotter, before he left to become AG, he told me there is never a time when you feel more like a governor than when you have the black phone. He had two on his watch. Two executions. He said you never forget these nights. Now I know what he meant." He looked at his watch. "This guy's going to die in an hour and forty-five minutes."

"Is he?" I asked.

He looked at me a moment before breaking eye contact. The last time the two of us were alone, it didn't end so well, and it was a fresh memory, having happened only last night. So far he hadn't acknowledged it, delegating the task to Hector, which was fine with me.

"Is he?" I repeated.

The governor glanced back at me, inclined his head a click, just enough to show what he thought of my perceived naïveté. "I didn't pull the trigger. I didn't prosecute him. I didn't convict him, and I didn't sentence him to death. People who know a whole lot more about Antwain Otis and his crimes did those things."

"True."

"I'm a safety valve. I'm there in case there's some reason to think, after all the legal process is done, that something is way off. And nothing's way off. Fair trial. No question of guilt."

He'd thought about this more than I'd realized. I'd begun to stereotype him as a soulless politician and nothing more.

"Then why am I here?" I asked.

He smiled, even laughed to himself. "Right."

"I don't do politics, Governor. You have people who do that, and they've told you what they think. And I have to say, I can't disagree with them. On the politics."

He drank from his bottle and fidgeted. This couldn't be easy for him, no matter how assured he was of the decision.

"You know what they call me down in the capital?" he asked. "You probably don't, do you?"

I shook my head, no.

"The 'accidental governor.' I'm not supposed to be here. I'm not one of them. I'm not entrenched. They don't want me. They want one of their own. They want Willie, because Willie's someone they know. He's been down there for twenty years. I'm talking about Democrats, too, not just the GOP. Nobody down there wants me."

I hadn't heard any of that. I was completely unplugged from capital politics, and I was sure that I was the better off for it.

"But you know what I am? Accidental or not, I'm the governor. And I'm the only Democrat who can win this thing. Willie can't win. I mean, we've had two Democratic governors in this state over the last thirty-five years. We like Republicans for our governors. The only Democrat who can win is the incumbent, and that's me. I'm the incumbent because everybody calls me Governor. "

He pointed at the black phone. "I do this—those guys are right. I might as well declare that I'm against the death penalty. Edgar Trotter or whoever comes out of the GOP primary will crucify me with this. I'll be a pussy liberal Democrat."

I rested my elbows on my knees and thought about that. I wasn't sure he was giving voters enough credit. But then, I didn't live in his political world. You run enough negative ads on one issue, it probably sinks in. It sticks. *Carlton Snow, soft on crime. Look at this beautiful white woman and her child, murdered by this black thug gangbanger. Carlton Snow let him off the hook!*

"You're the governor," I said. "Our constitution gives this power to you, without limitation. You're supposed to do what you think is right."

"What I think is *right*? Is that how you see the world, Jason?" He had turned on me. Something inside him had been stirred. "I get elected by people who want me to do things a certain way. So I do them that way. Do I get to do some things I care about? Yeah, sure I do. Health care for kids, for one. You pick your spots. But you can't do those things—you can't be a good governor unless you're governor."

The motto of this administration. He wasn't entirely off the mark, of course, but it depended on your perspective.

"When is enough enough?" I asked. "How much bullshit do you have to swallow to do the things you care about?"

The governor placed his palm on the window, like he was testing the outside temperature. "Good question."

"Yes, it is," I said. "I mean, Judge Ippolito, Governor. Judge George Ippolito. The guy you're appointing to the supreme court tomorrow?"

The governor pondered his hand for a moment. "You don't approve. But people want him. I'm doing what people want. Supporters."

"Gary Gardner wants him. And he's willing to trade a union endorsement for it."

Governor Snow turned to me. His lips parted but he didn't speak. "Who said that?"

"*Who said that?* That's exactly what's happening, Governor."

He looked away from me, otherwise immobile. I was having trouble reading this thing. Was he telling me that he didn't know?

The governor wagged his empty bottle and went to the fridge for another. After pulling a fresh, sweaty bottle out, he looked at me. "Sometimes I don't need to know all the details," he said. "Sometimes I don't want to."

"You didn't know," I said.

The governor came over and sat in the chair across from me. "Did I know that people supporting my candidacy wanted him? Yes. Did I know exactly how that played out? That's not my job. That's a detail. Because it's all the same."

"No, it's not."

"Sure it is. *Sure* it is. My actions respond to what voters, what *supporters* want. I get support from gun-control advocates because they know if a concealed-carry bill comes before me, I'll veto it. If I don't do what they want, they don't support me. That's wrong? That's how it works."

"But not an under-the-table deal, Governor."

"Oh, really?" He drew back. "What is the freaking difference, Jason? Really. See, here's what you don't get. Here's what you don't get." He framed his hands in the air. "You get elected governor by showing people you want it. That's how it's supposed to be. You have to really want it. You have to be willing to make sacrifices. You have to cut deals. Sometimes do things you don't want to do. If you aren't willing to do those things, then you don't want it bad enough, and you *shouldn't* get it. People *want* their politicians to scratch and claw to get the job."

"You don't think people want you to pick the best possible judge to sit on the supreme court?"

"They may want it, but they don't expect it." He took a long swallow of water. "They expect me to make a political judgment. They expect me to try to please my supporters."

"And you think that if they knew how George Ippolito got on the bench, they'd be okay with that? A side deal for a union endorsement?"

He sat back in the chair, crossed his leg, and smiled. "They don't want to know," he said.

I pulled on my tie, feeling a little hot and bothered at the moment. I wasn't sure what I was doing here. Chris Moody, were he listening to this in real time, would be having a heart attack. The last thing he'd want is for me to talk the governor out of appointing George Ippolito to the supreme court. I realized that I was giving the governor some rope here. But I wasn't sure why. I wasn't sure if I wanted to see if he'd hang himself with it, or if I was trying to decide whether to call off the hanging altogether.

My heartbeat had ratcheted up a few notches. I felt like I was doing a slow jog and preparing to kick it in for the final mile of the race. My watch said it was ten minutes to eleven.

"Are you trying to convince me or yourself?" I asked.

The comment surprised him. He wasn't accustomed, I suppose, to that level of bluntness.

"I mean, seriously, Governor. Why this impassioned defense? Why am I even here? You know what the politics dictate. What do you need me for?"

He rested his head on the chair and looked up at the ceiling. "Interesting question."

And the answer, I thought, was even more interesting. In the recesses of his soul, where political calculations hadn't yet infiltrated, he was thinking about commuting Otis's sentence. I was the guy who represented the opposite of politics, in some ways at least, and he wanted my opinion.

No—he wanted a *particular* opinion. He wanted me to come to the same conclusion as his political advisers. He wanted to be able to tell himself that he was doing the right thing tonight by letting Antwain Otis die.

"Tell me what you would do," he said.

I wouldn't want to be him, I knew that much. My principal objection, prior to tonight, had been the lack of due diligence on the governor's part. He hadn't been paying any attention to Antwain Otis, and that, itself, was criminal in my mind. I'd focused on that objection to the exclusion of actually formulating an opinion myself. Now, here it was, and I had to concede it wasn't easy having to make this decision.

But I knew this much: Carlton Snow still had a chance to pass my internal test. I'd been unsure whether he was a clueless leader or one who simply preferred to remain clueless to the crimes going on around him, who buried his head in the sand.

Now, I realized, there was another possibility: He might be someone who never had anyone whispering the *right* things in his ear. He had political animals around him. Everyone had more or less the same viewpoint; they might disagree about the political angle but it was always the political angle that mattered. He didn't have a voice of conscience. Maybe if he did—maybe there was something more to this guy.

"That minister who talked to us?" I said. "Remember what he said he preaches to the inmates? 'Don't look backward,' he said. 'Look forward. Make tomorrow a better day.'"

"Right, right." He pointed at me.

"Do you think tomorrow's a better day with Antwain Otis dead or alive?"

He watched me for a long time. I broke eye contact only to note that we were inside an hour before the execution.

"If I do what a majority of the people in this state want me to do," he said, "I don't touch that phone. Now, what's wrong with doing what the majority wants?"

"Because the majority wants you to exercise your judgment, not follow their lead like some permanent town hall meeting. You're supposed to make the tough call."

"I see." He ran his fingers through his hair. "Even if that tough call is against their wishes."

"That's why it's tough."

"Even if it fucks me in the election."

"Right again."

"You can't be a good governor unless you're gov—"

"Oh, Governor, spare me that, okay? I mean, what the hell's the *point* of being governor if you can't be a good one? To do the right thing as much as you can, as often as you can?"

He watched me, tolerating me like he might a child. "You'd commute the sentence."

"Yes," I said, "I would. Keep him in prison forever but let him make the world a slightly better place."

I exhaled. I'd tried to keep an open mind on this issue. I'd really been more concerned with the governor making the decision for the right reason than with any particular outcome. I'd surprised myself with the abrupt answer and with how strongly I held the sentiment, once iterated.

The governor opened his hands. "I just can't do that, son. I just can't."

"Yes, you can."

He gave me a grim smile. "You're right. I *won't* do that."

I felt the air go out of the room. There was nothing really left to say. I hadn't given the governor what he'd wanted—validation, reassurance—but it wasn't going to change his mind. It never was.

He looked at his watch. "I thought I wanted some company, but I'm not sure I do."

Right. He didn't want my disapproving eyes boring into him as the hour struck midnight and the venom seeped into the veins of Antwain Otis, strapped to a gurney.

I got up and straightened my suit coat, the F-Bird resting heavy in the inner pocket. I thanked him and walked to the door.

"I'm sorry, Jason," he said.

I stopped on my way back and turned to him. Antwain Otis aside, he'd probably said enough tonight about Judge Ippolito to buy himself an arrest warrant tomorrow.

"I'm sorry, too," I said.

I STOPPED AT THE HOTEL BAR IN THE LOBBY FOR a drink. I wasn't in a tremendous hurry to get back. Tucker and Moody would devour the contents of this F-Bird like it was their last meal, which in some sense of the word it was. They'd want to debrief me, and now that my job was all but completed, they might even want me to review the application for the arrest warrants, given that much of the information contained in it had been supplied by me. I didn't know, but I wasn't eager for a long night. I wanted to escape. I wanted to be anywhere but here.

The dirty martini was too dirty, too salty, but I drank it fast and then ordered a shot of whiskey, hot and bitter down my raw throat, which somehow felt more appropriate.

I walked from the Ritz toward the federal building. It wasn't all that cold out tonight, but there must have been rain, a damp musky odor on the emptying city streets. The fresh air helped.

"I'm done," I said into the cell phone to Lee Tucker.

"And? How did we do?"

"See you in ten minutes," I said.

I passed a couple arm in arm, drunk and amorous. I passed a homeless guy sitting against the wall of a building and handed him a crumpled five from my pocket. He made some noise, but I couldn't make out words. So much suffering in the world. So few people—including me—who did anything to help. That was what these guys were supposed to be doing, the governor and his crew. They were supposed to be helping the rest of us. Trying, at least. Giving us their honest best.

I gave Carlton Snow a chance tonight. I gave him a chance to show me that he could be the right kind of governor, that if pushed in the right direction he could take that path. He didn't take it. Maybe his ultimate decision was right. Plenty of people would believe that Antwain Otis's death sentence was just. Good people. Well-intentioned people. But deep down, Carlton Snow wanted to give Otis a reprieve, and he denied it anyway. No matter the correctness of his decision, he did it for the wrong reasons.

I walked along the bridge over the river that divided the commercial district from the near north side, which put me about three blocks south of the federal building. I didn't walk on the concrete pedestrian walkway but on the bridge surface itself, a grid design, a checkerboard of steel. I remember walking on this bridge as a kid with my father. My dad said the grid design was to prevent skidding. I didn't know if that was true, but I remembered getting on my hands and knees and poking my fingers through the diamond-shaped holes made by the grid and looking through the bridge down to the river itself.

I stopped on the bridge, hopped up on to the concrete walkway, and leaned over the railing, watching the misty fog that covered the river. I'd done the principal thing that brought me into this mess. I could always say that much. I found Ernesto's killer. In the process I'd played a role I never thought I would play, a snitch, a rat for the government. I suppose it was fair to say that I had performed a valuable service, but it didn't feel that way.

When I checked my watch, it was three minutes after midnight. It didn't matter anymore. I pushed off the railing and headed over the river.

My cell phone buzzed. I couldn't imagine being in the mood to talk to anyone, but I checked the phone. It was Madison Koehler. I had nothing to say to her but I answered, anyway.

"Hi, Madison."

"What the hell did you do?"

I sighed. I'd eaten a lot of shit from her for the greater good, but I'd hit my limit.

"I don't know, Madison, what did I do now?"

"You tell me," she said. "Please explain to me why the governor just halted the execution."

 I WATCHED HIM FROM THREE BLOCKS AWAY, ONCE HE turned the corner from the federal building, coming toward me. He was walking slowly. It was late, he had an enormous amount of work left ahead of him, and the temperatures were falling, but Assistant U.S. Attorney Christopher Moody was taking his time on his approach.

His gait seemed to slow even more as he got within earshot of me. He stopped at a distance of about ten feet. I wasn't sure why. It set the appropriate tone, I thought. Pistols and ten paces at dawn, that kind of thing.

"Okay, I'm here. All alone, as you asked. Is there some reason we had to do the hand-off on the middle of the Lerner Street Bridge?"

His distance from me, combined with the poor lighting, made it hard to distinguish his features. His face appeared to be set in a clench, like he was ready for battle. His tone was appropriately hostile but also cautious. He'd listened to my earlier F-Bird from this morning, my conversation with Hector Almundo. He had some reason to question my motives. And I had another F-Bird in my pocket right now, which was recording everything until he turned it off. That, more than anything, would make him careful with his words.

"Well?" he asked. "Do I get the F-Bird or not?"

I reached into the inner pocket of my suit coat, pulled out my little friend, and showed it to him.

Then I threw it into the river.

I never heard it splash. It just vanished into the darkness.

Moody followed the arc until it disappeared into the misty gray below. He probably wasn't happy, but he couldn't have been totally surprised, either. And he wasn't going to give me the satisfaction of a visceral reaction. If he was angry, he figured, he'd have plenty of ways to take it out on me.

"Okay, I'll bite," he said. "Why?"

"I think you're wrong about Snow," I said. "He's no saint. Maybe he's even a criminal. Maybe. The people around him? Most definitely. But I see a guy who was in a little over his head. If someone would have just given him the right advice, he might have been able to do better."

"That's really sweet."

"His people kept him in the dark, Chris. Maybe he didn't want to know, but still—he didn't know. Not exactly. That's why they always kept Hector in the dark, too. Because they knew Hector would tell the governor."

"Very touching, Jason. And what about the governor, all on his own, talking about shaking down those abortion groups? Way I heard it, that was all his idea."

"Yeah, and look how that turned out, Chris. A whole lot of nothing, that's what. They blew off what he said. That proves my point. His people are running that program, not him."

He was quiet a moment. "Well, you've got it all worked out, don't you?"

"Don't worry your little head, Chris. With the nooses you have around his people, there'll be plenty of flippers willing to sing. You'll get the governor. You'll probably put him away for a long time. It's just not going to be because of me."

I saw a faint shaking of the head from the prosecutor. From his perspective, what I was doing didn't make much sense—for exactly the reason I had just articulated. They were going to get Carlton Snow anyway. It would probably only take one of the dominoes—Charlie, Madison, Hector, MacAleer—to fall before the rest of them did. So why, Moody wondered, would I toss the F-Bird into the river and risk the ire of the man who held my fate in his hands, when ultimately it wouldn't help Snow all that much, anyway?

"This is all very noble of you, Mr. Kolarich. Maybe the governor can thank you while you're serving time together. I could recommend to the court that you serve in the same camp."

Maybe so. Maybe not. I nodded at him. "While it's just us girls talking," I said, "what did you think of that tape you heard this morning? Hector's confession."

I thought I saw a smile, or at least some change in his expression. "We already liked Hector for Connolly's murder. You didn't tell us anything we didn't know."

He enjoyed saying that, once again having the upper hand. I only knew what they let me know. They'd worked the case from other angles and gotten to Hector on their own.

"He copped to *three* murders," I said. "Wozniak, which you already fucked up, so he walks on that one. And Connolly, for which you now have a confession. But what did you think about Ernesto Ramirez, Chris?"

He paused. "I'm not sure I catch your meaning."

"Sure you do. Ernesto Ramirez had material information about the murder of Adalbert Wozniak. He and a good friend of his."

I didn't know the guy's name other than the moniker I gave him, Scarface. I wished I did, but I'd have to make do with what I had.

"I had a long talk with that friend of his," I said. "He told me that he and Ernesto told their story to law enforcement. He said 'cops,' actually, but he didn't mean cops. He meant federal agents. He meant *you*, Chris."

"Is that a fact?"

"Yes, it is. Ernesto and his friend came to see you during the Almundo trial. They told you they knew who killed Adalbert Wozniak and why. The 'who' was a member of the Latin Lords. Kiko. You know him. Every prosecutor's office knows Kiko. And the 'why' was a relationship with Delroy Bailey. The 'connection to Delroy.' Wozniak was going to expose someone's connection to Delroy and that someone had Kiko take Wozniak out."

Moody didn't say anything. I wouldn't, either, if I were he. But he couldn't deny it. The feds keep logs of all their interviews. It would be a very simple matter to prove that Ernesto Ramirez and Scarface paid them a visit, and who was in attendance. Hell, there would be surveillance cameras showing the two of them entering the federal building that day. And, above all that, surely Scarface himself—assuming I could ever find him again, but Moody didn't know that—would identify Chris Moody as the guy who threatened him that day.

I chuckled, but I wasn't having fun. "That must have really ruined your day, Chris."

I would've enjoyed watching Moody that day, seeing the look on his face. He'd spent three months in a trial blaming Wozniak's death on the Cannibals, when really it was the work of a rival gang, the Lords. He'd spent three months claiming that Wozniak died because he wouldn't pay the street tax, when in reality it was to cover up the illegal steering of a contract to Delroy Bailey's catering company—and Delroy's gay relationship with Hector Almundo.

"Funny thing," I said. "Ernesto and his buddy. When Kiko said he killed Wozniak to 'cover up a connection to Delroy,' they thought the guy doing the cover-up was your star witness, Joey Espinoza. Delroy's former brother-in-law. Which, from your perspective, was all the more devastating, seeing as how you cut a deal with Joey for eighteen months, and now he was your star witness at Hector's trial. How was that going to look? You're prosecuting Hector for murder and suddenly it's your star witness who did it?"

Moody was as still as a statue.

"Ironic," I went on. "Turns out, the 'connection to Delroy' was *Hector's* connection to Delroy. Ernesto and his buddy were handing you Hector on a silver platter, if you'd followed up on the evidence. But you didn't follow up on it, Chris, did you? You didn't do one shred of investigation. No, you buried that evidence. You withheld material evidence from the defense. You violated the first ethical rule of an honest prosecutor. Any of that ringing a bell, Chris?"

"I don't remember anything like that," Moody said. "And even if it happened, I'm under no obligation to chase red herrings."

"A red herring? Try that one again, Chris. It was *true*. Most everything they told you. A Latin Lord killed Wozniak, and it was to cover up a relationship with Delroy Bailey. Hard to call that a red herring when it was accurate. Maybe they were wrong on Joey Espinoza being behind it, but they still gave you almost the entire story right there."

"Twenty-twenty hindsight," he said.

"Okay, maybe—maybe you couldn't be *sure* what he was saying was true, at that moment. But you had an ethical obligation to turn that over to us, Mr. Moody. And you know it. Instead, you threatened Ernesto and his buddy with perjury, obstruction, the whole lot. You scared them into silence."

"Is that a fact?" said Moody.

I removed the Dictaphone from my pants pocket, the same one I used to record my conversation with Scarface in the alley that night. I hit play. Scarface's words echoed through the quiet city air.

They said I was a liar, ese. They told me, liars go to prison. We gonna lock you up. One thousand one, they kept sayin'. The fuckin' brownies, they pull out my sheet, they tell me, who'd believe you, convict? They tell me, ten years, man. Ten years for lying to us, the priors you got.

It was all there. "One thousand one," the federal crime for lying to a federal agent. "Brownies," the gangs' nickname for federal prosecutors, owing to their hideous brown building downtown. Scarface had never said Moody's name, but it wasn't much of a leap. Of course the lead prosecutor in the Almundo trial would have been called in at some point, once it was clear that Ernesto and Scarface had material information to disclose. And the threats Scarface described? They had Chris Moody's signature all over them.

Moody's stare carried beyond the bridge. His posture had become rigid, defensive mode, as if we were about to come to blows.

"That's not how it happened," he said. "You have the word of some scumbag with a sheet as long as my cock, versus a decorated supervisor in the U.S. attorney's office."

Moody had obviously done the calculus quickly in his head. His first instinct—to deny the meeting ever took place—wouldn't fly because of the records of the visit and the other federal agents who undoubtedly attended the interview. He went with his second instinct—admit the meeting took place but deny that it happened the way Scarface had described. He was right about his word versus Scarface's, but Moody still had problems. Other agents had been involved in the conversation. Someone below Moody would've handled the intake interview and would have brought in Moody only after there appeared to be something relevant. Moody would have overpowered the situation at that point and insisted these guys were lying, maybe even kicked out everyone else when he threatened Ernesto and Scarface. But still, given that what Scarface told Moody ultimately was mostly correct, the other agents might well revisit that session and remember Moody as more of a cover-up artist than anything else. If there were ever a *reason* to revisit that session— if anyone beefed Moody to the Division of Attorney Discipline, and everyone was interviewed. And that was assuming that Moody wouldn't be criminally prosecuted for misconduct; maybe a stretch but stranger things have happened.

Moody was boxed in, and we both knew it. His only defense to Attorney Discipline would be that he believed that the information was so lacking in credibility that it wasn't even worth mentioning to Hector's defense team. Given its ultimate accuracy, that argument wouldn't fly. And Moody already would have lost, with the publicity surrounding the controversy. A federal prosecutor withholding evidence in a major public corruption case? A case that he lost? He cheated and *still* lost? This was, to say the least, the very last thing he wanted. He wanted to go out with glory, having convicted the governor and all his cronies on public corruption charges, and then march into some silk-stocking law firm and reel in the big coin. He didn't want a very ugly ethics charge against him to stain his big moment.

And this was to say nothing of the fact that if I, the star prosecution witness in a public corruption trial that was forthcoming, filed an ethics beef against Moody, he'd probably be disqualified from trying the case against the governor. His swan song, his crowning achievement, would go out the window. He'd have to sit on the sidelines while someone else stole his glory. To Moody, that might be worse than anything else.

"So what do you want?" he asked. His posture wilted.

I exhaled, only then realizing that I'd been holding my breath. I didn't know if he'd say these words. There was, I must admit, a small part of me that wished he hadn't. There was a large part of me that knew he would.

"You want a walk," he said, answering his own question. "A get-out-of-jail-free card."

Did Moody actually believe what Scarface told him and then

blatantly cover it up? I didn't know and I never would. But I do know this much: The human inclination to believe what you want to believe runs very deep. Moody so deeply didn't *want* to believe what Scarface told him that he probably convinced himself it was bullshit and swept it under the rug.

"You can't record a conversation with that guy without his consent," he said, but his voice had weakened. He was flailing.

"Who said it was without his consent, Chris? You want to open an investigation and find out? You want your office to handle it? Attorney Discipline?"

I pulled out my cell phone and started dialing.

"What the hell are you doing?" Moody asked.

"Tucker," I said into the cell phone, "we're on the Lerner Street Bridge. Come down right away." I closed up the cell phone and put it back in my pocket.

I'd caught Moody off guard. He was losing control of the situation. "What the hell are you doing?"

I ejected the tape of Scarface's conversation. "You can have the tape. Catch," I said, and catch he did, wrapping it in his arms in a bear hug. He almost fell over doing so.

"That's my only copy of that tape," I said.

Moody stuffed it in his pocket. "Bullshit. You have a copy." He said it like he hoped he was wrong.

"I don't."

"What the fuck do you want, Kolarich?"

"From you? Nothing. I think you should turn yourself in to Attorney Discipline for withholding material evidence from Hector's defense team, but I'll leave that up to you. I'm not going to turn you in for that. Really. Even if you prosecute me."

"You made a copy," he said. "You want me to pass on prosecuting you, then when it's all over, you beef me to Attorney Discipline."

"No. Prosecute me," I said. "If that's what your conscience tells you to do. I'm not going to beef you, either way, for what you withheld in *Almundo*."

Moody watched me for a long time. This didn't make sense to him. I'd just hung this thing over his head, and now I was handing him my leverage. But all things considered, he was feeling a little better with the tape in his possession.

Finally, he let out a low chuckle.

"Okay, superstar. You'll get your pass. But you remember this. If you decide to go to DAD later, I'll fucking bury you. I'll be on you like ugly on a pig. Same goes for your girlfriend, Shauna, and your brother and anyone else I can think of. I'll be your worst fucking nightmare. Are we clear?"

"I'm not asking for a pass," I said. "I'm not blackmailing you. I'm advising you of this and hoping you'll do the right thing and turn yourself in to Attorney Discipline. But that's up to you, Christopher. I'm not a threat to you."

I looked over his shoulder. About three blocks away, someone—presumably Lee Tucker—had turned the corner and was heading toward the bridge. Moody turned and saw the same thing, then spun back and walked toward me so that his features came more fully into view. His eyes shone with an intensity I'd never seen. That was because I'd never seen Chris Moody scared.

"Now I guess we need to explain to Lee why there's no F-Bird tonight," he said. "How about we say it fell through the grid here on the bridge? That work for you, sport? A fumbled hand-off."

I snapped my fingers. "Glad you reminded me. I mean, that was the whole reason I came here, to deliver the F-Bird."

Chris Moody's eyes grew the size of Ping-Pong balls as I removed the F-Bird from my pocket.

"Handing off the F-Bird from tonight as promised," I said. "As always. Y'know, you guys really should have taught me how to turn this thing off."

Moody stared at the recording device in my hand, which was doing just that—recording our every word. Hey, to be fair, I never told him that I threw the F-Bird into the river. Moody just made that assumption. Can't a guy throw away a couple of used AA batteries from a stereo, wrapped together by some state-issued rubber bands, if he wants to? Sure, maybe my fingers were covering the rubber bands when I showed it to him, so from a distance it looked just like FeeBee, but who said I had to play fair?

In that short span of time, it must have crossed Moody's mind to lunge for it, try to get FeeBee away from me. But Tucker was well within sight distance now and would have seen the whole thing, and Moody was still far enough away that he'd have to struggle with me.

"Should I give the F-Bird to Lee?" I asked him. It was very hard not to smile.

"Put that fucking thing away," he said in a harsh whisper. He turned as Lee Tucker approached.

"You're the boss," I said.

"Hey. How we doing?" Tucker had walked out without a coat and was regretting it now. "What's—what's up?"

"You're never gonna believe this," Moody said. "Jason was handing me the Bird and we dropped it."

I eased between the two of them and started walking north.

"Oh, you gotta be—it fell through? It's in the *river*?"

"Craziest thing. A total accident."

Before I'd hit the other side of the bridge, Chris Moody was calling to me.

"Jason," he said. "Seriously, I want to thank you for everything you've done for us. You've performed a valuable service."

I didn't turn around. I didn't break stride. I didn't even smile, until I'd jumped into the back of a cab.

94 I WAS CALLED TO THE GOVERNOR'S OFFICE AT ELEVEN-fifteen the next morning. I'd slept in and hadn't arrived at the state building until about ten. The governor had been running from a prayer breakfast to a domestic violence shelter to a bill signing, and now he was briefly in his office before heading off to a fundraiser and then a downstate fly-around.

I'd spent the last hour or so reading the headline story in the paper as well as the follow-ups this morning online. The governor's dramatic, eleventh-hour reprieve of convicted double murderer Antwain Otis had overtaken everything else newsworthy that day. "Eleventh-hour" was an understatement; Governor Snow had made the call at four minutes to midnight. There was the predictable mix of jubilation and disgust. Antwain's mother and uncle were quoted as saying that Antwain had been touched by the hand of God; Anthony Newberry stated that he felt as if his family had been victimized one last time.

I was met with some glares as I walked into the governor's office. Madison was shooting daggers in my direction; Brady MacAleer mentioned something, meant for me to hear, about how the dramatic reprieve "stepped on our message" yesterday about the union endorsements and "probably cost us two percent downstate." I caught a glimpse of the governor, looking fresh and relaxed at his walnut desk, in his leather high-backed chair, as Peshke spoke to him.

"Good morning," said Madison, delivered with enough ice to sink the *Titanic*.

I simply nodded in return. I looked around the room. Madison, Hector, and Brady were all here, right here, with the governor. Charlie wasn't around.

"Jason, come in, come." The governor waved at me. He signed

a document and handed it to me. It was his official appointment of Judge George Henry Ippolito to the state supreme court.

"So I can do some good things once in a while," he said to me, winking. "Okay, what's next?"

I turned to Madison, holding the document in my hand. "I'll file it," I said. I hadn't been sure it would be me, but I was hoping.

I paused for a moment, wondering if I should offer some parting words, but no particular Solomonic pearl of wisdom came to mind so I excused myself. I took the stairs down to the secretary of state's office, where the index department received official filings such as the appointment of a supreme court justice.

I reached the door of the office and stopped. There, I handed the document to Special Agent Lee Tucker of the FBI, wearing his finest blue suit, pressed collar, and tie. He took the document with his left hand and offered me his right. I shook it and looked into his eyes a moment. Neither of us spoke. One of us was excited.

Tucker nodded. He put the document in his briefcase. Then he put on the blue jacket he'd been holding in his arm, the back of which said FBI in white block letters. He said something into his collar, and not three minutes later, six men and two women, all very serious customers in the same blue jackets, marched up the stairs and joined him.

"Let's do it," said Tucker.

The federal agents then walked up the same set of stairs I'd just descended, into the governor's office, armed with warrants to search and seize and warrants to arrest. I leaned against the wall and watched. It felt like a day's time, staring at the glass office doors bearing the state seal, the words CARLTON SNOW, GOVERNOR below it, before federal agents marched out with Madison Koehler, Brady MacAleer, and Hector Almundo in handcuffs.

I was a floor below, looking up. None of them could see me. I only saw their faces briefly, though I assumed the images would be burned into my memory forever, the humiliation and indignation in their expressions—but more than anything the look of being simply stunned. Each of them was experiencing something akin to having your life flash before your eyes. They were wondering what, exactly, were the bases for the criminal charges; how they'd been caught; how much the FBI knew; how they could escape the jam. They were calculating all the damage done to their lives and careers and how much of it was reparable. They were praying that they would open their eyes and discover that this had all been a dream.

I don't know how long I was there, staring at the governor's glass doors. Federal agents came and went, removing computers and entire file cabinets. A crowd, naturally, gathered around the office, and it wasn't long at all before the cameras began to appear.

The governor hadn't been arrested and he hadn't appeared outside his office. Had he the chance to think this over, he probably would have been best served to exit his office as soon as the arrests were made, before the press could arrive. Now, he was stuck. As far as I knew, there was only one way out, and now he was going to have to walk out into a carnivorous media.

My cell phone buzzed. I didn't recognize the number. I saw from the corner of my phone's face that I'd missed two calls in the last twenty minutes. I hadn't even noticed.

Before I could even say hello, Peshke was speaking harshly into the phone. "Jason, where are you? We need you in the governor's office right now. Don't you know what's going on?"

I closed the phone. I didn't enjoy turning my back, but it was the only option. Funny, it had never occurred to me that, in this dire moment, the governor would be calling his lawyer.

For some reason, I felt bad walking away from his call. It felt cruel. It was, I realized, a very curious reaction, given all the things I'd done to make this day happen.

I left the state building and headed back to my law office.

*   *   *

MARIE, MY RECEPTIONIST EXTRAORDINAIRE, opted to forgo the typical comment about my absenteeism in favor of this: "Did you hear the governor was arrested?"

I walked down the hall to my office and dropped onto my couch. Shauna was in my doorway moments later.

"Did you hear about the governor?" she said.

I turned my head slowly in her direction.

"Was it the governor or just some of his aides? They're saying both things. Nobody seems to know."

"Not the governor," I said. "Not yet."

"People you know? These were people you worked with?"

I sighed. I dropped my head against the couch and closed my eyes. My head was suddenly ringing. Everything started draining out of my body, all the tension and anger and worry and revulsion. All of that being gone, there was little of me remaining.

"I'm so tired," I said.

When I heard Shauna's voice again, she was closer. I felt the couch cushion depress next to me, and then her warm hand on my arm.

"You're shaking," she said. "Tell me. Jason, you never tell me anymore."

"I . . . miss that." I thought of all of the people with whom I'd come into contact over the last six months, almost all of them poison, ravenous, and unethical. Liars. Cheaters. I needed a hot shower that would last the rest of my life. I wanted to scrub and cleanse and purge all of the venom. I wanted to be anybody but me, anywhere but here.

I reached out for Shauna and found her hand. She covered it with her other hand. I must have fallen asleep there, awakening several hours later with a coat over my shoulder. I didn't remember letting go of her hand.

95

"THIS IS A SAD DAY FOR GOVERNMENT AND FOR THIS state. The complaint unsealed today exposes crimes in state government ranging from extortion and pay-to-play allegations to murder of a federal undercover witness. The complaint alleges that these crimes were committed at the highest levels of state government in Governor Carlton Snow's administration. Only hours ago, federal agents arrested Madison Koehler, chief of staff to the governor; Hector Almundo, deputy director of the Department of Commerce and Community Affairs; Brady MacAleer, chief of government administration; Ciriaco Cimino, Governor Snow's chief fundraiser . . ."

The U.S. attorney looked visibly angry as he spoke to reporters, the tremor in his voice unmistakable. He was flanked by Christopher Moody and other prosecutors, as well as other federal agents, including Lee Tucker.

Chris Moody was playing the sober part, but unlike his boss, I doubted he was truly angry. That wasn't how he operated. He was thrilled, exhilarated. It was all about personal ambition to him. I wondered if he worried about me at all, if last night was occupying his thoughts. After all, I had an F-Bird in my possession in which Moody had offered to decline to prosecute me if I kept quiet about his indiscretion during Hector's trial.

I'd never use it, and if he knew me better, he'd have known that. But he didn't. He lived in a black-and-white world. You were an ally or an enemy, a good guy or a bad one. He would always assume the worst about me. That probably suited my purposes. I would never be charged with a crime for anything related to this, nor had I taken a plea. I'd never admitted to wrongdoing. I would be the one whom they praised for coming forward, for risking my life, all to expose government corruption. I would be the star witness at trial, but I wouldn't be Joey Espinoza; I wouldn't be a flipper. I was a voluntary cooperator. I would come out of this better than anyone, at least on paper.

Shauna had found the complaint for the arrest warrant on the Internet and downloaded it. Although I told them they could use my name if they wished—"I don't give a rat's ass" was my official position—I wasn't identified by name in the complaint. Few people other than the defendants, whose names appeared always in all caps, would be named. I was "Private Attorney A" in the complaint. Shauna had already asked me if it was okay to use that as my nickname now.

Governor Snow, Madison, Hector, Charlie, MacAleer—they'd probably come up with other nicknames for me by now. Surely they'd put two and two together by this point. There were at least a dozen people in this city now who wished for nothing more than my violent death.

That might be viscerally pleasing to them but not tactically advantageous. Virtually everything I contributed to the case was caught on tape. The tapes would be the star witness. If I fell off the face of the earth, the United States could still bury everyone they'd charged.

Everyone, by the way, included more than the four top aides to the governor. Patrick Lemke, the nervous Nellie staffer at the Procurement and Construction Board, had been arrested. Top union officials Gary Gardner and Rick Harmoning were arrested. Judge George Ippolito was walked out of his courtroom in handcuffs. Four other men were charged for the murder of Greg Connolly and the assault committed on me, one of whom was Paul Patrino—Paulie, one of the guys who'd worked me over. Another of those guys surely was Leather Jacket, but I didn't know him by name.

Federico Hurtado—Kiko—was not named in this arrest warrant. Apparently he hadn't been involved in Greg Connolly's murder. But the feds would be looking at him hard on Ernesto Ramirez's murder, itself the murder of a potential government witness, but one that hadn't been charged yet. That could, theoretically, mean that Kiko would view me as a threat, but it would be a misplaced notion. The evidence against Kiko came, at the end of the day, principally from one man. If I were Hector Almundo, waiting in lockup on a federal murder charge, I'd be watching my back.

"I would like to add one more thing," said the U.S. attorney. "Greg Connolly was not the only person willing to cooperate with us to uncover corruption. Another individual agreed to cooperate with us at the early stages of this investigation and granted us windows into this political corruption that we otherwise wouldn't have had. He did so at great personal risk to himself, on one occasion narrowly escaping the same fate as Mr. Connolly. It's fair to say that we wouldn't be here today were it not for this individual. The people of this state owe him a debt of gratitude."

"Hey, look at you." Shauna flipped the back of her hand against my arm.

I almost laughed. That platitude to me, no doubt, was at the insistence of a certain assistant U.S. attorney who wanted to make sure I understood that we were still pals, and I wouldn't ever need to use that F-Bird I still kept from our friendly chat on the Lerner Street Bridge.

"I'm going home," I said, forcing myself out of a chair in Shauna's office.

"You probably need a lot of sleep."

"I don't need to sleep," I said. "I need to pack."

FIVE O'CLOCK THE FOLLOWING DAY. I'D JUST RETURNED from my second run of the day, the first taking place in the morning—a 10K, give or take—this follow-up shorter but more punishing. But still good, the cleansing from the cold fresh air and sweat and adrenaline.

Essie Ramirez was standing at my front door. Still with that sky-blue puffy coat, but this time no hat. Her silky hair was pulled back into a ponytail.

When she saw me, her expression eased but she didn't smile.

Inside, I helped her out of her coat, smelling her shampoo as her ponytail brushed against my mouth.

She turned to me. She was dressed in a blue suit, nothing fancy but formfitting, and her form was fit.

She looked up into my eyes, not faltering for a second. She put a hand on my cheek. A jolt of electricity ran through me.

"I'm ready," she whispered.

I didn't move, but internally, it was a different story. I felt a barrier break down, but I didn't know what to do about it.

Those wondrous dark eyes narrowed slightly. "But you're not. Did you lose your way, Jason Kolarich?"

I put my hand on hers. I was pretty sure I'd lost the map altogether.

"I told my children today that they caught the man who killed their father. And I told them that in catching him, they caught a lot of other people who were doing very bad things."

Her eyes glistened with tears, but she didn't falter. This was one strong woman.

"Something good came of it," she said. "Something always does."

I held my breath. I didn't know what to say or think.

She removed her hand from my cheek. She nodded as if something had been decided. Then she grabbed her coat and walked out the door.

CLOSING STATEMENT

"We're all good, Mr. Kolarich. See you over there?"

"Sure. Great," I said.

I looked out the window of my empty townhouse at the moving van parked at the curb. The back door was closing up, and all my possessions were moving about five blocks south. The only thing I hated more than packing was unpacking, so I wasn't looking forward to the next few weeks.

It would be Thanksgiving soon, and then of course Christmas, and I wasn't looking forward to the 2008 holiday season any more than I had the 2007 season, back when I'd been starting up with Charlie Cimino and everyone. It felt like more than eight months since the arrests. I wasn't sure I could pin down a sensation of time and distance. The whole thing felt, in many ways, like it had never happened.

But happened, it had. Three days ago, Edgar Trotter won election to the governor's mansion, having defeated Secretary of State Willie Bryant in an upset. Many people thought it would be a Democratic year, thanks to Barack Obama, but the scandal had tainted the Democrats too fiercely. We only had a Democratic governor for eighteen months, the argument went, and they managed to fuck it up that quickly with a sensational scandal.

Governor Carlton Snow had lost the primary, of course, after the scandal broke less than a week before the voters went to the booths in March. I didn't really follow the details but I recall a landslide. Many were surprised that Snow even stayed in the race, but the ballots were already printed, et cetera, and of course he denied any guilt.

The governor's indictment a few weeks ago couldn't have helped Willie Bryant, either. Turned out, everyone around Governor Snow flipped. Charlie Cimino, to my surprise, was first on board the federal bus in early April, but I understand he's not pleading guilty to the murder, only the extortion stuff that he and I did. Hector Almundo cut a deal in May—again, not to the murder but agreeing to testify to the governor's knowledge of certain wrongdoing. By the summer, Madison Koehler and Brady MacAleer were spilling their guts to Christopher Moody as well. I lost track of the order, but the two union guys, Gary Gardner and Rick Harmoning, have also been seen going in and out of grand jury rooms at the federal building.

The governor saw his indictment coming, naturally, and the word is his lawyers are trying to work something out with the feds as well. I don't know how that will play out.

Charlie and Hector will probably spend the rest of their lives in prison on the murder charges, which I highly doubt they can beat. Madison and Mac will probably do somewhere between five and ten. The governor? Probably the high side of that same range.

I probably will never have to testify. The corruption stuff will probably all go down in plea bargains, without a trial ever taking place. Perhaps I'll have to testify at a federal murder trial against Hector and Charlie, but my guess is that those guys will take a plea on that at some point. The evidence against them is overwhelming, my testimony aside, including the cooperation of all four of the goons who pulled off Greg Connolly's death. Hector and Charlie are toast.

Federico Hurtado—Kiko—is literally toast. Apparently the Latin Lords decided that he'd become a liability, given the federal government's interest and Kiko's depth of knowledge of criminal wrongdoing in their empire. Someone put a bullet in his brain, then doused him in gasoline and lit a match.

Me? I'm just "Private Attorney A." The papers had a field day with the arrest warrants issued back in March and the subsequent indictment, decoding all the described participants—"Lobbyist 1," "Public Official D," "State Contractor 39"—and they guessed correctly about me. I've never admitted it or offered comment of any kind, but I actually received some favorable coverage, in any event. The U.S. attorney's office had made me the big hero, after all.

"Okay, kiddo."

I turned back. Shauna had her coat on. One look at me, and she knew I wasn't ready to leave just yet. She walked up to me and lightly grabbed my arm.

"You okay?" she said. Her eyes moved to the mantel in the living room, the framed photograph of Talia in the hospital, holding Emily Jane, the only item of mine still remaining in the house.

She took the frame and handed it to me. "They're always with you, right? They always will be, Jason. Wherever you go. This is just a house."

I tried to smile. I couldn't find words.

"I'll be in the car," she said, breaking away from me. "Take all the time you want."

I took a deep breath. "No, that's okay," I said. "I'm ready."

I took Shauna's hand and walked out of the townhouse, the picture frame clutched against my chest.

Acknowledgments

I never stray too far into matters of federal law enforcement without consulting one of my closest friends, and one of the best lawyers I've ever known, Dan Collins, an assistant U.S. attorney in Chicago. Dan helped me understand the basics of a federal undercover operation, circa 2007–2008. He did not review this material before publication, and any mistakes I have made are purely my own.

For my knowledge of federal wiretap and surveillance technology, I must credit the testimony of former Assistant U.S. Attorney John Scully at the House Impeachment hearings concerning Governor Rod Blagojevich and at the Senate Impeachment Trial. It is sometimes scary what the federal government can do, but it's heartening to know that they have to jump through many legal hurdles and safeguards to do it.

My good friend Matt Stennes, a former federal prosecutor, gave me insight into prosecuting a political corruption case and patiently answered my questions. Again, any mistakes I may have made in translation are entirely my own.

I want to thank the federal prosecutors with whom I collaborated during the impeachment proceedings for their courtesy and professionalism, and for teaching me things without realizing it: U.S. Attorney Pat Fitzgerald and Assistant U.S. Attorneys Gary Shapiro, Tom Walsh, Dave Glockner, Reid Schar, and Ed Chang. Special thanks as well to FBI Special Agent Dan Cain. The prosecutor depicted in this novel bears absolutely no resemblance to these individuals.

Thank you to Ivan Held, for your friendship, confidence, and support. Thank you to Michael Barson and Summer Smith, for doing your best to make me look good. Thank you to Rachel Kahan, for an incredible eye for nuance, pace, and atmosphere and for putting up with me, and to the paperback publishers at Berkley—Leslie Gelbman, Susan Allison, and Tom Colgan—for making sure readers come back year after year. Thank you, as always, to Larry Kirshbaum and Susanna Einstein and everyone at LJK Literary for your enthusiasm and guidance.

Abigail and Julia are my oxygen, the two little human beings in this world who can lift me skyward with a smile or a hug. And Susan: Every day with you is better than the last. You ladies are my universe.

Author's Note

Good fiction mirrors reality. But writing about actual events isn't fiction at all. This book is fiction. The events depicted in this novel did not happen. The characters in this novel are not people I know. Like most fictional characters, they are a composite of a number of different people plus a very healthy dose of my own imagination. This is a work of fiction.